Come travel to the ends of the world and discover the secrets of the ruins of Salzarat . . .

Walk a path of fear to the mysterious rocks known as the "Toads of Grimmerdale" . . .

Venture to the city of sightless Dairine, who "sees" more with her hands than eyes dare behold . . .

Ride through a land of twisted, ancient magic as a warrior searches for his lost swordmate . . .

Enter into worlds of magic and delight. Welcome to the Wizards' Worlds, the worlds of Andre Norton.

Tor books by Andre Norton

Caroline (with Enid Cushing)
The Crystal Gryphon
Dare To Go A-Hunting
Flight in Yiktor
Forerunner
Forerunner: The Second Venture
Gryphon's Eyrie (with A. C. Crispin)
Here Abide Monsters
House of Shadows (with Phyllis Miller)
Imperial Lady (with Susan Shwartz)
The Jekyll Legacy (with Robert Bloch)*
Moon Called
Moon Mirror
The Prince Commands
Ralestone Luck
Stand and Deliver
Wheels of Stars
Wizards' Worlds

THE WITCH WORLD (editor)

Tales of the Witch World 1
Tales of the Witch World 2
Four from the Witch World
*Tales of the Witch World 3**

MAGIC IN ITHKAR (editor, with Robert Adams)

Magic in Ithkar 1
Magic in Ithkar 2
Magic in Ithkar 3
Magic in Ithkar 4

**forthcoming*

ANDRE NORTON

WIZARDS' WORLDS

Edited by Ingried Zierhut

A TOM DOHERTY ASSOCIATES BOOK
NEW YORK

This is a work of fiction. All the characters and events portrayed in this book are fictitious, and any resemblance to real people or events is purely coincidental.

WIZARDS' WORLDS

A Tor Book
Published by Tom Doherty Associates, Inc.
49 West 24th Street
New York, N.Y. 10010

Cover art by Lucy Synk

ISBN: 0-812-54750-0

First Tor edition: August 1989
First mass market printing: July 1990

Printed in the United States of America

0 9 8 7 6 5 4 3 2 1

Acknowledgments

"Falcon Blood" from *Amazons*, © 1979 by Jessica Amanda Salmonson. Reprinted by permission of the author.

"Toads of Grimmerdale" from *Flashing Swords!* #2, © 1973 by Lin Carter. Reprinted by permission of the author.

"Changeling" from *Lore of the Witchworld*, © 1980 by Andre Norton.

"Spider Silk" from *Flashing Swords!* #3, © 1976 by Lin Carter. Reprinted by permission of the author.

"Sword of Unbelief" from *Swords Against Darkness II*, © 1979 by Andrew J. Offut. Reprinted by permission of the author.

"Sand Sister" from *Heroic Fantasy*, © 1979 by Gerald W. Page and Hank Reinhardt. Reprinted by permission of the author.

Table of Contents

Falcon Blood

TANREE sucked at the torn ends of her fingers, tasted the sea salt stinging in them. Her hair hung in sticky loops across her sand-abraded face, too heavy with sea water to stir in the wind.

For the moment it was enough that she had won out of the waves, was alive. Sea was life for the Sulcar, yes, but it could also be death. In spite of the trained resignation of her people, other forces within her had kept her fighting ashore.

Gulls screamed overhead, sharp, piercing cries. So frantic those cries Tanree looked up into the gray sky of the after storm. The birds were under attack. Wider dark wings spread away from a body on the breast of which a white vee of feathers set an unmistakable seal. A falcon soared, swooped, clutched in cruel talons one of the gulls, bearing its prey to the top of the cliff, where it perched still within sight.

It ate, tearing flesh with a vicious beak. Cords flailed from its feet, the sign of its service.

Falcon. The girl spat gritty sand from between her teeth, her hands resting on scraped knees barely covered by her undersmock. She had thrown aside kilt, all other clothing, when she had dived from the ship pounding against a foam-crowned reef.

The ship!

She got to her feet, stared seaward. Storm anger still drove waves high. Broken backed upon rock fangs hung the Kast-Boar. Her masts were but jaggered stumps. Even as Tanree watched, the waters raised the ship once more, to slam her down on the reef. She was breaking apart fast.

Tanree shuddered, looked along the scrap of narrow beach. Who else had won to shore? The Sulcar were sea born and bred; surely she could not be the only survivor.

Wedged between two rocks so that the retreating waves could not drag him back, a man lay face down. Tanree raised her broken-nailed, scraped fingers and made the Sign of Wottin, uttering the age-old plea:

"Wind and wave,
Mother Sea,
Lead us home.
Far the harbor,
Wild thy waves—
Still, by thy Power,
Sulcar saved!"

Had the man moved then? Or was it only the water washing about him which had made it seem so?

He was— This was no Sulcar crewman! His body was covered from neck to mid-thigh by leather, dark breeches twisted with seaweed on his legs.

"Falconer!"

She spat again with salt-scoured lips. Though the Falconers had an old pact with her people, sailed on Sulcar ships as marines, they had always been a race apart—dour, silent men who kept to themselves. Good in battle, yes, so much one must grant them. But who really knew the thoughts in their heads, always hidden by their bird-shaped helms? Though this one appeared to have shucked all his fighting gear, to appear oddly naked.

There came a sharp scream. The falcon, full fed, now beat its way down to the body. There the bird settled on the sand just beyond the reach of the waves, squatted crying as if to arouse its master.

Tanree sighed. She knew what she must do. Trudging across the sand she started for the man. Now the falcon screamed again, its whole body expressing defiance. The girl halted, eyed the bird warily. These creatures were trained to attack in battle, to go for the eyes or the exposed face of an enemy. They were very much a part of the armament of their masters.

She spoke aloud as she might to one of her own kind: "No harm to your master, flying one." She held out sore hands in the oldest peace gesture.

Those bird eyes were small reddish coals, fast upon her. Tanree had an odd flash of feeling that this one had more understanding than other birds possessed. It ceased to scream, but the eyes continued to stare, sparks of menace, as she edged around it to stand beside the unconscious man.

Tanree was no weakling. As all her race she stood tall and strong, able to lift and carry, to haul on sail lines, or move cargo, should an extra hand be needed. Sulcarfolk lived aboard their ships and both sexes were trained alike to that service.

Now she stooped and set hands in the armpits of the mercenary, pulling him farther inland, and then rolling him over so he lay face up under the sky.

Though they had shipped a dozen Falconers on this last voyage (since the Kast-Boar intended to strike south into waters reputed to give sea room to the shark boats of outlaws), Tanree could not have told one of the bird fighters from another. They wore their masking helms constantly and kept to themselves, only their leader speaking when necessary to the ship people.

The face of the man was encrusted with sand, but he was breathing, as the slight rise and fall of his breast under the soaked leather testified. She brushed grit away from his nostrils, his thin-lipped mouth. There were deep frown lines between his sand-dusted brows, a masklike sternness in his face.

Tanree sat back on her heels. What did she know about this fellow survivor? First of all, the Falconers lived by harsh and narrow laws no other race would accept. Where their original home had been no outsider knew. Generations ago something had set them wandering, and then the tie with her own people had been formed. For the Falconers had wanted passage out of the south from a land only Sulcar ships touched.

They had sought ship room for all of them, perhaps some two thousand—two-thirds of those fighting men, each with a trained hawk. But it was their custom which made them utterly strange. For, though they had women and children with them, yet there was no clan or family feeling. To Falconers women were born for only one purpose: to bear children. They were made to live in villages apart, visited once a year by men selected by their officers. Such temporary unions were the only meetings between the sexes.

First they had gone to Estcarp, learning that the ancient land was hemmed in by enemies. But there had been an unbreachable barrier to their taking service there.

For in ancient Estcarp the Witches ruled, and to them a race who so degraded their females was cursed. Thus the Falconers had made their way into the no-man's-land of the southern mountains, building there their eyrie on the border between Estcarp and Karsten. They had fought shoulder to shoulder with the Borderers of Estcarp in the great war. But when, at last, a near exhausted Estcarp had faced the overpowering might of Karsten, and the Witches concentrated all their power (many of them dying from it) to change the earth itself, the Falconers, warned in time, had reluctantly returned to the lowlands.

Their numbers were few by then, and the men took service as fighters where they could. For at the end of the great war, chaos and anarchy followed. Some men, nurtured all their lives on fighting, became outlaws; so that, though in Estcarp itself some measure of order prevailed, much of the rest of the continent was beset.

Tanree thought that this Falconer, lacking helm, mail shirt, weapons, resembled any man of the Old Race. His dark hair looked black beneath the clinging sand, his skin was paler than her own sun-browned flesh. He had a sharp nose, rather like the jutting beak of his bird, and his eyes were green. For now they had opened to stare at her. His frown grew more forbidding.

He tried to sit up, fell back, his mouth twisting in pain. Tanree was no reader of thoughts, but she was sure his weakness before her was like a lash laid across his face.

Once more he attempted to lever himself up, away from her. Tanree saw one arm lay limp. She moved closer, sure of a broken bone.

"No! You—you female!" There was such a note of loathing in his voice that anger flared in her in answer.

"As you wish—" She stood up, deliberately turned her back on him, moving away along the narrow beach, half encircled by cliff and walls of water-torn, weed-festooned rocks.

Here was the usual storm bounty brought ashore, wood—some new torn from the Kast-Boar, some the wrack of earlier storms. She made herself concentrate on finding anything which might be of use.

Where they might now be in relation to the lands she knew, Tanree had no idea. They had been beaten so far south by the storm that surely they were no longer within the boundaries of Karsten. And the unknown, in these days, was enough to make one wary.

There was a glint in a half ball of weed. Tanree leaped to jerk that away just as the waves strove to carry it off. A knife—no, longer than just a knife—by some freak driven point deep into a hunk of splintered wood. She had to exert some strength to pull it out. No rust spotted the ten-inch blade yet.

Such a piece of good fortune! She sat her jaw firmly and faced around, striding back to the Falconer. He had flung his sound arm across his eyes as if to shut out the world. Beside him crouched the bird uttering small guttural cries. Tanree stood over them both, knife in hand.

"Listen," she said coldly. It was not in her to desert a helpless man no matter how he might spurn her aid. "Listen, Falconer, think of me as you will. I offer no friendship cup to you either. But the sea has spat us out, therefore this is not our hour to seek the Final Gate. We cannot throw away our lives heedlessly. That being so—" she knelt by him, reaching out also for a straight piece of drift lying near, "you will accept from me the aid of what healcraft I know. Which," she admitted frankly, "is not much."

He did not move that arm hiding his eyes. But neither did he try now to evade as she slashed open the sleeve of his tunic and the padded lining beneath to bare his arm. There was no gentleness in this—to prolong handling would only cause greater pain. He uttered no sound as she set the break (thank the Power it was a simple one) and lashed his forearm against the wood with strips slashed from his own clothing. Only when she had finished did he look to her.

"How bad?"

"A clean break," she assured him. "But—" she frowned at the cliff, "how you can climb from here one-handed—"

He struggled to sit up; she knew better than to offer support. With his good arm as a brace, he was high enough to gaze at the cliff and then the sea. He shrugged.

"No matter—"

"It matters!" Tanree flared. She could not yet see a way out of this pocket, not for them both. But she would not surrender to imprisonment by rock or wave.

She fingered the dagger-knife and turned once more to examine the cliffs. To venture back into the water would only sweep them against the reef. But the surface of the wall behind them was pitted and worn enough to offer toe and hand holds. She paced along the short beach, inspecting that surface. Sulcarfolk had good heads for heights, and the Falconers were mountaineers. It was a pity this one could not sprout wings like his comrade in arms.

Wings! She tapped her teeth with the point of the knife. An idea flitted to her mind and she pinned it fast.

Now she returned to the man quickly.

"This bird of yours—" she pointed to the red-eyed hawk at his shoulder, "what powers does it have?"

"Powers!" he repeated and for the first time showed surprise. "What do you mean?"

She was impatient. "They *have* powers; all know that. Are they not your eyes and ears, scouts for you? What else can they do beside that, and fight in battle?"

"What have you in mind?" he countered.

"There are spires of rock up there." Tanree indicated the top of the cliff. "Your bird has already been aloft. I saw him kill a gull and feast upon it while above."

"So there are rock spires and—"

"Just this, bird warrior," she dropped on her heels again. "No rope can be tougher than loops of some of this weed. If you had the aid of a rope to steady you, could you climb?"

He looked at her for an instant as if she had lost even that small store of wit his people credited to females. Then his eyes narrowed as he gazed once more, measuringly, at the cliff.

"I would not have to ask that of any of *my* clan," she told him deliberately. "Such a feat would be play as our children delight in."

The red stain of anger arose on his pale face.

"How would you get the rope up there?" He had not lashed out in fury to answer her taunt as she had half expected.

"If your bird can carry up a finer strand, loop that about one of the spires there, then a thicker rope can be drawn in its wake and that double rope looped for your ladder. I would climb and do it myself, but we must go together since you have the use of but one hand."

She thought he might refuse. But instead he turned his head and uttered a crooning sound to the bird.

"We can but try," he said a moment later.

The seaweed yielded to her knife and, though he could use but the one hand, the Falconer helped twist and hold strands to her order as she fashioned her ropes. At last she had the first thin cord, one end safe knotted to a heavier one, the other in her hands.

Again the Falconer made his bird sounds and the hawk seized upon the thin cord at near mid-point. With swift, sure beat of wings it soared up, as Tanree played out the cord swiftly hoping she had judged the length aright.

Now the bird spiralled down and the cord was suddenly loose in Tanree's grasp. Slowly and steadily she began to pull, bring upward from the sand the heavier strand to dangle along the cliff wall.

One moment at a time, think only that, Tanree warned herself as they began their ordeal. The heavier part of the rope was twisted around her companion, made as fast as she could set it. His right arm was splinted, but his fingers were as swift to seek out holds as hers. He had kicked off his boots and slung those about his neck, leaving his toes bare.

Tanree made her way beside him, within touching distance, one glance for the cliff face, a second for the man. They were aided unexpectedly when they came upon a ledge, not to be seen from below. There they crouched together, breathing heavily. Tanree estimated they had covered two thirds of their journey but the Falconer's face was wet with sweat which trickled down, to drip from his chin.

"Let us get to it!" he broke the silence between them, inching up to his feet again, his sound arm a brace against the wall.

"Wait!"

Tanree drew away, was already climbing. "Let me get aloft now. And do you keep well hold of the rope."

He protested but she did not listen, any more than she paid attention to the pain in her fingers. But, when she pulled herself over the lip of the height, she lay for a moment, her breath coming in deep, rib-shaking sobs. She wanted to do no more than lie where she was, for it seemed that strength drained steadily from her as blood flowing from an open wound.

Instead she got to her knees and crawled to that outcrop of higher rock around which the noose of the weed rope strained and frayed. She set her teeth grimly, laid hold of the taut strand they had woven. Then she called, her voice sounding in her own ears as high as the scream of the hawk that now hovered overhead.

"Come!"

She drew upon the rope with muscles tested and trained to handle ships' cordage, felt a responding jerk. He was indeed climbing. Bit by bit the rope passed between her torn palms.

Then she saw his hand rise, grope inward over the cliff edge. Tanree made a last great effort, heaving with a reviving force she had not believed she could summon, falling backward, but still keeping a grasp on the rope.

The girl was dizzy and spent, aware only for a moment or two that the rope was loose in her hands. Had—had he fallen? Tanree smeared the back of her fist across her eyes to clear them from a mist.

No, he lay head pointing toward her, though his feet still projected over the cliff. He must be drawn away from that, even as she had brought him earlier out of the grasp of the sea. Only now she could not summon up the strength to move.

Once more the falcon descended, to perch beside its master's head. Three times it screamed harshly. He was moving, drawing himself along on his belly away from the danger point, by himself.

Seeing that, Tanree clawed her way to her feet, leaning back against one of the rocky spires, needing its support. For it seemed that the rock under her feet was like the deck of the Kast-Boar, rising and falling, so she needs must summon sea-legs to deal with its swing.

On crawled the Falconer. Then he, too, used his good arm for a brace and raised himself, his head coming high enough to look around. That he was valiantly fighting to get to his feet she was sure. A second later his eyes went wide as they swept past her to rest upon something at her own back.

Tanree's hand curved about the hilt of the dagger. She pushed against the rock which had supported her, but she could not stand away from it as yet.

Then she, too, saw—

These spires and outcrops of rock were not the work of nature after all. Stones were purposefully piled upon huge stones. There were archways, farther back what looked like an intact wall—somber, without a break until, farther above her head than the cliff had earlier reached, there showed openings, thin and narrow as a giant axe might have cleft. They had climbed into some ruin.

A thrust of ice chill struck Tanree. The world she had known had many such ancient places and most were ill-omened, perilous for travelers. This was an old, old land and there had been countless races rise to rule and disappear once more into dust. Not all of those peoples had been human, as Tanree reckoned it. The Sulcar knew many such remained, and wisely avoided them—unless fortified by some power spell set by a Wise One.

"Salzarat!"

The surprise on the Falconer's face had become something else as Tanree turned her head to stare. What was that faint expression? Awe—or fear? But that he knew this place, she had no doubt.

He made an effort, pulling himself up to his feet, though he clung for support to a jumble of blocks even as she did.

"Salzarat—" His voice was the hiss of a warning serpent, or that of a disturbed war bird.

Once more Tanree glanced from him to the ruins. Perhaps a lighting of the leaden clouds overhead was revealing. She saw—saw enough to make her gasp.

That farther wall, the one which appeared more intact, took on new contours. She could trace—

Was it illusion, or some cunning art practiced by the unknowns who had laid those stones? There was no wall; it was the head of a giant falcon, the fierce eyes marked by slitted holes above an outthrust beak.

While the beak—

That closed on a mass which was too worn to do more than hint that it might once have been intended to represent a man.

The more Tanree studied the stone head, the plainer it grew. It was reaching out—out—ready to drop the prey it had already taken, to snap at her. . . .

"No!" Had she shouted that aloud or was the denial only in her mind? Those were stones (artfully fitted together, to be sure) but still only old, old stones. She shut her eyes, held them firmly shut, and then, after a few deep breaths, opened them again. No head, only stones.

But in those moments while she had fought to defeat illusion her companion had lurched forward. He pulled himself from one outcrop of ruin to the next and his Falcon had settled on his shoulder, though he did not appear aware of the weight of the bird. There was bemusement on his face, smoothing away his habitual frown. He was like a man ensorceled, and Tanree drew away from him as he staggered past her, his gaze only for the wall.

Stones only, she continued to tell herself firmly. There was no reason for her to remain here. Shelter, food (she realized then that hunger did bite at her), what they needed to keep life in them could only lie in this land. Purposefully she followed the Falconer, but she carried her blade ready in her hand.

He stumbled along until he was under the overhang of that giant beak. The shadow of whatever it held fell on him. Now he halted, drew himself up as a man might face his officer on some occasion of import—or—a priest might begin a rite.

His voice rang out hollowly among the ruins, repeating words—or sounds (for some held the tones of those he had used in addressing his hawk). They came as wild beating cadence. Tanree shivered. She had a queer feeling that he might just be answered—by whom—or *what?*

Up near to the range of a falcon's cry rose his voice. Now the bird on his shoulder took wing. It screamed its own challenge, or greeting—so that man-voice and bird-voice mingled until Tanree could not distinguish one from the other.

Both fell into silence; once more the Falconer was moving on. He walked more steadily, not reaching out for any support, as if new strength had filled him. Passing under the beak he was—gone!

Tanree pressed one fist against her teeth. There was no doorway there! Her eyes could not deceive her that much. She wanted to run, anywhere, but as she looked wildly about her she perceived that the ruins funneled forward toward that one place and there only led the path.

This was a path of the Old Ones; evil lurked here. She could feel the crawl of it as if a slug passed, befouling her skin. Only—Tanree's chin came up, her jaw set stubbornly. She was Sulcar. If there was no other road, then this one she would take.

Forward she went, forcing herself to walk with confidence, though she was ever alert. Now the shadow of the beak enveloped her, and, though there was no warmth of sunlight to be shut out, still she was chilled.

Also—there *was* a door. Some trick of the stone setting and the beak shadow had concealed it from sight until one was near touching distance. With a deep breath which was more than half protest against her own action, Tanree advanced.

Through darkness within, she could see a gray of light. This wall must be thick enough to provide not just a door or gate but a tunnel way. And she could see movement between her and that light; the Falconer.

She quickened step so that she was only a little behind him when they came out in what was a mighty courtyard. Walls towered all about, but it was what was within the courtyard itself which stopped Tanree near in mid-step.

Men! Horses!

Then she saw the breakage, here a headless body, there only the shards of a mount. They had been painted once and the color in some way had sunk far into the substance which formed them, for it remained, if faded.

The motionless company was drawn up in good order, all facing to her left. Men stood, the reins of their mounts in their hands, and on the forks of their saddles falcons perched. A regiment of fighting men awaiting orders.

Her companion skirted that array of the ancient soldiers, almost as if he had not seen them, or, if he had, they were of no matter. He headed in the direction toward which they faced.

There were two wide steps there, and beyond the cavern of another door, wide as a monster mouth ready to suck them in. Up one step he pulled, now the second. . . . He *knew* what lay beyond; this was Falconer past, not of her people. But Tanree could not remain behind. She studied the faces of the warriors as she passed by. They each held their masking helm upon one hip as if it was needful to bare their faces, as they did not generally do. So she noted that each of the company differed from his fellows in some degree, though they were all plainly of the same race. These had been modeled from life.

As she came also into the doorway, Tanree heard again the mingled call of bird and man. At least the two she followed were still unharmed, though her sense of lurking evil was strong.

What lay beyond the door was a dim twilight. She stood at the end of a great hall, stretching into shadows right and left. Nor was the chamber empty. Rather here were more statues; and some were robed and coiffed. Women! Women in an Eyrie? She studied the nearest to make sure.

The weathering which had eroded that company in the courtyard had not done any damage here. Dust lay heavy on the shoulders of the life-size image to be sure, but that was all. The face was frozen into immobility. But the expression. Sly exultation, an avid . . . hunger? Those eyes staring straight ahead, did they indeed hold a spark of knowledge deep within?

Tanree pushed aside imagination. These were not alive. But their faces—she looked to another, studied a third—all held that gloating, that hunger-about-to-be-assuaged; while the male images were as blank of any emotion as if they had never been meant to suggest life at all.

The Falconer had already reached the other end of the hall. Now he was silent, facing a dais on which were four figures. These were not in solemn array, rather frozen into a tableau of action. Deadly action, Tanree saw as she trotted forward, puffs of dust rising from the floor underfoot.

A man sat, or rather sprawled, in a throne-chair. His head had fallen forward, and both hands were clenched on the hilt of a dagger driven into him at heart level. Another and younger man, lunged, sword in his hand, aiming at the image of a woman who cowered away, such an expression of rage and hate intermingled on her features as made Tanree shiver.

But the fourth of that company stood a little apart, no fear to be read on *her* countenance. Her robe was plainer than that of the other woman, with no glint of jewels at wrist, throat or waist. Her unbound hair fell over her shoulders, cascading down, to nearly sweep the floor.

In spite of the twilight here that wealth of hair appeared to gleam. Her eyes—they, too, were dark red—unhuman, knowing, exulting, cruel—alive!

Tanree found she could not turn her gaze from those eyes.

Perhaps she cried out then, or perhaps only some inner defense quailed in answer to invasion. Snakelike, sluglike, it crawled, oozed into her mind, forging link between them.

This was no stone image, man-wrought. Tanree swayed against the pull of that which gnawed and plucked, seeking to control her.

"She-devil!" The Falconer spat, the bead of moisture striking the breast of the red-haired woman. Tanree almost expected to see the other turn her attention to the man whose face was twisted with half-insane rage. But his cry had weakened the spell laid upon her. She was now able to look away from the compelling eyes.

The Falconer swung around. His good hand closed upon the sword which the image of the young man held. He jerked at that impotently. There was a curious wavering, as if the chamber and all in it were but part of a wind-riffled painted banner.

"Kill!"

Tanree herself wavered under that command in her mind. Kill this one who would dare threaten *her,* Jonkara, Opener of Gates, Commander of Shadows.

Rage took fire. Through the blaze she marched, knowing what must be done to this man who dared to challenge. She was the hand of Jonkara, a tool of force.

Deep within Tanree something else stirred, could not be totally battered into submission.

I am a weapon to serve. I am—

"I am *Tanree!*" cried that other part of her. "This is no quarrel of mine. I am Sulcar, of the seas—of another blood and breed!"

She blinked and that insane rippling ceased for an instant of clear sight. The Falconer still struggled to gain the sword.

"Now!" Once more that wave of compulsion beat against her, heart high, as might a shore wave. "Now—slay! Blood—give me blood that I may live again. We are women. Nay, *you* shall be more than woman when this blood flows and my door is opened by it. Kill—strike behind the shoulder. Or, better still, draw your steel across his throat. He is but a man! He is the enemy—kill!"

Tanree swayed, her body might be answering to the flow of a current. Without her will her hand arose, blade ready, the distance between her and the Falconer closed. She could easily do this, blood would indeed flow. Jonkara would be free of the bonds laid upon her by the meddling of fools.

"Strike!"

Tanree saw her hand move. Then that other will within her flared for a last valiant effort.

"I am Tanree!" A feeble cry against a potent spell. "There is no power here before whom Sulcar bows!"

The Falconer whirled, looked to her. No fear in his eyes, only cold hate. The bird on his shoulder spread wings, screamed. Tanree could not be sure—was there indeed a curl of red about its feet, anchoring it to its human perch?

"She-devil!" he flung at her. Abandoning his fight for the sword, he raised his hand as if to strike Tanree across the face. Out of the air came a curl of tenuous red, to catch about his upraised wrist, so, even though he fought furiously, he was held prisoner.

"Strike quickly!" The demand came with mind-bruising force.

"I do not kill!" Finger by finger Tanree forced her hand to open. The blade fell, to clang on the stone floor.

"Fool!" The power sent swift punishing pain into her head. Crying out, Tanree staggered. Her outflung hand fell upon that same sword the Falconer had sought to loosen. It turned, came into her hold swiftly and easily.

"Kill!"

That current of hate and power filled her. Her flesh tingled, there was heat within her as if she blazed like an oil-dipped feast torch.

"Kill!"

She could not control the stone sword. Both of her hands closed about its cold hilt. She raised it. The man before her did not move, seek in any way to dodge the threat she offered. Only his eyes were alive now—no fear in them, only a hate as hot as what filled her.

Fight—she must fight as she had the waves of the storm lashed sea. She was herself, Tanree—Sulcar—no tool for something evil which should long since have gone into the Middle Dark.

"Kill!"

With the greatest effort she made her body move, drawing upon that will within her which the other could not master. The sword fell.

Stone struck stone—or was that true? Once more the air rippled, life overrode ancient death for a fraction of time between two beats of the heart, two breaths. The sword had jarred against Jonkara.

"Fool—" a fading cry.

There was no sword hilt in her hands, only powder sifting between her fingers. And no sparks of life in those red eyes either. From where the stone sword had struck full on the image's shoulder cracks opened. The figure crumbled, fell. Nor did what Jonkara had been vanish alone. All those others were breaking too, becoming dust which set Tanree coughing, raising her hands to protect her eyes.

Evil had ebbed. The chamber was cold, empty of what had waited here. A hand caught her shoulder, pulling at her.

"Out!" This voice was human. "Out—Salzarat falls!"

Rubbing at her smarting eyes, Tanree allowed him to lead her. There were crashing sounds, a rumbling. She cringed as a huge block landed nearby. They fled, dodging and twisting. Until at last they were under the open sky, still coughing, tears streaming from their eyes, their faces smeared with gray grit.

Fresh wind, carrying with it the clean savor of the sea, lapped about them. Tanree crouched on a mat of dead grass through which the first green spears of spring pushed. So close to her that their shoulders touched was the Falconer. His bird was gone.

They shared a small rise Tanree did not remember climbing. What lay below, between them and the sea cliff's edge, was a tumble of stone so shattered no one now could define wall or passage. Her companion turned his head to look directly into her face. His expression was one of wonder.

"It is all gone! The curse is gone. So she is beaten at last! But you are a woman, and Jonkara could always work her will through any woman—that was her power and our undoing. She held every woman within her grasp. Knowing that, we raised what defenses we could. For we could never trust those who might again open Jonkara's dread door. Why in truth did you not slay me? My blood would have freed her, and she would have given you a measure of her power—as always she had done."

"She was no one to command *me!*" Tanree's self-confidence returned with every breath she drew. "I am Sulcar, not one of your women. So—this Jonkara—she was why you hate and fear women?"

"Perhaps. She ruled us so. Her curse held us until the

death of Langward, who dying, as you saw, from the steel of his own Queen, somehow freed a portion of us. He had been seeking long for a key to imprison Jonkara. He succeeded in part. Those of us still free fled, so our legends say, making sure no woman would ever again hold us in bond."

He rubbed his hands across his face, streaking the dust of vanished Salzarat.

"This is an old land. I think though that none walk it now. We must remain here—unless your people come seeking you. So upon us the shadow of another curse falls."

Tanree shrugged. "I am Sulcar but there was none left to call me clan-sister. I worked on the Kast-Boar without kin-tie. There will be no one to come hunting because of me." She stood up, her hands resting on her hips and turned her back deliberately upon the sea.

"Falconer, if we be cursed, then that we live with. And, while one lives, the future may still hold much, both good and ill. We need only face squarely what comes."

There was a scream from the sky above them. The clouds parted, and, through weak sunlight, wheeled the falcon. Tanree threw back her head to watch it.

"This is your land, as the sea is mine. What make you of it, Falconer?"

He also got to his feet. "My name is Rivery. And your words have merit. It is a time for curses to slink back into shadows, allowing us to walk in the light, to see what lies ahead."

Shoulder to shoulder they went down from the hillock, the falcon swooping and soaring above their heads.

Toads of Grimmerdale

1

THE drifts of ice-crusted snow were growing both taller and wider. Hertha stopped to catch her breath, ramming the butt of the hunting spear she had been using as a staff into the drift before her, the smooth shaft breaking through the crust with difficulty. She frowned at the broken hole without seeing it.

There was a long dagger at her belt, the short-hafted spear in her mittened hand. And under her cloak she hugged to her the all too small bundle which she had brought with her out of Horla's Hold. The other burden which she carried lay within her, and she forced herself to face squarely the fate it had brought upon her.

Now her lips firmed into a line, her chin went up. Suddenly she spat with a hiss of breath. Shame—why should she feel shame? Had Kuno expected her to whine and wail, perhaps crawl before him so he could "forgive" her, prove thus to his followers his greatness of spirit?

She showed her teeth as might a cornered vixen and aimed a harder blow at the drift. There was no reason for her to feel shame, the burden in her was not of wanton seeking. Such things happened in times of war. She guessed that when matters worked so, Kuno had not been backward himself in taking a woman of the enemy.

It remained that her noble brother had sent her forth from Horla's Hold because she had not allowed his kitchen hags to brew some foul potion to perhaps poison her, as well as what she bore. Had she so died he could have piously crossed hands at the Thunderer's altar and spoken of Fate's will. And it would have ended neatly. In fact she might believe that perhaps that had been the intention.

For a moment Hertha was startled at the grim march of her thoughts. Kuno—Kuno was her *brother!* Two years ago she could not have thought so of him or any man! Before the war nearer the Hold. But that was long before she set out for Landendale. Before she knew the world as it was and not as she had believed it.

Hertha was glad she had been able to learn her lesson quickly. The thin-skinned maid she had once been could not have fronted Kuno, could not have taken this road—

She felt the warmth of anger, a sullen glowing anger, heating as if she carried a small brazier of coals under her cloak's edge. So she went on, setting her rough boots firmly to crunch across the drift edge. Nor did she turn to look back down at that stone-walled keep which had sheltered those of her blood for five generations. The sun was well westward, she must not linger on the trail. Few paths were broken now, times in number she must halt and use the spear to sound out the footing. But it was easy to keep in eye her landmarks of Mulma's Needle and the Wyvern's Wing.

Hertha was sure Kuno expected her to return to accept his conditions. She smiled wryly. Kuno was so very certain of everything. And since he had beaten off the attack of a straggling band of the enemy trying to fight their way to the dubious safety of the coast, he had been insufferable.

The Dales were free in truth. But for Kuno to act as if the victories hard-won there were his alone—! It had required all the might of High Hallack, together with strange allies from the Waste, to break the invaders, to hunt and harry them to the sea from which they had come. And that had taken a score of years to do.

Trewsdale had escaped, not because of any virtue, but by chance. But because fire and sword had not riven there was no reason to cry upon unbroken walls like gamecocks. Kuno had harried men already three-quarters beaten.

She reached the divide, to plod steadily on. The wind had been at work here, and her path was free of snow. It was very old, that road, one of the reminders to be found all across the dale land that her own people were late comers. Who had cut these ways for their own treading?

The well-weathered carvings at the foot of the Wyvern's Wing could be seen easily now. So eroded they were by time that none could trace their meaning. But men—or intelligent beings—had shaped them to a purpose. And that task must have been long in the doing. Hertha reached out her mittened fingers to mark one of the now vague curves. She did not believe they had any virtue in themselves, though the field workers did. But they marked well her road.

Downslope again from this point, and now the wind's lash did not cut at her. Though again snow drifted. Two tens of days yet to the feast of Year Turn. This was the last of the Year of the Hornet, next lay the Year of the Unicorn, which was a more fortunate sign.

With the increase of snow Hertha once more found the footing dangerous. The bits of broken crust worked in over the tops of her boots, even though she had drawn tight their top straps, melted clammily against her foot sacks. She plodded on as the track entered a fringe of scrub trees.

Evergreens, the foliage was dark in the dwindling light. But they arose to roof over a road, keep off the drifts. And she came to a stream where ice had bridged from one stony bank to the other. There she turned east to gain Gunnora's shrine.

About its walls was a tangle of winter-killed garden. It

was a low building, and an archway faced her. No gate or door barred that and she walked boldly in.

Once inside the outer wall she could see windows—round like the eyes of some great feline regarding her sleepily—flanking a door by which hung a heavy bell-pull of wrought metal in the form of Gunnora's symbol of a ripened grain stalk entwined with a fruit-laden vine.

Hertha leaned her spear against the wall that her hand might be free for a summons pull. What answered was not any peal of bell, rather an odd, muted sound, as if someone called in words she did not understand. That, too, she accepted, though she had not been this way before and had only a few whispered words to send her here.

The leaves of the door parted. Though no one stood there to give her house greeting, Hertha took that for an invitation to enter. She moved into gentle warmth, a fragrance of herbs and flowers. As if she had, in that single step, passed from the sere death of midwinter into the life of spring.

With the warmth and fragrance came a lightening of heart, so that the taut lines in her face smoothed a little and her aching shoulders and back lost some of the stiffening tension.

What light there was came from two lamps set on columns, one right, one left. She was in a narrow entry, its walls painted with such colors as to make her believe that she had truly entered a garden. Before her those ranks of flowers rippled, and she realized that there hung a curtain, fashioned to repeat the wall design. Since there still came no greeting, she put out her hand to the folds of that curtain.

But before she could finger it the length looped aside of itself, and she came into a large room. Inside was a table with a chair drawn up to it. The table was set with dishes, some covered as if they held viands which were to be kept warm, and a goblet of crystal filled with a green liquid.

"Eat—drink—" a voice sighed through the chamber.

Startled, Hertha looked about the room over her shoulder. No one— And now that hunger of which she had hardly been aware awoke full force. She dropped the spear to the floor, laid her bundle beside it, let her cloak fall over both, and sat down in the chair.

Though she could see no one, she spoke:

"To the giver of the feast, fair thanks. For the welcome of the gate, gratitude. To the ruler of this house, fair fortune and bright sun on the morrow—" The formal words rang a little hollow here. Hertha smiled at a sudden thought.

This was Gunnora's shrine. Would the Great Lady need the well-wishing of any mortal? Yet it seemed fitting that she make the guest speech.

There was no answer, though she hoped for one. At last, a little hesitantly, she sampled the food spread before her, and found it such fare as might be on the feast table of a Dales Lord. The green drink was refreshing, yet warming, with a subtle taste of herbs. She held it in her mouth, trying to guess which gave it that flavor.

When she had finished she found that the last and largest covered basin held warm water, on the surface of which floated petals of flowers. Flowers in the dead of winter! And beside it was a towel, so she washed her hands and leaned back in the chair, wondering what came next in Gunnora's hall.

The silence in the room seemed to grow the greater. Hertha stirred. Surely there were priestesses at the Shrine? Someone had prepared that meal, offered it to her with those two words. She had come here for a purpose, and the need for action roused in her again.

"Great Lady." Hertha arose. Since she could see no one, she would speak to the empty room. There was a door at the other end of the chamber, but it was closed.

"Great Lady," she began again. She had never been deeply religious, though she kept Light Day, made the harvest sacrifices, listened respectfully to the Mouth of Astron at Morn Service. When she had been a little maid her foster mother had given her Gunnora's apple as a pendant to wear. But according to custom that had been laid on the house altar when she came to marriageable age. Of Gunnora's mysteries she knew only what she had heard repeated woman to woman when they sat apart from the men. For Gunnora was only for womankind, and when one was carrying ripening seed within one, then she listened—

For the second time her words echoed. Now that feeling of impatience changed to something else—awe, perhaps, or fear? Yet Gunnora did not hold by the petty rules of men. It did not matter when you sought her if you be lawful wife or not.

As her distrust grew the second door swung silently open—another invitation. Leaving her cloak, bundle, spear where they lay, Hertha went on. Here the smell of flowers and herbs was stronger. Lazy curls of scented smoke arose from two braziers standing at the head and foot of a couch, set as an altar at the foot of a pillar carved with the ripened grain and fruited vine.

"Rest—" the sighing voice bade. And Hertha, the need for sleep suddenly as great as her hunger had been, moved to that waiting bed, stretched out her wearied and aching body. The curls of smoke thickened, spread over her as a coverlet. She closed her eyes.

She was in a place of half light in which she sensed others coming and going, busied about tasks. But she felt alone, lost. Then one moved to her and she saw a face she knew, though a barrier of years had half dimmed it in her mind.

"Elfreda!" Hertha believed she had not called that name aloud, only thought it. But her foster mother smiled, holding out her arms in the old, old welcome.

"Little dove, little love—" The old words were as soothing as healing salve laid on an angry wound.

Tears came as Hertha had not allowed them to come before. She wept out sore hurt and was comforted. Then that shade who was Elfreda drew her on, past all those about their work, into a place of light, in which there was Another. And that one Hertha could not look upon directly. But she heard a question asked, and to it she made truthful answer.

"No," she pressed her hands to her body, "what I carry I do not want to lose."

And that brightness which was the Other grew. But there was another question, and again Hertha answered:

"I hold two desires—that this child be mine alone, taking of no other heritage from the manner of its begetting and him who forced me so. And, second, I wish to bring to account the one who will not stand as its father."

There was a long moment before the reply came. Then a spear of light shot from the center core of the radiance, traced a symbol before Hertha. Though she had no training in the Mysteries yet, this was plain for her reading.

Her first prayer would be answered. The coming child would be only of her, taking naught from her ravisher. And the destiny for it was auspicious. But, though she waited, there was no second answer. The great One—was gone! But Elfreda was still with her, and Hertha turned to her quickly:

"What of my need for justice?"

"Vengeance is not of the Lady." Elfreda shook her veiled head. "She is life, not death. Since you have chosen to give life, she will aid you in that. For the rest—you must walk another road. But—do not take it, my love—for out of darkness comes even greater dark."

Then Hertha lost Elfreda also and there was nothing, only the memory of what happened in that place. So she fell into deeper slumber where no dreams walked.

She awoke, how much later she never knew. But she was renewed in mind and body, feeling as if some leechcraft had been at work during her rest, banishing all ills. There was no more smoke rising from the braziers, the scent of flowers was faint.

When she arose from the couch she knelt before the pillar, bowing her head, giving thanks. Yet still in her worked her second desire, in nowise lessened by Elfreda's warning.

In the outer room there was again food and drink waiting. And she ate and drank before she went forth from Gunnora's house. There was no kin far or near she might take refuge with. Kuno had made loud her shame when he sent her forth. She had a few bits of jewelry, none of worth, sewn into her girdle, some pieces of trade money. Beyond that she had only a housewife's skills, and those not of the common sort, rather the distilling of herbs, the making of ointments, the fine sewing of a lady's teaching. She could read, write, sing a stave—none of these arts conducive to the earning of one's bread.

Yet her spirit refused to be darkened by hard facts. From her waking that sense of things about to come right held. And she thought it best that she limit the future to one day ahead at a time.

In the direction she now faced lay two holdings. Nordendale was the first. It was small and perhaps in a state of disorder. The lord of the dale and his heir had both fallen at the battle of Ruther's Pass, two years gone. Who kept order there now, if there was any who ruled, she did not know. Beyond that lay Grimmerdale.

Grimmerdale! Hertha set down the goblet from which she had drained the last drop. Grimmerdale—

Just as the shrine of Gunnora was among the heights near the ancient road, so did Grimmerdale have a place of mystery. But no kind and welcoming one if rumor spoke true. Not of her race at all, but one as old as the ridge road. In fact perhaps that road had first been cut to run there.

Hertha tried to recall all she had heard of Grimmerdale. Somewhere in the heights there was the Circle of the Toads. Men had gone there, asked for certain things. By ill report they had received all they asked for.

What had Elfreda warned—that Gunnora did not grant death, that one must follow another path to find that. Grimmerdale might be the answer.

She looked about her, almost in challenge, half expecting to feel condemnation in the air of the room. But there was nothing.

"For the feast, my thanks," she spoke the guesting words, "for the roof, my blessing, for the future all good, as I take my road again."

She fastened the throat latch of her cloak, drew the hood over her head. Then with bundle in one hand and spear in the other, she went out into the light of day, her face to the ridges behind which lay Grimmerdale.

On the final slope above Nordendale she paused in the afternoon to study the small settlement below. It was inhabited, there was a curl of smoke from more than one chimney, the marks of sleds, foot prints in the snow. But the tower keep showed no such signs of life.

How far ahead still lay Grimmerdale she did not know, and night came early in the winter. One of those cottages below was larger than the rest. Nordendale had once been a regular halt for herdsmen with wool from mountain sheep on their way to the market at Komm High. That market was of the past, but the inn might still abide, at least be willing to give her shelter.

She was breathing hard when she trudged into the slush of the road below. But she had been right: over the door of the largest cottage hung a wind-battered board, its painted device long weathered away but still proclaiming this an inn. She made for that, passing a couple of men on the way. They stared at her as if she were a firedrake or wyvern. Strangers must be few in Nordendale.

The smell of food, sour village ale, and too many people too long in an unaired space was like a smothering fog as she came into the common room. At one end was a wide hearth, large enough to take a good-sized log, and fire burned there, giving off a goodly heat.

A trestle table with flanking benches, a smaller table stacked with tankards and settles by the hearth were the only furnishing. As Hertha entered, a wench in a stained smock and kirtle and two men on a hearth settle turned and started with the same astonishment she had seen without.

She pushed back her hood and looked back at them with that belief in herself which was her heritage.

"Good fortune to this house."

For a moment they made no answer at all, seemingly too taken aback at seeing a stranger to speak. Then the maidservant came forward, wiping her hands on her already well-besplattered apron.

"Good fortune"—her eyes were busy taking in the fine material of Hertha's cloak, her air of ease—"lady. How may we serve you?"

"With food, a bed—if such you have."

"Food—food we have, but it be plain, coarse feeding, lady," the girl stammered. "Let me but call mistress—"

She ran to an inner door, bolting through it as if Hertha was minded to pursue her.

But she rather laid aside her spear and bundle, threw back the edges of her cloak and went to stand before the hearth, pulling with her teeth at mitten fastenings, to bare her chilled hands. The men hunched away along the settle, mum-mouthed and still staring.

Hertha had thought her clothing plain. She wore one of the divided riding skirts, cut shorter for the scrambling up and down of hills, and it was now shabby and much worn, yet very serviceable. There was an embroidered edge on her jerkin, but no wider than some farm daughter might have. And her hair was tight braided, with no band of ribbon or silver to hold it so. Yet she might be clad in some festival finery the way they looked upon her. And she stood as impassive as she could under their stares.

A woman wearing the close coif of a matron, a loose shawl about her bent shoulders, a kirtle but little cleaner than the maid's, looped up about her wide hips and thick thighs, bustled in.

"Welcome, my lady. Thrice welcome! Up you, Henkin, Sim, let the lady to the fire!" The men pushed away in a hurry at her ordering. "Malka says you would bid the night. This roof is honored."

"I give thanks."

"Your man—outside? We have stabling—"

Hertha shook her head. "I journey alone and on foot." At the look on the woman's face she added, "In these days we take what fortune offers, we do not always please ourselves."

"Alas, lady, that is true speaking if such ever came to ear! Sit you down!" She jerked off her shawl and used it to dust along the settle.

Later, in a bed spread with coverings fire-warmed, in a room which manifestly had been shut up for some time, Hertha lay in what comfort such a place could offer and mused over what she had learned from her hostess.

As she had heard, Nordendale had fallen on dreary times. Along with their lord and his heir, most of their able-bodied men had been slain. Those who survived and drifted back lacked leadership and had done little to restore what had been a prosperous village. There were very few travelers along the road, she had been the first since winter closed in. Things were supposed to be somewhat better in the east and south, and her tale of going to kinsmen there had seemed plausible to those below.

Better still she had news of Grimmerdale. There was another inn there, a larger place, with more patronage, which the mistress here spoke of wistfully. An east-west road, now seeing much travel with levies going home, ran there. But the innkeeper had a wife who could not keep serving-maids, being of jealous nature.

Of the Toads she dared not ask, and no one had volunteered such information, save that the mistress here had warned against the taking farther of the Old Road, saying it was better to keep to the highway. Though she admitted that was also dangerous and it was well to be ready to take to the brush at the sighting of some travelers.

As yet Hertha had no more than the faint stirrings of a plan. But she was content to wait before she shaped it more firmly.

2

THE inn room was long but low, the crossbeams of its ceiling not far above the crown of a tall man's head. Smoking oil lamps hung on chains from those beams. But the light they gave was both murky and limited. Only at the far corner, where a carven screen afforded some privacy, were there tallow candles set out on a table. And the odor of their burning added to the general smell of the room.

The room was crowded enough to loosen the thin-lipped mouth of Uletka Rory, whose small eyes darted hither and yon, missing no detail of service or lack of service as her two laboring slaves limped and scuttled between benches and stools. She herself waited upon the candlelit table, a mark of favor. She knew high blood when she saw it.

Not that in this case she was altogether right, in spite of her years of dealing with travelers. One of the men there, yes, was the younger son of a dale lord. But his family holding had long since vanished in the red tide of war, and no one was left in Corriedale to name him master. One had been Master of Archers for another lord, promoted hurriedly after three better men had been killed. And the third, well, he was not one who talked, and neither of his present companions knew his past.

Of the three he was the middle in age. Though that, too, could not be easily guessed, since he was one of those lean, spare-framed men who once they begin to sprout beard hair can be any age from youth to middle years. Not that he went bearded now—his chin and jaw were as smooth as if he had scraped them within the hour, displaying along the jaw line the seam of a scar that drew a little at one corner of his lip.

He wore his hair cropped closer than most also, perhaps because of the heavy helm now planted on the table at his right hand. That was battered enough to have served through the war. And the crest it had once mounted was splintered down to a meaningless knob, though the protective bowl was unbreached.

His mail shirt, under a scuffed and worn tabbard, was whole. And the plain-hilted sword in his belt sheath, the war bow now resting against the wall at his back were the well-kept tools of a professional. But if he was a mercenary he had not been successful lately. He wore none of those fine buckles or studs which could be easily snapped off to pay for food or lodging. Only when he put out his hand to take up his tankard did the candlelight glint on something which was not dull steel or leather. For the bowguard on his wrist was true treasure, a wide band of cunningly wrought gold set with small colored stones, though the pattern of that design was so complicated that to make anything of it required close study.

He sat now sober-faced, as if he were deep in thought, his eyes half-veiled by heavy lids. But he was in truth listening, not so much to the half-drunken mumblings of his companions, but to words arising here and there in the common room.

Most of those gathered there were either workers on the land come in to nurse an earthen mug of home-brewed barley beer and exchange grumbles with their fellows, or else drifting men-at-arms seeking employment now that their lords were dead or so ruined that they had to release the men of their levies. The war was over, these were the victors. But the land they returned to was barren, largely devastated, and it would take much time and energy to win back prosperity for High Hallack.

What the invaders from overseas had not early raped, looted for shiploads sent back to their own lands, they had destroyed in a frenzy when the tide of war began to wash them away. He had been with the war bands in the smoking port, sent to mop up desperate enemies who had fallen back too late to find that their companions had taken off in the last ships, leaving them to be ground between the men of the dales and the sullen sea itself.

The smoke of the port had risen from piles of supplies set burning, oil poured over them and torches set to the spoilage. The stench of it had been near enough to kill a man. Having stripped the country bare—and this being the midwinter—the enemy had made a last defiant gesture with that great fire. It would be a long cold line of days before the coming of summer, and even then men would go pinched of belly until harvest time—harvest if, that is, they could find enough grain to plant, if enough sheep still roamed the upper dales and enough cattle, wild now, found forage in the edges of the Waste to make a beginning of new flocks and herds.

Many dales had been swept clean of people. The men were dead in battle; the women were fled inland, if they were lucky, or slaving for the invaders overseas—or dead also. Perhaps those were the luckiest of all. Yes, there had been a great shaking and leveling, sorting and spilling.

He had put down the tankard. Now his other hand went to that bowguard, turning it about, though he did not look down at it, but rather stared at the screen and listened.

In such a time a man with boldness, and a plan, could begin a new life. That was what had brought him inland, kept him from taking service with Fritigen of Summersdale. Who would be Master of Archers when he could be more, much more?

The invaders had not reached this Grimmersdale, but

there were other lands beyond with darker luck. He was going to find one of those—one where there was no lord left to sound the war horn. If there was a lady trying to hold a heritage, well, that might even fit well with his ambitions. Now his tongue showed for an instant on his lower lip, flicking across as if he savored in anticipation some dish which pleased him. He did not altogether believe in the over-ride of good or ill fortune. In his calculations a man mostly made his own luck by knowing what he wanted and bending all his actions toward that end. But he had a feeling that this was the time when he must move if he were ever to bring to truth the dream which had lain in him since early boyhood.

He, Trystan out of nowhere, was going to end Lord Trystan of some not inconsiderable stretch of land—with a keep for his home and a dale under his rule. And the time to move was here and now.

"Fill!" His near companion, young Urre, pounded his tankard on the table top so that one of the candles shook, spattering hot grease. He bellowed an oath and threw his empty pot beyond the screen to clatter across the flagstones.

The lame pot boy stooped to pick it up, casting a frightened look at Urre and a second at his scowling mistress, who was already on her way with a tray of freshly filled tankards. Trystan pushed back from the table. They were following a path he had seen too many nights. Urre would drink himself sodden, sick not only with the rank stuff they called drink back here in the hills, but also with his life, wherein he could only bewail what he had lost, taking no thought of what might be gained.

Onsway would listen attentively to his mumbling, willing to play liegeman as long as Urre's money lasted or he could use his kin ties to win them food and lodging at some keep. When Urre made a final sot of himself, Onsway would no longer wallow in the sty beside him. While he, Trystan, thought it time now to cut the thread which had brought them this far in uneasy company. Neither had anything to give, and he knew now that traveling longer with them he would not do.

But he was not minded to quit this inn soon. Its position on the highway was such that a man could pick up a wealth of information by just sitting and listening. Also, here he had already picked out two likely prospects for his own purposes. The money pouch at his belt was flat enough, he could not afford to spin a coin before the dazzled eyes of an archer or pike man and offer employment.

However, there were men like himself to be found, rootless men who wanted roots in better circumstances than they had known, men who could see the advantage of service under a rising man with opportunities for rising themselves in his wake. One did not need a large war band to overawe masterless peasants: half a dozen well-armed and experienced fighting men at his back, a dale without a lord—and he would be in!

Excitement awoke in him as it did every time his plan reached that place in his thoughts. But he had learned long since to keep a tight rein on his emotions. He was a controlled man, abstemious to a degree astounding among his fellows, though he did what he could to conceal that difference. He could loot, he could whore, he could kill—and he had—but always calculatingly.

"I'm for bed," he arose and reached for his bow, "the road this day was long—"

Urre might not have heard him at all, his attention was fixed on the tray of tankards. Onsway nodded absently; he was watching Urre as he always did. But the mistress was alert to the hint of more profit.

"Bed, good master? Three coins—and a fire on the hearth, too."

"Good enough." He nodded, and she screeched for the pot boy, who came at a limping waddle, wiping his grimed hands on the black rags of an apron knotted about him.

While the inn gave the impression of space below, on the second floor it was much more cramped. At least the room into which Trystan tramped was no more than a narrow slit of space with a single window covered by a shutter heavily barred. There was a litter of dried rushes on the floor and a rough bed frame, on which a pile of bedding lay as if tossed. The hearth fire promised did not exist. But a legged brazier with some glowing coals gave off a little heat, and a stool beside a warp-sided chest did service as a table. The pot boy set the candle down on that and was ready to scuttle away when Trystan, who had gone to the window, hailed him.

"What manner of siege have you had here, boy? This shutter has been so long barred it is rusted tight."

The boy cringed back against the edge of the door, his slack mouth hanging open. He was an ugly lout, and looked half-witted into the bargain, Trystan thought. But surely there was something more than just stupidity in his face when he looked to the window—there was surely fear also.

"Thhheee tooods—" His speech was thick. He had lifted his hands breast high, was clasping them so tightly together that his knuckles stood out as bony knobs.

Trystan had heard the enemy called many things, but never toads, nor had he believed they had raided into Grimmerdale.

"Toads?" He made a question of the word.

The boy turned his head away so that he looked neither to the window nor at Trystan. It was very evident he planned escape. The man crossed the narrow room with effortless and noiseless strides, caught him by the shoulder.

"What manner of toads?" He shook the boy slightly.

"Toodss—Thhheee toods—" the boy seemed to think Trystan should know of what he spoke. "They—that sit 'mong the Standing Stones—that what do men evil." His voice, while thick, no longer sputtered so. "All men know the Toods o' Grimmerdale!" Then, with a twist which showed he had long experience in escaping, he broke from Trystan's hold and was gone. The man did not pursue him.

Rather he stood frowning in the light of the single candle. Toads—and Grimmerdale—together they had a faintly familiar sound. Now he set memory to work. Toads and Grimmerdale—what did he know of either?

The dale was of importance, more so now than in the days before the war when men favored a more southern route to the port. That highway had fallen almost at once into invader hands, and they had kept it forted and patroled. The answer had been this secondary road, which heretofore had been used mainly by shepherds and herdsmen. Three different trails from upcountry united at the western edge of Grimmerdale.

However: had he not once heard of yet a fourth way, one which ran the ridges yet was mainly shunned, a very old way, antedating the coming of his own people? Now—he nodded as memory supplied answers. The Toads of Grimmerdale! One of the many stories about the remnants of those other people, or things, which had already mostly faded from this land, so that the coming of man did not dislodge them, for the land had been largely deserted before the first settlement ship arrived.

Still there were places in plenty where certain powers and presences were felt to this day, where things could be invoked—by men who were crazed enough to summon them. Had the lords of High Hallack not been driven at the last to make such a bargain with the unknown when they signed solemn treaty with the Were Riders? All men knew that it had been the aid of those strange outlanders which had broken the invaders at the last.

Some of the presences were beneficial, others neutral, still others dangerous. Perhaps not actively so in these days. Men were not hunted, harried, or attacked by them. But they had their own places, and the man who was rash enough to trespass there did so at risk.

Among such were the Standing Stones of the Toads of Grimmerdale. The story went that they would answer appeals, but that the manner of answer sometimes did not please the petitioner. For years now men had avoided their place.

But why a shuttered window? If, as according to legend, the toads (people were not sure now if they really *were* toads) did not roam from their portion of the dale, had they once? Making it necessary to bolt and bar against them? And why a second-story window in this dusty room?

Moved by a curiosity he did not wholly understand, Trystan drew his belt knife, pried at the fastenings. They were deeply bitten with rust, and he was sure that the window had not been opened night or day for years. At last the fastenings yielded to his efforts; he was now stubborn about it, somehow even a little angry.

Even though he was at last able to withdraw the bar, he had a second struggle with the warped wood, finally using sword point to lever it. The shutters grated open, the chill of the night entered, making him aware at once of how very odorous and sour was the fog within.

Trystan looked out upon snow and a straggle of dark trees, with the upslope of the dale wall beyond. There were no other buildings set between the inn and that rise. And the thick vegetation showing dark above the sweep of white on the ground suggested that the land was uncultivated. The trees there were not tall, it was mainly brush, and he did not like it.

His war-trained instincts saw there a menace. Any enemy could creep in its cover to within a spear-cast of the inn. Yet perhaps those of Grimmerdale did not have such fears, and so saw no reason to grub out and burn there.

The slope began gradually and shortly the tangled growth thinned out, as if someone had there taken the precautions Trystan thought right. Above was smooth snow, very white and unbroken in the moonlight. Then came outcrops of rock. But after he had studied those with an eye taught to take quick inventory of a countryside, he was sure they were no natural formations but had been set with a purpose.

They did not form a connected wall. There were wide spaces between as if they had served as posts for some stringing of fence. Yet for that they were extra thick.

And the first row led to a series of five such lines, though in successive rows the stones were placed closer and closer together. Trystan was aware of two things. One, bright as the moon was, it did not, he was sure, account for all the light among the stones. There was a radiance which seemed to rise either from them or the ground about them. Second, no snow lay on the land from the point where the lines of rock pillar began. And above the stones there was a misting, as if something there bewildered or hindered clear sight.

Trystan blinked, rubbed his hand across his eyes, looked again. The clouding was more pronounced when he did so. As if whatever lay there increased the longer he watched it.

That this was not of human Grimmerdale he was certain. It had all the signs of being one of those strange places where old powers lingered. And that this was the refuge or stronghold of the "toads" he was now sure. That the shutter had been bolted against the weird sight he could also understand, and he rammed and pounded the warped wood back into place, though he could not reset the bar he had levered out.

Slowly he put aside mail and outer clothing, laying it across the chest. He spread out the bedding over the hide webbing. Surprisingly the rough sheets, the two woven covers were clean. They even (now that he had drawn lungfuls of fresh air to awaken his sense of smell) were fragrant with some kind of herb.

Trystan stretched out, pulled the covers about his ears, drowsy and content, willing himself to sleep.

He awoke to a clatter at the door. At first he frowned

up at the cobwebbed rafters above. What had he dreamed? Deep in his mind there was a troubled feeling, a sense that a message of some importance had been lost. He shook his head against such fancies and padded to the door, opened it for the entrance of the elder serving man, a dour-faced, skeleton-thin fellow who was more cleanly of person than the pot boy. He carried a covered kettle, which he put down on the chest before he spoke.

"Water for washing, master. There be grain mush, pig cheek, and ale below."

"Well enough." Trystan slid the lid off the pot. Steam curled up. He had not expected this small luxury, and he took its arrival as an omen of fortune for the day.

Below the long room was empty. The lame boy was washing off table tops, splashing water on the floor in great scummy dollops. His mistress stood, hands on her hips, her elbows outspread like crooked wings, her sharp chin with its two haired warts outthrust like a spear to threaten the woman before her, well cloaked against the outside winter, but with her hood thrown back to expose her face.

That face was thin, with sharp features lacking any claim to comeliness, since the stretched skin was mottled with unsightly brown patches. But her cloak, Trystan saw, was good wool, certainly not that of a peasant wench. She carried a bundle in one hand, and in the other was a short-hafted hunting spear, its butt scarred as if it had served her more as a journey staff than a weapon.

"Well enough, wench. But here you work for the food in your mouth, the clothing on your back." The mistress shot a single glance at Trystan before she centered her attention once more on the girl.

Girl, Trystan thought she was. Though by the Favor of Likerwolf certainly her face was not that of a dewy maid, being rather enough to turn a man's thoughts more quickly to other things when he looked upon her.

"Put your gear on the shelf yonder," the mistress

gestured. "Then come to work, if you speak the truth on wanting that."

She did not watch to see her orders obeyed, but came to the table where Trystan had seated himself.

"Grain mush, master. And a slicing of pig jowl—ale fresh drawn—"

He nodded, sitting much as he had the night before, fingering the finely wrought guard about his wrist, his eyes half closed as if he were still wearied, or else turned his thoughts on things not about him.

The mistress stumped away. But he was not aware she had returned until someone slid a tray onto the table. It was the girl, her shrouding of cloak gone, so that the tight bodice of the pleated skirt could be seen. And he was right: she did not wear peasant clothes, that was a skirt divided for riding, though it had now been shortened enough to show boots, scuffed and worn, straw protruding from their tops. Her figure was thin, yet shapely enough to make a man wonder at the fate which wedded such to that horror of a face. She did not need her spear for protection; all she need do was show her face to any would-be ravisher and she would be as safe as the statue of Gunnora the farmers carried through their fields at first sowing.

"Your food, master." She was deft, far more so than the mistress, as she slid the platter of crisp browned mush and thin-sliced pink meat onto the board.

"Thanks given," Trystan found himself making civil answer as he might in some keep were one of the damosels there noticing him in courtesy.

He reached for the tankard and at that moment saw her head sway, her eyes wide open rested on his hand. And he thought, with a start of surprise, that her interest was no slight one. But when he looked again she was moving away, her eyes downcast like those of any proper serving wench.

"There will be more, master?" she asked in a colorless voice. But her voice also betrayed her. No girl save one hold-bred would have such an accent.

There had been many upsets in the dales. What was it to him if some keep woman had been flung out of her soft nest to tramp the roads, serve in an inn for bread and a roof? With her face she could not hope to catch a man to fend for her—unless he be struck blind before their meeting.

"No," he told her. She walked away with the light and soundless step of a forest hunter, the grace of one who sat at high tables by right of blood.

Well, he, too, would sit at a high table come next year's end. Of that he was as certain as if it had been laid upon him by some Power Master as an unbreakable geas. But it would be because of his own two hands, the cunning of his mind, and as such his rise would be worth more than blood right. She had come down, he would go up. Seeing her made him just more confident of the need for moving on with his plan.

3

THE road along the ridges was even harder footing after Nordendale, Hertha discovered. There were gaps where landslides had cut away sections, making the going very slow. However she kept on, certain this was the only way to approach what she sought.

As she climbed and slid, edged with caution, even in places had to leap recklessly with her spear as a vaulting pole, she considered what might lie ahead. In seeking Gunnora she had kept to the beliefs of her people. But if she continued to the shrine of the Toads she turned her back on what safety she knew.

Around her neck was hung a small bag of grain and dried herbs, Gunnora's talisman for home and hearth. Another such was sewn into the breast of her undersmock. And in the straw which lined each boot were other leaves with their protection for the wayfarer. Before she had set out on this journey she had marshaled all she knew of protective charms.

But whether such held against alien powers, she could not tell. To each race its own magic. The old ones were not men, and their beliefs and customs must have been far different. That being so, did she now tempt great evil?

Always when she reached that point she remembered. And memory was as sharp as any spur on a rider's heel. She had been going to the abbey in Lethendale, Kuno having suggested it. Perhaps that was why he had turned from her, feeling guilt in the matter.

Going to Lethendale, she must ever remember how it was, every dark part of it. For if she did not hold that in mind, then she would lose the bolster of anger for her courage. A small party because Kuno was sure there was naught to fear from the fleeing invaders. But after all it was not the invaders she had to fear.

There had come a rain of arrows out of nowhere. She could hear yet the bubbling cry of young Jannesk as he fell from the saddle with one through his throat. They had not even seen the attackers, and all the men had been shot down in only moments. She had urged her mount on, only to have him entangle hoofs in a trip rope. After that she could remember only flying over his head—

Until she awoke in the dark, her hands tied, looking out into a clearing where a fire burned between rocks. Men sat about the fire tearing at chunks of half-roasted meat. *Those* had been the invaders. And she had lain cold, knowing well what they meant for her when they had satisfied one appetite and were ready—

They had come to her at last. Even with tied hands she had fought. So they had laughed and cuffed her among them, tearing at her garments and handling her shamefully, though they did not have time for the last insult and degradation of all. No, that was left for some—some *man* of her own people!

Thinking on it now made rage rise to warm her even

though the sun had withdrawn from this slope and there was a chill rising wind.

For the ambushers had been attacked in turn, fell under spear and arrow out of the dark. Half conscious she had been left lying until a harsh weight on her, hard, bruising hands brought her back to terror and pain.

She had never seen his face, but she had seen (and it was branded on her memory for all time) the bowguard encircling the wrist tightened as a bar across her throat to choke her unconscious. And when she had once more stirred she was alone.

Someone had thrown a cloak over her nakedness. There was a horse nearby. There was for the rest only dead men under a falling snow. She never understood why they had not killed her and been done with it. Perhaps in that little her attacker had been overridden by his companions. But at the time she had been sorely tempted to lie where she was and let the cold put an end to her. Only the return of that temper which was her heritage roused her. Somewhere living was the man who should have been her savior and instead had rift from her what was to be given only as a free gift. To bring him down, for that she would live.

Later, when she found she çarried new life, yes, she had been tempted again—to do as they urged, rid herself of that. But in the end she could not. For though part of the child was of evil, yet a part was hers. Then she recalled Gunnora and the magic which could aid. So she had withstood Kuno's urging, even his brutal anger.

She held to two things with all the stubborn strength she could muster—that she would bear this child which must be hers only, and that she would have justice on the man who would never in truth be its father. The first part of her desire Gunnora had given. Now she went for answer to the second.

At last night came and she found a place among the rocks where she could creep in, the stone walls giving refuge from the wind, a carpet of dried leaves to blanket her. She must have slept, for when she roused she was not sure where she was. Then she was aware of the influence which must have brought her awake. There was an uneasiness of the very air about her, a tension as if she stood on the verge of some great event.

With the spear as her staff, Hertha came farther into the open. The moon showed her unmarked snow ahead, made dark pits of her own tracks leading here. With it for a light she started on.

A wan radiance, having no light of fire, shown in the distance. It came from no torch either, she was sure. But it might well mark what she sought.

Here the Old Road was unbroken though narrow. She prodded the snow ahead, lest there be some hidden crevice. But she hurried as if to some important meeting.

Tall shapes arose, stones set on end in rows. In the outer lines there were wide spaces between, but the stones of the inner rows were placed closer and closer together. She followed a road cut straight between these pillars.

On the crest of each rested a small cone of light, as if these were not rocks but giant candles to light her way. And that light was cold instead of warm, blue instead of the orange-red of true flame. Also here the moonlight was gone, so that even though there was no roof she could see, yet it was shut away.

Three stone rows she passed, then four more, each with the stones closer together, so that the seventh brought them touching to form a wall. The road dwindled to a path which led through a gate in the wall.

Hertha knew that even had she wanted to retreat, now she could not. It was as if her feet were held to the path and it moved, bearing her with it.

So she came into a hexagonal space within the wall. There was a low curbing of stone to fence off the centermost portion and in each angle blazed a flame at ground level. But she could go no farther, just as she could not draw away.

Within the walled area were five blocks of green stone. These glistened in the weird light as if they were carved of polished gems. Their tops had been squared off to give seating for those who awaited her.

What she had expected Hertha was not sure. But what she saw was so alien to all she knew that she did not even feel fear, but rather wonder that such could exist in a world where men also walked. Now she could understand why these bore the name of toads, for that was the closest mankind could come in descriptive comparison.

Whether they went on two limbs or four she could not be sure, the way they hunched upon their blocks. But they were no toads in spite of their resemblance. Their bodies were bloated of paunch, the four limbs seemingly too slender beside that heaviness. Their heads sat upon narrow shoulders with no division of neck. And those heads were massive, with large golden eyes high on their hairless skulls, noses which were slits only, and wide mouths stretching above only a vestige of chin.

"Welcome, seeker—"

The words rang in her head, not her ears. Nor could she tell which of the creatures had addressed her.

Now that Hertha had reached her goal she found no words, she was too bemused by the sight of those she had sought. Yet it seemed that she did not have to explain, for the mind speech continued:

"You have come seeking our aid. What would you, daughter of men—lose that which weighs your body?"

At that Hertha found her tongue to speak.

"Not so. Though the seed in me was planted not by lawful custom but in pain and torment of mind and body, yet will I retain it. I shall bear a child who shall be mine alone, as Gunnora has answered my prayers."

"Then what seek you here?"

"Justice! Justice upon him who took me by force and in shame!"

"Why think you, daughter of men, that you and your

matters mean aught to us, who were great in this land before your feeble kind came and who will continue to abide even after man is again gone? What have we to do with you?"

"I do not know. Only I have listened to old tales, and I have come."

She had an odd sensation then; if one could sense laughter in one's mind, she was feeling it. They were amused, and knowing that she lost some of her assurance.

Again a surge of amusement, and then a feeling as if they had withdrawn, conferred among themselves. Hertha would have fled, but she could not. And she was afraid as she had not been since she faced horror on the road to Lethendale.

"Upon whom ask you justice, daughter of men? What is his name, where lies he this night?"

She answered with the truth. "I know neither. I have not even seen his face. Yet"—she forgot her fear, knew only that which goaded her on—"I have that which shall make him known to me. And I may find him here in Grimmerdale, since men in many now pass along this road, the war being ended."

Again that withdrawal. Then another question.

"Do you not know that services such as ours do not come without payment? What have you to offer us in return, daughter of men?"

Hertha was startled, she had never really thought past making her plea here. That she had been so stupid amazed her. Of course there would be payment! Instinctively she dropped her bundle, clasped her hands in guard over where the child lay.

Amusement once more.

"Nay, daughter of men. From Gunnora you have claimed that life, nor do we want it. But justice can serve us too. We shall give you the key to that which you wish, and the end shall be ours. To this do you agree?"

"I do." Though she did not quite understand.

"Look you—there!" One of the beings raised a forefoot and pointed over her shoulder. Hertha turned her head. There was a small glowing spot on the surface of the stone pillar. She put out her hand and at her touch a bit of stone loosened, so she held a small pebble.

"Take that, daughter of men. When you find him you seek, see it lies in his bed at the coming of night. Then your justice will fall upon him—here! And so you will not forget, nor think again and change your mind, we shall set a reminder where you shall see it each time you look into your mirror."

Again the being pointed, this time at Hertha. From the forelimb curled a thin line of vapor. That gathered to form a ball which flew at her. Though she flinched and tried to duck, it broke against her face with a tingling feeling which lasted only for a second.

"You shall wear that until he comes hither, daughter of men. So will you remember your bargain."

What happened then she was not sure, it was all confused. When she was clear-headed again dawn was breaking, and she clawed her way out of the leaf-carpeted crevice. Was it all a dream? No, her fingers were tight about something, cramped and in pain from that hold. She looked down at a pebble of green-gray stone. So in truth she had met the Toads of Grimmerdale.

Grimmerdale itself lay spread before her, easy to see in the gathering light. The lord's castle was on the farther slope, the village and inn by the highway. And it was the inn she must reach.

Early as it was there were signs of life about the place. A man went to the stable without noticing her as she entered the courtyard. She advanced to the half-open door, determined to strike some bargain for work with the mistress, no matter how difficult the woman was reputed to be.

The great room was empty when she entered. But

moments later a woman with a forbidding face stumped in. Hertha went directly to her. The woman stared at her and then grinned maliciously.

"You've no face to make trouble, wench, one can be certain of that," she said when Hertha asked for work. "And it is true that an extra pair of hands is wanted. Not that we have a purse so fat we can toss away silver—"

As she spoke a man came down the steep inner stair, crossed to sit at a table half screened from the rest. It was almost as if his arrival turned the scales in Hertha's favor. For she was told to put aside her bundle and get to work. So it was she who took the food tray to where he sat.

He was tall, taller than Kuno, with well-set, wide shoulders. And there was a sword by his side, plain-hilted, in a worn scabbard. His features were sharp, his face thin, as if he might have gone on short rations too often in the past. Black hair peaked on his forehead, and she could not guess his age, though she thought he might be young.

But it was when she put down her tray and he reached out for an eating knife that it seemed the world stopped for an instant. She saw the bowguard on his wrist. And her whole existence narrowed to that metal band. Some primitive instinct of safety closed about her, she was sure she had not betrayed herself.

As she turned from the table she wondered if this was by the power of the Toads, if they had brought her prey to her hand so. What had they bade her—to see that the pebble was in his bed. But this was early morn and he had just risen. What if he meant not to stay another night but would push on? How could she then carry out their orders? Unless she followed after him, somehow crept upon him at nightfall.

At any rate he seemed in no hurry to be up and off, if that was his purpose. Finally, with relief, she heard him bargain with the mistress for a second night's stay. She found an excuse to go above, carrying fresh bedding for a second room to be made ready. And as she went down the narrow hall she wondered how best she could discover which room was his.

So intent was she upon this problem that she was not aware of someone behind her until an ungentle hand fell on her shoulder and she was jerked about.

"Now here's a new one—" The voice was brash and young. Hertha looked at a man with something of the unformed boy still in his face. His thick yellow hair was uncombed, his jaw beard stubbled, his eyes red-rimmed.

As he saw her clearly he made a grimace of distaste, shoved her from him with force, so she lost her balance and fell to the floor.

"—leave kiss a toad!" He spat, but the trail of spittle never struck her. Instead hands fell on him, slammed him against the other wall. While the man of the bowguard surveyed him steadily.

"What's to do?" The younger man struggled. "Take your hands off me, fellow!"

"Fellow, is it?" observed the other. "I am no liegeman of yours, Urre. Nor are you in Roxdale now. As for the wench, she's not to blame for her face. Perhaps she should thank whatever Powers she lights a candle to that she had it. With such as you ready to lift every skirt they meet."

"Toad! She is a toad-face—" Urre worked his mouth as if he wished to spit again, then something in the other's eyes must have warned him. "Hands off me!" He twisted and the other stepped back. With an oath Urre lurched away, heading unsteadily for the stair.

Hertha got to her feet, stooped to gather up the draggle of covers she had dropped.

"Has he hurt you?"

She shook her head dumbly. It had all been so sudden, and that *he*—this one—had lifted hand in her defense dazed her. She moved away as fast as she could, but before she reached the end of the passage she looked back. He was going through a door a pace away from where the one called Urre had stopped her. So—she had learned his room. But "toad-face"? That wet ball which had struck her last night—what had it done to her?

Hertha used her fingers to trace any alteration in her features. But to her touch she was as she had always been. A mirror—she must find a mirror! Not that the inn was likely to house such a luxury.

In the end she found one in the kitchen, in a tray which she had been set to polishing. Though her reflection was cloudy, there was no mistaking the ugly brown patches on her skin. Would they be so forever, a brand set by her trafficking with dark powers, or would they vanish with the task done? Something she had remembered from that strange voiceless conversation made her hope the latter was true.

If so, the quicker she moved to the end the better. But she did not soon get another chance to slip aloft. The man's name was Trystan. The lame pot boy had taken an interest in him and was full of information. Trystan had been a Marshal and a Master of Archers—he was now out of employment, moving inland probably to seek a new lord. But perhaps he was thinking of raising a war band on his own; he had talked already with other veterans staying here. He did not drink much, though those others with him, Urre, who was son to a dale lord, and his liegeman ordered enough to sink a ship.

Crumbs, yes, but she listened eagerly for them, determined to learn all she could of this Trystan she must enmesh in her web. She watched him, too, given occasion when she might do so without note. It gave her a queer feeling to look this way upon the man who had used her so and did not guess now she was so near.

Oddly enough, had it not been for the evidence of the bowguard she would have picked him last of those she saw beneath this roof. Urre, yes, and two or three others, willing to make free with her until they saw her face clearly. But when she had reason to pass by this Trystan he showed her small courtesies, as if her lack of comeliness meant nothing. He presented a puzzle which was disturbing.

But that did not change her plan. So, at last, when she managed close to dusk to slip up the stairway quickly, she sped down the hall to his room. There was a huddle of coverings on the bed. She could not straighten them, but she thrust the pebble deep into the bag-pillow and hurried back to the common room, where men were gathering. There she obeyed a stream of orders, fetching and carrying tankards of drink, platters of food.

The fatigue of her long day of unaccustomed labor was beginning to tell. And there were those among the patrons who used cruel humor to enliven the evening. She had to be keen-witted and clear-eyed to avoid a foot slyly thrust forth to trip her, a sudden grab at her arm to dump a filled platter or tray of tankards. Twice she suffered defeat and was paid by a ringing buffet from the mistress' hand for the wasting of food.

But at length she was freed from their persecution by the mistress (not out of any feeling for her, but as a matter of saving spillage and spoilage) and set to the cleaning of plates in a noisome hole where the stench of old food and greasy slops turned her stomach and made her so ill she was afraid she could not last. Somehow she held out until finally the mistress sourly shoved her to one of the fireside settles and told her that was the best bed she could hope for. Hertha curled up, so tired she ached, while the rest of the inn people dragged off to their holes and corners—chambers were for guests alone.

The fire had been banked for the night, but the hearth was warm. Now that she had the great room to herself, though her body was tired, her mind was alert, and she rested as best she could while she waited. If all went well, surely the stone would act this night, and she determined to witness the action. Beyond that she had not planned.

Hertha waited for what seemed a long time, shifting now and then on her hard bed. Near to hand were both her cloak and the spear staff, her boots, new filled with fresh straw, were on her feet.

She was aware of a shadow at the head of the stairs, or steps. She watched and listened. Yes, she had been right—this was the man Trystan, and he was walking toward the door. Whirling her cloak about her, Hertha rose to follow.

4

SHE clung to the shadow of the inn wall for fear he might look behind. But he strode on with the sure step of a man on some mission of such importance his present surroundings had little meaning, rounding the back of the inn, tramping upslope.

Though a moon hung overhead, there was also a veiling of cloud. Hertha dropped farther and farther behind, for the brambles of the scrub caught at her cloak, the snow weighted her skirt, and the fatigue of her long day's labor was heavy on her. Yet she felt that she must be near to Trystan when he reached his goal. Was it that she must witness the justice of the Toads? She was not sure any more, concentrating all her effort on the going.

Now she could see the stones stark above. They bore no candles on their crests this night, were only grim blots of darkness. Toward them Trystan headed in as straight a line as the growth would allow.

He reached the first line of stones; not once had he looked around. Long since Hertha abandoned caution. He was almost out of sight! She gathered up her skirts, panting heavily as she plunged and skidded to where he had disappeared.

Yes, now she could see him, though he was well ahead. But when he reached that final row, the one forming a real wall, he would have to move along it to the entrance of the Old Road. While she, already knowing the way, might gain a few precious moments by seeking the road now. And she did that, coming to better footing with her breath whistling through her lips in gasps.

She had no spear to lean on and she nursed a sharp pain in her side. But she set her teeth and wavered on between those rows of stones, seeing the gate ahead and in it a dark figure. Trystan was still a little before.

There came a glow of light, the cold flames were back on pillar top. In its blue radiance her hands looked diseased and foul when she put them out to steady herself as she went.

Trystan was just within the gate of the hexagon. He had not moved, but rather stared straight ahead at whatever awaited him. His sword was belted at his side, the curve of his bow was a pointing finger behind his shoulder. He had come fully armed, yet he made no move to draw weapon now.

Hertha stumbled on. That struggle upslope had taken much of her strength. Yet in her was the knowledge that she must be there. Before her now, just beyond her touching even if she reached forth her arm, was Trystan. His head was uncovered, the loose hood of his surcoat lay back on his shoulders. His arms dangled loosely at his sides. Hertha's gaze followed to the object of his staring concentration.

There were the green blocks. But no toad forms humped upon them. Rather lights played there, weaving in and out in a flickering dance of shades of blue—from a wan blight, which might have emanated from some decaying bit on a forest floor, to a brilliant sapphire.

Hertha felt the pull of those weaving patterns until she forced herself (literally forced her heavy hands to cover her eyes) not to look upon the play of color. When she did so there was a sensation of release. But it was plain her companion was fast caught.

Cupping her hands to shut out all she could of the lights, she watched Trystan. He made no move to step across the low curbing and approach the blocks. He might have been turned into stone himself, rapt in a spell which had made of him ageless rock. He did not blink an eye, nor could she even detect the rise and fall of his chest in breathing.

Was this their judgment then, the making of a man into a motionless statue? Somehow Hertha was sure that whatever use the Toads intended to make of the man they had entrapped through her aid, it was more than this. Down inside her something stirred. Angrily she fought against that awakening of an unbidden thought, or was it merely emotion? She drew memory to her, lashed herself with all shameful, degrading detail. This had he done to her and this and this! By his act she was homeless, landless, a nothing, wearing even a toad-face. Whatever came now to him, he richly deserved it. She would wait and watch, and then she would go hence, and in time, as Gunnora had promised, she would bear a son or daughter who had none of this father—none!

Still watching him, her hands veiling against the play of the ensorceling light, Hertha saw his lax fingers move, clench into a fist. And then she witnessed the great effort of that gesture, and she knew that he was in battle, silent though he stood, that he fought with all his strength against what held him fast.

That part of her which had stirred and awakened grew stronger. She battled it. He deserved nothing but what would come to him here, he deserved nothing from her but the justice she had asked from the Toads.

His fist arose, so slowly that it might have been chained to some great weight. When Hertha looked from it to his face she saw the agony the movement was causing him. She set her shoulders to the rock wall—had she but a rope she would have bound herself there, that no weakness might betray her plan.

Strange light before him and something else, formless

as yet, but with a cold menace greater than any fear born of battle heat. For this terror was rooted not in any ordinary danger, but grew from a horror belonging by rights far back in the beginnings of his race. How he had come here, whether this be a dream or no, Trystan was not sure. And he had no time to waste on confused memory.

What energy he possessed must be used to front that which was keeping him captive. It strove to fill him with its own life, and that he would not allow, not while he could summon will to withstand it.

Somehow he thought that if he broke the hold upon his body, he could also shatter its would-be mastery of his mind and will. Could he act against its desires, he might regain control. So he set full concentration on his hand—his fingers. It was as if his flesh were nerveless, numb—But he formed a fist. Then he brought up his arm, so slowly that had he allowed himself to waver he might have despaired. But he knew that he must not relax the intense drive of will centered in that simple move. Weapons—what good would his bow, his sword be against what dwelt here? He sensed dimly that this menace could well laugh at weapons forged and carried by those of his kind.

Weapons—sword—steel—there was something hovering just at the fringe of memory. Then for an instant he saw a small, sharp mind picture. Steel! That man from the Waste-side dale who had set his sword as a barrier at the head of his sleeping roll, plunged his dagger point deep in the soil at his feet the night they had left him on the edge of very ancient ruins with their mounts. Between cold iron a man lay safe, he said. Some scoffed at his superstition, others had nodded agreement. Iron—cold iron—which certain old Powers feared.

He had a sword at his belt now, a long dagger at his hip—iron—talisman? But the struggle of possession of his fist, his arm was so hard he feared he would never have a chance to put the old belief to the proof.

What did they want of him, those who abode here? For he was aware that there was more than one will bent on him. Why had they brought him? Trystan shied away from questions. He must concentrate on his hand—his arm!

With agonizing slowness he brought his hand to his belt, forced his fingers to touch the hilt of his sword.

That was no lord's proud weapon with a silvered, jeweled hilt, but a serviceable blade nicked and scratched by long use. So that the hilt itself was metal, wound with thick wire to make a good grip which would not turn in a sweating hand. His finger tips touched that and—his hand was free!

He tightened hold instantly, drew the blade with a practiced sweep, and held it up between him and that riot of blending and weaving blue lights. Relief came, but it was only minor he knew after a moment or two of swelling hope. What coiled here could not be so easily defeated. Always that other will weighted and plucked at his hand. The sword blade swung back and forth, he was unable to hold it steady. Soon he might not be able to continue to hold it at all!

Trystan tried to retreat even a single step. But his feet were as if set in a bog, entrapped against any move. He had only his failing hand and the sword, growing heavier every second. Now he was not holding it erect as if on guard, but doubled back as if aimed at his own body!

Out of the blue lights arose a tendril of wan phosphorescent stuff which looped into the air and held there, its tip pointed in his direction. Another weaved up to joint it, swell its substance. A third came, a fourth was growing—

The tip, which had been narrow as a finger, was now thickening. From that smaller tips rounded and swelled into being. Suddenly Trystan was looking at a thing of active evil, a grotesque copy of a human hand, four fingers, a thumb too long and thin.

When it was fully formed it began to lower toward

him. Trystan with all his strength brought up the sword, held its point as steady as he could against that reaching hand.

Again he knew a fleeting triumph. For at the threat of the sword, the hand's advance was stayed. Then it moved right, left, as if to strike as a foeman's point past his guard. But he was able by some miracle of last reserves to counter each attack.

Hertha watched the strange duel wide-eyed. The face of her enemy was wet, great trickles of sweat ran from his forehead to drip from his chin. His mouth was a tight snarl, lips flattened against his teeth. Yet he held that sword and the emanation of the Toads would not pass it.

"You!"

The word rang in her head with a cold arrogance which hurt.

"Take from him the sword!"

An order she must obey if she was to witness her triumph. Her triumph? Hertha crouched against the rock watching that weird battle—sword point swinging with such painful slowness, but ever just reaching the right point in time so that the blue hand did not close. The man was moving so slowly, why could the Toads not beat him by a swift dart past his guard? Unless their formation of the hand, their use of it was as great an effort for them as his defense seemed to be for him.

"The sword!" That demand in her mind hurt.

Hertha did not stir. "I cannot!" Did she cry that aloud, whisper it, or only think it? She was not sure. Nor why she could not carry through to the end that which had brought her here—that she did not understand either.

Dark—and her hands were bound. There were men struggling. One went down with an arrow through him. Then cries of triumph. Someone came to her through shadows. She could see only mail—a sword—

Then she was pinned down by a heavy hand. She heard laughter, evil laughter which scorched her, though her body shivered as the last of her clothing was ripped away. Once more—

No! She would not remember it all! She would not! They could not make her—but they did. Then she was back in the here and now. And she saw Trystan fighting his stumbling, hopeless battle, knew him again for what he was.

"The sword—take from him the sword!"

Hertha lurched to her feet. The sword—she must get the sword. Then he, too, would learn what it meant to be helpless and shamed and—and what? Dead? Did the Toads intend to kill him?

"Will you kill him?" she asked them. She had never foreseen the reckoning to be like this.

"The sword!"

They did not answer, merely spurred her to their will. Death? No, she was certain they did not mean his death, at least not death such as her kind knew it. And—but—

"The sword!"

In her mind that order was a painful lash, meant to send her unthinking to their service. But it acted otherwise, alerting her to a new sense of peril. She had evoked that which had no common meeting with her kind. Now she realized she had loosed that which not even the most powerful man or woman she knew might meddle with. Trystan could deserve the worst she was able to pull upon him. But that must be the worst by men's standards—not this!

Her left hand went to the bag of Gunnora's herbs where it rested between her swelling breasts. Her right groped on the ground, closed about a stone. Since she touched the herb bag that voice was no longer a pain in her head. It faded like a far-off calling. She readied the stone—

Trystan watched that swinging hand. His sword arm ached up into his shoulder. He was sure every moment he would lose control. Hertha bent, tore at the lacing of her bodice so that the herb bag swung free. Fiercely she rubbed it back and forth on the stone. What so pitiful an effort might do—

She threw it through the murky air, struck against that blue hand. It changed direction, made a dart past Trystan. Knowing that this might be his one chance, Trystan brought down the sword with all the force he could muster on the tentacle which supported the hand.

The blade passed through as if what he saw had no substance, had been woven of his own fears. There was a burst of pallid light. Then the lumpish hand and that which supported it were gone.

In the same moment he discovered he could move, and staggered back. And a hand fell upon his arm, jerking him in the same direction. He flailed out wildly at what could only be an enemy's hold, broke it. There was a cry and he turned his head.

A dark huddle lay at the foot of the stone door frame. Trystan advanced the sword point, ready, as strength flowed once more into him, to meet this new attack. The bundle moved a white hand clutched at the pillar, pulled.

His bemused mind cleared. This was a woman! Not only that, but what had passed him through the air had not been flung at him, but at the hand. She had been a friend and not an enemy in that moment.

But now from behind he heard a new sound, like the hiss of a disturbed serpent. Or there might be more than one snake voicing hate. He gained the side of the woman, with the rock at his back, looked once more at the center space.

That tentacle which had vanished at the sword stroke might be gone, but there were others rising. And this time the tentacles did not unite to form hands, but rather each produced something like unto a serpent head. And they arose in such numbers that no one man could stand to front them all—though he must try.

Once more he felt a light weight upon his shoulder, he

glanced to the side. The woman was standing, one hand tight to her breast, the other resting on his upper arm now. Her hood overshadowed her face so he could not see it. But he could hear the murmur of her voice even through the hissing of the pseudo-serpents. Though he could not understand the words, there was a rhythmic flow as if she chanted a battle song for his encouragement.

One of the serpent lengths swung at them, he used the sword. At its touch the thing vanished. But one out of a dozen, what was that? Again his arm grew heavy, he found movement difficult.

Trystan tried to shake off the woman's hold, not daring to take a hand from his sword to repell her.

"Loose me!" he demanded, twisting his body.

She did not obey, nor answer. He heard only that murmur of sound. There was a pleading note in it, a frantic pleading; he could feel her urgency, as if she begged of someone aid for them both.

Then from where her fingers dug into his shoulder muscles there spread downward along his arm, across his back and chest a warmth, a loosing—not of her hold, but of the bonds laid on him here. And within the center space the snake heads darted with greater vigor. Now and then two met in midair, and when they did they instantly united, becoming larger.

These darted forth, striking at the two by the gate, while Trystan cut and parried: And they moved with greater speed so he was hard put to keep them off. They showed no poison fangs, nor did they even seem to have teeth within their open jaws. Yet he sensed that if those mouths closed upon him or the woman they would be utterly done.

He half turned to beat off one which had come at him from an angle. His foot slipped and he went to one knee, the sword half out of his grasp. As he grabbed it tighter he heard a cry. Still crouched he slewed around.

The serpent head at which he had struck had only been a ruse. For his lunge at it had carried him away from the woman. Two other heads had captured her. To his horror he saw that one had fastened across her head, engulfing most of it on contact. The other had snapped its length of body about her waist. Gagged by the one on her head she was quiet, nor did she struggle as the pallid lengths pulled her back to the snakes' lair. Two more reached out to fasten upon her, no longer heeding Trystan, intent on their capture.

He cried out hoarsely, was on his feet again striking savagely at those dragging her. Then he was startled by a voice which seemed to speak within his head.

"Draw back, son of men, lest we remember our broken bargain. This is no longer your affair."

"Loose her!" Trystan cut at the tentacle about her waist. It burst into light, but another was already taking its place.

"She delivered you to us, would you save her?"

"Loose her!" He did not stop to weigh the right or wrong of what had been said, he only knew that he would not see the woman drawn to that which waited—that he could not do and remain a man. He thrust again.

The serpent coils were moving faster, drawing back into the hexagon. Trystan could not even be sure she still lived, not with that dreadful thing upon her head. She hung limp, not fighting.

"She is ours! Go you—lest we take more for feasting."

Trystan wasted no breath in argument, he leaped to the left, mounting the curb of the hexagon. There he slashed into the coils which pulled at the woman. His arms were weak, he could hardly raise the sword, even two-handed, and bring it down. Yet still he fought stubbornly to cut her free. And little by little he thought that he was winning.

Now he noted that as the coils tightened about her they did not touch her hand where it still rested clasping something between her breasts. So he strove the more to cut the coils below, severing the last as her head and shoulders were pulled over the edge of the curb.

Then it seemed that, tug though they would, the tentacles could not drag her wholly in. As they fought to do so Trystan had his last small grant of time. He now hewed those which imprisoned her head and shoulders. Others were rising for new holds. But, as she so lay, to do their will they must reach across her breast to take hold, and that they apparently could not do.

Wearily he raised the blade and brought it down again, each time sure he could not do so again. But at last there was a moment when she was free of them all. He flung out his left hand, clasped hers where it lay between her breasts, heaved her back and away.

There was a sharp hissing from the serpent things. They writhed and twisted. But more and more they sank to the ground, rolled there feebly. He got the woman on his shoulder, tottered back, still facing the enemy, readied as best he could be for another attack.

5

IT would seem that the enemy was spent, at least the snakes did not strike outward again. Watching them warily, Trystan retreated, dared to stop and rest with the woman. He leaned above her to touch her cheek. To his fingers the flesh was cold, faintly clammy. Dead? Had the air been choked from her?

He burrowed beneath the edges of her hood, sought the pulse in her throat. He could find none, so he tried to lay his hand directly above her heart. In doing so he had to break her grip on what lay between her breasts. When he touched a small bag there a throbbing, a warmth spread up his hand, and he jerked hastily away before he realized this was not a danger but a source of energy and life.

Her heart still beat. Best get her well away while those things in the hexagon were quiescent. For he feared their defeat was only momentary.

Trystan dared to sheath his sword, leaving both arms free to carry the woman. For all the bulk of her cloak and clothing she was slender, less than the weight he expected.

Now his retreat was that of a coastal sea crab, keeping part attention on the stew pot of blue light at his back, part on the footing ahead. And he drew a full breath again only when he had put two rings of the standing stones between him and the evil they guarded.

Nor was he unaware that there was still something dragging on him, trying to force him to face about. That he battled with will and his sense of self-preservation, his teeth set, a grimace of effort stiffening mouth and jaw.

One by one he pushed past the standing stones. As he went the way grew darker, the weird light fading. And he was beginning to fear that he could no longer trust his own sight. Twice he found himself off the road, making a detour around a pillar which seemed to sprout before him—and thereby heading back the way he had come.

Thus he fought both the compulsion to return and the tricks of vision, learning to fasten his attention on some point only a few steps ahead and wait until he had passed that before he set another goal.

He came at last, the woman resting over his shoulder, into the clean night, the last of the stones behind him. Now he was weak, so weary that he might have made a twenty-four-hour march and fought a brisk skirmish at the end of it. He slipped to his knees, lowered his burden to the surface of the Old Road where, in the open, the wind had scoured the snow away.

There was no moon, the cloud cover was heavy. The woman was now only a dark bulk. Trystan squatted on his heels, his hands dangling loose between his knees, and tried to think coherently.

Of how he had come up here he had no memory at all.

He had gone to bed in the normal manner at the inn, first waking to danger when he faced the crawling light in the hexagon. That he had also there fought a danger of the old time he had no doubt at all. But what had drawn him there?

He remembered forcing open the inn window to look upslope. Had that simple curiosity of his been the trigger for this adventure? But that the people of the inn could live unconcerned so close to such a peril—he could hardly believe that. Or because they had lived here so long, were the descendants of men rooted in Grimmerdale, had they developed an immunity to dark forces?

But what had the thing or things in the hexagon said? That she who lay here had delivered him to them. If so—why? Trystan hunched forward on his knees, twitched aside the edge of the hood, stooping very close to look at her. But it was hard to distinguish more than just the general outline of her features in this limited light.

Suddenly her body arched away from him. She screamed with such terror as startled him and pushed against the road under her, her whole attitude one of such agony of fear as held him motionless. Somehow she got to her feet. She had only screamed that once, now he saw her arms move under the hindering folds of her cloak. The moon broke in a thin sliver from under the curtain of the cloud, glinted on what she held in her hand.

Steel swung in an arc for him. Trystan grappled with her before that blade bit into his flesh. She was like a wild thing, twisting, thrusting, kicking, even biting as she fought him. At length he handled her as harshly as he would a man, striking his fist against the side of her chin so her body went limply once more to the road.

There was nothing to do but take her back to the inn. Had her experience in that nest of standing stones affected her brain, turning all about her into enemies? Resigned, he ripped a strip from the hem of her cloak, tied her hands together. Then he got her up so she lay on his back, breathing shallowly, inert. So carrying her he slipped and slid, pushed with difficulty through the scrub to the valley below and the inn.

What the hour might be he did not know, but there was a night lantern burning above the door, which swung open at his push. He staggered over to the fireplace, dropped his burden by the hearth, and reached for wood to build up the blaze, wanting nothing now so much as to be warm again.

Hertha's head hurt. The pain seemed to be in the side of her face. She opened her eyes. There was a dim light, but not that wan blue. No, this was flamc glow. Someone hunched at the hearth setting wood lengths with expert skill to rebuild the fire. Already there was warmth her body welcomed. She tried to sit up. Only to discover that her wrists were clumsily bound together. Then she tensed, chilled by fear, watching intently him who nursed the fire.

His head was turned from her, she could not see his face, but she had no doubts that it was Trystan. And her last memory—him looming above her, hands outstretched— To take her again as he had that other time! Revulsion sickened her so that she swallowed hurriedly lest she spew openly on the floor. Cautiously she looked around. This was the large room of the inn, he must have carried her back. That he might take his pleasure in a better place than the icy cold of the Old Road? But if he tried that she could scream, fight—surely someone would come—

He looked to her now, watching her so intently that she felt he read easily every one of her confused thoughts.

"I shall kill you," she said distinctly.

"As you tried to do?" He asked that not as if it greatly mattered, but as if he merely wondered.

"Next time I shall not turn aside!"

He laughed. And with that laughter for an instant he seemed another man, one younger, less hardened by time and deeds. "You did not turn aside this time, mistress, I had a hand in the matter." Then that half smile which had come with the laughter faded, and he regarded her with narrowed eyes, his mouth tight set lip to lip.

Hertha refused to allow him to daunt her and glared back. Then he said:

"Or are you speaking of something else, mistress? Something which happened before you drew steel on me? Was that—that *thing* right? Did I march to its lair by your doing?"

Somehow she must have given away the truth by some fraction of change he read in her face. He leaned forward and gripped her by the shoulders, dragging her closer to him in spite of her struggles, holding her so they were squarely eye to eye.

"Why? By the Sword Hand of Karther the Fair, why? What did I ever do to you, girl, to make you want to push me into that maw? Or would any man have sufficed to feed those pets? Are they your pets or your masters? Above all, how comes humankind to deal with *them?* And if you so deal, why did you break their spell to aid me? Why, and why, and why!"

He shook her, first gently, and then, with each question, more harshly, so that her head bobbed on her shoulders and she was weak in his hands. Then he seemed to realize that she could not answer him, so he held her tight as if he must read the truth in her eyes as well as hear it from her lips.

"I have no kinsman willing to call you to a sword reckoning," she told him wearily. "Therefore I must deal as best I can. I sought those who might have justice—"

"Justice! Then I was not just a random choice for some purpose of theirs! Yet I swear by the Nine Words of Min, I have never looked upon your face before. Did I in some battle slay close kin—father, brother, lover? But how may that be? Those I fought were the invaders. They had no women save those they rift from the dales. And would any daleswoman extract vengeance for one who was her master-by-force? Or is it that, girl? Did they take you and then you found a lord to your liking among them, forgetting your own blood?"

If she could have she would have spat full in his face for that insult. And he must have read her anger quickly.

"So that is not it. Then why? I am no ruffler who goes about picking quarrels with comrades. Nor have I ever taken any woman who came not to me willingly—"

"No?" She found speech at last, in a hot rush of words. "So you take no woman unwillingly, brave hero? What of three months since on the road to Lethendale? Is it such a usual course of action with you that it can be so lightly put out of mind?"

Angry and fearful though she was, she could see in his expression genuine surprise.

"Lethendale?" he repeated. "Three months since? Girl, I have never been that far north. As to three months ago—I was Marshal of Forces for Lord Ingrim before he fell at the siege of the port."

He spoke so earnestly that she could almost have believed him, had not that bowguard on his wrist proved him false.

"You lie! Yes, you may not know my face. It was in darkness you took me, having overrun the invaders who had taken me captive. My brother's men were all slain. For me they had other plans. But when aid came, then still I was for the taking—as you proved, Marshal!" She made of that a name to be hissed.

"I tell you, I was at the port!" He had released her and she backed against the settle, leaving a good space between them.

"You would swear before a Truth Stone it was me? You know my face, then?"

"I would swear, yes. As for your face—I do not need that. It was in the dark you had your will of me. But there is one proof I carry ever in my mind since that time."

He raised his hand, rubbing fingers along the old scar

on his chin, the fire gleamed on the bowguard. That did not match the plainness of his clothing, how could anyone forget seeing it?

"That proof being?"

"You wear it on your wrist, in plain sight. Just as I saw it then, ravisher—your bowguard!"

He held his wrist out, studying the band. "Bowguard! So that is your proof, that made you somehow send me to the Toads." He was half smiling again, but this time cruelly and with no amusement. "You did send me there, did you not?" He reached forward and before she could dodge pulled the hood fully from her head, stared at her.

"What have you done with the toad-face, girl? Was that some trick of paint, or some magicking you laid on yourself? Much you must have wanted me to so despoil your own seeming to carry through your plan."

She raised her bound hands, touched her cheeks with cold fingers. This time there was no mirror, but if he said the loathsome spotting was gone, then it must be so.

"They did it—" she said, only half comprehending. She had pictured this meeting many times, imagined him saying this or that. He must be very hardened in such matters to hold to this pose of half-amused interest.

"They? You mean the Toads? But now tell me why, having so neatly put me in their power, you were willing to risk your life in my behalf? That I cannot understand. For it seems to me that to traffic with such as abide up that hill is a fearsome thing and one which only the desperate would do. Such desperation is not lightly turned aside—so—why did you save me, girl?"

She answered with the truth. "I do not know. Perhaps because the hurt being mine, the payment should also be mine—that, a little, I think. But even more—" She paused so long he prodded her.

"But even more, girl?"

"I could not in the end leave even such a man as you to *them!*"

"Very well, that I can accept. Hate and fear and despair can drive us all to bargains we repent of later. You made one and then found you were too human to carry it through. Then later on the road you chose to try with honest steel and your own hand—"

"You—you would have taken me—again!" Hertha forced out the words. But the heat in her cheeks came not from the fire but from the old shame eating her.

"So that's what you thought? Perhaps, given the memories you carry, it was natural enough." Trystan nodded. "But now it is your turn to listen to me, girl. Item first: I have never been to Lethendale, three months ago, three years ago—never! Second: this which you have come to judge me on," he held the wrist closer, using the fingers of his other hand to tap upon it, "I did not have three months ago. When the invaders were close pent in the port during the last siege, we had many levies from the outlands come to join us. They had mopped up such raiding bands as had been caught out of there when we moved in to besiege.

"A siege is mainly a time of idleness, and idle men amuse themselves in various ways. We had only to see that the enemy did not break out along the shores while we waited for the coasting ships from Handelsburg and Vennesport to arrive to harry them from the sea. There were many games of chance played during that waiting. And, though I am supposed by most to be a cautious man, little given to such amusements, I was willing to risk a throw now and then.

"This I so won. He who staked it was like Urre, son to some dead lord, with naught but ruins and a lost home to return to if and when the war ended. Two days later he was killed in one of the sorties the invaders now and then made. He had begged me to hold this so that when luck ran again in his way he might buy it back, for it was one of the treasures of his family. In the fighting I discovered it was not only decorative but useful. Since he could not redeem it, being dead, I kept it—to my disfavor it would seem. As for the boy, I do not even know his name—for they called him by some nickname. He was befuddled with drink half the time, being one of the walking dead—"

"'Walking dead'?" His story carried conviction, not only his words but his tone, and the straight way he told it.

"That is what I call them. High Hallack has them in many—some are youngsters, such as Urre, the owner of this," again he smoothed the guard. "Others are old enough to be their fathers. The dales have been swept with fire and sword. Those which were not invaded have been bled of their men, of their crops—to feed both armies. This is a land which can now go two ways. It can sink into nothingness from exhaustion, or there can rise new leaders to restore and with will and courage build again."

It seemed to Hertha that he no longer spoke to her, but rather voiced his own thoughts. As for her, there was a kind of emptiness within, as if something she carried had been rift from her. That thought sent her bound hands protectively to her belly.

The child within her—who had been its father? One of the lost ones, some boy who had had all taken from him and so became a dead man with no hope in the future, one without any curb upon his appetites. Doubtless he had lived for the day only, taken ruthlessly all offered during that short day. Thinking so, she again sensed that queer light feeling. She had not lost the child, this child which Gunnora promised would be hers alone. What she had lost was the driving need for justice which had brought her to Grimmerdale—to traffic with the Toads.

Hertha shuddered, cold to her bones in spite of her cloak and the fire. What had she done in her blindness, her hate and horror? Almost she had delivered an innocent man to that she dared not now think upon. What had saved her from that at the very last, made her throw that stone rubbed with Gunnora's talisman? Some part of her that refused to allow such a foul crime?

And what could she ever say to this man who had now turned his head from her, was looking into the flames as if therein he could read message runes? She half raised her bound hands; he looked again with a real smile, from which she shrank as she might from a blow, remembering how it might have been with him at this moment.

"There is no need for you to go bound. Or do you still thirst for my blood?" He caught her hands, pulled at the cloth tying them.

"No," Hertha answered in a low voice. "I believe you. He whom I sought is now dead."

"Do you regret that death came not at your hand?"

She stared down at her fingers resting again against her middle, wondering dully what would become of her now. Would she remain a tavern wench, should she crawl back to Kuno? No! At that her head went up again, pride returned.

"I asked, are you sorry you did not take your knife to my gamester?"

"No."

"But still there are dark thoughts troubling you—"

"Those are none of your concern." She would have risen, but he put out a hand to hold her where she was.

"There is an old custom. If a man draw a maid from dire danger, he has certain rights—"

For a moment she did not understand; when she did her bruised pride strengthened her to meet his eyes.

"You speak of maids—I am not such."

His indrawn breath made a small sound, but one loud in the silence between them. "So that was the why! You are no farm or tavern wench, are you? So you could not accept what he had done to you? But have you no kinsman to trade for your honor?"

She laughed raggedly. "Marshal, my kinsman had but one wish: that I submit to ancient practices among women so that he would not be shamed before his kind. Having done so I would have been allowed to dwell by sufferance in my own home, being reminded not more than perhaps thrice daily of his great goodness."

"And this you would not do. But with your great hate against him who fathered what you carry—"

"No!" Her hands went to that talisman of Gunnora's. "I have been to the shrine of Gunnora. She has promised me my desire—the child I bear will be mine wholly, taking nothing from *him!*"

"And did she also send you to the Toads?"

Hertha shook her head. "Gunnora guards life. I knew of the Toads from old tales. I went to them in my blindness and they gave me that which I placed in your bed to draw you to them. Also they changed my face in some manner. But—that is no longer so?"

"No. Had I not known your cloak, I should not have known you. But this thing in my bed— Stay you here and wait. But promise me this, should I return as one under orders, bar the door in my face and keep me here at all costs!"

"I promise."

He went with the light-footed tread of one who had learned to walk softly in strange places because life might well depend upon it. Now that she was alone her mind returned to the matter of what could come to her with the morn. Who would give her refuge—save perhaps the Wise Women of Lethendale. It might be that this marshal would escort her there. Though what did he owe her except such danger as she did not want to think on. But although her thoughts twisted and turned she saw no answer except Lethendale. Perhaps Kuno would some day—no! She would have no plan leading in that path!

Trystan was back holding two sticks such as were used to kindle brazier flames. Gripped between their ends was the pebble she had brought from the Toads' hold. As he reached the fire he hurled that bit of rock into the heart of the blaze.

He might have poured oil upon the flames so fierce was the answer as the pebble fell among the logs. Both shrank back.

"That trap is now set at naught," he observed. "I would not have any other fall into it."

She stiffened, guessing what he thought of her for the setting of that same trap.

"To say I am sorry is only mouthing words, but—"

"To one with such a burden, lady, I can return that I understand. When one is driven by a lash one takes any way to free oneself. And in the end you did not suffer that I be taken."

"Having first thrust you well into the trap! Also—you should have let them take me then as they wished. It would only have been fitting."

"Have done!" He brought his fist down on the seat of the settle beside which he knelt. "Let us make an end to what is past. It is gone. To cling to this wrong or that, keep it festering in mind and heart, is to cripple one. Now, lady," she detected a new formality in his voice, "where do you go, if not to your brother's house? It is not in your mind to return there, I gather."

She fumbled with the talisman. "In that you are right. There is but one place left—the Wise Women of Lethendale. I can beg shelter from them." She wondered if he would offer the escort she had no right to ask, but his next question surprised her.

"Lady, when you came hither, you came by the Old Road over ridge, did you not?"

"That is so. To me it seemed less dangerous than the open highway. It has, by legend, those who sometimes use it, but I deemed those less dangerous than my own kind."

"If you came from that direction you must have passed through Nordendale—what manner of holding is it?"

She had no idea why he wished such knowledge, but she told him what she had seen of that leaderless dale, the handful of people there deep sunk in a lethargy in which they clung to the ruins of what had once been thriving life. He listened eagerly to what she told him.

"You have a seeing eye, lady, and have marked more than most given such a short time to observe. Now listen to me, for this may be a matter of concern to both of us in the future. It is in my mind that Nordendale needs a lord, one to give the people heart, rebuild what man and time have wasted. I have come north seeking a chance to be not just my own man, but to have a holding. I am not like Urre, who was born to a hall and drinks and wenches now to forget what ill tricks fortune plays.

"Who my father was"—he shrugged—"I never heard my mother say. That he was of no common blood, that I knew, though in later years she drudged in a merchant's house before the coming of the invaders for bread to our mouths and clothing for our backs. When I was yet a boy I knew that the only way I might rise was through this"—he touched the hilt of his sword. "The merchant guild welcomed no nameless man, but for a sword and a bow there is always a ready market. So I set about learning the skills of war as thoroughly as any man might. Then came the invasion, and I went from Lord to Lord, becoming at last Marshal of Forces. Yet always before me hung the thought that in such a time of upheaval, with the old families being killed out, this was my chance.

"Now there are masterless men in plenty, too restless after years of killing to settle back behind any plow. Some will turn outlaw readily, but with a half dozen of such at my back I can take a dale which lies vacant of rule, such as this Nordendale. The people there need a leader, I am depriving none of lawful inheritance, but will keep the peace and defend it against outlaws—for there will be many such now. There are men here, passing through Grimmerdale, willing to be hired for such a purpose. Enough so I can pick and choose at will."

He paused and she read in his face that this indeed was

the great moving wish of his life. When he did not continue she asked a question:

"I can see how a determined man can do this thing. But how will it concern me in any way?"

He looked to her straightly. She did not understand the full meaning of what she saw in his eyes.

"I think we are greatly alike, lady. So much so that we could walk the same road, to profit of both. No, I do not ask an answer now. Tomorrow"—he got to his feet stretching—"no, today, I shall speak to those men I have marked. If they are willing to take liege oath to me, we shall ride to Lethendale, where you may shelter as you wish for a space. It is not far—"

"By horse," she answered in relief, "perhaps two days west."

"Good enough. Then, having left you there, I shall go to Nordendale—and straightway that shall cease to be masterless. Give me, say, threescore days, and I shall come riding again to Lethendale. Then you shall give me your answer as to whether our roads join or no."

"You forget," her hands pressed upon her belly, "I am no maid, nor widow, and yet I carry—"

"Have you not Gunnora's promise upon the subject? The child will be wholly yours. One welcome holds for you both."

She studied his face, determined to make sure if he meant that. What she read there—she caught her breath, her hands rising to her breast, pressing hard upon the talisman.

"Come as you promise to Lethendale," she said in a low voice. "You shall be welcome and have your answer in good seeming."

Changeling

LITHENDALE, though no fortress for defense, rather an abiding place for the Dames who gave refuge to all, still held something of grim darkness in this early spring. Snow lay in ragged, mid-edged patches upon the ground, and the courtyards showed a gloss of damp upon worn stones. A chill wind moaned and cried at every window to the west, plucked at steamy panes with fingers just too weak to wrench a way within.

Hertha's forehead pressed against one of those thick panes. She leaned over the wide sill as if she could gain relief from the pains which rent her fiercely. The life she bore within her body might be a warrior, one who ruthlessly would tear her in twain, so eager was it ready to battle all the world.

She was not alone. There was the woman who now and then came to walk beside her and steady her. To Hertha that other was a faceless puppet, someone from a dream, or rather a dark night's sending which had no end. In one hand the girl clasped, so tightly that even its time-smoothed ridges drove deep into her flesh, her one talisman, Gunnora's amulet. Hertha did not pray—not now.

Would any petition to one of the Old Ones be heard arising from this abbey dedicated to another power?

Setting her teeth, Hertha lurched away from the window, took one step, then two, before, once more, grinding pain sent her staggering. She was on the bed, her body arching. Dank sweat plastered her hair to her forehead.

"Gunnora!" Had she screamed aloud or had the name only rung in her mind? A last thrust of pain was a spear within her, twisting agony. Then—

The peace, end of all pain. She drifted.

In the dark which enfolded her she heard a throaty, gurgling laughter, a laughter which was evil, a threat. In that same dark she saw—

There was a circle of stones and to these clung—no, they did not cling—only the deformity of their bloated bodies made it seem so. Rather they sat, their monstrous heads all turned, their bulbous eyes watching her with malicious joy and triumph. Hertha remembered. Now she cried out, not any petition to a Power of the Old Ones, rather with a fear she thought safely gone, buried in time.

She wanted to run, even to raise her hands as a barrier between those eyes and hers. Though the girl knew that even if she so veiled her own sight, she could not escape. The Toads of Grimmerdale! She had recklessly, wrongly sought them once, cheated them, fought them, and now they were here!

"My lady."

The words were faint, far off, had nothing to do with present horror and fear. Still it would seem that somehow they acted as a charm against the Toad things, for those faded. Hertha, shivering, spent, opened her eyes.

Inghela, the stout Dame, wise in herb lore and nursing, stood in the light of two lamps. That wan day Hertha had watched so endlessly through the distorted thick glass of the window must have ended. Dame Inghela's grasp held the girl's limp wrist. There was an intent searching in her eyes, so dark and clear under the line of her folded linen headdress.

Hertha summoned strength. Her mouth was parched, dry, as if she had fed on ashes.

"The child?" In her own hearing her voice was very thin and hoarse.

"You have a daughter, my lady."

A daughter! For one moment of pure joy Hertha's heart moved with a quicker beat. She willed her arms to rise, even though it felt that each was braceleted with lead. Gunnora's promise—a child who would have nothing in it of the ravisher who had forced its birth. Hertha's own, her own!

"Give me," her voice was still weak, yet life, and now will, were fast returning to her, "give me my daughter!"

The Dame did not move. There was no bundle of warm wrappings in her arms. It seemed to the girl that the woman's measuring glance was stronger, an emotion in it which Hertha could not read.

She tried to raise herself higher on the bed.

"Is the child dead?" She believed that she had managed to ask that without betraying the surge of emotion which tore her as sharply as had the pains earlier.

"No." Now Dame Inghela did move. Hertha watched as the Dame stooped to lift from a box-like bed a bundle that gave a sudden, ear-piercing squall, struggled against the confinement of the blanket about it.

Not dead—then what? There was ill fortune in the way the Dame had met her question, Hertha was sure. She held out her arms, willing them not to tremble, setting herself to bear any evil.

The baby must be far from death. Its battling against the swaddling was vigorous. Hertha grasped the bundle, resolutely turned back the coverings to look upon what Gunnora had promised, a child to be wholly and only hers.

She looked down upon a small wrinkled, reddened

body of the newborn, and she knew! Revulsion, for only a moment, burned in her as if she might still vomit forth the evil which must have lain dormant in her since this new life had been conceived.

Evidence of her sin, her dealing with the powers of evil, ancient and strong evil, only that lay now on this one, not on her. She stared down into the ill formed face. The child stared back, its croaking cries still. Those bulbous eyes seeming to thrust into hers as if already the small creature knew that fate had marked it. There was the faint hint of brownish patches already staining its skin. The Toads—yes—their mark!

Hertha cradled the child with fierce protectiveness, looked defiantly over its head at the Dame.

Inghela's hands moved in the signs of ritual against the Powers of Darkness, even as her lips shaped words which were whispered too low for Hertha to catch. One of her hands caught at the loop of prayer rings at her belt and fingers began to separate one from the other.

"Changeling!" The maidservant, whom Hertha had hardly been aware of during her hours of labor, crept from behind her mistress into the circle of lamplight.

That word aroused Hertha to greater awareness.

"This is," she said slowly, distinctly, in that moment taking unto herself all which might have misformed the child, all the burden of sin she had drawn to her in her madness and her hate, "this is my daughter, Elfanor, whom I proclaim is truly of my body, my fair child, and who rests within the name of my clan."

Elfanor? Hertha wondered at that name, how had it come to her? It was one which she had never heard before. Yet it seemed to her the proper one. As for the other formal words of her acknowledgment of the child, they were empty. She had no clan, no family name, no lord to raise the child in the central hall of a keep before all those of his holding.

She was utterly alone, the more so now because of what had been laid upon this child. Hearing the click of the prayer rings Inghela fingered, Hertha knew that already her daughter had been judged, and she had been, too.

That same stubborn pride which had made her withstand the demands of a family line she could no longer lay claim to, to court a certain revenge which had now recoiled upon her in this vile fashion, that was her shield, and, perhaps, still her weapon.

"My daughter," she repeated firmly, daring the Dame, the maidservant staring avidly at what she held, to raise any protest.

"Changeling—" Once more that dread word held a cursed sound.

Dame Inghela turned swiftly, her authority plain to read on her round face as she looked at the maid and issued a swift stream of orders. The girl fled, busied herself hastily in gathering stained linen, pouring slops into a waiting bucket. Then she scuttled from the chamber. Inghela had once more taken her place by the bedside. Her steady gaze met Hertha's defiant stare.

"The child—" she began slowly.

Hertha's chin raised a fraction. She would never reveal now to this, or any other living soul, the sorrow and the torment within her.

"Is cursed. Is that what you would say, Dame? If so, the curse is mine and mine must be the answer."

Dame Inghela showed no sign of affront at what might almost be considered blasphemy when uttered in this place. Those who followed the Flame were taught, and taught, that sin left its mark upon the sinner. In so much could Hertha's words be considered confession.

"Evil seeds itself when it is watered and cherished by the will," she said slowly. Yet the gaze which held Hertha's so levelly did not condemn.

"You know my story," Hertha replied harshly. Since

she had taken Elfanor into her arms the child lay quiet, the large, bulging eyes were half closed, as if, young as the babe was, she heard and understood. "Yes, I sought evil to draw upon my enemy, him who had defiled me. I sought an evil of the Old Ones openly, willingly, because all which filled me then was hate. Still the full evil did not come to fruit. He whom I sent to the Toads I fought for. He lives."

"Yet he was not the right man, as you have also said," Dame Inghela reminded her.

"That I did not know until after. I had already fought for him. Thus, this—" Her arms tightened about the small body. "I do not know any of the ancient wisdom, the sorcery of how any power could have reached within my body and changed new life I carried into this. Elfanor is mine, upon me let the burden fall. And—" it might be ill for her to speak so within this place, still that headlong need for defense, for the right to nurse some small hope within her now, led her to do so—"perhaps what one power had done to set awry, another can aid."

Once more Dame Inghela swung her hoop of rings. "Your speech is not good. Here we follow the true teachings. You have already had proof of what comes when one appeals to that which is no belief of ours!"

"True." Hertha repressed a shiver arising from cold within her, not in answer to that rebuke. At the same time she reckoned—they can put no walls about my thoughts. There are powers and powers.

She loosed one hand, her fingers found what lay upon her breast, the amulet of Gunnora. Again she recalled how she had sought out that shrine, heavy with her child, seeking what succor she could. Of how in dream—or perhaps more than dream—she had been made welcome and one of her boons granted. For she was certain at this moment that Elfanor had indeed no part of her father within her, that she was wholly Hertha's own.

As days passed Hertha never spoke again of what she might do. She was well aware that her child was the subject of many whispers, that such congratulations upon her safe delivery as were offered gave lip service only to custom.

Sudden warm winds came out of the south. The earth dried after the last of the snow's burden soaked into it. Spring was coming early. Hertha kept to her chamber much of the time, her thoughts busier than her hands, though she nursed her daughter and cared for her entirely, refusing any help from those who she knew looked upon the baby as cursed.

At the fourth week she asked for formal audience with the Abbess, her plans made.

Carrying the child, she made her courtesy of ceremony in the inner parlor, thinking fleetingly how different matters were since she had been previously received here. Then she had come wrapped in what she knew now was a false contentment, having laid upon another for a short space, the ordering of her life. At this moment she caught at that straying memory fiercely, pushed it away. She had been a fool, and must now pay for her folly, perhaps all her days.

"They say, Lady Hertha, that you desire to go forth from Lithendale." The Abbess was not a tall woman. Still the high-backed chair of age-darkened wood, all carven with Flame symbols, enthroned her. Hertha's first suspicion dulled. Perhaps she was a poor judge of the motives and thoughts of others, but here she read no malice, no accusation, only true concern.

"I must," she replied, sitting on the very edge of the stool to which the Abbess had waved her, Elfanor close against her. The baby never cried when Hertha held her so In fact she would lie still, open eyes upon her mother's face. Hertha had to keep herself from ever searching those too-large eyes for some hint of the marsh fires she had seen once in eyes so like them. "Your reverence, I—and mine—have no place within these walls."

"Has that been said to you?" The Abbess's demand came, quick and sharp.

"Such does not have to be said. No, none has given me

any unwelcome word. But it is the truth. Through me a shadow of evil has come into a place which should be at peace and holy."

"Peace we may strive for. Holiness is not of our fashioning," the Abbess returned. "If you leave here where do you go? My Lord of Nordendale—"

Hertha made a swift gesture. "Your Reverence, he was good to me when he had every right to draw steel across my throat. I brought him into such peril as perhaps none of our kind has seldom faced. You know my story, how I prayed for vengeance to creatures whose very nature is of black foulness, and later drew him into their net."

"Then fought for him again," the Abbess said slowly. "Did you not believe when you so fought that he was still the one who shamed you?"

"Yes. But what did that matter? If I had turned my own dagger point upon him for a clean death, that was my right, was it not?" Her old shame and hate clung for a moment to memory. "But no man, no matter what his sin, should be given to old evil."

"He did not hold your act against you. No, rather he did in a measure honor you for trying to uphold your battle against shame. This Trystan spoke with me before he rode forth, and, since then, have you not had twice messengers from him confirming that he has accomplished his desires in part, that he has taken command of the leaderless people of Nordendale, that he has brought peace and more than a small measure of hope to others, that he wishes you to come in all honor as his lady. He is a strong man, hard in some ways, but also, in his core, as good as the steel he carries. What of him? Do you go to him?"

"To him least of all, Your Reverence. He is but new come into his lordship. Strong and valiant a man though he may be, let him bring a bride with a 'changeling' already at her breast, and trouble shall rise about him, as water rises about a rock fallen into a swift flowing river which in time shall roll it over and over, doing with it as the water wills.

No, I do not go to Nordendale. Also I beg this humbly of Your Reverence, that you not send any message to Lord Trystan. If he or his messenger rides hither again you will say that I have gone to my own people."

"You have no people, so you have said," the Abbess returned sharply. "Falsehood shall not be uttered here either in a good or bad cause."

"My Lady Abbess, I have by my own action set myself apart from those once my kind. In truth I go to what perhaps is my own place."

"The Waste? That means your death. To seek death willingly is also a sin."

Hertha shook her head. "No, had I wished to travel that path I would have taken it easily months ago. I do not go out to die, but to seek an answer. If that seeking leads me into strange places, then that I shall face."

"*Their* ways have never been ours. You imperil more than your body in such a search."

"Lady, I imperiled myself so months ago. Now I have a battle before me. Do you believe—" the girl's face flushed, her eyes were bright, afire as those of a hunting falcon ready for the death swoop, "that I shall not fight for this little one, who is wholly mine? There are places of evil from the days when our people did not know this land, but there are also places of peace and good. Is it not true of a healer that often a small part of a dangerous herb may be given to counteract the illness that same herb or its like seeded in the body? If it takes me a lifetime of searching, I will seek healing."

For a long moment the Abbess made no answer. She studied Hertha's face, as if by the very force of her will she could see through flesh and bone to the thoughts of the mind within that skull.

"This is your choice," she said slowly. "We do not use strange powers, but sometimes the Flame grants *us* also a measure of foreseeing, even as a wise woman will look into her scrying cup. I cannot tell why, but I believe that if anything can be done to lift this curse, guidance will be given you."

"And if the Lord Trystan comes?" Hertha had drawn a deep breath. She had never expected such a response from a woman so deeply wedded to rituals which denied any dependence upon other and older arts.

"He will be told the truth. That you bore one for whose future you must strive, and that you have gone so to battle, we know not where. Whether such a man will accept these statements, I do not know. That is a matter for him to decide. I cannot give your search a blessing, but insofar as one vowed to our beliefs can well-wish another, so do I you, Lady Hertha. You have courage, and your will is like a sword blade, worn somewhat by this world's battles, still sunbright and keen of edge.

"You have the mount which the Lord Trystan left for you; that I advise you to accept, even though your pride may prickle. We shall also give you one of the baggage ponies, for of those we have many, brought here by refugees, some of whom did not survive and whose goods were left for kinsmen who never came. Supplies you shall have, with what traveler's gear you wish to select from our storehouse.

"And—" once more she hesitated. "I have given you well-wishing. I cannot add to that any blessed charm, for where you go such could be a hindrance rather than an aid. Nor will I ask in which direction you travel, though I will say do not ride the open road, as this is a land in chaos and there are many masterless men to prey on travelers."

"Lady Abbess, you have given me far more than I dared dream." Hertha arose to her feet. "Perhaps your greatest gift is that you have not said to me, 'Go not, this is a useless thing!'"

There was the faintest shadow of a smile about the Abbess's lips.

"And if I said so, and wrung my hands, and called upon authority—which I do not have since you are no daughter of this roof—would you have listened? No, I believe that you have thought much and that you believe this is your life burden. So be it. We all choose our own roads, some with less cause than you."

Hertha stood very straight. This woman had that in her which might have made them friends had the circumstances been otherwise. For a single moment Hertha wondered what it would have been like to be welcomed as a "daughter" into such a house of peace. But that was a very fleeting thought. She repeated the old guesting farewell of the traveler:

"For the feasting, for the roof, I give thanks and blessing. For the future all good to this place, as I take the road again."

The Abbess bowed her head slightly. "Go in peace, Lady Hertha. As you seek so may you find." Though she said she refused the flame blessing, still her hand raised and moved in some air-drawn sign between them.

Then Hertha and Elfanor went out of the place of peace. The Abbess had indeed been generous. The horse Hertha rode, astride, garments culled from the supply left by the refugees providing her with the wide, skirt-like breeches of a noblewoman's hunting garb, was that on which Trystan had brought her here. It was not a showy beast, and it was rather small, having much of the blood, she was sure, of the tough, wild mountain breed. But such were sought by travelers for hardiness.

Trailed behind by a leading rope was an even smaller pony, well-filled packs slung one on either side of his back. Belted at Hertha's waist was a long bladed sword-dagger which she had found among the stored gear. She also had strapped to her saddle a short boar spear, its wicked head needle sharp. Elfanor rode in a cradle-like basket against Hertha's back, leaving the girl's arms free for the managing for her two beasts.

She went out in the early morning, for it was her wish to get along the known road when it would be the least traveled, on into the hills, even as the Abbess had advised. The land was indeed filled with masterless men and outlaws. Many of the lords had died in the war, leaving their holdings to the weak and the easily preyed upon. It was such men as Trystan who might in the end bring order out of this present darkness. She thought of that, and then pushed it out of mind. That she could have stood beside him and perhaps given him aid, that was like a smoke fancy, quickly blown away by the grim truth of her burden.

Before the sun was well up she was off the road to pick a crisscross path among some stones which looked as if they were the chance product of a landslip, but which, she knew from her diligent questioning at the abbey, were instead a barrier or half-closed gate to disguise the beginning of another and much older way.

It was true those Old Ones who had once held the Dales, had a liking for roads which climbed along the crests of the hills rather than curled at more ease through the valleys. Such a way had, months before, taken her to Gunnora's shrine and later to the place of the Toads. What she sought now was a return to the shrine. Gunnora alone might grant her some direction. For the Great Lady was a lover of children, one who smiled upon those who bore them, and was well known to listen to any petition for a baby in need. Whether she would aid one who was cursed—No, Hertha told herself firmly, this sin was hers and not that of the child. Any payment which must be made was to be laid where it belonged. She would take the scaly spotted skin, the eyes, all visited on Elfanor. It was her hope that Gunnora might lead her by some dream of enlightenment to learn to do just that thing.

She rode at a slow amble, stopping at times to slide from her padded saddle and nurse Elfanor. The child had not cried. Her silence was one of the strange things about her. Also Hertha noted that, at times, those rounded eyes looked out upon the world with a measurement which certainly was not of the human kind. Nor should so young a baby focus so keenly on what lay about it.

Though the ancient road kept to the heights, those who had fashioned it had arranged that travelers could not easily be revealed. Brush and trees, both thick-growing, walled it on the valley side, here and there giving way to a screen of upstanding broken rocks, all blending with the countryside so that this safeguard was not, in itself, a sign that a highway lay so concealed.

Hertha and the child sheltered that night in what might even have been a contrived campsite, for here were rocks upsprouting, several leaning at an angle so that their tips touched to form a rude imitation of roof.

There was even a basin or pit there, blackened surely by ancient fires, into which she packed sticks and the dried moss she had had the forethought to cull from branches of the brush, setting a pocket of flames, over which she crouched, nursing the baby against her. To that fire she added a scant handful of dried leaves from a packet Dame Inghela had given her. The smoke puffing up as those were consumed brought a fresh, clean scent. But it was not for that that Hertha had added her material so sparingly. Such a combination of herbs had the ability to keep at bay dark dreams. The scent cleared the head, as those learned in plant lore knew. Hertha needed this.

To travel this old road deliberately put her again under the influence which ancient powers could still exert. Whatever small safeguards she could raise against evil, those she must use.

The beasts drew closer to the fire also, feeding on the grain she took from her journey bags. She dared not turn them loose to graze at will. But there was water nearby, a spring feeding a rill from which the horse and pony had drunk noisily, where she herself rinsed out her two bottles of water, refilling them both, slaking her own thirst after the dryness of a journeycake.

Sleep came fitfully, for she had set herself a kind of inner warning which did arouse her now and then through the night to feed the fire, while ever close to her hand was the hilt of the long knife, the shaft of the boar spear.

Her body ached in spite of the way she had tried to ease her travel. Near dawn, though she lay back once more in the cup of rock, she did not sleep, rather went over in her mind the direction in which she must head at the coming of true day.

The hill road ran on, now dipping a little into some valley, now climbing above. Hertha passed rock walls on which had been graven so deeply strange symbols that even long passing of time had not altogether erased them.

On the fourth day her road branched, one part turning south. She had seen no one, though once or twice, when the trail drew closer to the valley way, she had heard sounds of others. Each sound had frozen her into waiting with a fast-beating heart.

At the splitting of the trails Hertha took the northernmost, and began to look about her for some landmark. If she was right, this was the same way she had followed months ago to Gunnora's shrine. So she should catch sight of some rock spur, some stretch of country she could remember.

There was no good camping place on this fork. The wind swept down, holding no spring softness. She swung the cradle about from her back, steadying it across her saddle, bending a little over it so that the folds of her cloak could give protection to the baby.

Shadows formed by early evening drifted down the slope. Still she rode on, for there was no promising place to alight. Then, when Hertha had nearly given up hope, she saw the building she sought. There was a glow from the door on which was hung a strip of metal fashioned into Gunnora's own sign, a ripe grain sheath with a binding of fruit-laden vine.

Her mount, which had been plodding with down-drooping head, now whinnied. Its call was answered by the pony from behind. Hertha herself raised her voice, which in her own hearing sounded hoarse from cold and lack of use:

"Good fortune to this house and the dwellers therein!"

The door split open, each half sliding back into the wall; golden light streamed out. Nor did her mount give her time to slip clumsily from her saddle, rather the horse paced on and stood, blowing, in what was an outer chamber, not a real courtyard. Still both beasts seemed quiet and content as if they had indeed come to their proper place.

Hertha, stiff and sore, feeling as if she had been riding forever, dismounted.

"Enter into peace."

The voice came from the air. She remembered how it had also done so upon her visit to the shrine. She looked doubtfully at the horse and the pony. Their loads must be shed. They had served her well and should be eased.

"Enter." A second door opened for her. "The good beasts will be tended, as will all who come in peace."

Already the warmth, the feeling of being burdenless, filled her. She did not linger, but walked forward. At that second doorway she slipped the long knife from her belt sheath and left it lying, for steel was not worn in Gunnora's hall.

The second room was as she had remembered it—a table set with food, all ready to refresh the traveler. In her basket nest Elfanor stirred, gave a small mewling cry. Her large eyes stared up into her mother's face, and never had Hertha been so sure that within the small misshapen body there was a mind which saw, which knew, which was older than the flesh and bone that contained it.

She half expected a protest from the child, or perhaps from whatever presence abode in this chamber. Could one bring a cursed being into the light which was its opposite? Save for that one cry Elfanor did not make another sound, nor was there any answer. Hertha dropped into the chair, held the baby close to her with her left arm, stretched out her right hand to pick up a goblet from which arose faint steam, the scent of wine mulled with herbs which was a traveler's welcome on a night of cold and long wayfaring.

She drank. She spooned into her mouth the richness of a stew, food which satisfied, filled the body and eased the mind as no mouthful had done since her first visit to the shrine.

Satisfied, she sat back in her chair at last and spoke as much to the leaping flame of the two lamps on the table as to the room.

"To the giver of the feast, fair thanks from the heart. For the welcome of the gate, gratitude. To She who rules here—" Hertha hesitated. She could no longer find the proper words. For the first time the idea arose, hard and harsh, of what she had done. Into a place of peace and light she had brought sin and evil—her own sin and evil!

On the far side of the table a second door swung open. There was dimmer light beyond. Now, filling the room, came the sweet scent of flowers at the height of their summer blooming, a kind of voiceless murmur as one might hear in the flowing of a merry stream, the hum of contented bees about their harvest, the faintest breath of wind stirring blossom-laden branches.

It would seem that the Presence here did not judge as she knew she should be judged. In her heart there was a small spring of real hope. Her travel-stained divided skirt dragging at her boots, she went forward, not slowly, reluctantly, but as one who has a purpose and knows that it must be carried out.

Smoke tendrils ringed about her, the scent grew stronger. It seemed to Hertha as if that smoke took on tangible substance, forming many arms to draw her on. Half-amused by the herb scent, she stumbled a little as she came up against a couch. There she lay down wearily. Her eyes closed.

There was a light, golden as the ker-apples of autumn, rich in its seeming as the metal men prized. It arose as a pillar stretching from the floor or ground so far into the upper regions of this other place that Hertha, no matter how far back she turned her head, could not see its crown. She saw now that it was not solid, even though her sight could not pierce it. Rather it pulsed in rhythm, as if it were tuned to the beating of a heart.

Beautiful as that column was, there was something awesome, near threatening about it. Hertha had knelt unconsciously. She wanted to reach out her hands to that light, to pray for pardon; only her hands, her arms, were locked about what she carried. She turned her eyes from the light to that burden.

The child had human form, true human form, yet it was dark, sullenly dark. Still, in its small breast, the light of the pillar awoke an answer, a spark as clear and glowing golden.

"Lady—" Hertha did not believe she spoke aloud. In this place the words came straight from the heart, from innermost thought, and that part of any who came here which was the whole truth. "I have sinned against the life which is of the good. Let not punishment fall upon the child, but rather on me. For the innocent should not suffer for the guilty."

The light flashed brightly to scald her eyes. Tears ran. Or were those tears she had not shed since first the evil that all her kind could do had caught her in a foul net?

Hertha waited for an answer. When nothing came, fear awoke. She had to hold to all her strength and courage to keep her eyes upon that searing light. She shivered, for it seemed to her that a cold wrapped around her, cutting her off not only from the mercy of the light, but from the life of her own kind as well.

She cried out. If this was death, then—

"Not the child!" Her words were not as a plea, rather a demand. Then she was more frightened, for one did not demand from the Powers, one wooed and prayed.

The light vanished as if a blink of her tormented eyes had sent it into extinction. She saw something else—

There spread now before her a place of rocks standing in a pattern, a wheel pattern. That stretched as if she were suspended in the air above. Though it had looked different from the ground, as she had seen it twice before, she knew what she envisioned now—the place of the Toads.

Devilish greenish lights glowed upon the sitting rocks at its heart. Hertha half expected those to reach for her, fearing that any protection she might once have had against those Dark Ones had been withdrawn.

However, they did not appear to be aware of her, if indeed the Toads were present. Now she moved, as one might who wore wings and used them in slow even beats. She traveled above that maze of rock ways outward to its circumference. Something else appeared. At the ends of several of the ways which led into the web of the Toads there stood straight and fast in the middle (as if they were closed doors to bar entrance) stones which shown faintly blue. Three such roads were so closed, three were open. Into Hertha's mind swept knowledge, as if this were something she had always known and which had been asleep in her mind, to be now awakened.

So had the Toads of Grimmerdale once been confined and kept from troubling the dreams of men, kept from drawing to them such foolhardy or evil people as she had been when she had first sought them out. So must they be confined again. Hertha drew a deep breath. If this was the task set her, then she was ready for it.

There came to her then a warning. Because she had once attempted to use the Toads to achieve her end, she was now vulnerable to them. To come so close to their own place was a risk of death worse than any failure or hurt of body. The choice was hers alone. Would it save Elfanor? Of even that she could not be sure, only hope, but hope was strong, it could carry one far, be meat and drink, rest and surcease. Now Hertha held to it with the full force of her will.

Once more the girl faced the winds of the heights. There had been food again waiting her when she had awakened. In the outer court she had discovered the animals, fed, saddled and burdened, ready. The sun already touched the upstanding peaks of the hills as she set out, turning once more eastward, picking a way to avoid the closer settled dales.

As she went Hertha searched for landmarks she had seen but once. Above all she must avoid any meeting with a far-roving hunter or herder out of Nordendale. The fact that the dalesmen avoided the places of the Old Ones, shunned their roads, was her only advantage.

The track which had been a clear guide to Gunnora's shrine became dimmer on its twisting way east. Beyond the reaches of Nordendale she should cut south once again for the circle of the Toads, perhaps over land where there was no trace at all of any road.

She dared not quicken pace. This track was treacherous with a winter slippage of stones and rock. With Elfanor in her carrying cradle upon her back, Hertha had to dismount now and again to lead her horse, testing the stability of the trail with the haft of the spear. Her mount had not so far refused to advance and that she took as a good sign, accepting that the animal's sense, so much keener than her own in many ways, would give any warning of trouble.

After a full day's travel she slept but fitfully, Elfanor in her arms beneath the huddle of her cloak, their rest a nest of last year's leaves and grass which Hertha scooped into place among a tangle of storm-downed trees. The second day had no sun, instead a thick mist which was half drizzle dampened her dank clothing against her.

Nordendale she passed—with a feeling of relief. She

had allowed herself a short period of viewing what lay below, marking the changes which had come to that half-deserted, once masterless holding since last she had come this way. There were people in the garden patches, a movement of sheep along one hillside. But her eyes had sought at once the tower of the keep. No banner cracked in the crisp wind. Which meant the lord was not in residence. Where? Hertha bit down on her mittened hand. There could well be one place to which Trystan was now bound—Lithendale! If he had gone seeking her— She shook her head as if her jumble of thoughts could be so reduced to order. No, there was only one thing which mattered, that stone wheel above Grimmerdale!

There was little forage for the horse and pony here. They pulled toward the green now coating hillside meadows. She had to use all her skill and determination to keep them moving. At noon she bribed them with broken bits of journey cake which they mouthed eagerly, licking up the last of the crumbs from the rocks where she had dropped the pieces.

The drizzle never became true rain, only a gray misery which wrapped her around. One of those lesser irritations which could eat away at one's determination. Her garments clung to her, and she shivered continually as she rode. Tonight—if she did not halt too long at an eating or rest break—tonight she should be within such distance of Grimmerdale that the next morn she could face her task.

She had this much in her favor, Hertha decided. The Powers of the Dark Ones were fed by the night, by any absence of light. If she could get to her task by the day she would have that small advantage. Providing she could finish before dusk deepened again.

Twilight came early. Again she camped at a place from which she could see the lantern above the door of that inn where once she had served and waited with what patience she could muster, for the one man whom her singleminded purpose had sent her to deliver to vengeance. She longed for a hot drink, for shelter even as squalid as that inn had been, the sound of voices of her own kind. Instead she crouched alone, her two beasts uneasy beside her, sucking at a stick of dried meat, and nursing her child. In the last of the light she saw that once more that knowing, measuring look was back in Elfanor's eyes. Something which was not of proper mankind gazed out at her, slyly, maliciously, with anticipation.

Hertha refused to believe that this was more than her imagination. She cradled the baby in her arms, after giving her the breast, rocking back and forth, crooning in a whisper one of the old, old songs she remembered her own old nurse had used to hold at bay the dark and all which might glide within thick shadows.

That night she did not sleep. It was as if the driving purpose which had brought her here fostered within her a frenetic energy, so that she had to use all her power and determination not to leave the half shelter she had found, to go straightway to the place where *they* waited.

So strong did that pull become that she knelt upon the ground, fighting with all the strength of her being the desire to move, to go—

That night might have lasted for a year, a century, more than her own lifetime, or so it seemed when the first grayish finger-claws of dawn came clutching over the hills. Hertha got stiffly to her feet. She was numb with cold, cramped in every muscle by the battle she had fought. Still lay the task ahead.

Now placing the baby's cradle on the ground, the girl opened the bag which Dame Inghela had given her. There were packets of leaves so dried and crushed that their condition was dry powder, others, withered to be sure, but still clinging to the branches from which they had sprung.

Hertha made her choices, lifting each pinch she used close to her nose to make sure that she dealt with the right one. Five such pinches she worked into a thick grease contained in a small pot, then three more, and lastly one, which was the strongest and most pungent of them all, making her sneeze, even gag when she smelled it closely.

The salve which had absorbed all these she rubbed in wide circles about her eyes. It beaded in her brows, making her squint a little from its strength of emanation. Again she used more as an ointment. Taking off her damp cap, she thrust her braids of hair back impatiently that she might anoint her ears. Last of all what was left she spread across the palms of her hands. Having so prepared herself, and fasting as required, she picked up the basket cradle and took Elfanor to the nearest shelter, a bush very thick with budding branches which overhung the ground. Slipping the cradle back under that rough canopy, Hertha set on end about the open side of the hiding place those branches of twigged herbs, forcing them into the earth, bolstering them erect with small stones.

The horse and pony had followed her. Now she recklessly crumbled all she had left of her journey cakes, leaving the bits in two piles at which they eagerly nuzzled. Getting to her feet, Hertha started forward, refusing to let herself look back. All she could do to protect Elfanor she had. She dared not let any apprehension steal into her mind, she must remember only what she had come to do.

The circle of the outer stones which was the rim of the Toad's wheel were clear enough. She held her hands together so that the greased palms were as one. Using them both then she pointed her fingertips forward, the smell of the herbs very strong.

Hertha edged along, making the circuit of the wheel's outer wall. Nor would she allow herself to glance down any of the avenues formed between the spokes of upstanding stones, but kept her gaze on the ground. She found the first of the "stopper stones" at the third such aisle.

Hertha faltered. The thing was a rough hunk of rock, not even worked as were the pillar stones, and it was as tall as her knees, so well embedded in the ground that perhaps it might be even larger. She wet her chapped lips with the tip of her tongue and considered its size, her own strength. Could she move such?

She might only find one of the missing ones and try. The girl dropped her cloak to the ground, its sodden folds hindered her shoulders and arms. Already she had sighted what she wanted. This was one! All points and angles, its blue surface standing out vividly in this place. Hertha reached it quickly, set her palms to it and pushed, to find the boulder set in the ground as securely as any forest tree.

So—but it could be moved! Having been in place once, it must be put so again. Now she exerted more strength, strove to rock it back and forth, her hands chafed by the roughness of its surface. The stone moved!

So small a triumph, but enough to encourage her. Panting, fighting, rubbing her hands near raw in spite of their protective covering (for in this place she knew that she dare not use the mittens which dangled from her wrists), she edged the rock on, brought it into place at last midpoint of one unguarded aisle, and leaned against it, panting for a space.

There was something building about her, a kind of soundless laughter, of jeering at one who dared so much surely to fail. Hertha straightened. Her lips were one firm line, her chin set. One! Now for the next—

She found a second stone, but this was half buried in rubble. She had to pull and dig to free it before she could once more try to move the rock on. It was stubborn, leaving its bed with such reluctance that once or twice she despaired of ever getting it out. Her hands left bloody prints upon its surface when she dragged it at last to the doorway it must lock. Two—

Hunger gnawed at her. She swayed dizzily now and again as she went to search for the last. Surely she could find and set that. Her wide divided skirt dragged at her legs. She felt as one wading through a vast quagmire of sucking mud, having to fight for each forward step.

There was no stone! There must be! She could not have

been misled in her vision in the shrine. Those of the Power who turned to the light played no such cruel tricks. They could refuse help, but they did not deliberately deceive. Somewhere near the stone must lie. Hertha turned slowly, examining the ground. There were tumbled stones, yes, plenty of them, both large and small, but none of a blue sheen.

Could it be wholly buried in some pile as the second was half concealed? She could sight no heap in that clutter of rocks which was large enough to hide totally what she sought. Once more she made the dragging round of the outer circumference of the wheel. As she went, so did that sly laughter seem to grow within her mind, buffet her like the wind of a rising storm. She was certain that the Toads knew what she attempted, that they watched her in amusement, somehow certain that her efforts would fail. But those would not!

The circling of her search grew wider, farther away from the edge of the wheel. Now she sought out Elfanor and nursed the whimpering baby, not realizing her own fatigue until her legs seemed to fold under her and the bleeding hands with which she clasped the child to her shook with tremors she could not control.

Her hunger was gone, leaving only a dull pain in her body as she hunched forward, impatient but waiting that the child might be satisfied. The horse and the pony stood on either side of the tangled bush. They had again licked up all the food she had left but they had not strayed.

Suddenly the mount which had carried her threw up its head and nickered before Hertha could stop it. A neigh answered. She stiffened where she crouched, taking the baby from her breast and placing it quickly in the basket behind her. Elfanor opened her mouth and gave forth a furious yell.

Somehow Hertha got to her feet, stood there wavering, one hand making fast her clothing, the other resting ready on the hilt of her dagger. Though the drizzle of rain no longer fell, the clouds still hung overhead. Not dark nor close enough however to hide the fact that there was a rider coming.

There were outlaws enough in this war-torn land who had the desperate courage, or perhaps even the inclination, to follow the Old Roads. She remembered, too, nightmare tales of *things* which prowled, or were said to run the ridges. Surely no one would come here unless he was bent on some form of mischief, so evil was the reputation of this place.

The newcomer fronted the rise, and she saw he wore war mail, a snouted helm which hid much of his face. A shield swung by his saddle horn, and its device had been new painted. That was the only bit of color about him, for the horse he rode was of the same dull gray as his half armor, as dusky of mane as his surcoat.

Once she might have known him by the shield device, but the lords of the dales lay in many unknown graves up and down the lands, and new men had risen, choosing their own markings. Hertha could not put name to who would bear what he carried. The painting was crude as if someone hardly versed in such work had made an effort to picture something only imperfectly described. There was a strange cloudy representation of what might be some kind of monstrous head, cutting across it, straight and far better pictured, the blade of a drawn sword, as if that weapon barred the monster behind from some prey. Cold iron—

The thought ran in her head as if he who rode so shouted it aloud. Cold iron, which was indeed the bane of some of the Old Ones, a counter to their magic in itself.

Some outlaw, more foolhardy and reckless than most of their breed? Or a wanderer who did not know the danger he unwittingly courted in such a place? With that snouted helm so overshadowing his face she could not see him any clearer than if he wore a mask. But the voice which hailed her! Hertha drew a deep breath of protest—yes, *that* she knew!

His mount, a war charger of good breed, paced slowly onward, the reins lying easy on its neck as if the rider had no reason to control it to his will. She wanted to run, but there was no refuge, no place to go where he could not follow—even into the den of the Toads where once they did venture together.

"My lady—" His hail seemed to hang in the air between them as if she refused to let her ears hear it. His horse stood quiet as he swung down with the practiced ease of a fighting man, leaving that shield still hung in place. Now he came toward her, his booted feet making a small crunching sound on the gravel. Somehow Hertha found her voice, was able to raise hand and ward him off with the only gesture she could make.

"No!"

If he heard her he did not listen. Now she could see his sunbrowned jaw, his firm-lipped mouth below the half mask of the helm. He paused and dragged his mail-enclosed gauntlets from his hands, thrust them into his belt and then dealt expertly with the fastening snaps of the helm, pulled it off to free his head with its frosted hair blowing free in the breeze. His eyes were slightly narrowed as he regarded her with such a speculative look that Hertha longed to be away from here, safe hid from all the thoughts which his coming had awakened in her, nothing must defeat her purpose here. So, hardening her resolve, it was her turn to take a step forward, both hands up, grimed, broken of nail, raw of finger, between them, in that warding off gesture.

"My Lord Trystan—why?"

Somehow she could not find more words, though thoughts plagued her.

"I went to Lithendale; you were gone." He spoke simply, as one might to a troubled child. "They told me that you sought help in a strange and perilous place. So I came."

Hertha ran her tongue across her lips, tasted a little of the bitter coating she had laid upon her face.

"This—it is my task—" She tried to lash herself into saving anger. Always, save once, she had defended her independence, carried her own burden without any help.

"I do not know witcheries," he said gravely. "Perhaps it is true that yours may be the only hands," he glanced at her misused fingers then, "which can accomplish this. Then again, my lady, it may also be that two can do better and quicker than one what must be done."

Before Hertha could retreat he was at her side in one swift stride, trying to catch her hands. But she jerked away.

"Do not!" she cried. "They have protection."

"Protection!" One eyebrow arched upward in an odd slant which she remembered of old. "It would seem by the looks of those that you have had little of that this day. Tell me," now his voice had the ring of that which had been raised many times to command men, "what do you do here and why?"

"Why?" She must disgust him and quickly, get rid of one who had no part of this and who must not be drawn into her troubles. With a flap of her earth-stained clothing she turned and stooped to catch up the basket. Settling that against her hip, she pulled free the covers about Elfanor's face. Even under these clouds the light was without pity, showing the clear marks of the curse. While the baby's eyes were open, staring outward with that evil, knowing look. "See you?" she demanded fiercely, studying him intently, watching for the first sign of revulsion.

However he had himself well schooled, that she must admit. He did not display the disgust she was certain she would see.

"They told me—a changeling—" His voice was slow, even, again as if he were afraid to alarm. "But you think, lady, that you have found an answer here?"

"Perhaps, only perhaps." She felt odd, having prepared herself to counter the shrinking she had expected from him. What kind of a man was he who faced the results of dark evil without a change of eye or expression?

"Perhaps is sometimes all one can ask for." Again he made one of those swift, sure moves and she found the basket whirled out of her torn hands, held firm and secure in his, as he looked down at the child. "What is it that you think must be done?" he asked briskly.

She wanted to take the basket from him, to draw tight the coverings which made Elfanor safe from prying eyes as well as this cold. But her tired body made her clumsy as she stumbled, half fell forward, so that now he held the cradle upon one hip and his other arm was about her, both drawing her close and supporting her.

"Come." He countered her small attempt to pull away, led her to a pile of stones and there seated himself, the cradle resting across his knees, she herself beside him, unable to summon any strength to pull free from his hold.

She shivered, her hands lying uselessly on her knees. Then, to her great disgust, she felt tears on her cheeks. So much of her wanted to yield, to let someone else take command. Only—she need only look down at Elfanor, who as usual lay quiet, only stared up into the face of the man who held her with those unblinking eyes, the sly fires well alive deep in their depths.

Hertha summoned up all the strength she could muster, and broke free from his grip, somehow got to her feet.

"The rocks—the last one—" She must keep to her task!

"Which rock?" He did not try to hold her back, only stood himself and then placed the cradle carefully on the ground.

Hertha had already lurched away, afraid now that he would attempt to hold her again. If he did, she might yield to that traitor part of her which his coming here had awakened in a way which bewildered and weakened her resolve.

"The blue one, the last—I have searched, and searched. Two I found. The third—I cannot." She stumbled on, her torn hands outstretched as if to implore the ground itself to produce the stone she must have. "The rocks," she spoke more to herself than to him, trying to return to her singleminded hunt, shut out all which was not atuned to that, "one must be placed at each of the entrances, as a sealing. That is the task laid upon me now."

She was only half aware then he had passed her, to go to the nearest of the spoked lanes and look down at the earth-encrusted boulder she had worked so hard to set in place.

"This kind?" Trystan did not wait for her to answer. Instead, having studied the stone, he too swung out in search among the tumble of rocks which lay spread out along the crest of the ridge.

Hertha dragged her way on, stopping now and then to pull at a pile of smaller stones, hoping each time to see hidden beneath them the blue she sought. She had been near three-quarters of the way around the wheel now and there was no sign of the last one. Did it exist at all?

"Ha!"

She turned. So quickly that she lost her balance and fell painfully to her knees. For a moment she did not see him at all and then his head appeared nearly at ground level and she remembered a notch of gully which ran there.

"I think that it is down here!"

Somehow Hertha got across the ground between them. Trystan was stooped, hurling small rocks away from him with vigor. As Hertha came to the lip of that cut she could see it too, buried, only a small bit showing above the soil now that he cleared it from the rock fall. Blue like the others. But how could she raise it?

Having thrown aside the rocks, Trystan drew his sword and stabbed the earth, throwing chunks of winter-hardened clay aside, yet working more slowly and with care for the safety of his tool which was not to be foolishly blunted.

Hertha wiped the back of her hand across her forehead, smearing the herb grease on her face. She stared down at where Trystan worked with a dull despair. He might free the stone, yes, but how could she get it out of that tight lodging, then drag or roll it to the final resting place? Strength seemed to have melted out of her body.

"There it is, my lady!" He stepped away, thrusting his sword once more into its scabbard, looking down at the boulder he had uncovered with an expression of satisfaction.

From somewhere Hertha summoned croaking words. "Up—how does one get it up?"

That she could lift that piece of rock she had to acknowledge was beyond her powers. Yet the task was hers alone, she was sure of that, as she had been since the first of this ordeal.

"There is the rope which kept your pony's sacks in place." He stood, pinching his lips as he looked down at the rock. "With the aid of the horses it can be pulled out."

Hertha blinked. What he said made sense. She had been so bemused by her own fatigue that such a move had not occurred to her. It gave her a spurt of energy and she was on her feet once more, heading to where she had piled the pony's gear. There was the rope, sure enough, a strong one. Whether its strength was enough to carry through Trystan's suggestion she could not be sure until it was tried. Looping the coil over her arm and shoulder, she brought it back and tossed the end to him.

He caught it neatly out of midair as it fell, then knelt to work a length around the rock, taking advantage of any projecting angle to make the stone more secure. Finally he looked up to her.

"Bring your horse, mine, and we shall see if this will serve."

Her own placid mount caused no trouble, plodding

easily enough to the gully. But his beast pulled back on the reins he had left dangling to the ground, the traditional "earth tie" of a fighting man, rolling its eyes and snorting. Hertha pulled steadily on the reins and was glad that there was no battle—the horse followed her at last, one reluctant step after another.

Trystan clambered out of the cut, was already making one end of the rope into a loop about the horn of her saddle. The other he still gripped in his hand as he mounted up, giving the now foreshortened piece of cordage a second twist about his own horn.

At his signal not only the horse he bestrode, but her own moved and she saw the rope become as taut as a bowstring, snapping hard against the edge of the gully. She feared to hear the crack of a breaking rope. Still that did not come. Trystan's horse went slowly on, step by step, her own following while the rope remained taut. The rock, indeed, freed from its earth setting, was drawn up the side of the gully as it gouged and scraped against the wall along which it swung.

The boulder arose at last over the edge, plopped near Hertha's feet. She hurried to it, worrying at the knotted rope, she would have nothing left to draw upon. Trystan was beside her, his hands pushing her aside as they competently freed the stone.

"Now where? Where is this road which must be so guarded?"

She shook her head. "I must do it! Mine the sin, mine the payment!" She tried to edge past him, to set her hands to the stone's earth-grimed side. It must be done—she *must* do it!

"No." His voice seemed to come from very far away, as if her head were so full of the need for keeping her mind on action that she could not catch the words quickly. "If it needs your touch, well enough. But remember, I, too, faced the Toads once in a time."

"Because then I tricked you." Hertha was not aware

again that she was crying until she tasted the salt of her own tears. "All was of my doing. Let me go. It must be placed before sundown—it must be!"

He did not answer her. Instead he bent and braced both hands to the boulder, releasing his strength, sending it rolling in a wobbling fashion across the ground. Hertha hurried after it with a cry of dismay. She reached it first, set her own energy, what remained of it, to the pushing, and felt that it gave only inches.

He was once more beside her. "Together we once fought here, my lady. So shall we fight again. I have not sought you out to lose you again in any battle which means all this one does. Heave if you will and must, but with my help also. Surely whatever power sent you here cannot deny you my aid, not now!"

Hertha could not raise breath to answer him. She labored at the stone, and it was moving more easily, rocking from side to side. If she was not fulfilling the task laid upon her, *she* would suffer. But she could not accomplish it all alone, of that she was sure.

The stone moved so slowly. Above was the darkening of clouds which were of no storm's signal but that of coming night. Night was when the Dark Ones arose to power, if they could not get the stone in place before the last of daylight reached them! Hertha's breath came in shallow gusts of panting. Before them to the left was the last of the open ways. Trystan changed position, coming about behind her so as to exert pressure from the other side.

It seemed to Hertha that the very ground denied them aid, that certain shadows crept out from the pillar bases to cover the rough portions and hide obstacles from them as they labored.

"On now, my lady, just a short way—" He, too, was panting. Then he bent even closer to the ground, going down on one knee as he set his shoulder firmly against the side of the rock.

"Stand away!" he ordered her.

She saw the strain of his body, his flushed face. For a long moment it would seem that the rock had caught past their moving. Then—

Slowly, and with a wavering from side to side (which Hertha watched with anguished anxiety, her bleeding hands pressed to her mouth) it went forward, came to a stop in the center of the way.

There was a sudden sweep of wind, sword-sharp with cold, whirling out her clothing, raising dust to blind her eyes. Somewhere from within that gritty haze came hands, arms, a body which steadied her. Was it the wailing of the wind which carried that strange chorus of grunting cries? Or did she imagine it only?

She could barely keep her feet. A moment later he caught her up, carried her out of the whirlwind of noise and grit, back toward the bush which still sheltered Elfanor.

The wind died, she heard another sound, the vigorous crying of a baby. Trystan set her down and Hertha staggered to the cradle. It was not dark yet, the twilight was still holding off a little. She caught the basket up into her arms as she fell to her knees. Holding it tight against her with one arm, she clawed at the covering blanket. Elfanor was screaming steadily.

Hertha stared down. Her eyes were tearing, perhaps the grit of the wind storm had irritated them. She blinked and blinked furiously, fighting against that distortion of her sight. Then she could see clearly.

Her daughter's face was red with effort, her eyes screwed shut as she howled, flailing at the air with the fists she had managed to loose from her swaddling.

A red face, but—

Hertha's fear melted away. This was no changeling! She had won! The curse was gone. The eyes in the baby's face opened. They were dark, but there was no alien knowledge in them, just as that anger-reddened skin held no scaled patch of brown.

"Free! She is free!" Hertha crooned, rocking the baby, cradle and all, against her as she swayed back and forth. Firm hands clasped her shoulders. Dimly she realized that a new strength had come, that she was no longer alone.

"You freed her." His voice was clear to her.

She turned her head to look at him, all her gratitude swelling up within her like an inner fire.

"With you only could I have done it."

"Did you think I would not help?" He looked stern, harsh and hard, in the failing light. But that was not Trystan in truth, that she was sure of. For the first time in days, months, even years which she could remember, Hertha let her stiff independence seep away, allowed herself the precious safety of his hold.

"With you only," she repeated softly. She knew from the light suddenly aglow in his eyes, the softening of his lips that he heard. "Many are Gunnora's gifts—many and good."

"May her name be praised," he said then, though Gunnora was the holder of women's Power and no man worshiped at her shrine. "She has given us both much in this hour. My lady, it grows dark, shall we go?"

Hertha looked at Elfanor. Whatever rage had possessed her at the sundering of the dark power was gone. The baby blinked sleepily.

"Yes," Hertha cried. "Let us go—home!"

The delight in his face was such at her words that she believed she had nothing else to wish for.

Spider Silk

1

THE Big Storm in the Year of the Kobold came late, long past the month when such fury was to be expected. This was all part of that evil which the Guardians had drawn upon Estcarp when they summoned up their greatest power to blast and twist the mountain lands, seal off passes through which had come the invasion from Karsten.

Rannock lay open to that storm. Only the warning dream-sending to the Wise Woman, Ingvarna, drew a portion of the women and children to the higher lands, there to watch with fear and trembling the sea's fierce assault upon the coast. So high dashed those waves that water covered and boiled about the Serpent Teeth of the upper ledges. Only here, in pockets among the Tor rocks, could a fugitive crouch in almost mindless terror, awaiting the end.

Of the fishing fleet which had set out yesterday morn, who had any hopes now of its return save perhaps a scattering of wreckage, playthings of the storm waves?

There was left only a handful of old men and boys, and one or two such as Herdrek, the Twist-Leg, the village smith. For Rannock was as poor in men as it was in all else since the war years had ravaged Estcarp. To the north perched Alizon, a hawk ready to be unleashed upon its neighbor; from the south Karsten boiled and bubbled, if aught was still left alive beyond the wrecked mountain passages.

Men who had marched with the Borderers under Lord Simon Tregarth or served beneath the Banners of the Witch Women of Es—where were they? Long since, their kin had given up any hope of their return. There had been no true peace in this land since old Nabor (who could count his years at more than a hundred) had been in his green youth.

It was Nabor now who battled the strength of the wind to the Tor, dragged himself up to stand, hunched shoulder to shoulder, with Ingvarna. As she, he looked to the sea uneasily. That she expected still their own fleet, he could not believe, foresighted as all knew her to be.

Waves mounted, to pound giant fists against the rock. Nabor caught sight of a ship rising and falling near the Serpent's dread fangs. Then a huge swell whirled it over those sharp threats into the comparative calm beyond. Nabor sighed with the relief of a seaman who had witnessed a miracle, life won from the very teeth of rock death. Also, Rannock had the right of storm wrack. If that ship survived so far, its cargo was forfeit now to any who could bring it to shore. He half turned to seek the shelter of the Tor hollows, rouse Herdrek, the others, with this promise of fortune.

However, Ingvarna turned her head. Through the drifts of rain her eyes held his. There was a warning in her steady gaze. "One comes—" He saw her lips shape the words rather than voice them above the roar of wind and wave.

At the same moment, there was such a crash as equaled the drum of thunder, the lash of lightning. The strange ship might have beaten the menace of the reef's fangs, but now had been driven halfway up the beach, where it was fast breaking up under the hammer blows of the surf.

Herdrek stumped out to join them. "It is a raider," he commented during a lull of the wind. "Perhaps one of the Sea Wolves of Alizon." He spat at the wreck below.

Ingvarna was already scrambling over the rocks towards the shore, as if what lay there were of vast importance. Herdrek shouted after her a warning, but she did not even turn her head. With a curse at the folly of females, which a second later he devoutly hoped the Wise Woman had not been able to pick out of the air, the smith followed her, two of the lads venturing in his wake.

At least when they reached the shore level, the worst of the storm was spent. Waves drew a torn seaweed veil around the broken vessel. Herdrek made fast a rope about his waist, gave dire warnings to his followers to keep a tight hold upon it. Then he ventured into the surf, using that cordage from wind-rent sails, hanging in loops down the shattered sides, to climb aboard.

There was a hatch well tamped down, roped shut. He drew belt knife to slash the fastening.

"Ho!" His voice rolled hollowly into the dark beneath him. "Anyone below?"

A thin cry answered, one which might issue from the throat of a seabird such as already coasted over the subsiding surface of the sea on hunt for the bounty of the storm. Yet he thought not. Gingerly, favoring his stiff leg, the smith lowered himself into the stinking hold. What he found there made him retch, and then heated in him dull anger against those who had mastered this vessel. She had been a slaver, such as Rannock's men had heard tell of—dealing in live cargo.

But of that cargo, only one survived. Her, Herdrek carried gently from the horror of that prison. A little maid, her small arms no more than skin slipped glovelike on bones, her eyes great, gray, and blankly open. Ingvarna took the strange child from the smith as one who had the authority of clan and home hearth, wrapping the little one's thin, shivering body in her own warm cloak.

From whence Dairine came, those of Rannock never learned. That slavers raided far was no secret. Also, the villagers soon discovered the child was blind. Ingvarna, though she was a Wise One, greatly learned in herbs and spells, the setting of bones, the curing of wounds, shook her head sadly over that discovery, saying that the child's blindness came from no hurt of body. Rather, she must have looked upon some things so horrible that thereafter her mind closed and refused all sight.

Though she must have been six or seven winters old, yet also speech seemed driven from her, and only fear was left to be her portion. Although the women of Rannock would have tried to comfort her, yet secretly in their hearts they were willing that she bide with Ingvarna, who treated her oddly, they thought. For the Wise Woman did not strive to make life easier in any way for the child. Rather, from the first, Ingvarna treated the sea waif not as one maimed in body, and perhaps in mind, but rather as she might some daughter of the village whom she had chosen to be her apprentice in the harsh school of her own learning.

These years were bleak for Rannock. Full half the fleet did not return from out of the maw of that storm. Nor did any of the coastwise traders come. The following winter was a lean one. But in those dark days, Dairine showed first her skill. Though her eyes might not see what her fingers wrought, yet she could mend fishing nets with such cleverness that even the experienced women marveled.

And in the following spring, when the villagers husked the loquth balls to free their seeds for new plantings, Dairine busied herself with the silken inner fibers, twisting and turning those. Ingvarna had Herdrek make a small spindle, and showed the child how this tool might be best put to work.

Good use did Dairine make of it, too. Her small,

birdclaw fingers drew out finer thread than any had achieved before, freer from knotting than any the villagers had seen. Yet never seemed she satisfied, but strove ever to make her spinning yet finer, more smooth.

The Wise Woman continued her fosterling's education in other ways, teaching her to use her fingers, her nose, in the herb garden. Dairine learnt easily the spelling which was part of a Wise Woman's knowledge. She absorbed such very quickly, yet always there was about her an impatience. When she made mistakes, then her anger against herself was great. The greatest when she tried to explain some tool or need which she seemed unable to describe but for which she evinced a need.

Ingvarna spoke to Herdrek (who was now village elder), saying that perhaps the craft of the Wise Woman might aid in regaining a portion of Dairine's lost memory. When he demanded why she had not voiced such a matter before, Ingvarna answered gravely:

"This child is not blood of our blood, and she was captive to the sea wolves. Have we the right to recall to her past horrors? Perhaps Gunnora, who watches over all womankind, has taken away her memory of the past in pity. If so—"

He bit his thumb, watching Dairine as she paced back and forth before the loom which he had caused to be set up for her, now and then halting to slap her hand upon the frame in frustration. It seemed as if she longed to force the heavy wood into another pattern which would serve her better.

"I think that she grows more and more unhappy," he agreed slowly. "At first she seemed content. Now there are times when she acts as a snow cat encaged against her will. I do not like to see her so."

The Wise Woman nodded. "Well enough. In my mind, this is a right choice."

Ingvarna went to the girl, taking both her hands, drawing her around so that she might look directly into those blind eyes. At Ingvarna's touch, Dairine stood still. "Leave us!" the Wise Woman commanded the smith.

Early that evening as Herdrek stood at his forge, Dairine walked into the light of his fire. She came to him unhesitatingly. So acute was her hearing that she often startled the villagers by her recognition of another presence. Now she held out her hands to him as she might to a father she loved. And he knew all was well.

By midsummer, when the loquths had flowered and their blossoms dropped, Dairine went often into the fields, fingering the swelling bolls. Sometimes she sang, queer, foreign-tongued words, as if the plants were children (now knee height, and then shoulder height) who must be amused and cherished.

Herdrek had changed her loom as the girl suggested might be done. From Ingvarna, she learned the mysteries of dyes, experimenting on her own. She had no real friend among the few children of the dying village. Firstly, because she did not range much afield, save with Ingvarna, of whom most were in awe. Secondly, because her actions were strange and she seemed serious and more adult than the years they believed to be hers.

In the sixth year after her coming, a Sulcar ship put in at Rannock, the first strange vessel they had sighted since the wreck of the slaver. Its captain brought news that the long war was at last over.

The defeat of the Karsten invaders, who so drained the powers of the rulers of Estcarp, had been complete. Koris of Gorm was now Commander of Estcarp, since so many of the Guardians had perished when they turned the full extent of their power upon the enemy. Yet the land was hardly at peace. The sea wolves of the coast had been augmented by ships of the broken and defeated navy of Karsten. And as in times of chaos, other wolfheads, without any true lands or allegiance, now ravaged the land wherever they might. Though the forces under Captain

General Koris sought to protect the boundaries, yet to clearly defeat such hit-and-run raids was yet well beyond the ability of any defending force.

The Sulcar Captain was impressed by the latest length of Dairine's weaving, offering for it, when he bargained with Ingvarna, a much better price than he had thought to pay out in this forgotten village. He was much interested also in the girl, speaking to her slowly in several tongues. However, she answered him only in the language of Estcarp, saying she knew no other.

Still, he remarked privately to Ingvarna that somewhere in the past he had seen those like unto her, though where and when during his travels he could not bring to mind. Still, he thought that she was not of common stock.

It was a year later that the Wise Woman wrought the best she could for her sea-gift foundling.

No one knew how old Ingvarna was, for the Wise Woman showed no advance of age, as did those less learned in the many uses of herbs and medicants. But it was true that she walked more slowly, and that she no longer went alone when she sought out certain places of Power, taking Dairine ever with her. What the two did there no one knew, for who would spy on any woman with the Witch Talent?

On this day, the few fishing boats had taken to sea before dawn. At moonrise the night before, the Wise Woman and her fosterling had gone inland to visit a certain very ancient place. There Ingvarna kindled a fire which burned not naturally red, but rather blue. Into those flames, she tossed small, tightly bound bundles of dried herbs so that the smoke which arose was heavily scented. But she watched not that fire. Rather, a slab of stone set behind its flowering. That stone had a surface like unto glass, the color of a fine sword blade.

Dairine stood a little behind the Wise Woman. Though Ingvarna had taught her so much over the years, to make her other senses serve her in place of her missing sight, so that her fingers were ten eyes, her nostrils, her ears could catch scent and sound to an extent far outreaching the skill of ordinary mankind; yet at moments such as this, the longing to be as others awoke in her a sense of loss so dire that to her eyes came tears, flowing silently down her cheeks. Much Ingvarna had given her. Still, she was not as the others of Rannock. And ofttimes loneliness settled upon her as a burdensome cloak. Now the girl sensed that Ingvarna planned for her some change. But that it would make her see as others saw—that she could not hope for.

She heard clearly the chanting of the Wise Woman. The odor of the burning herbs filled her nose, now and then made her gasp for a less heavy lungful of air. Then came a command, not given in words, nor by some light touch against her arm and shoulder. But into her mind burst an order and Dairine walked ahead, her hands outstretched, until her ten fingers flattened against a throbbing surface. Warm it was, near to a point which would sear her flesh, while its throb was in twin beat to her own heart. Still, Dairine stood firm, while the chant of the Wise Woman came more faintly, as if the girl had been shifted from farther away in space from her foster mother.

Then she felt an inward flow from the surface she touched, a warmth which spread along her hands, her wrists, up her arms. Fainter still came the voice of Ingvarna petitioning on her behalf, strange and half-forgotten powers.

Slowly the warmth receded. But how long Dairine had stood so wedded to that surface she could not see, the girl never knew. Except that there came a moment when her hands fell, as if too heavily burdened for her to raise.

"What is done, is done." Ingvarna's voice at the girl's left sounded as weighted as Dairine's hands felt. "All I have to give, this I have freely shared with you. Though being blind as men see blindness, yet you have sight such as few can own to. Use it well, my fosterling."

From that day it became known that Dairine did indeed have strange powers of "seeing"—through her hands. She could take up a thing which had been made and tell you of the maker, of how long since it had been wrought. A shred of fleece from one of the thin-flanked hill sheep put into her fingers would enable her to guide an anxious owner to where the lost flock member had strayed.

There was one foretelling which she would not do, after she came upon its secret by chance only. For she had taken the hand of little Hulde during the Harvest Homing dance. Straightway thereafter, Dairine dropped her grasp upon the child's small fingers, crying out and shrinking away from the villagers, to seek out Ingvarna's house and therein hide herself. Within the month, Hulde had died of a fever. Thereafter, the girl used her new sight sparingly, and always with a fear plain to be seen haunting her.

In the Year of the Weldworm, when Dairine passed into young womanhood, Ingvarna died, swiftly. As if foreseeing another possible end, she summoned death as one summons a servant to do one's bidding.

Though Dairine was no true Wise Woman, yet thereafter she took on many of the duties of her foster mother. Within a month after the Wise Woman's burial, the Sulcar ship returned.

As the Captain told the forgotten village the news of the greater world, his eyes turned ever to Dairine, her hands busy with thread she spun as she listened. Among those of the village, she was indeed one apart, with her strange silver-fair hair, silver-light eyes.

Sibbald Ortis, Sibbald the Wrong-Handed—thus they had named him after a sea battle had lopped off his hand, and a smith in another land had made him one of metal—was that captain. He was new come to command and young—though he had lived near all his life at sea after the manner of his people.

Peace, after a fashion, he told them, had encompassed

the land at least. For Koris of Gorm now ruled Estcarp with a steady hand. Alizon had been defeated in some invasion that nation had attempted overseas. And Karsten was in chaos, one prince or lord always rising against another. While the sea wolves were being hunted down, one after another, to a merciless end.

Having made clear that he was in Rannock on lawful business, the Captain now turned briskly to the subject of trade. What had they, if anything, which would be worth stowage in his own ship?

Herdrek was loathe to spread their poverty before these strangers. Also, he wanted, with a desire he could hardly conceal, some of the tools and weapons he had seen in casual use among them. Yet what had Rannock? Fish dried to take them through a lean winter, some woven lengths of wool.

The villagers would be hard put even to give these visitors guest-right, with the feast they were entitled to. And to fail in that was to deny their own heritage.

Dairine, listening to the Captain, had wished she dared touch his hand, and thus learn what manner of a man he was who had journeyed so far and seen so much. A longing was born in her to be free of the narrow, well-known ways of Rannock, to see what lay beyond in the world. Her fingers steadily twirled her thread, but her thoughts were elsewhere.

Then she lifted her head a little, for she knew someone was now standing at her side. There was the tang of sea-salted leather, and other odors. This was a stranger, one of the Sulcar men.

"You work that thread with skill, maid."

She recognized the Captain's voice. "It is my skill, Lord Captain."

"They tell me that fate has served you harshly," he spoke bluntly then. But she liked him the better for that bluntness.

"Not so, Lord Captain. These of Rannock have been ever kind. And I was fosterling to their Wise Woman. Also, my hands serve well, if my eyes are closed upon this world. Come, you, and see!" She spoke with pride as she arose from her stool, thrusting her spindle into her girdle.

Thus Dairine brought him to the cottage which was hers, sweet within for all its scents of herbs. She gestured to where stood the loom Herdrek had made her.

"As you see, Lord Captain, I am not idle, even though I may be blind."

For she knew that there, in the half-done web, there was no mistake.

Ortis was silent for a moment. Then she heard the hiss of his breath expelled in wonder.

"But this is weaving of the finest! There is no fault in color or pattern . . . How can this be done?"

"With one's two hands, Lord Captain!" She laughed. "Here, give me a possession of yours that I may show you better how fingers can be eyes."

Within her there was a new excitement, for something told her that this was a moment of importance in her life. She heard then a faint swish as if some bit of woven stuff were being shaken free. A clinging length was pressed into the hand she held out.

"Tell me," he commanded, "from whence came this, and how was it wrought?"

Back and forth between her fingers, the girl slipped the riband of silken stuff.

Woven—yes. But her "seeing" hands built no mind picture of human fingers at the business. No, strangely ill-formed were those members engaged in the weaving. And so swift were they also that they seemed to blur. No woman, as Dairine knew women, had fashioned this. But female—strongly, almost fiercely female.

"Spider silk—" She was not aware that she had spoken aloud until she heard the sound of her own words.

"Yet not quite spider. A woman weaving—still, not a woman. . . ."

She raised the riband to her cheek. There was a wonder in such weaving which brought to life in her a fierce longing to know more and more.

"You are right." The Captain's voice broke her preoccupation with that need to learn. "This comes from Usturt. And had a man but two full bolts of it within his cargo, he could count triple profits from such a voyage alone."

"Where lies Usturt?" Dairine demanded. If she could go there—learn what could be learned. "And who are the weavers? I do not see them as beings like unto our own people."

She heard his breath hiss again. "To see the weavers," he said in a low voice, "is death. They hate all mankind—"

"Not so, Lord Captain!" Dairine answered him then. "It is not mankind that they hate—it is all males." For from the strip between her fingers came that knowledge.

For a moment she was silent. Did he doubt her?

"At least no man sails willingly to Usturt," he replied. "I had that length from one who escaped with his bare life. He died upon our deck shortly after we fished him from a waterlogged raft."

"Captain," she stroked the silk, "you have said that this weaving is a true treasure. My people are very poor and grow poorer. If one were to learn the secret of such weaving, might not good come of it?"

With a sharp jerk he took the riband from her.

"There is no such way."

"But there is!" Her words came in an eager tumble, one upon the other. "Women—or female things—wove this. They might treat with a woman—one who was already a weaver."

Great, calloused hands closed upon her shoulders.

"Girl, not for all the gold in Karsten would I send any woman into Usturt! You know not of what you speak. It is true that you have gifts of the Talent. But you are no confirmed Guardian, and you are blind. What you suggest is such a folly—Aye, Vidruth, what is it now?"

Dairine had already sensed that someone had approached.

"The tide rises. For better mooring, Captain, we need move beyond the rocks."

"Aye. Well, girl, may the Right Hand of Lraken be your shield. When a ship calls, no captain lingers."

Before she could even wish him well, he was gone. Retreating, she sat down on her hard bench by the loom. Her hands trembled, and from her eyes the tears seeped. She felt bereft, as if she had had for a space a treasure and it had been torn from her. For she was certain that her instinct had been right, that if any could have learned the secret of Usturt, she was that one.

Now, when she put a hand out to finger her own weaving, the web on the loom seemed coarse, utterly ugly. In her mind, she held queer vision of a deeply forested place in which great, sparkling webs ran in even strands from tree to tree.

Through the open door puffed a wind from the sea. Dairine lifted her face to it as it tugged at her hair.

"Maid!"

She was startled. Even with her keen ears, she had not heard anyone approach so loud was the wind-song.

"Who are you?" she asked quickly.

"I am Vidruth, maid, mate to Captain Ortis."

She arose swiftly. "He has thought more upon my plan?" For she could see no other reason for the seaman to seek her out in this fashion.

"That is so, maid. He awaits us now. Give me your hand—so. . . ."

Fingers grasped hers tightly. She strove to free her hand. This man—there was that in him which was—wrong— Then out of nowhere, came a great, smothering cloak, folded about her so tightly she could not struggle. There were unclean smells to affront her nostrils, but the worst was that this Vidruth had swung her up across his shoulder so that she could have been no more than a bundle of trade goods.

2

SO was she brought aboard what was certainly a ship, for in spite of the muffling of the cloak, Dairine used her ears, her nose. However, in her mind, she could not sort out her thoughts. Why had Captain Ortis so vehemently, and truthfully (for she had read that truth in his touch), refused to bring her? Then this man of his had come to capture her as he might steal a woman during some shore raid?

The Sulcarmen were not slave traders, that was well known. Then why?

Hands pulled away the folds of the cloak at last. The air she drew thankfully into her lungs was not fresh, rather tainted with stinks which made her feel unclean even to sniff. She thought that her prison must lie deep within the belly of the ship.

"Why have you done this?" Dairine asked of the man she could hear breathing heavily near her.

"Captain's orders," he answered, leaning so close she not only smelt his uncleanly body, but gathered with that a sensation of heat. "He has eyes in his head, has the Captain. You be a smooth-skinned, likely wench—"

"Let her be, Wak!" That was Vidruth.

"Aye, Captain," the other answered with a slur of sly contempt. "Here she be, safe and sound—"

"And here she stays, Wak, safe from your kind. Get out!"

There was a growl from Wak, as if he were close to questioning the other's right to so order him. Then Dairine's ears caught a sound which might have been that of a panel door sliding into place.

"You are not the Captain," she spoke into the silence between them.

"There has been a change of command," he returned. "The Captain, he has not brought us much luck in months agone. When we learned that he would not try to better his fortune—he was—"

"Killed!"

"Not so. Think you we want a blood feud with all his clan? The Sulcarmen take not lightly to those who let the red life out of some one of their stock."

"I do not understand. You are all Sulcar—"

"That we are not, girl. The world has changed since those ruled the waves about the oceans. They were fighters and fighting men get killed. The Kolder they fought, and they blew up Sulcarkeep in that fighting, taking the enemy—but also too many of their own—on into the Great Secret. Karsten they fought, and they were at the taking of Gorm, aye. Then they have patrolled against the sea wolves of Alizon. Men they have lost, many men. Now if they take a ship out of harbor, they do it with others than just their kin to raise sails and set the course. No, we do not kill Sibbald Ortis, we may need him later. But he is safe laid.

"Now let us to the business between us, girl. I heard the words you spoke with Ortis. Also did I learn much about you from those starvelings who live in Rannock. You have some of the Talents of the Wise Women, if you cannot call upon the full Power, blind as you are. You yourself said it—if any can treat with those devil females of Usturt, it must be one such as you.

"Think on that spider silk, girl. You held that rag that Ortis has. And you can do mighty things, unless all those at Rannock are crazed in their wits. Which I do not believe. This is a chance which a man may have offered to him but once in a lifetime."

She heard the greed in his voice. And perhaps that greed would be her protection. Vidruth would take good care to keep her safe. Just as he held somewhere Sibbald Ortis for a like reason.

"Why did you take me so, if your intentions are good? If you heard my words to the Captain, you know I would have gone willingly."

He laughed. "Do you think those shore-side halflingmen would have let you go? With three-quarters of the Guardians dead, their own Wise Woman laid also in her grave shaft, would they willingly have surrendered to us even your small Talent? The whole land is hard pressed now for any who hold even a scrap of the Power.

"No matter. They will welcome you back soon enough after you have learned the secret of Usturt. If it then still be in your mind to go to them."

"But how do you know that in Usturt I shall work for you?"

"Because you will not want the Captain to be given over to them. They do not have a pleasant way with captives."

There was fear behind his words, a fear born of horror, which he fought to control.

"Also, if you do not do as we wish, we can merely sail and leave you on Usturt for the rest of your life. No ship goes there willingly. A long life for you perhaps, girl, alone with none of your own kind—think of that."

He was silent for a moment before he added, "It is a bargain, girl, one we swear to keep. You deal with the weavers, we take you back to Rannock, or anywhere else you name. The Captain, he can be set ashore with you even. No more harm done. And a portion of the silk for your own. Why, you can buy all of Rannock and make yourself a Keep lady!"

"There is one thing—" She was remembering Wak. "I am not such a one as any of your men can take at his will. Know you not what happens then to any Talent I may possess?"

When Vidruth answered her, there was a deep note of menace in his voice, though it was not aimed at her.

"All men know well that the Talent departs from a woman who lies with a man. None shall trouble you."

"So be it," she returned, with an outward calm it was hard for her to assume. "Have you the bit of silk? Let me learn from it what I can."

She heard him move away the grate of whatever door kept snug her prison. As that sound ceased, she put out her hands to explore. The cubby was small, there was a shelflike bunk against the wall, a stool which seemed bolted to the deck, nought else. Did they have Captain Ortis pent in such a hole also? And how had this Vidruth managed so well the take-over of the Captain's command? What she had read of Sibbald Ortis during their brief meeting had not been such as to lead her to think he was one easily overcome by an enemy.

But she was sitting quietly on the stool when Vidruth returned to drop the length of riband across her quiet hands.

"Learn all you can," he urged her. "We have two days of sail if this wind continues to favor us, then we shall raise Usturt. Food, water, what you wish, shall be brought to you, and there is a guard without so that you need not be troubled."

With the silk between her hands, Dairine concentrated upon what it could tell her. She had no illusions concerning Vidruth. To him and the others, she was only a tool to their hands. Because she was sightless, he might undervalue her, for all his talk of Talent and Power. She had discovered many times in the past that such was so.

Deliberately, Dairine closed out the world about her, shut her ears to creak of timber, wash of wave, her nose to the many smells which offended it. Once more her "sight" turned inward. She could "see" the blur of those hands (which were not quite hands) engaged in weaving. Colors she had no words to describe were clear and bright. For the material she saw so was not one straight length of color, but shimmered from one shade to another.

Dairine tried now to probe beyond that shift of color to the loom from which it had come. She had an impression of tall, dark shafts. Those were not of well-planed and smooth wood; no, they had the crooked surface of—trees—standing trees!

The hands—concentrate now upon the moving hands of the weaver.

But the girl had only reached that point of recognition when there was a knock to distract her concentration. Exasperated, she turned her head to the door of the cubby.

"Come!"

Again the squeak of hinge, the sound of boots, the smell of sea-wet leather and man-skin. The newcomer cleared his throat as if ill at ease.

"Lady, here is food."

She swirled the riband about her wrist, put out her hands, for suddenly she was hungry and athirst.

"By your leave, lady," he fitted the handle of a mug into her right hand, placed a bowl on the palm of the other. "There is a spoon. It is only ship's ale, lady, and stew."

"My thanks," she said in return. "And what name do you go by, ship's man?"

"Rothar, lady. I am a blank shield and no real seaman. But since I know no trade but war, one venture is nigh as good as another."

"Yet of this venture you have some doubts." She had set the mug on the deck, kept upright between her worn sandals. Now she seized his hand, held it to read. For it seemed to Dairine that she must not let this opportunity of learning more of Vidruth's followers go, and she sensed that this Rothar was not of the same ilk as Wak.

"Lady"—his voice was very low and swift—"they say that you have knowledge of herb craft. Why then has

Vidruth not taken you to the Captain that you may learn what strange, swift illness struck him down?"

There was youth in the hand Dairine held and not, she believed, any desire to deceive.

"Where lies the Captain?" she asked in as low a voice.

"In his cabin. He is fevered and raves. It is as if he has come under some ensorcelment and—"

"Rothar!" From the door, another voice sharp as an order. The hand she held jerked free from hers. But not before she had felt the spring of fear.

"I promised no man shall trouble you. Has this cub been at such tricks?" Vidruth demanded.

"Not so." Dairine was surprised her voice remained so steady. "He has been most kind in bringing me food and drink, both of which I needed."

"And having done so—out!" Vidruth commanded. "Now"—she heard the door close behind the other—"what have you learned, girl, from this piece of silk?"

"I have had but a little time, lord. Give me more. I must study it."

"See that you do" was his order as he also departed.

He did not come again, nor did Rothar ever once more bring her food. She thought, though, of what the young man had said concerning the Captain. Vidruth's tale made her believe that the whole ship's company had been behind the mate's scheme to take command and sail to Usturt. There were herbs which, put in a man's food or drink, could plunge him into the depths of fever. If she could only reach the Captain, she would know. But there was no faring forth from this cubby.

Now and again Vidruth would suddenly appear to demand what more she had learned from the riband. There was such an avid greediness in his questions that sometimes rising uneasiness nearly broke through her control. At last she answered with what she believed to be the truth.

"Have you never heard, Captain, that the Talent

cannot be forced? I have tried to read from this all which I might. But this scrap was not fashioned by a race such as ours. An alien nature cannot be so easily discovered. For all my attempts, I cannot build a mind picture of these people. What I see clearly is only the weaving."

When he made no answer, Dairine continued:

"This is a thing not of the body, but the mind. Along such a road one creeps as a babe, one does not race as one full grown."

"You have less than a day now. Before sundown, Usturt shall rise before us. I know only what I have heard tell of witch powers, and that may well be changed by the telling and retelling. Remember, girl, your life can well ride on your 'seeing'!"

She heard him go. The riband no longer felt so light and soft. Rather, it had taken on the heaviness of a slave chain binding her to his will. She ate ship's biscuits from the plate he had brought her. It was true time was passing, and she had done nothing of importance.

Oh, she could now firmly visualize the loom and see the silk come into being beneath the flying fingers. But the body behind those hands, that she could not see. Nor did any of the personality of the weavers who had made that which she held come clear to her, for all her striving.

Captain Ortis—he came in the reading, for he had held this. And Vidruth also. There was a third who was more distant, lying hid under a black cloud of fear. Was this day or night? She had lost track of time. That the ship still ran before the wind, she sensed.

Then—she was not alone in the cubby! Yet she had not heard the warning creak of the door. Fear kept her tense, hunched upon the stool, listening with all her might.

"Lady?"

Rothar! But how had he come?

"Why are you here?" Dairine had to wet her lips with her tongue before she could shape those words.

"They move now to put you ashore on Usturt, lady!

Captain Ortis, he came up leaning on Vidruth's arm, his body all atremble. He gives no orders, only Vidruth. Lady, there is some great wrong here—for we are at Usturt. And Vidruth commands. Such is not right."

"I knew that I must go to Usturt," she returned. "Rothar, if you have any allegiance to your captain, know he is a prisoner to Vidruth in some manner, even as I have been. And if I do not do as Vidruth says, there will be greater trouble—death—"

"You do not understand." His voice was very husky. "There are monsters on this land. To see them even, they say, makes a man go mad!"

"But I shall not see them," Dairine reminded him. "How long do I have?"

"Some moments yet."

"Where am I and how did you get here?"

"You are in the treasure hold, below the Captain's own cabin. I have used the secret opening to reach you as this is the first time Vidruth and the Captain have been out of it. Now they must watch carefully for the entrance to the inner reef."

"Can you get me into the Captain's cabin?" If, in those moments, she might discover what hold Vidruth had over Captain Ortis, she perhaps would be able to help a man she trusted.

"Give me your hands, then, lady. I fear we have very little time."

She reached out, and her wrists were instantly caught in a hold tight enough to be painful, but she made no sound of complaint. Then she found herself pulled upward with a vast heave as if Rothar must do this all in a single effort. When he set her on her feet once more, she sensed she was in a much larger space. And there was the fresh air from the sea blowing in as if through some open port.

But the air was not enough to hide from her that telltale scent—a scent of evil.

"Let me go, touch me not now," she told Rothar. "I seek that which must be found, and your slightest touch will confuse my course."

Slowly she turned away from the wind, facing to her right.

"What lies before me?"

"The Captain's bed, lady."

Step by step she approached in that direction. The sniff of evil was stronger. What it might be she had no idea, for though Ingvarna had taught her to distinguish that which was of the shadow, she knew little more. The fetid odor of some black sorcery was rank.

"The bed," she ordered now, "do you strip off its coverings. If you find aught which is strange, be sure you do not touch it with your hand. Rather, use something of iron, if you can, to pluck it forth. And then throw it quickly into the sea."

He asked no questions, but she could hear his hurried movements. And then—

"There is a—a root, most misshapen. It lies under the pillow, lady."

"Wait!" Perhaps the whole of that bed place was now impregnated by what evil had been introduced. To destroy its source might not be enough. "Bundle all—pillow, coverings—give them to the sea!" she ordered. "Let me back then into the treasure cubby, and if there be time, make the bed anew. I do not know what manner of ensorcelment has been wrought here. But it is of the Shadow, not of the Power. Take care that you keep yourself also from contact with it."

"That will I do of a certainty, lady!" His answer was fervent. "Stand well back, I will get rid of this."

She retreated, hearing the click of his sea boots on the planking as he passed her toward the source of the sea wind.

"Now"—he was back at her side—"I shall see you safe, lady. Or as safe as you can be until the Captain comes to his mind once more and Vidruth be removed from command."

His hands closed upon her, lowered her back down into the cubby. She listened intently. But if he closed that trap door, and she was sure that he had, it had fallen into place without a sound.

3

SHE had not long to wait, for the opening on the floor level of the cubby was opened and she recognized Vidruth's step.

"Listen well, girl," he commanded. "Usturt is an island, one of a string of islands, reaching from the shore. At one time, they may all have been a part of the coast. But now some are only bare rock with such a wash of sea around them as no man can pass. So think not that you have any way of leaving save by our favor. We shall set you ashore and keep down-sea thereafter. But when you have learned what we wish, then return to the shore and there leave three stones piled one upon another. . . ."

To Dairine, his arrangements seemed to be not well thought out. But she questioned nothing. What small hopes she had she could only pin on Rothar and the Captain. Vidruth's hand tightened about her arm. He drew her to a ladder, set her hands upon its rungs.

"Climb, girl. And you had better play well your part. There are those among us who fear witchcraft and say there is only one certain way to disarm a witch. That, you have heard. . . ."

She shivered. Yes, there was a way to destroy a witch—by enjoying the woman. All men were well versed in that outrage.

"Rothar shall set you ashore," Vidruth continued. "And we shall watch your going. Think not to talk him out of his orders, for there is no place elsewhere. . . ."

Dairine was on the deck now, heard the murmur of voices. Where stood Captain Ortis? Vidruth gave her no time to try to sort out the sounds. Under his compelling, the girl came up against the rail. Then Vidruth caught her up as if she were a small child and lowered her until other hands steadied her, easing her down upon a plank seat.

Around her was the close murmur of the sea, and she could hear the grate of oars within their locks.

"Do you believe me witch, Rothar?" she asked.

"Lady, I do not know what you are. But that you are in danger with Vidruth, that I can swear to. If the Captain comes into his own mind again—"

He broke off and then continued. "Through the war, I have come to hate any act which makes man or woman unwillingly serve another. There is no future before me, for I am wastage of war, having no trade save that of killing. Therefore, I will do what I may to help you and the Captain."

"You are young to speak so, of being without a future."

"I am old in killing," he told her bleakly. "And of such men as Vidruth leads, I have seen amany. Lady, we are near the shore. And those on the ship watch us well. When I set you on the beach, take forth carefully what you find in my belt, hide it from all. It is a knife made of the best star-steel, fashioned by the hand of Hamraker himself. Not mine in truth, but the Captain's."

Dairine did as he ordered when he carried her from the sand-smoothing waves to the drier reach beyond. Memory stirred in her. Once there had been such a knife and—firelight had glinted on it—

"No!" she cried aloud to deny memory. Yet her fingers remained curled about that hilt.

"Yes!" He might not understand her inner turmoil, but his hold on her tightened. "You must keep it.

"Walk straight ahead," he told her. "Those on the ship have the great dart caster trained on you. There are trees ahead—within those, there the spiders are said to be. But, lady, though I dare not move openly in your aid now, for that would bring me quick death to no purpose, yet what I can do, that I shall."

Uncertainty held Dairine. She felt naked in this open which she did not know. Yet she must not appear concerned to those now watching her. She had the riband of silk looped about her wrist. And within the folds of her skirt, she held also the knife. Turning her head slightly from one side to another, she listened with full concentration, walking slowly forward against the drag of the sand.

Coolness ahead—she must be entering the shade of the trees. She put out her hand, felt rough bark, slid around it, setting the trunk as a barrier between that dart thrower of which Rothar had warned, and her back.

Then she knew, as well as if her eyes could tell her, that it was not alone the ship's company who watched. She was moving under observation of someone—or something—else. Dairine used her sense of perception, groping as she did physically with her hands, seeking what that might be.

A moment later she gasped with shock. A strong mental force burst through the mind door she had opened. She felt as if she had been caught in a giant hand, raised to the level of huge eyes which surveyed her outwardly and inwardly.

Dairine swayed, shaken by that nonphysical touch, search. It was nonhuman. Yet she realized, as she fought to recover her calm, it was not inimical—yet.

"Why come you here, female?"

In Dairine's mind, the word shaped clearly. Still, she could build up no mental picture of her questioner. She faced a little to the right, held out the hand about which she had bound the riband.

"I seek those able to weave such beauty," she replied aloud, wondering if they could hear, or understand, her words.

Again that sensation of being examined, weighed. But this time she stood quiet, unshaken under it.

"You think this thing beautiful?" Again the mind question.

"Yes."

"But you have not eyes to see it." Harshly that came, as if to deny her claim.

"I have not eyes, that is the truth. But my fingers have been taught to serve me in their place. I, too, weave, but only after the manner of my own people."

Silence, then a touch on the back of her hand, so light and fleeting Dairine was not even sure she had really felt it. The girl waited, for she understood this was a place with its own manner of barriers, and she might continue only if those here allowed it.

Again a touch on her hand, but this time it lingered. Dairine made no attempt to grasp, though she tried to read through that contact. And saw only bright whirls.

"Female, you may play with threads after the crude fashion of your kind. But call yourself not a weaver!" There was arrogance in that.

"Can one such as I learn the craft as your people know it?"

"With hands as clumsy as this?" There came a hard rap across her knuckles. "Not possible. Still, you may come, see with your fingers what you cannot hope to equal."

The touch slid across her hand, became a sinewy band about her wrist as tight as the cuff of a slave chain. Dairine knew now there was no escape. She was being drawn forward. Oddly, though she could not read the nature of the creature who guided her, there flowed from its contact a sharp mental picture of the way ahead.

This was a twisted path. Sometimes she brushed against the trunks of trees; again she sensed they crossed clear areas—until she was no longer sure in what direction the beach now lay.

At last they came into an open space where there was

some protection other than branches and leaves overhead to ward off the sun. Her ears picked up small, scuttling sounds.

"Put out your hand!" commanded her guide. "Describe what you find before you."

Dairine obeyed, moving slowly and with caution. Her fingers found a solid substance, not unlike the barked tree trunk. Only, looped about it, warp lines of thread were stretched taut. She transferred her touch to those lines, tracing them to another bar. Then she knelt, fingering the length of cloth. This was smooth as the riband. A single thread led away—that must be fastened to the shuttle of the weaver.

"So beautiful!"

For the first time since Ingvarna had trained her, Dairine longed for actual sight. The need to *see* burned in her. Color—somehow as she touched the woven strip, the fact of color came to her. Yet all she could "read" of the weaver was a blur of narrow, nonhuman hands.

"Can you do such, you who claim to be a weaver?"

"Not this fine." Dairine answered with the truth. "This is beyond anything I have ever touched."

"Hold out your hands!" This time Dairine sensed that the order had not come from her guide, but another.

The girl spread out her fingers, palms up. There followed a feather-light tracing on her skin along each finger, gliding across her palm.

"It is true. You are a weaver—after a fashion. Why do you come to us, female?"

"Because I would learn." Dairine drew a deep breath. What did Vidruth's idea of trade matter now? This was of greater importance. "I would learn from those who can do this."

She continued to kneel, waiting. There was communication going on about her, but none she could catch and hold with either eye or mind. If these weavers would shelter her, what need had she to return to Vidruth? Rothar's plans? Those were too uncertain. If she won the good will of these, she had shelter against the evil of her own kind.

"Your hands are clumsy, you have no eyes." That was like a whiplash. "Let us see what you *can* do, female."

A shuttle was thrust into her hand. She examined it carefully by touch. Its shape was slightly different from those she had always known, but she could use it. Then she surveyed, the same way, the web on the loom. The threads of both warp and woof were very fine, but she concentrated until she could indeed "see" what hung there. Slowly she began to weave, but it took a long time and what she produced in her half inch of fabric was noticeably unlike that of the beginning.

Her hands shaking, the girl sat back on her heels, frustrated. All her pride in her past work was wiped out. Before these, she was a child beginning a first ragged attempt to create cloth.

Yet when she had relaxed from concentrating on her task and was aware once more of those about her, she did not meet the contempt she had expected. Rather, a sensation of surprise.

"You are one perhaps who can be taught, female," came that mind voice of authority. "If you wish."

Dairine turned her face eagerly in the direction from which she believed that message had come. "I do wish, Great One!"

"So be it. But you will begin even as our hatchlings, for you are not yet a weaver."

"That I agree." The girl ran her fingers ruefully across the fabric before her.

If Vidruth expected her return into his power now—she shrugged. And let Rothar concentrate upon the Captain and his own plight. What seemed of greatest importance to her was that she must be able to satisfy these weavers.

They seemed to have no real dwelling except this area

about their looms. Nor were there any furnishings save the looms themselves. And those stood in no regular pattern. Dairine moved cautiously about, memorizing her surroundings by touch.

Though she sensed a number of beings around her, none touched her, mind or body. And she made no advances in turn, somehow knowing such would be useless.

Food they did bring her, fresh fruit. And there were some finger-lengths of what she deemed dried meat. Perhaps it was better she did not know the origin of that.

She slept when she tired on a pile of woven stuff, not quite as silky as that on the looms, yet so tightly fashioned she thought it might pass the legendary test of carrying water within its folds. Her sleep was dreamless. And when she awoke, she found it harder to remember the men or the ship, even Rothar or the Captain. Rather, they were like some persons she had known once in distant childhood, for the place of the weavers was more and more hers. And she *must* learn. To do that was a fever burning in her.

There was a scuttling sound and then a single order: "Eat!"

Dairine groped before her, found more of the fruit. Even before she was quite finished, there came a twitch on her skirt.

"This ugly thing covering your body, you cannot wear it for thread gathering."

Thread gathering? She did not know the meaning of that. But it was true that her skirt, if she moved out of the open space about the looms, caught on branches. She arose and unfastened her girdle, the lacings of her bodice, allowed the dress to slip away into a puddle about her feet. Wearing only her brief chemise, Dairine felt oddly free. But she sought out her girdle again, wrapped it around her slim waist, putting there within the knife.

There came one of those light touches, and she faced about.

"Thread hangs between the trees"—her guide gave a

small tug—"touch it with care. Shaken, it will become a trap. Prove that you have the lightness of fingers to be able to learn from us."

No more instructions came. Dairine realized they must be again testing her. She must prove she was able to gather this thread. Gather it how? Just as she questioned that, something was pushed into her hand. She discovered she held a smooth rod, the length of her lower arm. This must be a winder for the thread.

Now there was a grasp again on her wrist, drawing her away from the looms, on under the trees. Even as her left hand brushed a tree trunk came the order:

"Thread!"

There would be no profit in blind rushing. She must concentrate all her well-trained perceptive sense to aid her to find thread here.

Into her mind slid a very dim picture. Perhaps that came from the very far past which she never tried to remember. A green field lay open under the morning sun and on it were webs pearled with dew. Was what she sought allied to the material of such webs?

Who could possibly harvest the fine threads of such webs? A dark depression weighed upon Dairine. She wanted to hurl the collecting rod from her, to cry aloud that no one could do such a thing.

Then she had a vision of Ingvarna standing there. That lack of self-pity, that belief in herself which the Wise Woman had fostered, revived. To say that one could not do a thing before one ever tried was folly.

In the past her sense of perception had only located for her things more solid than a tree-hung thread. But now it must serve her better.

Under her bare feet, for she had left her sandals with her dress, lay a soft mass of long-fallen leaves. Around here there appeared to be no ground growth—only the trees.

Dairine paused, advancing her hand until her finger-tips rested on bark. With caution, she slid that touch up and around the trunk. A faint impression was growing in her. Here was what she sought.

Then—she found the end of a thread. The rest of it was stretched out and away from the tree. With infinite care, Dairine broke the thread, putting the freed end to the rod. To her vast relief, it adhered there as truly as it had to the tree trunk. Now. . . . She did not try to touch the thread, but she wound slowly, with great care, moving to keep the strand taut before her, evenly spread on the rod.

Round and round—then her hand scraped another tree trunk. Dairine gave a sigh of relief, hardly daring to believe she had been successful in harvesting her first thread. But one was little enough, and she must not grow overconfident. Think only of the thread! She found another end and, with the same slow care, began once more to wind.

To those without sight, day is as night, night is as day. Dairine no longer lived within the time measure of her own kind. She went forth between intervals of sleep and food to search for the tree-looped thread, wondering if she so collected something manufactured by the weavers themselves or a product of some other species.

Twice she made the error she had been warned against, had moved too hastily, with overconfidence, shaken the thread. Thus she found herself entrapped in a sticky liquid which flowed along the line, remaining fast caught until freed by a weaver.

Though she was never scolded, each time her rescuer projected an aura of such disdain for this clumsiness that Dairine cringed inwardly.

The girl had early learned that the weavers were all female. What they did with the cloth they loomed, she had not yet discovered. They certainly did not use it all, neither had she any hint that they traded it elsewhere. Perhaps the very fact of creation satisfied some need rampant in them.

Those who, like her, hunted threads were the youngest of this nonhuman community. Yet she was able to establish no closer communication with them than she did with the senior weavers.

Once or twice there was an uneasy hint of entrapment about her life in the loom place. Why did everything which had happened before she arrived now seem so distant and of such negligible account?

If the weavers did not speak to her save through mind speech—and that rarely—they were not devoid of voices, for those at the looms hummed. Though the weird melody they so evoked bore little resemblance to human song, it became a part of one. Even Dairine's hand moved to its measure and by it her thoughts were lulled. In all the world, there were only the looms, the thread to be sought for them—only this was of any importance.

There came a day when they gave her an empty loom and left her to thread it. Even in the days of her life in the village, this had been a matter which required her greatest dexterity and concentration. Now, as she worked with unfamiliar bars, it was even worse. She threaded until her fingertips were sore, her head aching from such single-minded using of perception, while all about her the humming of the weavers urged her on and on.

When fatigue closed in upon her, she slept. And she paused to eat only because she knew that her body must have fuel. At last she knew that she had finished, for good or ill.

Now her fingers, as she rubbed her aching head, were stiff. It was difficult to flex them. Still, the hum set her body swaying in answer to its odd rhythm.

To Dairine's surprise, no weaver came to inspect her work, to say whether it was adequately or poorly done. When she had rested so that she could once more control her fingers, she began to weave. As she did so, she discovered that she too hummed, echoing the soft sound about her.

As she worked, there was a renewal of energy within her. Maybe her hands did not move as swiftly as the blur of elongated fingers she had seen in her mind, but they followed the rhythm of the hum and they seemed sure and knowing, not as if her own will but some other force controlled them. She was weaving—well or ill she did not know or care. It was enough that she kept to the beat of the quiet song.

Only when she reached the end of her thread supply, and sat with an empty shuttle in her hand, did Dairine rouse, as one from a dream. Her whole body ached, her hand fell limply on her knee. In her was the sharpness of hunger. There was no longer to be heard the hum of the others.

The girl arose stiffly, stumbled to her sleeping place. There was food which she mouthed before she lay down on the cloth, her face turned up to whatever roof was between her and the sky, feeling drained, exhausted—all energy gone from her body, as was logical thought from her mind.

4

DAIRINE awoke into fear, her hands were clenched, long shivers shook her body. The dream which had driven her into consciousness abruptly faded, leaving only a sense of terror behind. However, it had broken the spell of the weavers, her memory was once more sharp and clear.

How long had she been here? What had happened when she had not returned to the shore? Had the ship under Vidruth's control left, thinking her lost? And Rothar? the Captain?

Slowly she turned her head from side to side, aware of something else. Though she could not see them, she knew that the looms ringing her in were vacant, the weavers were gone!

Now Dairine believed she must have been caught in some invisible web, and had only this moment broken free.

Why had she chosen to come here? Why had she remained? The riband of stuff was gone from her wrist—had that set some ensorcelment upon her?

Fool! She could not see as the rest of the world saw. Now it appeared that even her carefully fostered sense of perception had, in some manner, deceived her. As Dairine arose, her hand brushed the loom where she had labored for so long. Curiosity made her stoop to finger the width her efforts had created. Not quite as smooth as the riband, but far, far better than her first attempt.

Only—where were the weavers? The shadow of terror lingering from her dream sent her moving purposefully about the clearing. Each loom was empty, the woven cloth gone. She kicked against something—groped to find it. A collecting rod for thread.

"Where—where are you?" she dared to call aloud. The quiet seemed so menacing she longed to set her back to some tree, to raise a defense. Against whom—or what?

Dairine did not believe that Vidruth and his men would dare to penetrate the wood. But did the weavers have other enemies, and had fled those, not taking the trouble to warn her?

Breathing faster, she set hand on the hilt of the knife at her girdle. Where *were* they? Her call had echoed so oddly that she dared not try again. Only her fear grew as she tried to listen.

There was the rustle of tree leaves. Nothing else. Nor could she pick up by mind touch any suggestion of another life form nearby. Should she believe that the cloth missing from each loom meant her co-workers had left for an ordered purpose, not in flight? Would she be able to track them?

Never before had she put to such a use that sense Ingvarna had trained in her. Also, that the weavers had their own guards, Dairine was well aware. She was not sure that she herself mattered enough in their eyes for them to set any defense against her seeking their company. Suppose, with a collecting rod in her hand, she was to leave the loom place as if on the regular mission of hunting thread?

First she must have food. That she located, by scent, in two bins. The fruit was too soft, overripe, and there was none of the dried sticks left. But she ate all she could.

Then, rod conspicuously in hand, the girl ventured into the woods. All the nearby threads must have been harvested, her questing fingers could find none as she played out her game for any who might watch.

And there *were* watchers! Not the weavers, for the impression these gave her was totally different—more feeble sparks as compared to a well-set fire. As she moved, so did they, hovering near, yet making no attempt to come in contact with her.

She discovered a thread on a tree. Skillfully, she wound it on her rod, took so a second and third. However, at the next, she flinched away. Any thread anchored here must have been disturbed, for she smelled the acrid odor of the sticky coating.

The next two trees supported similarly gummed threads. Did that mean these had been prepared to keep her prisoner? Dairine turned a little. Already, she was out of familiar territory. Thus she expected to meet at any moment opposition, either from the threads or those watchers.

Next was a tree free of thread. Trusting to her sense of smell, she sought another opening, hoping that the unthreaded trees would mark a trail. Though she moved a little faster, she kept to her pretense of seeking threads from each tree she encountered. The watchers had not left her, though she picked up no betraying sound, only knew they were there.

Another free tree—this path was a zigzag puzzle. And she had to go so slowly. One more free tree, and then, from her left, a sound at last—a faint moaning.

It was human, that sound, enough to feed her fear. This—somehow this all seemed a shadow out of her now-forgotten dream. In her dream she had known the sufferer—

Dairine halted. The watchers were drawing in. She could tell they had amassed between her and the direction from which the moan came. Thus she had a choice—to ignore the sound or to try to circle around.

No sign, make no sign that she heard. Keep on hunting for threads—strive to deceive the watchers. All her nature rebelled against abandoning one who might be in trouble, even if he were one of Vidruth's men.

She put out her hand as if searching for thread, more than half expecting to touch a sticky web. From those watchers she believed she picked up an answering sensation of uncertainty. This might be her only chance.

Her fingers closed about a thick band of woven stuff. That led in turn downward to a bag, the flap of the top turned over and stuck to the fabric so tightly she could not open it. The bag was very large, pulling down the branch from which it was suspended. And within it—something had been imprisoned!

Dairine jerked back. She did not know if she had cried out. What was sealed within that bag, her perception told her, had been alive, was now only newly dead. She forced herself to run fingers once more along the surface of the dangling thing. Too small—surely too small to be a man!

Now that the girl knew no human was so encased, she wanted no greater knowledge of the contents. As she stepped away, her shoulder grazed a second bag. She realized that she moved among a collection of them, and all they held was death.

Only, she could still hear that moaning. And it was human. Also, at last the watchers had dropped behind. As if this place were one they dared not enter.

Those bags—Dairine hated to brush against them. Some seemed far lighter than others and twirled about dizzily as she inadvertently touched them. Others dipped heavily with their burdens.

The moans—

The girl made herself seek what hung before her now. Her collecting rod was in her girdle. In its place, she held the knife. When she touched this last bag, feeble movement answered. There was a muffled cry which Dairine was sure was one for help.

She ripped at the silk with knife point. The tightly woven fabric gave reluctantly, this was no easily torn material. She hacked and pulled until she heard a half-stifled cry!

"For Sul's sake—"

Dairine dragged away the slashed silk. There was indeed a man ensnared. However, about him now was sticky web, for its acrid scent was heavy on the air. Against that, her knife was of no avail. To touch such would only make her prisoner, too.

She gathered up the folds of the torn bag and, using pieces to shield her fingers, tore and worried at the web. To her relief, she was succeeding. She could feel that his own struggles to throw off his bonds were more successful.

Also, she knew whom she fought to free—Rothar! It was as if he had been a part of that dream she could not remember.

Dairine spoke his name, asking him if he were near free.

"Yes. Though I still hang. But that now is a small matter—"

Dairine heard a threshing movement, then the sound of his weight touching the ground. His breath hissed heavily in and out.

"Lady, in nowise could you have come at a better time." His hand closed about her arm. She felt him sway and then recover balance.

"You are hurt?"

"Not so. Hungry and needful of a drink. I do not know

how long I have hung in that larder. The Captain—he will think us both dead."

"Larder!" That one grim word struck her like a blow.

"Did you not know? Yes, this is the spider females' larder, where they preserve their males—"

Dairine fought rising nausea. Those bags of silk, the beautifully woven silk! And to be used so.

"There is someone—something—out there," he said.

The watchers, her protective sense, alerted her. They were now moving in again.

"Can you see them?" Dairine asked.

"Not clearly." Then he changed that to "Yes!"

"They have throwing cords of web, such as they used on me before. No blade can cut those—"

"The bag!"

"What do you mean?"

Covered with the bag's rent material, she had been able to pull loose his bindings. Those sticky cords could not find purchase against the woven silk. As she explained that, her knife was wrenched from her hold and she heard sounds of ripping.

The watchers—as Rothar worked to empty other bags, Dairine strove to perceive them by mind. They had neared, but once more had halted, as if this were a place which they feared to enter even if ordered to do so to hold the humans captive.

"They spin their lines now," Rothar told her. "They plan to wall us in."

"Let them believe us helpless," she commanded.

"But you think we are not?"

"With the bags, perhaps not."

If she could only *see!* Dairine could have cried aloud in her frustration. Who were the watchers? She was sure they were not the weavers themselves. Perhaps these were the ones who supplied the thread she had harvested so carefully in the past.

Rothar once more was back at her side, a bundle of silk

from plundered bags. The girl dared not let herself remember *what* had been in those bags.

"Tell me," she said, "what is the nature of those spinning out there?"

She could sense his deep aversion, revulsion. "Spiders. Giant spiders. They are furred and the size of hounds."

"What are they doing?"

"They are enwebbing an opening. Beyond that on either side are already nets. Now they are disappearing. Only one is left, hanging in the center of the fresh web."

Through her grasp on his wrist, Dairine could read his thoughts, his mind picture, even more clearly, to add to the scene his words had built for her.

"Those others may have gone to summon the weavers"—she made an alarming guess. "So for the present, we have only that one guard to deal with."

"And the web—"

She loosed her hold upon him, clutched a length of the raggedly cut silk. "This we must bind about our bodies. Do not touch the web save with this between your flesh and it."

"I understand."

Dairine moved forward. "I must loose the web," she told him. "The guard will be your matter. Lead me to a tree where the web is anchored."

His hand was on her shoulders. Under his gentle urging, she was guided to the left, was moved forward step by cautious step.

"The tree is directly before you now, lady. Have no fear of the guard." His promise was grim.

"Remember, let nothing of the web touch your flesh."

"Be sure I am well shielded," he assured her.

She fingered rough bark, around her hand and arm the silk was well and tightly anchored. There—she had discovered the end of an anchoring thread. But this was far stronger and thicker than any she had harvested before.

"Ha!" Rothar gave a cry—was no longer beside her.

Dairine found a second thread, felt vibrations along it.

The guard must be making ready to defend its web. However, she must concentrate on the finding of each thread, of breaking such loose from the tree.

There was no way for her to know how many threads she must snap so. From her right came the sound of scuffling, heavy breathing.

"Ah!" Rothar's voice fiercely triumphant. "The thing is safely dead, lady. You are right, the cords it threw at me were well warded by the cloth."

"Keep watch. Those which were with it may still return," she warned.

"That I know!" he agreed.

The girl moved as swiftly as she could, discovering thread ends, snapping them. Not only might the spiders return, but the weavers. And them she feared even more.

"The web is down," he told her.

However, she felt little relief at what might be a small victory.

"Lady, now it would be well to wrap our feet and legs with this silk, they could well lay ground webs for our undoing."

"Yes!" She had not thought of that, only of the threading cords from tree to tree.

"Let me get more silk."

Dairine stood waiting, her whole body tense as she strained to use ears and inner senses to assess what might lie in wait beyond. Then he was back and, with no by-your-leave, busied himself wrapping her feet and legs with lengths of silk, tying the strips tightly in places.

While she, who had once so loved the riband Captain Ortis had shown her, wanted to shrink from any touch of that stuff. Save now it might be their salvation.

"That is the best I can do." He released her foot after tying a last knot about her ankle. "Do you hear aught, lady?"

"Not yet. But they will come."

"Who—what are the weavers?" he asked.

"I know not. But they do not hold our kind high in esteem."

He laughed shortly. "How well do I know that! Yet they did you no harm."

"Because, I think, I am without sight, and also a female who knows a little of their own trade. They are proud of their skill and wished to impress me."

"Shall we go then?"

"We must watch for trees bare of threads."

"Those I can see, lady. Perhaps trusting in my kind of sight, we can go the quicker. There has been much happened. The Captain, though he is still weak, again commands his ship. Vidruth is—dead. But the Captain could not get that scum which his mate has signed to come ashore. And only he can hold them in control."

"Thus you alone are here?"

He did not answer her directly. "Set your hand to my belt. And I shall take heed in my going, I promise," was all he said.

Such a journey was humiliating for Dairine. So long had it been since she must turn to one of her kind as a guide. But she knew that he was right.

So Captain Ortis, released from the evil spell, had taken command. She wondered briefly how Vidruth had died, there had been a queer little hesitancy in Rothar's telling of that. For now she must put her mind on what lay immediately before them. That the weavers would allow them to escape easily she did not believe.

A moment later she knew she was right. They were once more under observation, she sensed. This new, stronger contact was not that of the watchers.

"They come!" she warned.

"We must reach the shore! It is among the trees that they set their traps. And I have a signal fire built there, ready to be lighted, which will bring in the *Sea Raven.*"

"Can you see any such traps?"

She could feel his impatience and doubt in the slight contact of her fingers against his body where they were hooked about his belt.

"No. But there are no straight trails among the trees. Webs hang here and there; one can only dodge back and forth between those."

Dairine was given no warning, had no time to loose her hold. Rothar suddenly fell forward and down, bearing her with him. Her side scraped painfully against a broken end of branch. It was as if the very earth under them had opened.

5

THE smell of freshly turned soil was thick in her nostrils. She lay against Rothar and he was moving. In spite of her bruises, the jarring shock of that fall, Dairine sat up. Where they had landed she did not know, but she guessed they were now under the surface of the ground.

"Are you hurt?" asked her companion.

"No. And you?"

"My arm caught under me when I landed. I hope it is only a bad bruising and no break. We are in one of their traps. They had it coated over." There was a note of self-disgust bleak in his voice.

Dairine was glad he had told her the bald truth. Rising to her feet, the girl put out her hands to explore the pit. Freshly dug, the earth of its sides was moist and sticky. Here and there a bit of root projected. Could they use such to pull themselves out? Before she could ask that of Rothar, words shot harshly into her mind.

"Female, why have you stolen this meat from us?"

Dairine turned her head toward the opening which must be above. So close that voice, she could believe that a head bobbed there, eyes watched them gloatingly.

"I know not your meaning," she returned with all the spirit she could summon. "*This* is a man of my people, one who came seeking me because he felt concern."

"That with you is our meat!"

Cold menace in that message brought not fear, but a growing anger to Dairine. She would not accept that any man was—*meat.* These weavers—she had considered them creatures greater than herself because of the beauty they created, because of their skill. She had accepted their arrogance because she also accepted that she was inferior in that skill.

Yet to what purpose did they put their fine creations? Degrading and loathsome usage by her own belief. With a flash of true understanding, she was now certain that she had not been free here, never so until she had awakened in the deserted loom place. They had woven about her thoughts a web of ensorcelment which had bound her to them and their ways, just as at this moment they had entrapped her body.

"No man is your meat," she returned.

What answered her then was no mind words, rather a blast of uncontrolled fury. She swayed under that mental blow, but she did not fall. Rothar called out her name, his arm was about her, holding her steady.

"Do not fear for me," she said and tried to loosen his grip. This was her battle. Her foot slipped in the soft earth of the pit and she stumbled. She flung out her arms to keep herself off the wall. There was a sharp pain just above her eyes, and then only blackness in which she was totally lost.

Heat—heat of blazing fire. And through it screaming —terrible screaming—which tortured her ears. There was no safety left in the world. She had curled herself into a small space of blessed dark, hiding. But she could still see—see with her *eyes!* No, she would not look, she dared not look—at the swords in the firelight—at the thing streaming with blood which hung whimpering from two knives driven like hooks into the wall to hold it upright. She willed herself fiercely *not* to see.

"Dairine! Lady!"

"No—" She screamed her denial. "I will not look!"

"Lady!"

"I will not—"

There were flashes of color about her. No mind pictures these—the fire, the blood, the swords—

"Dairine!"

A face, wavery, as if she saw it mirrored in troubled water, a man's face. His sword—he would lift the sword and then—

"No!" she screamed again.

A sharp blow rocked her head from side to side. Oddly enough, that steadied her sight. A man's face near hers, yes, but no fire, no sword dripping blood, no wall against which a thing hung whimpering.

He held her gently, his eyes searching hers.

They—they were not—not in the Keep of Trin. Dairine shuddered; memory clung about her as a foul cloak. Trin was long, long ago. There had been the sea, and then Ingvarna and Rannock. And now—now they were on Usturt. She was not sure what had happened.

But she *saw.*

Had Ingvarna believed that some day this sight would return to her? Not sight totally destroyed, but sight denied by a child who had been forced to look upon such horrors that she would not let herself face the true world openly again.

Her sight had returned. But that was not what the weavers had intended. No, their burst of mind fury had been sent to cut her down. Not death had they given her, but new life.

Then *she,* who had sent that thrust of mind power, looked over and down upon the prey.

Dairine battled her fear. No retreat this time. She must make herself face this new horror. Ingvarna's teachings went deep, had strengthened her for this very moment of her life, as if the Wise Woman had been enabled to trace the years ahead and know what would aid her fosterling.

The girl did not raise her hand but she struck back, her new-found sight centering upon that horror of a countenance. Human it was in dreadful part, arachnoid in another, such as to send one witless with terror. And the thought strength of the weaver was gathering to blast Dairine.

Those large, many-faceted eyes blinked. Dairine's did not.

"Be ready," the girl said to Rothar, "they are preparing to take us."

Down into the pit whirled sticky web lines hurled by the weaver's spider servants. Those caught and clung to root ends and then fell upon the two.

"Let them think for this moment," Dairine said, "that we are helpless."

He did not question her as more and more of the lines dropped upon them, lying over their arms, legs. Dull gray was the cloth which they had wound about them. That had none of the shimmering quality her mind had given to it. Perhaps the evil use to which this had been put had killed that opalescence.

While the cords fell, the girl did not shift her gaze, but met straightly the huge, alien eyes, those cold and deadly eyes, of the weaver. In and in, Dairine aimed her power, that power Ingvarna had fostered in her, boring deep to reach the brain behind the eyes. Untrained in most of the Wise Woman's skills, she intuitively knew that this was her only form of attack, an attack which must also serve as defense.

Were those giant eyes dulling a little? The girl could not be sure, she could not depend upon her newly restored sight.

About them, the web lengths had ceased to fall. But there was new movement around the lip of the pit above.

Now! Gathering all her strength, pulling on every reserve she believed she might have, Dairine launched a direct thought blow at the weaver. That weird figure writhed, uttered a cry which held no note of human in it. For a moment, it hunched so. Then that misshapen, nightmare body fell back, out of Dairine's range of sight. She was aware of no more mental pressure. No, instead came a weak panic, a fear which wiped away all the weaver's strength.

"They—they are going!" Rothar cried out.

"For a while perhaps." Dairine still held the creatures of the loom in wary respect. They had not thought her a worthy foe, so perhaps they had not unleashed against her all that they might. But while the weavers were still bewildered, shaken, at least she and Rothar had gained time.

The young man beside her was already shaking off the cords. Those curled limply away from his fabric-covered body, just as they fell from hers as he jerked at them. She blinked. Now that the necessity for focusing her eyes on the weaver was past, Dairine found it hard to see. It was a distinct effort for her to fasten on any one object, bring that into clear shape. This was something she must learn, even as she had learned to make her fingers see for her.

Though he winced as he tried to use his left arm, Rothar won out of the pit by drawing on the root ends embedded in the soil. Then he unbuckled his belt and lowered it for her aid.

Out of the earth prison, Dairine stood still for a long moment, turning her head right and left. She could not see them in the dusky shadows among the trees, yet they were there, weavers, spinners, both. But she sensed also that they were still shaken, as if all their strength of purpose had lain only in the will of the one she had temporarily bested.

All were that weaver's own brood—the arachnoid-human, the arachnoid complete. They were subject to the Great One's will, her thoughts controlled them, and they were her tools, the projections of herself. Until the Great Weaver regained her own balance, these would be no menace. But how long could such a respite last for those she would make her prey?

Dairine saw mistily a brighter patch ahead, sunlight fighting the dusk of this now-sinister wood.

"Come!" Rothar reached for her hand, clasped it tight. "The shore must lie there!"

The girl allowed him to draw her forward, away from the leaderless ones.

"The signal fire," he was saying. "But let me give light to that and the Captain will bring in the ship."

"Why did you come—alone from that ship?" Dairine asked suddenly, as they broke out of the shade of the forest into a hard brilliance of the sun upon the sand. So hurting was that light that she needs must shelter her eyes with her hand.

Peering between her fingers, Dairine saw him shrug. "What does it matter how a man who is already dead dies? There was a chance to reach you. The Captain could not take it, for that rogue's spell left him too weak, though he raged against it. None other could he trust—"

"Except you. You speak of yourself as a man already dead, yet you are not. I was blind—now I see. I think Usturt has given us both that which we dare not throw lightly away."

His somber face, in which his eyes were far too old and shadowed, became a little lighter as he smiled.

"Lady, well do they speak of your powers. You are of the breed who may make a man believe in anything, even perhaps himself. And there lies our signal waiting."

He gestured to a tall heap of driftwood. In spite of the slippage of the sand under his enwrapped feet, he left her side and ran toward it.

Dairine followed at a slower pace. There was the Captain and there was this Rothar who risked his life, even though he professed to find that of little matter. Perhaps now there would be others to touch upon her life, mayhap even her heart in years to come. She had these years to weave, and she must do so with care, matching each strand to another in brightness, as all had heretofore been wrought in darkness. The past was behind her. There was no need to glance back over her shoulder unto the dusk of the woods. Rather must she search out seaward whence would come the next strand to add to her pattern of weaving.

Sword of Unbelief

1
Fury Driven

MY eyes ached as I forced them to study the hard ground. From them a dull pain spread into the bony sockets that were their frames. The tough, mountain-bred mount I had saved from our desperate encounter with the wolf-ravagers stumbled. I caught at the saddle horn as vertigo struck with the sharp thrust of an unparried sword.

I could taste death, death and old blood, as I ran my tongue over lips where the salt of my own sweat plastered the dull gray dust of this land to my unwashed skin. Again I wavered. But this time my pony's stumble was greater. Strong as he was, and war-trained, he had come near to the end of endurance.

Before me the Waste was a long tongue of gray rock, giving rootage only to sparse and twisted brush, so mis-shapen in its growing that it might well have been attacked by some creeping evil. For there *was* evil in this country, every sense of mine warned that, as I urged Fallon on at a slow walk.

That wind which whipped at my cloak was bitter, carrying the breath of the Ice Dragon. It raised fine grains of gray sand to scour my face beneath the half shading of my helm. I must find some shelter, and soon, or the fury of a Dune-Moving Storm would catch me and provide a grave place which might exist for a day, a week, or centuries—depending upon the caprice of that same wind and sand.

An outcrop of angular rock stood to my left. Towards that I sent Fallon, his head hanging low as he went. In the lee of that tall fang I slipped from the saddle, keeping my feet only by a quick grasp of the rock itself. The ache in my head struck downwards through my shoulders and back.

I loosed my cloak a little and, crouching by the pony, flung it over both his head and mine. Little enough shelter against the drive of the punishing grains, but it was the best I had. However another fear gnawed at me. This flurry would wipe out the trail I had followed these two days past. With that gone, I must depend upon myself, and in myself I had lesser confidence.

Had I been fully trained as those of my Talent and blood had always been—then I could have accomplished what must be done with far less effort. But, though my mother was a Witch of Estcarp, and I was learned in the powers of a Wise Woman (and had indeed done battle using those powers in the past), yet at this moment I knew fear as an ever-present pain within me, stronger than any ache of body or fatigue of mind.

As I crouched beside Fallon, this dread arose like a flood of bile into my throat, the which I would have vomited forth had I could. Yet, it was too great a part of me to allow itself to be so sundered. Feverishly I drew upon those lesser arts I had learned, striving so to still the fast beating of my heart, the clouding of my thoughts by panic. I must think rather of him whom I sought, and of those who had taken him, for what purpose I could not imagine. For it is the way of the wolfheads to kill; torment, yes, if they were undisturbed, but kill at the end of their play. Yet they had drawn back into this forbidden and forbidding land taking with them a prisoner, one worth no ransom. And the reason for that taking I could not guess.

I set a bridle of calmness upon my thoughts. Only so might I use that other Talent which was mine from birth. So now I set my mind picture upon him whom I sought—Jervon, fighting man, and more, far more to me.

I could see him, yes, even as I had sighted him last by the fire of our small camp, his hands stretched out to warm themselves at the flames. If only I had not—! No, regret was only weakening. I must not think of what I had not done, but what I must now be prepared to do.

There had been blood on the snow-shifted ground when I had returned, the fire stamped into cold charred brands. Two outlaws' bodies hideously ripped—but Jervon . . . no. So they had taken him for some purpose I could not understand.

The dead wolfheads I left to the woods beasts. Fallon I had discovered, shivering and wet with sweat, within the brush and brought him to me by the summoning power. I had waited no longer, knowing that my desire to look upon the shrine of the Old Ones, which I had turned aside to do, might well mean Jervon's death, and no pleasant death either.

Now, crouching here, I cupped one hand across my closed eyes.

"Jervon!" My mind call went out even as I had brought Fallon to me. But I failed. There arose a cloud between me and the man I would find. Yet I was as certain that behind that shadow he still lived. For when one's life is entwined with another's and death comes, the knowledge of that passing through the Last Gate is also clear—to one trained in even the simplest of the Great Mysteries.

This Waste was a grim and much-hated place. Many were the remains of the Old Ones here, and men of true human blood did not enter it willingly. I am not of High Hallack, though I was born in the Dales. My parents came from storied Estcarp overseas, a land where much of the Old Knowledge has been preserved. And my mother was one of those who used that knowledge—even though she had wed, and so, by their laws, put herself apart.

What I knew I had of Aufrica out of Wark, a mistress of minor magic and a Wise Woman. Herbs I knew, both harmful and healing, and I could call upon certain lesser powers—even upon a great one, as once I had done to save him who was born at the same birth with me. But there were powers beyond powers here that I knew not. Only I must take this way and do what I could for Jervon who was more to me than Elyn, my brother, had ever been, and who had once, without any of the Talent to aid him, come with me into battle with a very ancient and strong evil, which battle we had mercifully won.

"Jervon!" I called his name aloud, but my voice was only a faint whisper. For the wind shrieked like a legion of disembodied demons around me. Fallon near jerked his head from my hold on his bridle, and I speedily set myself to calming him, setting over his beast mind a safeguard against panic.

It seemed to last for hours, that perilous sheltering by the fang rock. Then the wind died and we pulled out of sand drifted near to my knees. I took one of my precious flasks of water and wet the corner of my cloak, using that to wash out Fallon's nostrils, the sand away from his eyes. He nudged at my shoulder, stretching his head towards the water bottle in a voiceless plea for a drink. But that I did not dare give him until I knew what manner of country we would cross and whether there would be any streams or tarns along the way.

Night was very near. But that strangeness of the Waste banished some of the dark. For here and there were scattered rock spires which gave off a flickering radiance, enough to travel by.

I did not mount as yet, knowing that Fallon must have a rest from carrying a rider. Though I am slender of body, I am no light weight with mail about me, a sword and helm. So I plowed through the sand, leading Fallon. And heard him snort and blow his dislike of what I would have him do—venture farther into this desolation.

Again, I sent forth a searching thought. I could not reach Jervon. No—that muddling cloud still hung between us. But I could tell in what direction they had gone. Though the constant concentration to hold that thread made my head throb with renewed pain.

Also there were strange shadows in this place. It would seem that nothing threw across the land a clear dark definition of itself, as was normal. Rather those shadows took on shapes which made the imagination quicken with vague hints of things invisible which still could be seen in this way, monstrous forms and unnatural blendings. And, if one allowed fear the upper hand, those appeared ripely ready to detach themselves and move unfettered by any trick of light or dark.

I wondered at those I followed. War had been the harsh life of this land now for so many years it was hard to remember what peace had been like. High Hallack had been overrun by invaders whose superior arms and organization had devastated more than half the Dales before men were able to erect their defense. There had been no central over-lord among us; it was not the custom of the men of High Hallack to give deference beyond the lord in whose holding they had been born and bred. So, until the Four of the North had sunk their differences and made a pact, there had been no rallying point. Men had fought separately for their own lands, and died, to lie in the earth there.

Then had come the final effort. Not only did the Dale lords unite for the first time in history to make a common cause, but they had also treated with others—out of this same Waste—the Wereriders of legend. And together what was left of High Hallack arose with all the might it could summon to smash the Hounds of Alizon, driving them back to the sea, mainly to their own deaths therein. But a land so rent produces in turn those with a natural bent towards evil, scavengers and outlaws, ready to plunder both sides if the chance offered. Now such were the bane of our exhausted and warworn country.

These were such that I followed. And it could well be that, since they were hardy enough to lair within the Waste, they might not be wholly human either. Rather be possessed by some emanation of the Dark which had long lurked here.

For the Old Ones, when they withdrew from the Daleland, had left behind them pools of energy. Some of these granted peace and well being, so that one could enter therein timorously, to come forth again renewed in spirit and body. But others were wholly of the Dark. And if he was destroyed at once the intruder was lucky. It was worse, far worse, to live as a creature of a shadow's bidding.

The ghostly light streamed on before me. I lifted my head, turned this way and that, as might a hound seeking scent. All traces of trail had been wiped away by the wind. However I was sure that I followed the right path. So we came to two stelae which fronted each other as if they might once have formed part of an ancient gate. Yet there was no wall, just these pillars, from the tip of which streamed cloudwards thin ribbons of a greenish light. And they had been formed by men, or some agency with intelligence, for they had the likenesses of heavy bladed sabers. Yet on their sides I could see, half eroded by time, pits and hollows which, when the eye fastened straightly upon them, took on the semblance of faces—strange faces—long and narrow, with large noses overhanging pointed chins. Also it seemed that the eyes (which were pits) turned upon me, not in interest or in warning, but as if in deep, age-old despair.

Though I felt no emanation of evil, neither did I like to pass between those sword pillars. Still it was that way my road ran. Quickly I sketched with my hand certain symbols before I stepped forward, drawing Fallon on rein-hold behind me.

These pillars stood at the entrance of a narrow gash of valley which led downwards, the steep sides rising ever higher. Here the dark had full sway, for there were no more of the luminous stones. So that I went with that slow caution I had learned in the years I had ridden to war.

I listened. Outside this valley I had heard the murmur of the wind, but here was a deep quiet. Until my straining ears caught a sound which could only be that of running water. And there was a dampness now in the air, for which I was momentarily grateful. Fallon pushed against me, eager to slake his thirst.

But where there was water in this desert land there could also well be a camp of those I pursued. So I did not hasten, and I held back the pony. He snorted and the sound echoed hollowly. I froze, listening for any answer which might mean my coming was marked. But if the wolves I followed were human, certainly their sight here would be no better than mine, even more limited for they did not have—or so I hoped—the Talent to aid it.

On we went step by hesitant step. Then my boot, slipping across the ground, struck against some obstruction. I stooped, to feel about with my hands. Here was a cluster of small rocks, and beyond that, not too far, the water. I felt a path as clear as I could. As far as I could tell, a spring broke ground on my left, some way up the wall of the valley, and the water poured from that into a basin which in turn must have some outlet on the other side.

I scooped up a handful of the liquid, smelled it. There was no stench of minerals or of other deadliness. I splashed it over my face below the edge of my helm, washing away storm grit. Then I drank from my cupped hands, and squeezed aside to let Fallon have his way. The noise of his gulping was loud enough, but I no longer feared detection. Those I sought had come this way, yes. My refreshed mind assured me of that. But there was no camp hereabout.

"Jervon!" I pressed both hands over my eyes, pushing back my helm, reaching out in mind search again. For a moment it was as if my touch found a weakness in that mist I had encountered before. I touched— He was alive, mauled yet not badly injured! But when I tried to deepen contact, that I might read through him the numbers and nature of the force which held him, there was once more a cutting off of communication, as suddenly as a sword might descend between us.

The nature of that interference I could judge. There was that ahead which was aware of me, but only when I tried to reach Jervon. For as I hunkered there, my mind barrier up, I did not sense any testing of that. In me now fear was lessened; instead another emotion woke to life. Once before I had fought against very ancient evil—with love—for the body and soul of a man. Then I had sought my brother Elyn trapped in a cursed place. Though what I felt for Elyn, though we were of one blood and birth, was but a pale shadow to that which filled me when Jervon looked upon me. I am not one who speaks easily of what she thinks the deepest upon, but in that moment I knew how completely Jervon's fate and mine were rooted together. And I experienced fury against that which had cut the cord between us.

Recognizing that fury, I drew deep upon it, used the hot emotion to fill me with new strength. For, even as fear weakened that which was my own, so could anger give it sword and shield, providing I might control that anger. And there in the dark, by that unseen pool, I fashioned my invisible armor, sharpened those weapons which no one but myself could ever wield. For they were forged out of my wit and my emotion even as a smith beats a true-edged sword out of clean metal.

2

The Shadow Hunter

IT was folly to advance farther into the dark. I dared not risk a fall and perhaps a broken bone for me or for Fallon. Though every surge of emotion urged me on, I held to logic and reason. Here dark was so thick it was as if the ground about generated some blackness. Above hung clouds to veil even the stars.

I fumbled in my saddle bag and brought out a handspan of journey bread, hard enough perhaps to crack teeth gnawing it unwarily. This I soaked in water and fed the greatest portion to Fallon, whose lips nuzzled my hand to search out the smallest crumb. Then I used my will and forced upon his mind the order that he was not to stray, before I settled in between two rocks and drew my cloak about me as poor protection against this damp chill.

Though I had not thought to sleep, the fatigue of my body overcame the discipline of my mind and I dropped into a dark even deeper than that which enfolded me here. In that dark, presences moved and I was aware of them, only not clearly enough to draw any meaning from such fleetings.

I woke suddenly, into the gray of early dawn. And I awoke because I had been summoned as if someone had clearly called my name, or a battle trumpet had blown nearby. Now I could see the dim pool with the runnel of water leaping down the rocks to feed it. On the other side of that Fallon grazed on clumps of tough grass, which were not green but sickly ashen, withered by the chill of the season.

There was indeed an outlet for the pool basin, a kind of trough which ran on into the morning fog beyond. I moved stiffly, but, now that my mind was once more alert, I cast ahead for that blankness which hid Jervon and his captors.

It was there and this time I did not make the mistake of trying to pierce it, and so alert whatever I had touched the night before. At any rate, for the present, there was only one road, that walled by rises of stone on which I could not even see finger holds. Yet there were markings there—eroded and time-worn as those upon the stelae guardians—too regular to be nature's work, too strange to be read by me. Save that I misliked the general outlines of some of those symbols, for with their very shape they aroused misgivings.

As I broke my fast with another small portion of water-soaked bread, I kept my eyes resolutely turned away from those shadowy scrawls. Rather did I strive to see into the mist which filled this cut in the earth. And again I listened—but there was nothing to hear save the water.

Having filled my two saddle bottles I mounted, but I let Fallon for the moment take his own pace. For the way was much cluttered with rocks, with here and there a landslip over or around which we crept with care.

The sense of new danger crept slowly upon me, so intent was I on keeping contact with that peculiar blankness which I believed imprisoned Jervon. This was first like a foul smell which is but a suggestion of rottenness, but which gradually grows the stronger as one approaches the source of corruption. Fallon snorted, tossing his head, only kept to the path by my will.

Oddly enough I could not sense any of the ancient evil in this thing, though I bent my mind and my Talent to test it by all which I had learned from Aufrica and the use of my own power. It was not of any source I knew—for the taint was that of human not of the Old Ones. Yet also during our hunting of the Waste outlaws this I had not met either.

Now my flesh roughed as if more than the chill of the fog struck at me. Fear battled for release from the iron guard I had set upon my emotions. With that fear came a disgust and anger—

I found myself riding with hand upon sword hilt. Listening—ever listening—but my ears caught nothing but the thud of Fallon's hooves, now and again the ring of an iron shoe against an edge of rock.

The fog closed about, beads of moisture dripped from my helm, shone oily wet upon my mail, dampened Fallon's heavier winter coat into points.

Then—

Movement!

Fallon threw up his head to voice a shrill squeal of fear. At the same instant that which I had sensed struck and lapped me round.

For, through the rim of the fog, came horror unleashed. The thing was mounted even as I, and some trick of the fog made it loom larger than it was. But that which it rode was no horse of flesh and blood—rather a rack of bones held together by a lacing of rotted and dried flesh. And it was as its mount, a thing long dead and yet given a terrible life.

Its weapon was terror, not any sword. As I stiffened and drew deeply upon my power I realized it for what it was—a thoughtform born out of ancient fear and hatred. So did it continue to feed upon such emotions, drawing in to it at each feeding a greater substance.

My fear, my anger, must have both summoned and fed it. But it was real. That I could swear to, as much as if I laid hand upon that outstretched arm of bone. And Fallon's wide-eyed terror was meat to it also. While it trailed behind it, like a cloak, a deep depression of the spirit.

Fallon reared, screamed. That mount of bone opened wide its jaws in answer. I struggled with the panic-mad horse under me, glad for a moment that I had this to fight, for it awoke my mind from the blast of fear the spectre brought with it.

I raised my voice and shouted, as I would a battle cry, certain Words. Yet the rider did not waver, nor did the mount. And I summoned my will to master my own senses. This thing needed terror and despair to live, let me clamp tight upon my own and it would have no power—

Fallon sweated so that the smell was rank in the narrow defile of that way. My will had clamped upon him also, held him steady. He no longer screamed, but from his throat issued a sound not unlike the moaning of a man stricken close to death.

It was a thing fashioned of fear, and, without fear . . . I made myself into a bulwark, once more spoke my defiance. But I did not shout this time, rather I schooled my voice into obedience, even as I held Fallon.

The thing was within arm's length, the stench of it thick in my nostrils, the glare of its eyeless skull turned upon me. Then . . . it faded into the mist. Fallon still gave forth that unanimal-like moaning and great shudders ran through his body. I urged him forward, and he went one unsteady step at a time, while the fog coiled and spun around as if to entrap us.

It was enough for a moment that the horror had been vanquished. I hoped dimly that what I knew of such was the truth, that they were tied to certain places on earth where raw emotions had first given them birth.

As we paced along beside the small stream I heard sounds, not from ahead, but from behind. Faint they were at first, but growing stronger—there was the beat of hooves in such a loud tattoo that I thought some rider came at a speed far too reckless for the stony way. I heard also voices calling with the mist, though never could I make out the words, for the sounds came muffled and distorted. Still there reached me the impression of a hunt behind. And a strange picture flashed into my mind of one crouched low on a wild-eyed horse, behind him, unseen, the terror which drove him.

So keen and clear was this picture that I swung around when I reached a pile of rocks against which I could set my back. And I drew my sword. There was a rushing past where I crouched, my left hand tangled within Fallon's reins, for he was like to bolt. But nothing material cleared the mist. Again ancient shadows had deceived me.

Though I waited tensely for whatever pursued that lone rider of the distant past, there was nothing. Nothing save the uneasy sense that here were remnants of ancient terror caught forever in the mist. Then, ashamed at my own lack of self-control, I started on again, this time leading Fallon, stroking his head and talking softly to him, urging into his mind a confidence I did not wholly feel.

The walls about us began to widen out. Also that mist was tattered and driven by a wind which whistled down the valley, buffeting us with the frost it carried. But also it brought me something else, the scent of wood smoke, of a fire which has been recently dampened out.

We came to a curve in the near wall which served as a guide through the now disappearing mist. I dropped Fallon's reins and ordered him to stand so, cautiously crept forward; though the probe of my Talent picked up no whisper of a human mind. Still so strange was the Waste that I could believe those who harbored here might well have some defense against my power.

There had been a camp there right enough. A drowned fire still gave off a strong odor. And there were horse droppings along one side. I could see tracks crossing and recrossing each other, though the sand and gravel did not hold them clearly. But plainest of all was what had been painted on one massive rock which jutted forth from the wall. And that was no work of years before; the symbols must have been freshly drawn, for they were hardly weathered or scoured by sand.

One was a crudely drawn head of some animal—a wolf or hound—it could have been either. It interlaced the edge of the other, a far more complex and better executed symbol. I found myself standing before that, my forefinger almost of itself following its curves by tracing the air.

When I realized what I was doing I snatched my hand back to my side, my fingers balled into a fist. This was not of my learning, though it was a potent thing. And dangerous . . . There was an unpleasant *otherness* about the symbol which aroused wariness. However, I believed, though I did not understand its complete meaning, I did pick up the reason for those mated drawings. For among the Dales there was an old custom that, when a lasting truce or alliance was made, the lords of both parties chose a place on the boundaries of their domains and there carved the Signs of their two Houses so twined in just the same fashion.

So here I had come upon a notice that the outlaws I hunted had indeed made common cause with some dweller of the Waste who was not of their blood or kind. And, though I had suspected no less, having trailed them through the haunted valley, yet I could wish it otherwise.

To have some knowledge but not enough is a thing which eats upon one. If I might have read that other symbol I could be warned as to what—or who—I had to face. As I began a careful search about the deserted camp I alerted the Talent to sniff out any clue to the nonhuman. But the impressions my mind gathered were only of the same wolfish breed as we had hunted—desperate and dangerous enough.

Jervon had been there and he still lived. I had half steeled my mind to find him dead, for the Waste wolves did not take captives. What did they want with him? Or were they but the servants and hands of another force? The impression grew on me that the latter was so. That they had some purpose in bringing him hither could not be denied.

My years with Aufrica had taught me well that there are two kinds of what the untalented term "magic" or "witchery." It was contagious magic which I used to track Jervon, for about my throat I wore the amulet of a strange stone shaped not unlike an eye, which he had found and carried for a luck piece since he was a boy, and then had put into my keeping upon our handfasting, having in those years of war no other bride-jewel to offer.

But there was also sympathic magic which works according to the laws of correspondence and now I prepared to call upon that. From my healer's bag I brought forth a length of ash stick, peeled, blessed by the moon, bound with a small ring of silver wire, which is moon metal. Now I faced that symbol on the rock, pointed to it with ash rod which was no longer than my palm and fingers together.

Immediately the wand came to life in my hold, not to trace the characters, rather turning and twisting in a manner to suggest it would leap from my grasp rather than face what was so carven there. So I knew what I suspected was true and that this was a thing of the Dark from which the Light recoiled.

Now I touched the wand with the eye-stone which I drew forth from beneath my mail, rubbing the stone down one side and up the other. Then I held out my hand with the lightest hold upon the ash. Again it twisted, pointing ahead.

My battle with fear in the mist had drawn too heavily upon my inner resources; I could no longer depend upon mind search to follow those whom I sought. However, with the wand I had a sure pointer, in which I could trust. So I continued to hold it as I mounted Fallon and rode out of that camp, turning my back upon the entwined symbols of an unholy alliance.

The valley widened even farther, as if it had been but a narrow throat to open country beyond. I saw trees now, as misshapen as the brush, and monoliths, as well as tumbles of stone, which suggested ruins so old they could not be dated by my own species.

There were tracks again. But within a very short time we came to a place where those turned to the right at an abrupt swing. Only, in my hand, the wand did not alter course, but still pointed straight ahead. There was only one solution to accept: Jervon was no longer with the wolf pack which had pulled him down.

Had there been some monstrous meeting beneath

those symbols and he whom I sought been given to that Other whose sign was set boldly on the rock? I dismounted to search the ground with a scout's patience. And was rewarded with faint traces at last. The main body I hunted had indeed turned here. But two mounts had kept to the straight track. One of those must carry Jervon.

If he rode with only one outlaw as guard—I drew a sharp swift breath . . . This might well herald a chance for rescue with the odds much in my favor. I mounted again and urged Fallon to a faster pace than he had kept during that day's travel, watching keenly the country ahead.

3

The Frozen Flame

HERE in the open the mist was tattered by the wind and one could see farther. So my eyes caught a flash of light. Yet it was plain that this did not rise from any fire but rather sparked into the sky, perhaps as a beacon.

Now the stones of the forgotten ruins drew together, formed tumbled walls, with here or there some uprise of worked rock which might have once been a stele, or even a statue. But these were now so worn away by erosion that such shapes remained only vaguely unpleasant ones, hinting of ancient monstrous beings. Gods or guardians? What man now living could say?

The sun broke through, yet here it had not even the pallid light of mid-winter, rather a drained, bespoiled radiance, with nothing to warm either body or heart. And still shadows clung to the rocks, though I resolutely refused more than to glance at them. I knew the power of illusion, for much of that lies within the Talent.

Before me rose a wall, massive in its blocks, some larger than myself, even when mounted on Fallon. This time had not used so harshly. The pale sun struck points of icy fire from gray-white crystals embedded in its surface. The way I followed led to the single break in that wall, a gateway so narrow that it would seem no more than one had ever been meant to pass therein at a time.

Now the wand in my hand flipped so that I barely prevented it from slipping through my fingers. Its silver-bound tip pointed to a dark stain smeared on that wall near the height of my thigh, riding as I was. Blood—and that of him whom I now sought!

I could only draw hope because the smear was so small a one. That Jervon had not been overborne without a fight, that I was already sure of. He was too seasoned in war to be easily taken, and the bodies I had found at our last camp had testified to his skill in defense. Yet this was the first sign I had seen that he had been wounded. Now I glanced at the pavement under foot, expecting to sight more splotches thereon.

The wall was the first of three such. And they varied in color, for the outer one, in spite of its clusters of crystals, was a gray as the rest of this Waste. The second, some twenty places beyond, was dull green. Yet it was not any growing thing which had clothed it, but part of the blocks themselves.

While the third was the rusty-brown-red of dried blood and in it the stones were smaller. The entrance through to it was still narrower; so that, despite my misgivings, I was forced to dismount, and essay that on foot.

If there were any blood smears here to mark Jervon's passing, those were cloaked by the natural coloring of the stone. Before me stood a squat building, only a fraction higher than the wall, windowless and dour, the stone of its making a lustreless, thick black, as if it had been fashioned from shadows themselves. From the roof of this issued, straight up to defy the sullen sun, the beam of light that had shone across the land.

Now that I drew nearer I could see that beam pulsated

in waves, almost like the ever-changing and moving flames of a fire. Yet I was sure it was not born from any honest burning of wood.

Windowless the place might be, but there existed a deeply recessed doorway; so deep and dark a portal I could not be sure if any barrier stood within. I paused, using my senses to test what lay about me, for to go blindly into danger would not serve either Jervon's cause or my own.

Hearing? There was no sound, not even the sigh of wind across twisted shrub and sliding sand. Smell? I could not pick up any of the faint rottenness which had alerted me to the coming of the phantom in the valley. Sight? The deep door, the pulsing flame, unmarked ground between me and that doorway. Touch . . .?

I held up my hand, the wand lying across the palm. That moved again, wavering from side to side with a growing speed until it had switched around and the wire-wound tip pointed to me, or back of me to the wall entrance through what I had just squeezed. There was warning enough in that. What lay ahead was highly inimical to such forces as I dared call upon. And I was somehow certain if I took these last few strides, passed within that portal, I would be facing danger worse than any wolf blade or phantom hunter.

If only I knew more! Once before I had gone to battle with one of the evil Old Ones, in ignorance and using only my few poor weapons. And Jervon, at that hour (having far more to fear than I, for he possessed none of the safeguards of the Talent), had come with me, trusting only in the power of cold iron and his own courage.

Could I do less now? As I stood there, the fluttering wand in my hand, I thought of what Jervon was to me. First an unwanted road companion through a hostile land, one who made me impatient for I feared that he might in some way turn me from my purpose. Then—

My life was bound to Jervon's. I could not deny that. Whatever force had brought him here, it was for no purpose except his destruction—and perhaps also mine. Yet I accepted that and walked toward the doorway.

There was no door to face me. Only, once I had stepped under the shadow of that overhang, there was a cloud of darkness so thick it might seem one might gather together folds of it in one's fingers as one could a curtain woven on a Dale loom. I raised the hand I could no longer see until I thought the wand was level with my lips. Then I breathed upon that and spoke three words.

So tiny a light, as if a candle no thicker than my own little finger, shone feebly. But as that sparked into being I drew a deep breath. There was not yet any pressure on me. In so little had I won a token victory.

That other time I had had an advantage because what dwelt anciently in such a place had been all-powerful for so long that it had not seen in me a worthy opponent. Therefore it had not unleashed its full strength against me until too late. I did not know that lay ahead, nor could I hold any hope that it would be the same here.

Time is often distorted and altered in those places of the Old Ones. All human memory is filled with legends of men who consorted with Those of Power for what seemed a day or year, and returned to find that their own world had swept on far faster. Now it appeared otherwise to me.

The very darkness, which was hardly troubled by the light on which my spirit fed, was like a flood of sticky clay or quicksand catching at my feet, so that it was a physical effort to fight against that in order to advance. As yet there had been no other assault upon me. Slowly, I gained the impression that what intelligence had raised this place for its shell of protection was otherwise occupied, so intent upon that concentration that it was not yet aware of me.

Even as the pinpoint of flame I held before me, that thought strengthened my courage. Yet I dared not depend upon such concentration holding. At any moment it might be broken, by some unknown, unseen system of alarm, to turn the force of Its interest in my direction.

I fought against the sticky dark, one step, two. It seemed to me that this journey had consumed hours of time. My body ached once more with the effort I must exert in order to advance. One more stride—

Thus I passed from complete dark into light so suddenly that, for two breaths, three, I was blinded. Then, blinking, I was able to see. The space in which I stood was round, with two great chairs, by their dimensions made for bodies larger than humankind, facing each other across a dazzling pillar which formed the innermost core.

Then I saw that it was not really a pillar, but rather a rounded shaft of ceaseless rolling radiance. No heat radiated from it, only an inner flickering suggested the flames it mimicked.

My inner warning sounded an alarm. Instantly I averted my eyes. There stood the force and purpose of this place. I had come out behind the nearer chair, its back a barrier, but I could see the other. Something had fallen from its wide seat to lie like a pile of wrung out rags on the floor.

Jervon—?

But even as I took a step towards that body, for dead that man must be by the very limpness of his form, I saw more clearly the face turned towards the light, the eyes wide in horror. And a stubby beard pointed outward from the chin. One of the outlaws!

Then Jervon—?

Carefully averting my gaze from that challenging, beckoning fire, I edged around the chair before me. Yes, he whom I sought sat there. There were bonds about his arms, loops bringing together his booted ankles. His helm was gone and there was a gash on his forehead which had been only roughly bandaged so that congealed red drops lay on the cheek beneath.

He was—alive?

I reached forth my hand. The wand trembled. Yes, there still was a spark of life in him, held so by the stubbornness of his own will and courage. But his eyes were locked on the pillar of fire and I knew that what was the man I knew was being rift out of him into that flame.

I could do two things. Recklessly, I first tried mind seek. No, his consciousness was too depleted to respond. If I attempted to break the binding of the flame I could overturn the result of his own courage, loose him and lose him. There was a great strength in Jervon. I had seen it in action many times over during the seasons we had ridden together as comrades and lovers (seldom can those two be made one, but so it was with us).

So—I must follow him—into the flame. Front that Power on its own ground.

If only I knew more! I beat my hands together in my impotent frustration. This was a great force, and one I had no knowledge of. I did not know if I could face it with any Talent of my own. It might be invincible in its own stronghold.

I moved slowly on to look at the dead outlaw. He had been emptied of life force, easier prey by far than Jervon. The way he had fallen made it seem he had been contemptuously thrown aside.

But I knew Jervon. And upon that knowledge I could build now. It would do me no good to take his body from this place, even if the flame power would allow that. For then he could never regain what he had already lost—what must be returned to him . . .

Returned—how?

Desperate I was, for I might lose all, his life, mine, and perhaps more than just the lives of our bodies. But I could see no other way.

Deliberately I went to that other throne, careful not to touch the wasted body as I stepped over it. I am glad I did not hesitate now, that my inner strength carried me up unflinchingly to where that dead man had sat. I settled myself within the curve of the arms, under the shadow of the high back. My wand I took in both hands, forcing it up against the power which tried to forestall me, until the point was aimed at Jervon's breast.

I did not believe that the power I would confront was of my plane of existence at all. Rather I thought that the frozen flames were but a small manifestation visible to our world. I must seek it on its own ground if I were to have a chance.

The outlaw had been its creature already. Doubtless he had lain under its spell even before he had entered here, perhaps sent by it to find such strong meat as Jervon. And Jervon it had not completely taken. Also it might never have tried to absorb one learned in the Talent.

Such a hope was very thin; I could count on nothing save my own small learning and my determination. But it was not in me to leave this place without Jervon. We would win or lose together.

So—the battlefield lay within the flame—

My grip on the wand was iron tight. Now I deliberately raised my eyes, stared straight into that play of curbed fire. I need only release my will for a very little.

4

Elsewhere and Elsewhen

I was—elsewhere. How can one summon words to describe what is so wholly alien to all one's experience? Colors rippled here that had no name I knew, sensations wrenched at the inner core of my determination and Talent as if they would pull me apart while I yet lived. Or did I live now? I was aware of no body in this place, five senses no longer served me, for I realized I did not "see" but rather depended upon a different form of perception.

Only seconds, breaths long, was I given; then a compelling force swept up the consciousness which was all that remained of my identity and drew me forward across a fantastic and awesome country.

For *country* it was—! Though it was subtly *wrong,* my human instinct told me. There were growing things, which did not in the least resemble any I had ever seen, of eye-searing yellow, threatening red. These writhed and beat upon the air as if they fought against their rooting, would be free to do their will, and yet were anchored by another's ordering. Branches tip-clawed the earth or swept high into the air in ceaseless movement.

Then I was beyond them, carried so by the force which I had momentarily surrendered to. And I put aside my preoccupation with the strangeness of this place, to fasten inwardly, nurse my Talent with all my strength.

Yet must I also conceal from that which summoned me that I had that hard core of defiance within me. For I was sure that I must not dissipate that before I fronted the Power which ruled here.

I had heard legends through Aufrica (though from whom she had gained them she never said) that when the Old Ones held the Dales they had meddled with the very stuff of life itself, and that the adepts among them had opened "gates" which led to other dominions in which the human was as unnatural as that which passed swiftly below me now. That this might be such a "gate" I have begun to believe. But its guardianship was alien.

Here was a stretch of yellow ground unbroken by any of the monstrous growths. Patterned deeply on its surface were many tracks and trails, some deep-worn as well-used roads. Yet my own feet, if I still possessed those appendages, did not seek to tread there. Rather I had the sensation of being wafted well above that broken surface.

Those tracks and ways converged, angling toward some point ahead. And, as I passed on, I began to see moving figures, ones which pressed forward step by reluctant step. Yet none was clear, but rather cloaked in ever-shifting color so that one could not define their true outlines. Some were dully gray, one or two a deep black that reminded me of the dark through which I had passed to reach the chamber of the flame. Others showed as sickly green, or a sullen, blood/rust red. As I swept over them I longed to shriek aloud my pain, for it seemed that from each there came some thrust of despair and horror which was like the cut of a sword one could not guard against. Thus I realized that these were victims of this place even as I might be.

Why I winged my way rather than trode theirs I could not guess. Unless that which ruled here knew me for what I was and would have me quickly within its grasp! And it was not good to think of that. But I had made my choice, and must hold firmly to my resolution.

Thicker became the figures plodding so slowly. Now I began to believe that their doom was deliberately prolonged by purpose, that their helpless suffering was meat and drink to something—

Was Jervon one of those?

I tried to delay my own passage, hover above those misty lights which were still substantial enough to leave tracks on the plain. But then a second thought came to me, that in allowing myself to show interest in any of those tormented wayfarers I could in turn betray the more plainly what I was and why I had come.

So I turned my new sense of perception from those travelers, and allowed the compulsion full rein to draw me in. I came at last to where that yellow plain gave way abruptly to a chasm.

The walls of that were the dull red of the final wall which had guarded the flame building, and in shape it was round. Down its sides the lights which tracked the plain made a painful descent, now so thronged together that their colors seemed to blend and mingle. Though I thought in truth no entity was aware of its fellows, but only of its own sore fate.

Down I was drawn, past those toiling victims. Once more into a pool of dead blackness and loss of all perception. Here I began to exercise those safeguards I had learned, seeds of which had been mine from birth. I was myself, me, Elys—a woman, a seer, a fighter. And I must remain me and not allow That Other to take away my oneness with myself and my past.

Still I raised no opposition save that belief in myself which I kept within me. At this moment I must put even Jervon from my conscious mind and concentrate on my own personality. Instinct told me this, and for a Wise Woman such instinct is a command.

The dark began to thin and I could see light again. But in that sickly yellowish glow there was nothing to be marked, save directly under me, or that part of me which had come seeking this grim venture, a throne.

It was fashioned of the black, the dark itself, and on it there wavered a ruddy mist in which whirled gemlike particles.

"Welcome—"

It was not sound which reached me, rather a vibration which shuddered through whatever form I now wore.

Slowly I settled down, until I fronted that towering throne and the unstable form it contained. Very small was I, so that this was like looking up at the face of some high Dale hill.

"Good—"

Again the word vibrated through me, bringing with it both pain and—may the Power I serve forgive me—also a kind of pleasure which defiled that which I held to be the innermost core of my being.

"It has been long and long since this happened—"

The glittering mist of the throne was melting, developing more of a form.

"Are there then again those to summon for the Gate?"

That *form* leaned forward on its throne. The glitter points flowed together, formed two discs which might serve the alien for eyes. Now those centered upon me.

"Where is the gift then, servant of ——" The name the thing mouthed was like a flame lapping about me, so strong was the Power that carried, even though I was no follower of It.

Before I could frame an answer, its shadowy head bobbed in what might be a nod.

"So the gift comes—yet I think it not of your devising. Think you I can be so easily deceived?" And the form shook with what might be silent and horrible laughter. The contempt in which it held me and all my species was like a loathsome stench in the air of that place.

"Your kind has served me," the vibration which was speech continued. "Long and well have they served me. Nor have I ever withheld their rewards. For when I feed, *those* feed— Behold!"

It stretched forth an extension of the upper body which might well serve it for arm, and then I could perceive indeed that all it had fed upon was a part of it. But not in peace. For the torment of those it consumed and yet nourished within its own substance was that they were conscious of what had happened to them, and that consciousness lasted throughout ages without respite. While as a part of this Thing they were also forced to feed in turn, damning themselves to further torture which was endless.

Even as I watched one of those long appendages flickered even farther out and returned, grasped in it a writhing core of grayness which was one with those shapes I had watched on the plain above. This it clasped to its body so that the gray sank into its mass and another life force was sentenced to an existence of terror and despair.

Seeing that, my mind stirred. Even as that rider I had seen in the valley was a thoughtform fed into life by the terror of those whose emotions strengthened it, so was this Thing a product of similar forces.

I had heard it said that men are apt to make their gods in their own images, attributing to those gods their own emotions, save that those emotions are deemed far greater than any human mind and heart can generate. Thus this Thing might once have been born—to serve a people whose god it was, who fed it for generations. So that at last it was no longer dependent upon their willingly brought sacrifices, but could indeed control mankind and so exert its own dominion.

But if that were indeed the truth, then the weapon against it was . . . *unbelief.* And, in spite of the evidence of my senses, here I must bring that weapon into being.

The glittering eyes that were set so on me did not change and the despair and horror which it exuded in waves wrapped me around with all the force long generations of worship could generate within it.

"Small creature—" again it shook with that unvoiced demonic laughter. "I am, I exist—no matter from what small seed of thought I was born. Look upon me!"

Now its substance grew even thicker and it indeed formed a body. This unclothed body was godlike in its beauty—its tainted beauty—brazenly male. And the eyes shrank, to become normal-sized in a face whose features were those truly of some super being without a flaw.

Except the flaw of knowledge of what it was and from what it had come. And that knowledge I clung to. It did not show bones and rotting flesh, but that was its true state.

"Look upon me!" Once more the command rang out. "Females of your kind found me good to look upon in the old days before I grew tired of your world, and that which closed Gates swept across the land. Look—and come!"

And that vile pleasure, which had troubled me before, again assailed me. Against that I set the training of my Talent—the austerity in which we learn to master all that which is of the body. Though I felt myself waver a little forward, yet my determination held me fast.

Then those perfect lips smiled—evilly.

"You are more than I have tasted for a long time. This shall indeed be a dainty feasting—" Now it raised a fine muscled arm, beckoned to me with its long fingers. "Come—you cannot withstand me. Come willingly and the reward will be very great indeed—"

My thought arose in answer and I shaped the name it had given me and with that name certain words. It was a forlorn hope. And, as that head tossed back and it laughed openly, I knew how vain that hope was.

"Names! You think that you can lay upon me your will by *names?* Ah, but that which I gave you is but the name men—some men—called me. It is not the name by which I know myself. And without that—you have no weapon. However, this is exciting—that you dare to stand against *me!* I have fed, and I have gathered strength, and I have waited for those who closed the Gates perhaps to hunt me. But they have not come, and you, worm thing who dares to face me—you are of such as they would not trouble themselves to look upon, far less do you stand equal to them.

"Only you shall give me sport, and that will be pleasant. You have come seeking one, have you not? Others have been led by pride and kinship to do so. They were fitly rewarded as you shall see when you join them. But name me no names which have not power!"

This time I did not try to answer. But feverishly I went seeking in my memory for the smallest trace of knowledge I had. Aufrica's learning had been shared with me to the best of her ability. We had visited certain forgotten shrines in the old days and sometimes dared to summon influences, long weakened by the years, which had once been dwelling in them. Spells I knew, but before this creature such were but as the rhyming games small children play.

No—I would not allow room to that despair which insidiously nibbled at my mind! What I could do I would—!

The creature on the throne laughed for the third time.

"Very well. Struggle if you wish, worm one. It amuses me. Now—look what comes—"

It pointed to the left and I dared to look. There had come, very slowly, plainly fighting the compulsion which drew it, one of those columns of light. This one was not black, not gray, nor yet red, but a yellow which was clear and bright. And in that moment I knew that this was what this world would see of Jervon.

Nor did it crawl abjectly as had the one the false god had claimed in my sight, but stood erect, as it fought against the power of the thing on the throne.

"Jervon!" I dared at that moment to send forth a thought call. And instantly and valiantly was it answered:

"Elys!"

But the thing who commanded here looked from one of us to the other and smiled its evil smile.

5

Together We Stand

"So sweet a feasting—" A tongue tip appeared between the lips of the handsome face, swept back and forth as if indeed savoring some pleasant taste. "You give me much, small ones—much!"

"But not all!" I made answer. And that yellow flame which was Jervon no longer advanced, but stood with me, as we had stood together through the years when there was a blooding of swords and a need for defense. For I knew that this was not all of Jervon, that still in his ensorceled body he held stubbornly to his identity even as I went armed behind the wall of mine.

That which sat enthroned leaned forward a little, its beautiful and vile face turned to us.

"I hunger—and I feed—so simple is it."

It stretched out one of those seeming arms to an unnatural length, gathering to its bosom another crawling blob. In my mind there was a shriek of despair.

"You see how easy it is?"

Rather did I in turn reach with the Power for Jervon. And it was indeed as if we now stood hand-linked before this thing that should never have been. All the clean strength of Jervon's manhood was at war with what abode here. And to that I joined my Power, limited as it might be. I formed symbols and perceived them glow in the air, as if written in fire.

But the Thing laughed and stretched out a hand of mist to sweep those easily away.

"Small are your gifts, female. Do you think I cannot wipe them from sight? So and so and so—" That hand of mist moved back and forth.

"Jervon," I sent my own message, "it feeds upon fear—"

"Yes, Elys, and upon the souls of men also." And it seemed to me that his reply was so steady it was as if I had indeed found an anchorage which I needed.

Twice more the creature fed upon those blobs which crawled about the base of its throne. But always its eyes were on us. For what it waited, save that it must have our greater fear to season its feasting, I could not guess.

But that pause gave me time to draw in all which I knew, suspected, or hoped might aid us. How does one kill a god? *With unbelief,* my logic told me. But here and now unbelief was nigh impossible to summon.

We who have been burdened with the Talent must believe, yes. For we know well that there are presences beyond our comprehension, both good and evil, who may be summoned by man. Though we cannot begin to understand their true nature, limited as we are by the instincts and emotions of our corporal bodies. I seek certain of these intangible presences every time I exercise the Power which is mine, small that it is. And in Jervon also there is belief—though his presences might not be mine. For we do not all walk the same roads, though in the end those roads must meet at a certain Gate which is the greatest of all, and beyond which lies what we cannot begin to imagine with our earthbound minds and hearts.

Only to this Thing I owed no belief. I was not one who had bowed in the courts of its temple nor sought its evil aid in any undertaking. Therefore—for me—it was no god!

"So do you think, female," flashed its thought back in answer. "Yet you are of a like kind to those who gave me creation. Therefore in you lie certain matters which I can touch—"

It was as if a slimy, rotting finger sleeked across my shrinking flesh. And in its wake—yes—there was that in me ready to respond to that nauseating touch. I have weaknesses as inborn as my Talent, those it could summon into battle against me. Once more it laughed.

"Elys—" The thought that was Jervon's overrang that laughter. "Elys!"

It was no more than my name, but it broke through that feeling of abasement that anything in me could respond to this horror. I drew once more upon logic. No man or woman is perfect. There is much lying within us which we must look upon with cold, measuring eyes and hate. But if we do not yield to that hatred, nor to what gave it birth, but stand aside to let one balance the other, then we do what those trained in the Way can do to fight that which is base. Yes, I had in me that which could quicken from this thing of the utter dark. But it was how I met that weakness, not the weakness itself which counted.

I was Elys, a Wise woman, even as Jervon had reminded me by the speaking of my name. Therefore I was no tool of that which had led me to this throne. I had come of my own free will in order to face it, not been dragged by dark forces overcoming my spirit.

"Elys—" It was the enthroned creature that uttered my name now, and there was enticement in that naming.

But I stood fast, summoning up all which was born of my long training to armor me. And the beautiful head so far above me shifted a little. Now, though keeping me still in its gaze, it also could see Jervon. It raised its hand to beckon.

The yellow flame which was my fulfillment in this life wavered towards the throne. Yet it was not muddied as were those others which crawled about us. Nor did Jervon ask aught of me in that moment, but made the struggle his own, for I knew, without his telling, that he feared I would be depleted should I undertake his defense as well as mine.

Then I moved whatever form this world had left me, standing between Jervon and the thing which reached now with its shadow hand to grasp him.

Once more I pronounced the name men had given him in their fear and horror of this baneful worship. But I sent no symbols into the air for him to sweep aside. Rather I did send a thought picture and this was of an empty throne crumbling in long decay.

Fear I fought, and anger I reined in, making both feed and serve *me* in what I would do. This was—not!

I could not close off that sense of perception which assured me that it was. But I held valiantly to the small weapon I had. I did not worship, I did not believe, nor did Jervon. Therefore: this thing was *NOT!*

Yet it was growing more and more solid even as I so denied it. Beckoning—BEING!

The imagination of countless generations of men had fashioned it, how could I hope to dismantle it with only a denial?

An empty throne—a nonbeing—!

I threw all that was me, all which I sensed I drew now from Jervon with his willing consent, into that picture. This was no god of mine, I did not feed it—it could not exist!

Torment indeed was that denial, for ever it called to a part of me, to force homage and worship. Yet that I held out against. No god of mine! There must be faith to bring a god alive, to perform deeds in his name—without faith there was no existence.

I knew better than to summon the Powers I did kneel before. In this place all worship the enthroned thing would take to itself, whether given in its filthy name or not. No, this was the bareness of my spirit and my belief in myself, and Jervon's belief in himself—(the which he was loosing to me)—that mattered. I did not accept, and I refused homage because it was—*NOT!*

The thing lost its lazy assurance, its evil smile and laughter, even the quasi-human form it had assumed to tempt me. There was nothing in the throne place now but a ravening flame touched with the deep black of its evil. That swept back and forth as might the head of a great serpent elevated above a coiled body, waiting to strike.

Its rage was that of madness. The long years it had existed had not prepared it for this. It was here, it could seize my kind, absorb into it their spirits—

But could it?

Humans are composed of many layers of consciousness, many emotions. Any who deal with the Talent—and many who do not—knew this. The throned thing fed upon fear and those viler parts of us. The miserable blobs it drew to it, which were now packed tightly around me, swaying in time to the swaying of that flame on the throne, were dominated by the worst that had lain in the humanity they had once been, not the best. They had been held prisoner by their fears and their belief, until they had been summoned here to be delivered helplessly to their master.

A master who could in turn not hold them unless they surrendered, whom they had created and could now destroy—if they so willed it!

I threw that thought afield as I might whirl about me an unsheathed sword. If they were all lost in the depths of their foul belief then it would avail me nothing. But if only a few could join us—only a few!

The thing on the throne was quick. It lapped out and down, and took with that lapping the first row of the blob things, swelling in power as it absorbed their energy.

"Elys—Elys—"

Only my name, but into it Jervon put all he could to hearten and sustain me. I was aware of a brighter burst of the clear golden flame to my left.

Again the false god pounced to feast. There was something too hasty in its movements, as if time was no longer its servant, but might speedily be its enemy. It wanted to cram itself with life force, swell its power.

But it could not feed on unbelief. That logic I held to as one holds to a rope which is one's only hope of aid.

An empty throne—

Now that rusted and diseased flame uttered a kind of shriek, or perhaps that was not any cry but a vibration meant to shake me, loose me from my rope of hope. It flickered out and out towards me, towards the light which was Jervon.

We did not believe, therefore we could not be its prey.

I was in the dark; my perception was totally gone. I was—in . . . No, I could not be within something which did not exist. I was *me,* Elys, and Jervon. We were no meat for a false god whose creators were long since dust, its temple forgotten.

It was as if my bare body were seared by a cold so intense that it had the same effect as fire. I was one with—no, I was not! I was Elys. And Jervon was Jervon! I would feel him through the torture of the cold, holding as I did to his own identity. We were ourselves and no servants —victims—of this thing which had no place in the world. We had no fear for it to batten on now, and those parts of us which it could awaken, those we could control.

There was an empty throne—there was nothingness —nothingness but Elys and Jervon who did not believe—

Pain, cold, pain, and still I held and now Jervon called to me and somehow I found the strength to give to him even as earlier he had loosed his for me. Together we stood, and because of that both of us were the stronger, for in our union was the best part of us both—mind and spirit.

Darkness, cold, pain—and then a sense of change, of being lost. But I would not allow fear to stir. A god who was naught could not slay—

I opened my eyes—for I saw with them now and not with that special sense I had had in that other place. Before me was a column of light, but it was wan, sinking, growing paler even in the space of a blink or two. I moved; my body was stiff, cold, my hands and feet had no feeling in them as I slid forward on the wide seat where I had awakened, looking about me for something familiar and known.

This—this was the round chamber where I had found Jervon—

Jervon!

Stumbling, weaving, I staggered to that other chair, fumbling with my dagger so that I might cut the ropes which bound his stiff body. His eyes were closed, but he had not tumbled flaccidly down as had the outlaw who had been drained. I sawed at his hide bonds with my numb and fumbling hands, twice dropping the blade so I had to grope for it in the half light. For the flaming pillar in the center gave forth but little radiance now—more like the dread glow which sometimes gathers on dead bodies.

"Jervon!" I called to him, shook him as best I could with those blockish hands. His body fell forward so his head rested on my shoulder and his weight nearly bore me tumbling backward. "Jervon!"

It seemed in that moment that I had lost. For if I alone had won out of that evil place then there was no further hope for me.

"Jervon!"

There was a breath against my cheek, expelled by a moan. I gathered him to me in a hold, which even the false god could not have broken, until his voice came, low and with a stammering catch in it:

"My dear lady, would you break my ribs for me—" and there was a thread of weak laughter in that which set me laughing too, until I near shook with the force of that reaction.

I almost could not believe our battle won. But before us, where we crouched together on the wide seat of that throne, the last glimmer of light died. There was no gateway now into elsewhere. Outside the outlaws of the Waste might be waiting, but we two had battled something greater than any malice of theirs, and for the moment we were content.

Sand Sister

1

THE moment of birth came in the early dawning when the mists of Tormarsh night still curled thick and rank about the walls of Kelva's hall. This in itself was an ill thing, for, as all well knew, a child who is to have the foresight and the forereach must come into the world at that time: the last moment of one day and the first of the next; while under a full moon of the Shining One is indeed the best time to welcome a new Voice among the People.

Also this was no lusty child who entered the world crying a demand for life and the fullness thereof. Rather the wrinkled skin on its undersized body was dusky, and it lay across the two hands of the healer limply. Nor did it seek to draw a breath. But because all children were necessary for the Torfolk and each new life was a barrier against the twilight of their kind, they labored to save this one.

The healer set lips upon the cold flaccid ones of the baby and strove to breathe air into its lungs. They warmed it and nursed it, until at last it cried feebly—not to welcome life but to protest that it must receive it. At the sound of that cry Mafra's head inclined to one side as she listened to that plaint which was more like the cry of a luckless bird trapped in a net than that of any true child of Tor.

Though her eyes were long since blind to what the Folk could see, being covered with a film which no light could hope now to pierce, Mafra had the other sight. When they brought the child to her for the blessing of the Clan and House Mother, she did not hold out her hands to receive the small body. Rather she shook her head and spoke:

"Not of the kindred is this one. The spirit who was chosen to fill this body came not. What you have drawn to life in it is—"

She fell silent then. While the women who had brought the child drew away from the Healer, now staring at the baby she held as if the wrap cloth of the clan birthing enfolded some slimy thing out of the encroaching bogland.

Mafra turned her head slowly so that her blind eyes faced each for the space of a breath.

"Let no one think of the Dark Death for this one." She spoke sharply. "The body is blood of our blood, bone of our bone. This much I also say to you: what now dwells within that body we must bind to us, for there is a strength indwelling in it which the child must learn to use for herself. Then when she uses it for those she favors it will be both a mighty tool and a weapon."

"But you have not named her, Clan Mother. How can she dwell in the clan house if she bears not our name freely given?" ventured then the boldest of those who had faced Mafra.

"It is not in my gift to name her," Mafra said slowly. "Ask that of the Shining One."

It was now morning and the mist was curtain heavy, blanking out the sky. However, as if her very words had summoned the creature out of the air, there swooped across the women there gathered one of the large, silver-gray moths that were dancers in the night air. This settled for an instant on the wrapping of the child, fanning gently its palm-wide wings. Thus the healer spoke:

"Tursla—" Which was a name of the Moth-maid in the very ancient song-tale of Tursla and the Toad Devil. Thus it was that the child who-was-not-of-the-clan spirit was given a name which was in itself uncanny and even a little tinged with ill-fortune.

Tursla lived among the Torpeople. After the fashion of their ways she who had borne the child was never known to her as "mother," for that was not the custom. Rather all the children of one clan were held in love by the elders of their House and all were equal. Since Mafra had spoken for her, and the Tormarsh itself had sent her a name, there was no difference made between Tursla and the other children —who were very few now.

For the Torfolk were very old indeed. They spoke in their Remember Chants of a day when they had been near unthinking beasts (even less than some of the beasts of this old land) and how Volt, The Old One (he who was not human at all but the last of a much older and greater race than man dared to aspire to equal) had come to be their guide and leader. For he was lonely and found in them some spark of near thought which intrigued him so he would see what he might make of them.

Volt's half-avian face still was one they carved on the guard totems set about the fields of loquths and in their dwelling places. To his memory they offered the first fruits of their fields, the claws and teeth of the dire wak-lizard, if they were lucky enough to slay such. By Volt's name they swore such oaths as they must say for weighty reasons.

Thus Tursla grew in body, and in knowledge of Tormarsh. What lay across its borders was of no consequence to the Torfolk, though there was land and sea and many strange peoples beyond. Not as old naturally as Torfolk, nor with the same powers, for they had not been blessed by Volt and his learning in the days their clans were first shaped.

But Tursla was different in that she dreamed. Even before she knew the words with which she might tell those dreams they caught her up and gave her another life. So that many times the worlds which encased her periods of sleep were far more vivid and real than Tormarsh itself.

She discovered as she grew older that the telling of her dreams to those of her own age made them uncomfortable and they left her much to herself. She was hurt, and then, angered. Later, perhaps out of the dreams, there came to her a newer thought that these were for her alone and could not be shared. This brought a measure of loneliness until she discovered that Tormarsh itself (though it might not be the worlds through which her dreams led her) was a place of mystery and delight.

Such opinion, however, could only be that of one who wore a Tor body and was reared in a Tor Clan; for Tormarsh was a murky land in which there were great stretches of noisome bog from which reared the twisted skeletons of long-dead trees—and those were oftentimes leprous seeming with growths of slimy substances.

There were the remnants of very ancient roads, which tied together in a network the islands raised from these marshy lands, and age-old stone walls enclosed the fields of the Torfolk, rearing also to form the clan halls. Always the mists gathered at night and early morning and wreathed around the crumbling stones.

But to Tursla the mists were silver veiling, and in the many sounds of the hidden boglands she could single out and name the cries of birds, the toads, frogs, and lizards, though even those were not like their distant kin to be found other places.

Best of all she loved the moths which had given her her own name. She discovered they were drawn to the scent of certain pale flowers which bloomed only at night. This scent she came to love also and would place the blossoms in the silvery fluff of her shoulder-length hair, weave garlands of them to wear about her neck. Also she learned to dance, swaying as did the marsh reeds under the winds, and as she danced the moths gathered about her, brushing against her body, flying back and forth in their own measures about her upheld, outstretched arms.

But this was not the way of the other Tormaidens, and when Tursla danced she did so apart and for her own pleasure.

The years are all the same in Tormarsh and they pass with a slow and measured beat. Nor do the Torfolk reckon them in any listing. For when Volt left his people they no longer cared to reckon time. They knew that there was war and much trouble in the outer world. Tursla had heard that before she had been born a war leader of that other land had been brought into Tormarsh by treachery and had been taken away again by his enemies with whom the Torfolk had made an uneasy and quickly broken pact.

Also there was still an older story—but that was whispered and could only be learned if one plucked a hint there, added a word here. Even further back in time there had been a man from outside whose ship had foundered on the strip of shore where Tormarsh actually came down in a point to the sea. And there he had been found by one who was a clan mother.

She had taken pity on the man who had been sore hurt and had, against all custom, brought him to the healers. But the end to that had been sadness, for he had laid a spell of caring on the First Maiden of that clan and she had chosen, against all custom, to go forth with him when he was healed.

There had come a time when she returned—alone. Though to her clan she had said the name of a child. Later she had died. Yet the name of the child remained in the chant of the Rememberer. Now it was said that he, too, was a great warrior and a ruler in a land no Torfolk would ever see.

Tursla often wondered about that story. To her it had more meaning (though why she could not have said) than any of the other legends of her people. She wondered about the ruler who was half Tor. Did he ever feel the pull of his part blood? Did the moon at night and perhaps one of the lesser mists which might lay in his land awake in him some dream as real as the strange ones which haunted her? Sometimes she said his name as she danced.

"Koris! Koris!" She wondered if his mate among the stranger people held his heart in truth and if so, what was she like? Did he feel divided in his heart as Tursla did? She was by all the rights of blood fully of Tor and yet had this ache in her spirit which would never be stilled and which waxed stronger with every year of her life.

She grew out of childhood and she set herself obediently to the learning which she should have. Her fingers were clever at the loom and her weaving was smooth, with delicate pale patterns quite new among the Torfolk. Yet no one remarked upon any strangeness in those designs and she had long since ceased to mention her dreams. Lately she had indeed come to feel that there was a certain danger in allowing herself to become too deeply immersed in such. For sometimes they filled her with an odd feeling that if she was not careful she would lose herself in that other world, unable to return.

There was an urgency in those dreams, which plucked at her, wishing her to do this or that. The Torfolk themselves had strange powers. Among them such talent was not accounted in any way alien. Not all of them could use these—but that, too, was natural. Was it not true that all had each his or her own gift? That one could work in wood, another weave, a third prove a hunter or huntress skilled in tracking the quarry. Just so could Mafra, or Elkin, or Unnanna, transport a thing here or there by will alone. The range of such talents was limited, and the use of them drew upon the inner strength of the user to a high degree so that they were not for common employment.

In her dreams lately Tursla had not roamed afar in those strange landscapes. Rather she had come always to stand beside a pool of water, not murky or half overgrown with reed and plant as were the pools of Tormarsh, but rather a clear green blue.

More important, what she had felt in each of those recurring dreams was that the reddish sand which rimmed it around, as the old soft gold the Torfolk used would rim a gem, had great meaning. It was the sand which drew her—always the sand.

Twice with the coming of the Shining One in full sighting, she had awakened suddenly, not in Kelva's House but in the open, awakened and was afraid, for she knew not how she had come there. So mused that she might have wandered into one of the sucking bogs and been trapped forever. She came to be afraid of the night and sleep, although she did not share with any the burden she bore. It was as if one of the geas set by Volt himself bound her thoughts, laid a silencing finger across her lips. She grew unhappy and restless. The isle of the clan houses began to feel like a prison.

It was on the night of the highest and brightest coming of the Shining One that the women of the Torfolk must gather and bathe in the radiance of the One's lamp (for so was the body quickened and made ready that children might come forth) and there were too few children. But Tursla had never come to the Shining One's place of blessing, nor had this been urged upon her. This night when the others arose to go she stirred, meaning to follow. But out of the darkness there came a quiet voice:

"Tursla—"

She turned and saw now that some of the light insects had crawled from their crevices to form a circle on the wall, giving the light of their bodies to illuminate the woman sitting on the bed place there. Tursla bowed her head even though that woman could not see her.

"Clan Mother—I am here."

"It is not for you—"

Tursla did not need Mafra to tell her what was not for

her. But in her was the heat of shame, and also a little anger. For she had not chosen to be what she was; that fate had instead been thrust upon her from the hour of her birthing.

"What then is for me, Clan Mother? Am I to go unfulfilled and give no new life to this House?"

"You must seek your own fulfillment, moth-child. It lies not among us. Yet there is a purpose in what you are and a greater purpose in what awaits you—out there." Mafra's hand pointed to the open door of the House.

"Where do I find it, Clan Mother?"

"Seek and it will find you, moth-child. Part of it already lies within you. When that awakes you will learn and learning—know."

"This is all you will tell me then, Clan Mother?"

"It is all I can tell you. I can foresee for the rest. But between your spirit and mine rolls a mist thicker and darker than any Tormarsh gives birth to in the night. There is this—" She hesitated a long time before she spoke again.

"Darkness lies before us all, moth-child. We who foresee can see, in truth, only one of many paths. From every action there issues at least two ways, one in which one decision is followed, one in which it is made in opposition to that. I can see that such a decision now lies before the folk. Ill, great ill may come from it. There is one among us who chooses even now to ask for the Greater Power."

Tursla gasped. "Clan Mother, how can this thing be? The Greater Power comes not by a single asking. It is called only when there is danger to all whom Volt taught."

"True enough in the past, moth-child. But time changes all things and even a geas may fade to a dried reed easily snapped between the fingers. Such a calling needs blood to feed it. This I say to you now, moth-child. Go you out this night—not to seek the place of the Shining One—there are those there who tend strange thoughts within. Rather go where your dreams point you and do what you have learned within those dreams."

"My dreams!" Tursla wondered. "Are they of use, Clan Mother?"

"Dreams are born of thought—ours—or another's. All thought is of some use. That which entered into you at your birthing cannot be denied, moth-daughter. You are now ripe to seek it out and deal with it. Go. Now!"

Her last word had the force of an order. Tursla still hesitated however. "Clan Mother, have I your blessing, the good will of this House?"

When Mafra did not reply at once Tursla shivered. This was like being before the House and seeing the door barred, shutting one out of all touch with kin and heart-ties.

But Mafra was raising her hand.

"Moth-daughter, for what it may be worth to you as you go to fulfill the future laid before you, you have the goodwilling of this House. In return you must open your mind to patience and to understanding. No, I will not tell this foreseeing, for you must be guided not by any words of mine but by what comes from your own heart and mind when you are put to the test. Now, go. Trust to what the dreams have laid in your mind and go!"

Tursla went into the moonlight, into a world which was the black of bog-buried wood, the silver of mist and the pallid moonlight. But where was she to go? She flung out her arms. This night no moths came to dance with her.

Trust to what the dreams had laid in her mind. Would such point her in the direction she must take? Following the discipline of those who used the talent, she strove to clear her mind of all conscious thought.

Tursla began to walk, steadily, as one who has a purpose and a definite goal. She did not turn to the east, but faced westward, her feet on the blocks of one of the lesser roads. Though her eyes were open, she was not aware of what she saw, or even of her moving body. Somewhere before her lay the pool of her dreams and about it the all-important sand.

The mist clung about her like a veiling, now concealing what lay ahead, what she had left behind. She crossed one of the islands and another. The road failed at last but unerringly her feet found tussocks and hillocks of solid land to support her. At last the mist itself was tattered by a wind, strong, carrying in it a scent which was not that of the Tormarsh.

That wind awoke Tursla from her trance. She slowed to a halt at the highest point of a hillock covered with grass, shaped like the finger of a giant, pointing due west. The girl used both hands to keep the silk-soft strands of her hair out of her eyes. Now the moon was bright enough to show her that this ridge of land ran on to further rises beyond.

Then, she began to run—lightly. In her some barrier had broken and she was swallowed up by this great need to find what lay ahead; that which had waited for her so long—so very long!

Nor was she surprised to come at last into that very place of her dreams. Here was the clear pool, and the sand. Though in the moonlight the colors of her dream had been leached away, the sand was dark and so was the pool.

She tore off her robe, letting the length of cloth, spattered with the mud and slime of her marsh journey, fall from her. But she did not allow it to drop onto the sand. It was as if nothing must sully or mark that sand.

Nor did Tursla step upon its smooth surface. Rather she climbed a small rock just beyond its edge and from that sprang out, to dive into the waiting water. That closed about her body, neither cold nor hot, but rather silken smooth, caressing. It held her as might a giant hand cupped about her, soothing, gently. She surrendered to the water, floating on the surface of the pool.

Did she sleep then, or was she entranced by some

magic beyond the knowledge of those who had bred her? Tursla was never quite sure. But she was aware that there came a change within her. Doors opened and would never close again. What lay behind those doors she was not yet sure, but she was free to explore, to use. Only the first thing—

As she lay floating on the soft cushion of the water Tursla began to hum, and then to sing. There were no words in her song, rather she trilled as might a bird, first gently, quietly, then with a rising—call? Yes, a call!

Though she lay with her face turned up to the sky, the moon, the stars, those far-off night jewels, she was aware that about her was a stirring; not in the water which cradled her, but in the sand. It was arising, partly to her will, or rather her call, partly to the need of—of—someone.

Still Tursla sang. Now she dared to turn her head a little. There was a pillar of sand from which came a tinkling, a faint chiming, caused as one grain of its substance rubbed against the other in a whirl so fast it would seem that there was no sand but only a solid column of the dark grit. Louder grew Tursla's song, more and more the pillar thickened. It no longer reached skyward, rather kept to a height no greater than her own.

The contours of the pillar began to alter, to thin here, thicken there. It took on the appearance of a statue—crude at first, a head which was a ball, a body with no grace or shape to it. But still the sand changed, the figure it formed became more and more humanlike.

At last the sense of movement was gone. A figure stood there on rock from which her birth had drawn all the sleeping sand. Tursla trod water, drew into the shore, and climbed out to front this being for whom her song had opened the door and wrought a shaping.

Into her mind there came the name she must now speak—the name which would anchor this other, make sure and safe the bridge between her world and another one that she could not even imagine, so alien was its existence.

"Xactol!"

The sand woman's eyelids quivered, raised. Eyes which were like small red-gold coals of fire regarded Tursla. The girl saw the rise and fall of the stranger's breasts, the moonlight was reflected from a dark skin as smooth seeming as her own.

"Sister—"

The word from the other was hardly more than a whisper. It held in it still some of the sound of sand slipping over sand. But neither woman nor voice wrought any fear in Tursla. Her open hands went out, offering kinship to the sand woman. And hands as firm to the touch as her own caught and held, in a clasp which welcomed her in return.

"I have hungered—" Tursla said, realizing in this moment that she spoke the truth. Until those hands closed about hers there had been this deep lack, this hunger in her which she had not even truly known she carried until it was so assuaged.

"You have hungered," Xactol repeated. "Hunger no more, sister. You have come—you will have what you seek. You shall do thereafter what must be done."

"So be it."

Tursla took another step forward. Their hands fell apart, but their arms were wide. They embraced as indeed close kin welcomed one another after some long time apart. Tursla found tears on her cheeks.

2

WHAT is asked of me?" The girl drew back from that embrace, studied the face so close to her own. It was calm and still as the sand had been before her power had troubled it.

"Only what you yourself choose," came the murmured reply. "Open your mind, and your heart, sister-one, and it shall be shown to you in the appointed time. Now—" The right hand of the sand woman arose, and the slightly rough fingertips touched Tursla's forehead, held so for the space of several heart beats. Then they slid down, over the eyelids the girl instinctively closed and again held so, before going on to her lips. The touch withdrew, came again to her breast over the faster beating of her heart.

From each of those touches there issued an inflowing of strength so that Tursla's breathing quickened; she felt a kind of impatience, of a need to be busy, though with what task she could not have said. This inflow of energy made her flesh tingle, alive in a way she had never experienced.

"Yes—" her voice was swift, her words a little slurred. "Yes, yes! But how—and when? Oh, how and when, sand sister?"

"The how you shall know. The when is shortly."

"Then—then I shall find the door? I shall be free in the place of my dreaming?"

"Not so. For each her own place, sister-one. Seek not any gate until the time. There is that for you to do here and now. The future is the threaded loom upon which there is not yet any weaving. Sit before it, sister-kin, and fix the pattern you desire in your mind, then take up the shuttle and begin your task. In one sense we, in turn, are shuttles in the service of a greater purpose and we are moved to form a pattern we cannot see, for to its weaving we are too close. We can know the knotting and the breakage and perhaps even mend and reweave a little—but we are not that Great One who views it all. The time has come for you to set your portion of the pattern into the unseen design."

"But with you—"

"Younger sister, my bridging of the space between us cannot be held for long. We must hasten to the task set upon us both. Your mind is open, your eyes can now see, your lips are ready for the words, and your heart is prepared for what must come. Listen!"

So there by the dream pool Tursla listened. It was as if her mind was as porous and empty as one of those leaves of the draw-well, a sponge ready to be filled when one dipped it into water. She drew in strange words, and heard stranger sounds which she must shape her lips to form. Though that was a difficult thing, for it would seem that some of those sounds were never meant for her to utter. Her hands moved to pattern designs in the air. While following the movements of her fingers there remained for an instant thereafter a faint tracing of color—that which was red-brown like the sand which had formed the body of her teacher, or else green-blue as the pool beside which they sat.

Again she got to her feet and moved her body in the measures of a dance—to no music save that which seemed to be locked into her own mind. All this had a meaning, though she was not sure what that might be, save that what she learned now was her true birthright and also both a weapon and a tool.

At last her companion was silent and Tursla, now slumped upon the sand, felt as if that energy which had filled her had seeped away little by little, driven out of her again by the learning which she had so eagerly grasped.

"Sand sister, you have given me much. To what purpose? I cannot set aside Volt's ways and be ruler here."

"So was never intended. In what manner you can serve these people—that you will see from time to time. Give them what is best for their needs, but not openly, not claiming for yourself any powers. Give it only when such giving shall not be marked. There will be a time when your giving will set another part of the design to work—then, oh, younger sister, give with all your heart!"

She who answered to the name Xactol and whose true form and kind Tursla only dimly could perceive (and then only in her mind) arose. She began to turn, and that turning became faster and faster, a blur of movement. Just as she had put on the substance of the sand so now she lost it. Tursla covered her face with her hands, protecting her eyes against the trails of grit which spun out and away from what was becoming once more only a pillar.

The girl sank forward, feeling the drift of the sand over her. She was so tired, so very tired. Let her sleep now dreamlessly, she asked something beyond, the nature of which she recognized no more than she did the real form of Xactol. As the sand arose about her body, covered her lightly as might a soft cloth of spider silk, she indeed slept without dreams, even as she had petitioned to do.

It was the warmth of the midday sun beaming down upon her which roused her at last. She sat up, sand cascading from her. The colors of her dream were here, bright—green of pool, red of sand. But last night had not been a dream. It could not be! Tursla gathered up a palmful of the sand and allowed it to sift between her fingers. It was very fine, more like powder-ash than the grit she expected.

She brushed it from her body and then she knelt by the pool, troubling its mirror-smooth surface to wash the sand from her hand, her arms, her face, splashing the water over her body. The wind blew steadily and, after she had retrieved the robe she had discarded, she went on, past the rocks which rimmed the pool site.

So she came to the sea and for the first time looked out onto that part of the outside world which she had heard spoken of but had never seen. The play of the waves as they crashed in shore and broke, leaving that which had formed them to drain away, enchanted her. She ventured out upon the water-smoothed sand. The wind, so much stronger here, whipped her robe and tugged at her hair. She flung her arms wide to welcome the wind which had none of the marsh scent.

It was good to be so in the open. Tursla settled down on the sand to watch the breaking waves, singing softly to herself in wordless sounds which were not meant to evoke any answer but which were an attempt to match the music of wind and wave.

She saw shells in the sand and picked them up in wonder and delight. Like and yet unlike they were, for, seeing them closely, she could perceive that each had some small difference to set it apart from its kind. Not unlike those of her own species—each with some part of him or her which was only his or hers.

At last she reluctantly turned her face from the sea to the Tormarsh. The sun was already westering. For the first time Tursla wondered if any had sought her and what she must say when she returned which might cloak this thing which had happened to her.

Slowly she dropped her harvest of shells. There was no need to advertise her visit to a place which custom forbade any desire to see. But that was no reason why she might not come this way again. No rule of Volt said definitely that the sea was forbidden to those who followed his ancient rules of living.

Tursla found the marsh oddly confining as she passed swiftly along the trail toward the House island. So as she went she plucked certain leaves which were for dyeing, glad that fortune favored her in that several plants were of the Corfil—a rarity much prized as it produced a scarlet dye which was mainly used for the curtains of Volt's own shrine, thus was always eagerly sought.

As Tursla came along the westward road she had her skirt upheld into a bag, a goodly harvest in that. But one moved out to intercept her before she gained Kelva's House.

"So, moth-sister—you have thought to return to us? Did the winged ones tire of you so soon, night walker?"

Tursla tensed. Of all those she wished the least to meet Affric was the one. He leaned now on his spear, his eyes regarding her mockingly. There was a belt with a fringe of wak-lizard teeth about his middle, attesting to both his courage and skill. For only a man with both nearly supernormal reflex and cunning dared hunt those great lizards.

"Fair day to you, Affric." She did not warm her words. He flouted custom in his familiar greeting. The very fact he did so was disturbing.

"Fair day—" he repeated. "And what of the night, moth-sister? Others danced with the moon."

She was more than startled. For any Torman to speak of the Calling, and to such as her who had not named any man before Volt for a choosing!

He laughed. "Send me no spears from your eyes, moth-sister. Only daughters of Volt—true daughters—need make a man watch his tongue by custom." He took a step nearer. "No, you did not seek the moon last night, so then whom *did* you seek, moth-sister?" There was an ugly set to his mouth.

She did not make any answer. To do so would be indeed lessening herself in the eyes of all. For there were those who listened, if from a distance. What Affric said and did was a raw affront.

Tursla looked away and walked forward. He would not dare, she was sure, attempt to stop her. And he did not. But the fact that he could publicly address her in that manner was frightening. Also not one of those listening had spoken up in rebuke. It was almost as if this had been deliberately arranged to insult her. Her hands tightened on her improvised bag of leaves. Why—?

None stood before the door of Kelva's House and she walked head high, back straight, from the day into the dusk.

"Back at last, are you, then?" Parua, who tended the store cupboards and served as eyes for Mafra, regarded her sourly. "What have you there which needed to be cropped by night? A night when your duty lay elsewhere?"

Tursla shook out the leaves to fall upon a mat.

"Parua—do you really think that such as I should

dance for the Shining One's favor?" she asked in a voice from which she was able to keep all emotion.

"What do you mean? You are woman grown. It is your duty to bring forth children—if you can!"

"If I can—you yourself say that, Mother-one. Have I not heard otherwise all my life? That I am one who is not true Tor-born, and therefore I must not give life to a child because of the strangeness which is a part of me?"

"We grow too few—" Parua began.

"So thus the clan will welcome even the flawed? But that is not custom, Parua. And when custom is broke it must be done openly before Volt's shrine, with all his People assenting."

"If we grow few enough," Parua countered, "Volt will have none here to raise his name. There are to be changes, even in custom. There will be a Calling, a Great Calling. So it has been decided."

Tursla was astounded. Great Callings she had heard talked of; the last had been years ago when the Torfolk had allowed their stronghold to be invaded for a short time by strangers. It was then that the war leader of the outside lands had been prisoner here—together with her who, it was whispered, had been Koris' chosen lady. There had come no great ill from that, save that it had reached them later that, even as they had closed the marsh, so was now the outer world closed to them in turn. But even then there had been two minds about the right and the wrong of what they did.

It was true that births grew fewer each year. She had heard that Mafra and one or two of the other Clan Mothers speculated as to the reason for that. Perhaps even that their race was too old, had taken mates only among themselves too long so that their blood thinned, their creative powers were dimming. Thus it might be a fact that they would try to force her to their purposes. For it would only be by force that she would come to a Choosing—there was no Torman she had ever looked upon with favor. And now, she was not conscious she was pressing her hands against her breast; even less was she a daughter of Volt!

"So, moth-one," Parua continued, looking at her, Tursla thought, slyly and near maliciously, "your body being Tor-born, that might well serve Volt's purposes. Consider that."

Tursla turned quickly toward that wall alcove which was Mafra's. The Clan Mother seldom left her private niche nowadays. She had hands whose skill had outrun her vanished sight, and, by touch, alone, she made those useful to her people, shaping small pots to be fired, or spinning fibers more smoothly than any of her house descendants could.

Now Tursla saw that those hands lay strangely still, loosely clasped in the old woman's lap. Her head was held up, just slightly a-tip as if she listened. As the girl stood hesitantly before her, uncertain if she dared break into that trancelike state, Mafra spoke:

"Fair day, moth-child. Fair be your going, fair be your coming, firm your steps upon the crossing places, full your hands with good labor, your heart with warmth, your mind with thoughts which will serve you."

Tursla sank to her knees. That was no common greeting! It was—it was that given to any clan daughter who knew she was at last with child! But—why—

Mafra raised one hand, stretched it forth. Tursla quickly bent her head to kiss those long, age-thinned fingers.

"Clan Mother—I am not—not as you have welcomed me," she said hurriedly.

"You are filled," Mafra said. "Not all filling is with a life which will separate itself in time from yours and become all in all to itself. There is life within you now and, in due time, it will come forth. If it does so in a different fashion, then that is the will of Volt, or of what power stood behind him when he came to lead our people up out of savagery. It shall be with you as with the Filled. So shall it be said in this House and Clan. And if it is said so among those who are your own, then it will be the same elsewhere among the Folk."

"But, Clan Mother, if my body does not contain a life they will understand, and the time passes when I should bear the fruit which House and Clan need, then will there not be a reckoning? What can be said then for one who had misled House and Clan?"

"There will be no misleading. There is set before you a task, that you shall do by virtue of the life you hold. What will follow from that will lead the two roads of which I told you—one this way—" Her hand swept to the right. "One that way." She indicated the left. "I cannot foresee past that choice which shall be yours. But I think what you will choose shall be of wisdom. Parua—" she raised her voice and the other woman came near, going to her knees as did Tursla.

"Parua, this Tursla, moth-daughter, is Filled and so let House and Clan be guarded according to custom."

"But she—there was no Choosing, no moon dance," Parua protested.

"She was sent out by my wisdom, Parua, do you question that?" Mafra's tone was chill. "Into the night she went with my blessing. What she sought—and found—was by the will of Volt as revealed to me in foresight. She has returned, filled. I recognize it so, and, by my Volt-given gift, I proclaim that now."

Parua's mouth opened again as if she would protest and then it closed. Clan Mother had spoken, she had said that Tursla was Filled. And, if she who had the farsight for her own said this, then no one dared question the truth of it. Parua bowed her head submissively and kissed the hand held out to her. She backed away, her gaze still on Tursla, and the girl sensed that she might have to admit openly Mafra's judgment was right, but her own reservations were still stubbornly alive.

"Clan Mother," the girl said quickly, as soon as she

was sure Parua must be beyond hearing the murmur of a voice she held to the edge of a whisper, "I do not know what is expected of me."

"This much I can tell you, moth-child. There will soon come one whom Unnanna will summon—not with voice or message—but by the Calling itself. He has such blood ties that this calling can catch and hold him as one snared in a net. But the purpose for which they would bring him—" There was a new note in Mafra's voice. "That is, in the end, death. If his blood is spilt upon the ground before Volt's shrine, that blood shall call aloud. And *its* calling will bring the forces of the outer world upon us with fire and steel. Volt's people will die and Tormarsh shall be a barren and cursed place.

"We count our children as the fruit of all of us together. No one claims any child as his or hers alone. But this is not the way of the Outside. There they hold not to House Clans, but are split into smaller gatherings. There a child has but two on which to call in trouble—she who gave him birth and he who filled her at some time of choosing. This seems strange and wrong to us, a breaking up of the bonds which are our strength. But it is their way of life.

"However, this different way also gives other bonds which we do not understand. Strange indeed are these bonds. Let anyone there raise hand against a child—and the mother-one and he who filled her will take up the hunt with the fury of a wak-lizard who sights man. The one whom Unnanna would summon for her purposes is son to a man who is perhaps the greatest threat the Outside can raise against us. I fear for our people, moth-child.

"It is true that we grow fewer, that only a hand-finger count of children may be born after any choosing. But that is our sorrow and perhaps the will of life itself. To bring in blood-giving—no."

"And my part in this, Clan Mother?" Tursla asked. "Do you wish me to stand against Unnanna then? But even though you have named me Filled, who would listen to my words? She is a Clan Mother, and, since you go no more to the moon dance, it is she who leads."

"That is so. No, I lay no task on you, moth-daughter. When the time comes for you to do as you must, you yourself will know it, for that knowledge will be inside you. Give me now your hands."

Marfa held out both of her own palm up, and Tursla placed hers thereupon, palm down. Again, just as it had been when she and Xactol had communed with one another, there was a feeling of quickening within her, a stirring of energy she longed to use but did not yet know how to put to any testing.

"So—" Mafra's voice was but a whisper, as if this were a very secret thing. "I knew that you were from elsewhere at your birthing, but this is indeed a strange thing."

"Why did this happen to *me,* Clan Mother?" Tursla voiced her old protest.

"Why do many things happen—those for which we can see no meaning or root? Somewhere there is a master pattern of which we must all be a part."

"So did *she* say also—"

"She? Ah, think of her, picture her in your mind, moth-child!" There was an eagerness in Mafra now. "See her for me!" she ordered.

Obediently Tursla pictured the spinning pillar of sand, and she who had been formed by that.

"Indeed you have been Filled, moth-child," sighed Mafra after a long moment. "Filled with such knowledge that perhaps you alone in this world can begin to comprehend. I wish we might talk of this and of your learning, but that cannot be. For it was not meant for me to gain any other than I have. Do not share it, moth-daughter, even if you are so moved. A basket woven to hold loquth seeds, no matter how skillfully made, cannot carry water which is intended to fill a fired clay jar. Go you now and rest. And live after the manner of the Filled until the time comes and you know it."

So dismissed, Tursla went to her own portion of the clan house—that small section given to her when she was judged more girl than child. She pulled close the woven reed mats which made it into a private place and sat upon her double cushion to think.

Mafra's pronouncement would not only excuse her from any moon dancing, but would speedily put to punishment any speeches such as Affric had made to her, any gesture even from any man of any House. She would be excused also from certain kinds of work. The only difficulty she might face at first would be that she could not leave the settlement island alone from now on. The Filled were ever under guard for their own protection.

She ran her hands down her own slender body. How long before the fact that her belly did not swell would be noted? The women were sharp-eyed about such matters, since birth was their great mystery and they were jealous of the keeping of it. Perhaps she could devise some sort of padding within her robe. Also the Filled often had unusual desires for different food, altered their habits of living. Maybe she could turn such fancies to her account.

But eventually the time would come when she would be found out. Then what? To her knowledge no one among the Folk had ever made a false statement concerning such a thing. It would strike at the very root of all of their long-held beliefs. What punishment could be harsh enough for that? Why had Mafra done this?

No one of the Torfolk, Tursla was sure, would accept the idea of a Filling with knowledge. And Mafra—she, Tursla, had not made the claim—it had been the Clan Mother. Such a deliberate flouting of custom, just so that she would be left to hold herself ready for this other action of which Mafra had only given her hints.

A Calling for the purpose of blood. Tursla drew a deep breath. If Mafra meant by that what Tursla could guess, then that was a great breaking of custom also. Sacrifice—of a—*man?* But there were no such sacrifices ever made to Volt; a man whose killing might bring down a doom of ending on Tormarsh and Torfolk. What part would she have?

She could—no, something within Tursla forbade that for now. This was no time to open that door in her mind which guarded what she had learned from Xactol.

Patience must be hers and this role must be played well. The girl drew aside her private curtain and arose. What she wanted most was food and drink. Suddenly she was very hungry and thirst made her mouth dry. She started for the supply jars, intent only on tending her body, sternly closing down the whirl of thoughts in her mind.

3

THREE days went by; Tursla spent the time quietly at work with her spindle in her hands, but, more to her own desires, also with her thoughts. Mafra's word had been accepted by the House clan—how could it not be? She was given the deference accorded the Filled, served first with the choicest of foods, left to her own thoughts since she seemed to wish it so.

But on the third day the girl aroused from the half trance in which she had allowed herself to drift as she attempted to sort out and store what she had learned. Much of what she discovered lay only in hints. Yet she was sure that such hints were only way markers to deeper knowledge that she must have and that she still could not now remember. The struggle to do so only made her tense and restless, her head ache, and sleep hard to come by.

Nor could she summon up any of her dreams. When she slept now it was fitfully, more like a light doze from which she could be awakened by such a small thing as a sleeper in the next mat place turning over.

Knowledge was of no help if one could not tap it, Tursla believed with an ever-growing distress. What lay before her?

Wishing to be alone with that spark of fear which was fast growing into a flame, she arose from her stool before the loom and went from the Kelva's House. She neared the group of women before she noted them, so entangled was she in her thoughts.

Unnanna stood there, the others facing her as if she were laying upon them some duty. Now her gaze rested on Tursla, and a small smile—a smile which held no kindness in it—lifted the corners of her thin-lipped mouth.

"Fair be the day—" She raised her voice a little, plainly to address the girl. "Fair be your going. Fair be the end of the waiting for you."

"I give thanks for your good wishing, Clan Mother," Tursla replied.

"You have not spoken before Volt the name of your Choosing—" Unnanna's smile grew wider. "Are you not proud enough for that, Filled One?"

"If I choose to spread Volt's cloak about me and am challenged for so doing," Tursla returned, hoping to hold her pretense of serenity, "then there must be a changing of custom."

Unnanna nodded. Her outer pose was one of good will. It was not unheard of that some maid at her first Filling chose not to announce the name of her partner in the moon ritual. Though generally it was a matter of common knowledge as soon as her Clan Mother proclaimed the fact to the satisfaction of the clan.

"Wear Volt's cloak then, moth-daughter. In days to come you will have sisters in aplenty." There was an assenting murmur from the women about her, an eager assenting.

But Unnanna was not yet through with Tursla.

"Do not go a-roaming, moth-daughter. You are precious to us all now."

"I go only to the fields, Clan Mother. To Volt's shrine that I may give thanks."

That was a worthy enough reason for leaving the place of Houses and no one could deny her such a small journey. She passed Unnanna and started down the moss-greened pavement of the ancient road. Nor did any follow her there, for again custom decreed that one who so sought Volt's shrine should be granted privacy for any petition or thanks the worshipper desired to raise.

Volt's shrine—time had not dealt well with it. Walls had sunk into the ever-hungry softer ground of the marsh, or else tumbled the stone of their making across pavement, because no man could put hand to any rebuilding here.

For these were the very stones which Volt himself had laid hands upon in the very long ago, set up to make his shelter. It had been a large hall, Tursla guessed, as she traced the lines of those crumbling walls. But by all legend Volt himself was larger in body than any of the Torfolk.

Now she wove a way between those crumbling walls. Under her feet the earth and stone was beaten hard into a path during the countless years Torfolk had sought comfort here. Thus she came into the inner room. Though the roof was gone, and the light of sun shone down upon what was the very heart of Volt's domain—a massive chair seemingly carved of wood (but such a wood—strange to Tormarsh —which no damp could rot). On either side of the chair stood tall vases wrought of stone and set in them, ready for any call to Volt, the quick firing pith of those trees waterlogged in the marsh whose spongy outer bark could be flaked away, leaving an inner hardness which burned so brightly. Here were no light insects, but fire which destroyed and yet was so brilliant in its death.

For a long moment Tursla hesitated. What she would do now was allowed by custom, yes, but only if one was greatly moved by some happening which could not be understood and from which there seemed to be no answer in any human mind. Was that her case now? She believed she could claim it was.

Tursla put out her hand, setting her palm flat on the petrified wood of the chair's wide arm. Then she drew herself up the one shallow step which raised the seat above the flooring of that near destroyed hall, and seated herself upon the chair of Volt.

It was as if she was a small child settling herself into the chair of some large-boned adult. Tall as she was among the Torfolk, here her feet did not meet the pavement as she wriggled back until her shoulders touched the wood behind her. To lay her hands out upon the arms was a strain but this she did before she closed her eyes.

Did Volt indeed listen from wherever he had gone when he withdrew from Tormarsh? Did that essence of Volt which might just still exist somewhere in the world care now what happened to those he had once protected and cherished? She had no answer to those questions, nor could any within the bounds of Tor give her more than such guesses as she herself might make.

"Volt—" her thought shaped words she did not speak aloud—"we give you honor and call upon your good will in times of need. If you still look upon us— No, I do not cry now for help as a helpless child calls upon those of the clan house. I wish only to know who or what I am, and how I must or may use what has Filled me as Mafra swears I have been Filled. It is no child that I carry in truth; perhaps it is more—or less. But I would know!"

She had closed her eyes, and her head rested now upon the back of the chair. There was the faint scent of the tree candles from either hand, less than they would give off at their igniting. She had seen the Clan Mothers hold such before them and the smoke had wreathed them around while they chanted.

She—

Where was she? Green grass grew out before her, a fan

which stretched to the feet of rises of gray rock. Scattered in the grass, as if someone had carelessly flung wide a handful of bright and shining stones, were flowers, their petals wide, their shapes and colors differing as the shells on the shore had differed. Above the flowers fluttered moths—or winged things which resembled moths. Those were also brightly colored, sometimes bearing more than one shade or hue on their wings.

There was nothing of Tormarsh in this place. Nor was it, she was sure, another sighting of her dream land. She willed to move forward and her will gave birth to action, for she passed, not on her feet step by step, but rather drifted in the air, as might those flying things.

So Tursla was wafted by her will to those rocks which rose above the grass. Again her desire lifted her higher, to the topmost pinnacle of the rocks. Now she gazed down into a greater valley wherein there ran a river. Across that wide ribbon of water spanned a bridge of stone, and the bridge served a road which ran across the green of the land.

While on the road, approaching the bridge, there was—

Horse—that was a horse. Though Tursla had never seen such an animal she knew it. And on the horse—a man.

Her will to see drew him to her sight in a strange way, though in truth she had not moved from her place on the hill, nor had he yet come upon the bridge. Still she saw him as clearly as if he and his mount were within such distance that she could put forth a hand and lay it on the horse's shoulder.

He wore metal like a silken shirt, for it had been fashioned of small rings linked one upon the other. Above that a cloak dropped down his shoulders, fastened at his throat with a large brooch set with dull green and gray stones. There was a belt with like stones about his waist and from that hung a sheathed sword.

His head was covered with a cap also of metal, but this was a solid piece, not chained rings. It had a ridge beginning above the wearer's forehead and running back to a little below the crown of his head. This ridge possessed sockets into which were fastened upstanding feathers of a green color.

But Tursla's attention only marked that in passing, for it was the man himself she would see. So she studied the face beneath the shadow of the cap.

He was young, his skin was fair, hardly darker than a Torman's. There was strength in his face, as well as comeliness. He would make a good friend or clan brother, she decided, and a worse enemy.

As he rode he had been looking ahead, not truly as if he saw the road, but rather as if he were busied with his thoughts, and those not pleasant ones. Now, suddenly, his head jerked up a fraction and his eyes were aware—and they looked upon her! While a quick frown marked a sharp line between his brows.

Tursla saw his lips move, but she heard nothing, if he had spoken. Then one hand lifted, was held out toward her. At that same moment all was gone. She whirled away in a dizzy, giddy retreat. When she opened her eyes she sat once more in Volt's chair, and she saw nothing save the time breached walls of his shrine. But now—now she knew! Volt had indeed answered her wish! She was linked with the horseman and in no easy way. Their meeting lay before her and from it would come danger and such a trial of strength as she could not now measure.

Slowly the girl arose, drawing a deep breath, as one preparing for a struggle, though she knew that the time for that was not yet. He had been aware of her, that horseman, nor did he in the mind's eye grow blurred with the passing of moments. No, somewhere he rode and was real!

In the later afternoon she sought out Mafra again. Perhaps the Clan Mother could or would give her no answers, yet she must share Volt's vision with someone. And in all this place only Mafra did she trust without reservation.

"Moth-child—" Though Mafra turned sightless eyes in her direction never was she mistaken concerning the identity of those who came to her. "You are a seeker—"

"True, Clan Mother. I have sought in other places and other ways, and I do not understand. But this I have seen; from Volt's own chair did I venture out in a strange way beyond explaining." Swiftly she told Mafra of the rider.

For a long moment the Clan Mother sat silent. Then she gave a quick nod as if she affirmed some thought of her own.

"So it begins. How will it then end? The foreseeing reaches not to that. He whom you saw, moth-child, is one tied to us by part blood—"

"Koris!"

Mafra's hand, where it rested upon her knee, tightened, her head jerked a fraction as if she strove to avoid a blow.

"So that old tale still holds meaning," she said. "But Koris was not your rider. This is he whom I told you about—the child of those who would move mountains with spells, slay men with steel, that naught comes to harm him. He is Koris' son, and his name is Simond, which in part was given by that outlander who fought so valiantly beside his father to free Estcap of the Kolder."

Mafra paused and then continued. "If you wonder how these things are known: when I was younger, strong in my powers, I sometimes visited in thought beyond the edge of Tormarsh, even as this day you have done. It was Koris' friend Simon Tregarth who was brought hither through strangers' magic and delivered to his enemies. Also with him was she who was Koris' choice of mate after the manner of the outlanders. Then we chose ill, so that in turn the outlands set their own barriers against us. We cannot go, even if we wish, outside the Marsh, nor can anyone come to us."

"Is the seashore also barred, Clan Mother?"

"Most of the shore, yes. One may look at it, but the mist which rises between is a wall as firm as the stone ones about us now."

"But, Clan Mother, I have trod the sand beside the sea, found shells within it—"

"Be silent!" Mafra's voice was a whisper. "If this much was given you let no other know it. The time may come when it will be of worth to you."

Tursla allowed her voice to drop also. "Is that a foreseeing, Clan Mother?"

"Not a clear one, I only know that you will have need for all your strength and wit. This I can tell you, Unnanna calls tonight and, if she is answered, then—" Mafra lifted her hands and let them fall again to her lap. "Then I leave it to your wit, moth-daughter. To your wit and that which is in you from that other place."

She gave the sign of dismissal and Tursla went to her own place and took up her spindle, but if any watched her for long they would know that she had little profit from her labors.

Night came and around her the women of the clan stirred and spoke to one another in whispers. None addressed her, being Filled she was carefully set apart that nothing might threaten that which she was supposed now to carry. Nor did they approach Mafra either, rather ranged themselves with Parua and slipped quietly away.

There were no guards set about the House isle, save on the two approaches by which a wak-lizard might come. No one would watch those bound for the Shrine in any case, so that Tursla, pulling a drab cloak about her, even over the soft silver of her hair, thought she could follow behind without note.

Once more she crept along the same path she had

taken earlier that day. Those ahead carried no lighted torches; there was no gleam save the moonlight, but she saw that every house must be represented. But this could not be a complete Calling after all, for there were no men. Or so she had thought until she caught sight of moon gleam on a spear head and noted those cloaked men, ten of them, standing in a line facing the Chair. While in that seat huddled a figure who raised her face to the light even as Tursla found a hiding place back behind a pile of fallen rock.

Unnanna sat in the place of Seeking. Her eyes were closed, her head turned slowly from side to side. Those standing below began to croon, first so softly that it was hardly to be heard over the lap of water, the wing rustle of some flying thing. Then that hum grew stronger—no words, but rather a sound which made Tursla's skin tingle, her hair move against her neck. She found that her head was swinging also in the same way as Unnanna's and, at that moment, realized the danger which lay in being trapped into becoming a part of what they would do here.

She raised her hands and covered her eyes so that she might not see that swaying, while she thought, as one catches a line of safety thrown wide, of the sand sister, or the racing sea waves. Though a pulse now beat within her, Tursla also fought her own body; and, without being fully conscious of what she did, she rose to her full height and began to move her feet, not in the pattern Unnanna's head had set, but in another fashion, to break for herself the spell the Clan Mother was raising.

There was power building here; her body answered to it. Force pressed in upon her like a burden, trying to crush her. Still Tursla countered that, her lips moving in words which sprang from behind those doors in her mind which she had earlier tried to open and could not. Only such danger as this would free them for her.

She opened her eyes. All was as before—save that Unnanna had moved forward on the chair of Volt. One after another those waiting men came to her. She touched them on the forehead, on the eyes. Then each made way for his fellow. From the tips of those fingers which she used to touch them came small cones of light, and those who stepped back from her anointing carried now a mark on the forehead of the same eerie radiance.

When all had been so marked they turned and made their way from the hall, the women giving back to open their path. As they passed by Tursla she saw that their eyes were set and they stared as men entranced. Their leader was Affric; and those who followed him were all young, the most skilled of the hunters.

When they had gone from her sight, Tursla looked back to the hall. Once more Unnanna sat with closed eyes. Power surged; it came from each of them there. Unnanna in some manner drew that unseen energy from them, consolidated it, shaped from it a weapon, aimed that weapon, and sent out on course.

Tursla was not one of them. Now she stood tense, seeking within herself something she sensed must be ready to answer her call. She used her thought to mould it, thinking of what she would hurl—not as the spear Unnanna's wish had fostered—no, what then? A shield? She did not hold strength enough in herself to interpose any lasting barrier. But perhaps there was something else she could mind-fashion. She thought of the likenesses of all the weapons known to the Torfolk, and fastened in the space of a breath upon—a net!

Clenching her hands until her nails cut into her own flesh, the girl centered all of her unknown energies, untested to their full extent since that night by the pool, and thought of a net—a net to entangle feet, to impede those who marched by night, those who would set a trap. Let they themselves be now entrapped.

As blood draining from a grievous, mortal wound, the energy Tursla summoned seeped from her. If she could only call upon that greater well of strength which Unnanna could tap for herself! But a net—surely a net! Let it catch about the feet of Affric; let it ensnare him where he would go. Let it *be!*

The girl stumbled back against the wall, weakness in her legs, her arms hanging heavily by her sides, as she had neither the will nor strength now to raise them. With her back against the rough stone she slipped downward, the ruins rising around her like a protective shield. Her head fell forward on her breast as she made her last attempt to send what remained in her to reinforce the net her vivid mind picture had set about Affric's stumbling feet.

It was cold and she was shivering. Dark lay about her, and she no longer heard that sound which had built up the energy for Unnanna's mind dart. Rather what came was the whisper of wings. Lifting her head, Tursla looked upward to the night sky above the pocket in the ruins where she rested.

There were two moths a-dance, their beautiful shadowy wings outlined with the faint night shine which was theirs when they flew in the deep dark. Back and forth they wove their meetings and partings. Then the larger spiralled down, and for just a moment it clung to the dew-wet robe on her breast, fanning its wings, tiny eyes which were alight looking into hers . . . or so it seemed to the bemused girl.

"Sister," Tursla whispered. "I give you greeting. Fair flying for your night. May the blessing of Volt himself be with you!"

The moth clung for another instant and then flew away. Stiffly Tursla pulled herself up. Her body ached as if she had done a full day's stooping at the loom, or at harvest in the fields. She felt stupid, also, when she tried to think clearly.

She tottered along, one hand against the wall to support her. There was no one here—Volt's chair was empty. For a moment she wavered as she gazed upon that seat. Should she try again? There was a longing in her, a strange longing. She wanted to see how the rider fared.

What had Mafra named him? Simond, an odd name. Tursla repeated it in a whisper as if a name could be tasted, said to be either sweet or sour.

"Simond!"

But there was no answer. And she knew that, even if she mounted Volt's chair again, this time there would be no answer. What she had done or tried to do here this night had exhausted for a time her power. She had nothing to aid her to reach out.

Walking slowly, catching now and then on some half-broken wall or pile of stones, she won out of Volt's hall. But she needed to sit and rest several times before she got back to the clan house.

Then it took all the skill she had to be able to make her way through Mafra's house to her own corner. Should she tell the Clan Mother what had been done this night? Perhaps—but not in this hour. To rouse any of the nearby sleepers would be the last thing she wished.

She lowered herself onto the sleeping mat. In her mind then there was only one picture, already becoming fuzzed with sleep—the image of Affric fighting a web about his feet, his sneering mouth open as if he shouted aloud in fear. Though she was not conscious of it, Tursla smiled as she fell asleep.

4

MIST was heavy about the island where the ancient clan houses stood, hanging curtains between house and house, turning those who went outside into barely seen shadows moving in and around through the fog. The moisture in it pearled on every surface in large drops which gathered substance and then trickled downward. That same damp clung to skin, matted hair, made clammy all garments.

Such fen mists had been known to Tursla all her life.

Still this one was far thicker than any she could remember; and it would seem her uneasiness was matched within the clan house, for no hunters went forth, while those within stirred higher the fires, drawing in closer for the light and heat. Perhaps they did this not for any warmth to send their garments steaming but because the very brightness of the flames themselves had a kind of cheer.

Tursla had sought out Mafra again. But the Clan Mother appeared unwilling to talk. Rather she sat very still, her blind eyes staring unwinking at the fire and those about it, though she made no move to add herself to the circle of company there. At length Tursla's foreboding of a shadow to come made her greatly daring and she touched timidly one of Mafra's hands where it lay palm up on the woman's lap.

"Clan Mother—?"

Mafra's head did not turn, yet Tursla was sure she knew that the girl was beside her. Then she spoke, in so low a voice Tursla was sure it could not carry beyond her own ears.

"Moth-child, it comes close now—"

What—the fog? Or that other thing which Tursla felt, though she had no part of Mafra's powers.

"What may be done, Clan Mother?" The girl shifted her body restlessly.

"Nothing to stop these witless ones. Not now." There was a bitter note in that. "You cannot trust in anything or anyone save yourself, moth-child. The ill act has been begun."

At that moment there sounded, through the doorway of the clan house (like the bellow of some great beast), a call which brought Tursla and all the rest sheltering within to their feet. Never before had the girl heard such a sound.

Then the cries of those by the fire, who were now all turning to the mist-hidden doorway, running toward that, made her understand. That had been the Great Alarm, which had never been sounded in her lifetime, perhaps even in the lifetimes of all now here. Only some action of overpowering peril could have brought the sentries on the outer road to give that alert.

"Girl!" Mafra was also standing. Her hand tightened about Tursla's arm. "Give me your strength, daughter. Ill, thrice ill, has been this thing! Dark the ending thereof!"

Then she, who so seldom left her own alcove nowadays, tottered beside Tursla. At first her slight body bore heavily upon the girl's support. Then she straightened, and it appeared that strength returned to her limbs as she took one step and then another.

They came into the open but there the mist was very thick. Figures could only be half seen and that just when close by. Mafra's pressure on her arm drew Tursla in a way which it would seem the blind woman knew well.

"Where—?"

"To Volt's Hall," Mafra answered her. "They would carry this through to the end—profane the very place which is the heart of all we are, have ever been. They will slay, in the name of Volt. And, if such a slaying comes, why, then their own deaths must follow! They have decided upon their road—and evil is the end of it!"

"To stop—" Tursla got out no more than those two words when her companion interrupted her.

"Stop—yes. Girl, open now your inner thoughts, give yourself freely to what may lie within you. That is the only way! But it must be quick."

She had never believed that Mafra's strength might still be such as to send the Clan Mother at so fast a pace. There were others around them, all were heading in the same direction. The stones of the ancient road under their feet were slimed with water, yet Mafra, for all her lack of sight, made no missteps.

About them loomed the broken walls of Volt's Hall. Still on they pressed, until they were in the place of the chair. Here through some trick perhaps of emanations from the ancient stones themselves, the mist thinned, raised, to lay above their heads like a ceiling, yet allow them full sight of all which was below.

Those torches set upright in the vases to either side of the chair were ablaze. Other brands were in the hands of those standing along the walls. In Volt's chair sat Unnanna once again. Braced with a hand on either arm of the giant seat she leaned forward, an eager, avid expression on her face.

Those she so eyed were gathered immediately below. Affric stood there; but he had not the arrogant pride which he had worn so confidently when he had strode forth from this place at the Clan Mother's bidding. He was pale of countenance, and his clothing was smeared with swamp slime, while one arm was bound to his side with vine fiber, as if bones had been broken that must be straightened and protected for healing.

Seeing him so brought a picture into Tursla's mind: that of Affric unsure of foot as if he had been caught in some snare, stumbling and falling, falling against one of the upright pillars which bore Volt's own face deep carven. Her wish—dream! Had that indeed left Affric like this?

If so, she had not done all that she had wished. For between two of Affric's followers was the stranger she had seen mounted on the road, the one Mafra had named Simond.

His helm was gone, so his fair hair, near as bleached as her own, shown in the torch light. But his head rolled limply forward on his breast. It was plain his legs would not support him and he had to be kept on his feet by the help of his guards. There was a matting of blood in his hair.

"Done!" Unnanna's voice rang out silencing the murmurs of those gathered there, producing a quiet through which the sounds of the marsh life without could be heard. "Done, well done! Here is that which shall give us new life! Did I not say it? Into our hands has Volt brought this one that we may drink of his strength and—"

Tursla did not know if she had made some signal but

the guards suddenly released their hold upon Simond and he fell forward. There must have remained some spark of awareness in him, for he put out his hands, though he was on his knees, to catch at the edge of the step on which the chair stood. Now he raised his head by visible effort and lurched forward and up, for he grasped at the chair itself, and dragged himself to his feet.

The girl could not see his face. Without knowing she had done so, she broke from Mafra's side and edged along, pushing by others, seeing none of them, coming closer to where the captive stood.

"What do you want of me?" he asked as he edged around, so that he half faced the Torfolk.

Affric took a step forward and spat. His mouth was a vicious slit.

"Half-blood! We want from you what you have no right to—that part which is of Tormarsh!"

There was a sound like the far-off squall of a wak-lizard. Unnanna laughed.

"They are right, half-blood. You are part of Tor. Let that part now give us what we need." Her tongue curled over her lower lip, swept from side to side as if she licked moss-honey and savored the sweetness of that delicacy.

"We need life," she leaned closer to the arm of the chair where Simond still had his hand, using that hold to support him. "Blood is life, half-breed. By Volt's word we dare not take it from our own kind, and we cannot take from one who is full outlander, for between the twain of us there is no common heritage. You are neither one nor the other; therefore you are ripe for our purpose."

"You know of what House I am." Simond held his head high and now his eyes caught the Clan Mother's in a compelling stare. "I am the son of he who took Volt's axe—by Volt's own wishing. Do you think then that Volt will look with approval on the fate you would give me?"

"Where is the axe now?" Unnanna demanded. "Yes, Koris of Gorm took it; but is it not now gone from him?

Volt's favor follows the axe. With it destroyed, he has lost interest in you."

The murmur which had begun at Simond's words died away. Tursla pushed closer. She had done as Mafra had urged, laid her mind open to whatever power lay in her. But she felt no swelling of force, no new warmth within. How then could she stop this thing which was of dark evil and which would indeed bring an end to the Torfolk?

"Take him—" Unnanna was on her feet, her arms spread wide. In her pale face there was exultation.

Tursla moved. Those about her were so intent upon the scene before them that they were not aware of her until she was through their line and had shoved past one of Affric's followers to reach Simond. Once there she stationed herself before him, facing the man moving in to obey Unnanna's order.

"Touch me if you dare," she said. "I am one Filled. And this one I take under my protection."

The nearest man had raised his hands to sweep her aside. Now he stood as rooted as one of the dead trees, while those behind him retreated a step or two. Unnanna leaned closer from her perch upon the chair.

"Take him!" She lifted her hand as if to strike Tursla in the face, so drive her away. The girl did not flinch.

"I am one Filled," she repeated.

The Clan Mother's face twisted with stark rage. "Stand aside," she hissed as might one of the pallid vipers of the deep muck. "In Volt's name, I order, stand aside! And if you are truly Filled—"

"Ask it of Mafra!" challenged the girl. "She has said it—"

"Shall it be needful then—" Mafra's voice rang out from the gathering of the Torfolk, "for a Clan Mother to state this again? Do you aver that on such a thing there can be a false swearing, Unnanna?"

The crowd stirred, fell away to form a lane. Along that Mafra advanced. She did not totter now, but walked as firmly as if she could indeed see what lay before her, bumping into no one, but keeping straight course down that open way until she, too, came to stand before the chair of Volt.

"You take much upon you, Unnanna, very much."

"You take more!" Unnanna shrilled. "Yes, once you sat here and spoke for Volt, but that day is past. Rule your own clan house as you may until the messenger of Volt comes to call you. But do not try to speak for all in this time."

"I say no more than is my right, Unnanna. If I say this house daughter is Filled, then do you deny it?"

Unnanna's mouth worked. "It is your word before Volt, then? You take on you much in that, Mafra. This one came not to the moon dancing—who then filled her?"

"Unnanna—" Mafra raised her right hand. Her fingers moved in the air as if gathering threads of mist and rolling them into a ball. In the silence which now fell between them, she made a tossing motion, as if what she had pulled out of invisibility had indeed substance. Unnanna shrank back until her shoulders touched the high back of the chair.

Suddenly she flung both hands up before her face. From behind that slight defense she sputtered words which had no meaning as far as Tursla was concerned. But that Unnanna was, for the moment, at bay, the girl understood. Turning a little she caught at Simond's arm which was closest to her.

"Come!" she ordered.

Whether they could win from Volt's Hall, and if so what she might do then, Tursla had no idea. For the moment all she could think of was to get away from this place where only the slender thread spun by custom had so far protected her.

She did not even look to Simond. But he apparently yielded to her urging, for when she stepped away from Volt's chair he did in truth come with her. Hoping that he would continue to be able to stay on his feet, Tursla led him forward.

Affric moved into their path. His good arm raised, he balanced a short stabbing spear. Tursla met his gaze squarely and moved closer to Simond. She said no word but her intention was plain. Any attack upon the stranger would be met by her. To raise a weapon against a Filled One—Affric snarled, but he gave way when she did not, just as those others made a path for her, even as they had for Mafra.

Somehow they reached the outer wards of the Hall. Tursla was breathing as fast as if she had run all the way. Where now—? They could not return to the clan houses. Not even Mafra could hold back the weight of outraged custom long enough for Simond to escape. And the trails out from here would be speedily covered.

The trail to the pool, the sea! That flashed into her mind even as if some voice out of the mist had reminded her. For the first time she spoke to her companion:

"We dare not stay here. I do not think even Mafra can long hold Unnanna. We must go on. Can you do it?"

She had noted that he staggered though he kept his feet. Now she could only hope.

"Lady—by the Death of the Kolder—I shall try!"

So they went into the boiling of that strange, heavy mist. She could not even see beyond the length of an outheld hand before her. This was the strongest folly. If they missed the road, the step-tussocks farther on, the marsh itself might claim them and no one would ever know how they passed.

Still she walked, and brought him with her. After a space they went side by side, as she drew his arm about her shoulders, took a measure of his weight. He muttered now and then—broken words without any meaning.

They were well away from the clan-house isle when once again the deep-throated alarm trumpet of the Torfolk aroused echoes across the marsh. Now they could expect pursuit. Would this mist which enclosed them work as well to delay the hunters? She feared because such as Affric knew the outer ways of the Tormarsh far better than she.

On and on, Tursla fought a desire to hurry. For he whom she now half supported could never step up the pace. The surface of the road was still under them. She was, she realized, trusting in an inner guide which was an instinct and something she had never called upon before. Unless it was that same feeling of rightness which had led her this way when she had met Xactol under the moon. Always she listened, after the echoes of the alarm died away, for any sounds which might mean they were closely followed.

There were ploppings from swamp sloughs where small creatures, disturbed by their passing, leapt into hiding; and the hoarse cries and calls of other life. They did not move out of the mist, nor did that grow any thinner.

Time lost any measurement. From one moment to the next Tursla could only hope that they were still well ahead of any pursuers. That she had been proclaimed Filled would save her, for a space, until her false claims would be proven. But she could not hope to protect Simond.

Why did she risk all for this stranger? Tursla could not have answered that. But when she had seen him in that vision which had visited her in Volt's Hall she had known that, in some way, they were linked. It was as if some geas of power had been laid upon her; there was no avoiding what must be done.

They were nearly to the end of the pavement now. Though she could see nothing, the girl could sense that in an odd way as if the knowledge came to her by a talent which had nothing to do with sight, hearing, or touch. She halted and spoke sharply to her companion, striving to bring him, by the very force of her will, out of the daze of mind in which he walked.

"Simond!" Names had power; the use of his might well awaken him to reality. "Simond!"

His head raised, turned a little so he could eye her. Like the Tormarsh men he was of a height such that they could see each other on a level. His mouth hung a little open; there was a runnel of blood from one temple clotting on his cheek. But in his eyes there was also the look of intelligence.

"We must take to the swamp itself here." She spoke slowly, pausing between words as one might do with a small child or a person gravely ill. "I cannot hold you—"

He closed his mouth and his jaw line firmed. Then he tried to nod, winced, and his eyes blinked in pain.

"What I can do—that I shall," he promised.

She looked on into the mist. Folly to venture so blindly. But this mist might lie for hours. With the Torfolk aroused they had no hours; they might not even have more than the space of a dozen breaths. She had as yet heard no sounds of pursuit, for Torfolk were wily and had learned long since to move with practiced silence through their territory.

"You must come directly behind me," Tursla bit her lip. That they could do this at all she was dubious. But there was no other choice.

He drew himself straight. "Go—I'll follow," he told her quietly.

With a last glance at him the girl stepped out into the mist. That inner guide had led her aright; her foot came down on the firmness of the hassocks he could not see. She went slowly, lingering before she took each step to make that he saw her, though for him this blind journey must be much worse, for he did not have the same certainty which was hers.

Step by step she wove a way, trying hard to remember how long this most perilous part of their flight must last. Still he did not call to her, and each time she turned her head she could see him well upright, safely balanced on a foothold.

Then she stumbled out on firm ground, the tenseness of her body leading to pain in her back and shoulders, a warning tremble in her legs. This was, at last, that island like a finger which marked the last part of the way to the pool. With her feet firmly planted she waited once more for him to draw close to her. When he gained that solid stretch of land he fell to his knees and his body swayed from side to side. Swiftly she knelt beside him, steadied him.

There was the sheen of sweat across his face and the clotting blood melted under that. He breathed heavily through his mouth, and his eyes, when he looked at her, were dull. He frowned as if she were difficult to see and he must expend much effort to hold her within his range of vision.

"I—am—near—done—Lady—" he gasped, word by painful word.

"There is no more. From here the footing is good. It is only a little way."

His mouth stretched in a stark shadow of a smile. "I can—crawl—if—it—not—be—too far—"

"You can walk!" she said firmly. Rising, she stooped and locked both her hands under his nearer armpit. Exerting the full of her remaining strength, Tursla indeed brought him to his feet. Then, pulling his arm once more about her shoulders, she led him on, until they were on the rocks above the silent pool encircled in sand.

Her hands fumbled first with the fastenings of her robe. She moved now in answer to her knowledge of what must be done. The answer slipped into her mind as the maker of dye might measure and add a handful of this, a counter of that, while intent on boiling some fire-cradled mixture. There was custom to be faced here also. Only by a certain ritual might that which she must summon be approached.

Tursla's robe fell about her feet. Now she stooped once more above the recumbent man, her fingers seeking buckles, the fastening of mail. His eyes opened and he looked up to her, puzzled.

"What—do—?"

"These—" She tugged at the mail where it lay across his shoulders, her other hand picking at the stuff of his breeches. "Off—we must go where these cannot be worn."

He blinked. "One of the Old Powers?" he asked.

Tursla shrugged. "I know not of your Old Powers. But I know a little of what we can summon here. If—" She put her forefinger to her mouth and bit upon that as she considered a point which had only that moment occurred to her. This place would welcome her, had welcomed her, because she was what she was (and what in truth was she? one small part of her now asked. But the time for any such questioning was not now). Would he also be accepted? There was no way of proving that except to try.

"We must—" She made the decision firm—"do this thing. For I have no other way of escape for you."

She helped his fumbling hands with the fastenings, the clasps, and belting, until his body with the wide powerful shoulders, the long arms which marked him as of Torblood, was bare. Then she pointed to the rock from which she had leaped that other time.

"Do not tread upon the sand," she cautioned. "Not while it lays thus. We must leap from there—into the pool."

"If I can—" but he pulled himself along as she mounted the rock.

Out she leapt and down. Once more that water closed about her. But she moved swiftly away toward the farther side of the pool, clearing the spot where he should land. Then she looked up as she trod water.

"Come!"

His body looked as white as the mist curling behind him. He had climbed onto the stone she had just quitted, and she saw his muscles tense. Then he stretched out his arms and dove, cleaving the water with a loud splash.

Tursla turned on her back and floated as she had before. He was no longer her charge, for she had brought him to what safety her instinct told her was all they could hope for, and the pool had not repelled him.

Tursla, her eyes up to the sky which she could see through ragged patches of mist which was being tattered by the sea wind, began to sing—without words—the notes rising and falling like the call of some bird.

5

AS before at her call that sand stirred. The girl could feel no wind, yet the grains of powdery stuff arose, began to twirl as she had seen them on that night. A pillar was born, now moving faster and faster, each turn making it more solid to the eye. Now came the rounding of a head, the modeling of the body below that.

Still Tursla sang her hymn without words as the vessel was formed to hold that which she summoned. She had half forgotten Simond. If he watched in astonishment he made no sound to disturb the voice spell she wove with the same certainty as her hands could follow a design upon her loom.

At last Xactol stood there. Seeing her waiting, Tursla came from the pool, standing erect on stone from which the forming of that other had swept the last minute grain of sand.

"Sand sister—" The girl raised her arms, but did not quite embrace the other.

"Sister—" echoed the other, in her hissing, sand-sliding voice. "What is your need?" Now her hands came forth also and Tursla's lay palm down upon them, flesh meeting sand.

"There is this one." Tursla did not turn her head to look upon Simond in the water still. "He is hunted. They must not find him."

"This is your choice, sister?" inquired that other. "Think well, for from such a choice may come many things you could have reason to look upon as ills in the future."

"Ills alone, Xactol?" asked the girl slowly.

"Nothing is altogether ill, sister. But you must think of this—you are now of Tor. If you go forth there will be no return. And those of Tor are not well looked upon by the Outlanders."

"Of Tor," Tursla repeated. "Only part of me, sand sister. Only part of me. Even as it is with him. I have the body of Tor but the—"

"Do not say it!" commanded Xactol, interrupting her sharply. "But even if it be so, Tor body may betray you. There is a spell set upon the Marsh boundaries. Torfolk cannot go forth—and live."

"And this one?"

"He is divided. He was drawn in by the spelling of Tor, for there was that in him which answered to such a call. But his outland blood will help him to win forth again. Do you try to go with him—" Now it was the woman of sand who left unfinished a warning.

"What will happen to me?"

"I do not know. This spelling is none of ours. The Outlanders have their own witcheries and their learning in such is very old and very deep. You would go at your own peril."

"I stay at even more, sand sister. You know what cloak of safety Mafra dared to throw over me; and, in the way they understand that claim, it is false."

"The decision is yours. What now would you have of me?"

"Can you buy us time, sand sister? There are those who will trail us to the death."

"That is so. Their rage and fear reaches out even to this place. It is like the mists which they love." The woman withdrew her right hand from where it rested under

Tursla's. Now she raised that so that her finger touched the girl's forehead between and just above her eyes.

"This I give you. Use it as you will," she said in a soft voice. "I must go—"

"Will I see you again?" Tursla asked.

"Not if this choice is yours, sister, this choice I read in your thoughts. My door between the worlds is here alone."

"Then I can't—" Tursla cried out.

"But you have already chosen, sister. In your spirit's innermost place that choice lies. Go with peace. Accept what may lie before you with the courage of your spirit. There is a meaning behind what has happened to you. If we don't see it now, all will be made clear in time. Do as you know how to do."

Her arms dropped to her sides and Tursla fell once more to her knees, and veiled her eyes with one hand. But the other she rested on one knee, palm up and slightly cupped.

Xactol began to turn, her spin grew ever faster. The fine sand which had formed her whirled out and away as the body became a pillar, and the pillar, in turn, sand falling to the rock. But in Tursla's hand there remained a small pile of the sand.

When the rest of that substance was once more spread out upon the rim of the pool she arose, cupping her fingers tightly about what she held. Now she hailed Simond.

"You may come forth. We must go on."

Her head jerked around. There was a sound behind. The hunters may have been questing, at last they had the trail. Like Xactol, she could now sense the rage and fear which drove them. Not even her claim of being Filled would be a protection against what moved them now. She shivered. Never before had emotions other than her own been fed to her in this way. The alienness of this was frightening. But there was no time to hesitate, to learn fear fostered by that hate.

Simond came ashore. He walked more steadily, his head was up, but his attention was not for her, rather on their back trail as if he, too, had picked up some emanation from their pursuers.

Tursla climbed the rock to where she had left her robe. She held it up in one hand and spoke:

"Can you tear from this a portion of cloth? What I carry—" she showed him the fist which grasped the sand-dust—"must be safe until we have need for it."

He caught the cloth from her and tore a portion from the mud-stained hem. Into this she emptied the sand, making a packet of it. Then she drew on her robe. But though he had breeches and boots on now, he fastened on only the leather undershirt, left his mail lying.

When he caught her attention he stirred the mail with his boot. "It will slow me. Where do we go?"

"To the sea." Already she was on her way.

The stay in the pool might have refreshed Simond's body, brought beginning healing to his wound, for he kept pace with her as she climbed and slipped among the rocks. She could hear the come and go of the waves, the wind sweeping mist and marsh air away from her.

They came to the shore. Simond looked north and then south, finally standing to face south. "That is the way for Estcarp. Let us go—"

If I can, she thought. *How strong is that spell laid upon the Torfolk? Does it rule body only, or body and spirit both? Can my spirit break a bond laid upon the body?* But she asked none of this aloud.

So they sped along the sand just beyond the reach of the waves. From behind came a shout, and a spear flashed over the wash of the water. A warning, Tursla guessed. The hunters wanted them not dead but captive. Perhaps Unnanna still would have her sacrifice.

Suddenly the girl gasped and cried out, stumbling back. It was as if she had run into a wall and rebounded, her body bruised from the force of that encounter. Simond was already several strides farther on. He whirled about at her cry and started back.

Tursla put out her hands. There was a surface there—invisible—but as tight as the stone side of her place in the clan house. She could feel its substance.

The wall the outlanders had set about the Tormarsh! It would seem that it was indeed a barrier she could not pierce.

"Come!" Simond was back at her side, apparently what was the wall for her did not exist for him. He caught at her, tried to drag her on.

The force of his attempt again brought her hard against that barrier.

"No—I cannot! The spells of your people—" she gasped. "Go—they cannot follow you through this!"

"Not without you!" His face was grim as he stood beside her. "Try by sea. Can you swim?"

"Not well enough." She had splashed now and then in some of the marsh pools, but to entrust herself to the sea was another matter. Yet what choice had she? That heat of hate behind was warning enough of what might happen!

"Come—"

"Stand!" That shout was from behind. Affric— She did not even have to look around to know who led the hunters.

"Go—" Tursla tried to push her companion on, through that wall which was no wall for him.

"The sea!" he repeated.

But it would seem they were too late. Another spear expertly thrown, flashed between them, struck the unseen wall and rebounded. Tursla faced around, her hand going to the breast of her robe, closing upon what she had brought from the pool side.

Affric, yes, and Brunwol, and Gawan. Behind them a score of others, closing in, their eyes avid with a lust of hatred such as she had never met before. Consciously or unconsciously they were using that hatred as a weapon, beating at her; and the hurtful blows of it made her sway, sick and spirit wounded.

But Tursla still had strength enough to bring out the packet she had made. With one hand she tore that open as she balanced the fold of cloth upon the palm of the other. Now that the sand was uncovered, she raised it level with her lips and gathered a great breath to blow it outward. As it swirled she cried aloud. Not a word, for such spelling as this was not summoned by the words of this world. Rather she shaped a sound which seemed to roar, even as the alarm trumpet of the Torfolk had done.

There was no sighting the disappearance of the sand that her breath had dispersed. From the shore itself there uprose small curlings of white grit. Those began to whirl, even as Xactol had formed her body. Higher they grew by the instant, drawing more and more of the shore's substance into them. But they remained pillars, not taking on any other form. Far taller they were now than any of those who stood there.

Affric and his men backed away a little, eyeing the pillars with the uncertainty of men who face a hitherto-unknown menace. Yet they did not retreat far, and Tursla knew well that they still held to their deadly purpose.

The top of the tallest pillar began to nod—toward the Tormen. Tursla caught at Simond's shoulder. The strength that moved the pillars was draining from her. That she could order them much longer she doubted.

"The sea!"

Had she cried that aloud, or had he read it in her mind? She was not sure. But Simond's arm was about her and he was striding toward the wash of the waves, bearing her with him.

As the waves struck against her, the water rising from knee to waist, Tursla strove still to keep her mind upon the columns of sand. But she did not turn her head to watch how effectively her energy wrought.

There was shouting there, not now aimed at the

fugitives. Some of the voices were muffled or ceased abruptly. The water was high about her now. Simond, sparing no glance for what might be happening on the shore, gave an order:

"Turn on your back. Float! Leave it to me!"

She tried to do as he wanted. So far there had been no barrier. Now as she splashed she could see the shoreline again. There was a mist. No, not a mist—that must be a whirl of sand thick enough to half hide the figures struggling in it as if they could not win forth from its embrace, rather were caught fast held in the storm of grit.

Then she was on her back and Simond was swimming, towing her with him. No longer did he head out to sea, but rather altered course to parallel the shore. Tursla had held the sand, sent it raging as long as she could. She was drained now, not able to move to aid herself even if she had known how to swim.

That shouting grew louder. Then—

Force—force pushing her back, sending her under the water. She gasped, and the salt flood was in her mouth, drawn chokingly into her lungs. She fought for breath. The barrier! this was the barrier. She wanted to shout to Simond, tell him that all her efforts were useless. There was no escape for her.

No escape! Her body, her body was sealed into Tormarsh by the spells of the outlanders! No—hope—

Aroused to a frenzy by the danger of drowning, Tursla tried to get free of the hold upon her, to strike at Simond and make him let go before she was pushed completely under the water.

"—go! Let me go!" Her mind shrieked and water once more flooded into her mouth and nose.

Out of nowhere came a blow. She felt a flash of pain as it landed. Then, nothing at all.

Slowly she came back from that place of darkness. Water—she was drowning! Simond must let her go.

But there was no water. She lay on a surface which was

steady, which did not swing as did the waves. And she could breathe. No water filled her nose, covered her head. For a long moment it was enough to know that she was indeed safe from being drawn under. But—

They must be back on the shore then. With her releasing of mind control the sand would have gone. Perhaps Affric was—

Tursla opened her eyes. Above her the sky arched—clear except for a drifting cloud or two. There was no hint of the Tormarsh mist about. She raised her head—though that small action seemed very hard—she was weak, drained.

Sand, white, marked with the ripples of waves which curled in, drained away again. And rocks. And the sea. But no Affric, no Torman standing over her. She was— Tursla sat up, bracing herself by her hands.

Her wet robe was plastered thick with sand. She could even taste the grit between her teeth. There was no one—no one at all. Yet a few moments of study showed her that this was not that tongue of beach to which the Tormarsh reached.

She inched around to face inland. To her left now, a goodly distance away, rising into the air as if a hundred—no, a thousand fires burned (for it stretched along there inland as far as she could see), the mists of the marsh arose like smoke, cloaking well what might lie on the other side.

They had passed the barrier! This was the Outland.

Tursla wavered to her knees, striving to see more of this unknown world. The sand of the beach stretched for a space. Then there was a sparse growth of tough grass; beyond that, bushes. But there was no smell of the swamp.

Where was Simond?

Her loneliness, which had been good when she feared Affric and the others, now was a source of uneasiness. Where had he gone—and why?

His desertion, for her, was frightening. Was it that she was of the Torfolk? Could it be that the Outlanders' hatred for the marsh dwellers was so great, that, having saved her life, he felt he had paid any debts between them and had wished no more of her company?

Bleakly Tursla settled on that fact. Perhaps in the Outlands Koris himself hated his Torblood and his son had been raised to find it a matter of shame. Just as a Torman might, in turn, look upon half-Outland blood as something to lessen him among his fellows.

She was Tor—as much as Simond knew. And as Tor—

Tursla supported her head upon her hands and tried to think. It might well be that, having made one of those decisions she had been told to consider seriously, she had cut herself totally adrift from all people now. Xactol had warned her fairly. When she left the country of the pool she would no longer have communication with that one mind?—spirit?—entity?—who could understand what she was.

Mafra—for the first time Tursla wondered, with a little catch of breath, how had it gone with the Clan Mother who had faced Unnanna and worked some magic of her own to cover their escape; though what manner of Torfolk would dare to raise either hand or voice against Mafra? The girl wished passionately at that moment that she could reverse all that had happened to her, be once more in the clan house—as it had been on the night before she had gone to keep her meeting with the sand sister.

To look back, Tursla shook her head, that was only a waste of effort. No man or woman might ever turn again and decide upon some other path once their feet were firm set on one of their choice. She had made her decision, now by that she must live—or perhaps die.

Bleakly she looked landward. The sea was empty and she expected no help to arise out of that. Now she was hungry. Already the sun was well down in the western sky. She had not even a knife at her belt; and who knew what manner of danger might prowl the Outland at the coming of true darkness?

But if she tried to go hence it must be on hands and

knees. When she attempted to rise to her feet she found herself so weak and giddy that she tottered and fell. Hunger and thirst—both were an emptiness crying to be filled.

Filled! At least now the clan would never discover her deception. If she had been filled with something else as Mafra had averred, what *was* it?

She brought her knees up against her breast, put her arms about them, huddling in upon herself, for the wind was growing colder and had a bite to it which the winds of Tormarsh never held. Now she tried to think. What was good fortune for her now? What was ill? The latter seemed a longer list. But the good—she had escaped Affric and the rest—the anger of the Torfolk which would have been dire when they discovered she would bring forth no child to swell their dwindling numbers. She had certain knowledge which she as yet did not know how to use, that which Xactol had granted her.

But if the sand sister was forever barred from her, when and how could she ever learn?

And where might she go for shelter? Where was there food? Water? Would the hands of all dwellers in this land be raised against her when they knew her for Tor?

She—

"Holla!"

Tursla's head came up instantly.

There was a mounted man—riding through the inland brush! His head—bare head—Simond! Somehow she wobbled to her feet, called out in return though her voice sounded very thin and weak in answer to that shout of his:

"Simond!"

Now, it was as if something tight and hurting inside her had suddenly broken apart. She wavered to her feet, staggered, one foot before the other. She was not alone! He had not left her here!

The horse was coming at a trot. She could sight a second animal following; Simond had it on lead. He came in a shower of sand sent up by the pounding feet of his mount. Then he was out of the saddle and to her, his arms around her.

Tursla could only repeat his name in a witless fashion, letting him take the weight of her worn out and aching body.

"Simond! Simond!"

"It is well. All is well." He held her steady, letting the very fact that he was there, that she was not alone, seep into her mind and bring her peace.

"I had to go," he told her. "We needed horses. There is a watch tower only a little away. I came back as soon as I could."

Now she gained a measure of control.

"Simond." She made herself look directly into his eyes, sure that he would in no way try to soothe her with any false promise. "Simond, I am of Tormarsh. I do not know how you brought me past that spell your people used as a barrier to keep us from the Outland. But I remain Tor. Will your people give me any welcome?"

His hands now cupped her face, and his eyes did not shift.

"Tor chose to stand our enemy, but in return we have never sought that enmity. Also, I am partly Tor. And Koris has made Torblood a blessing not a curse in Estcarp, as all men know. He held the Axe of Volt which would come only to him. And he intended that Estcarp not be meat for those who were worse than any winter wolf! Tor holds no stigma here."

Then he laughed, and the lightness of his smile made his whole face different.

"This is an odd thing. You know my name, but I do not know yours. Will you trust me with that much to show your belief in my good will?"

She found that her face, sticky with sea water and rough with sand, stretched an answering smile.

"I am Tursla of —No, I am no longer of any clan house. Just what I am now—or whom—that I must learn."

"It will not be hard that learning. There will be those to help," he promised her.

Tursla's smile grew wider. "That I do not doubt," she replied with conviction.

Toys of Tamisan

1

SHE is certified by the Foostmam, Lord Starrex. A true action dreamer to the tenth power."

Jabis was being too eager, or almost so; he was pushing too much, Tamisan sneered mentally, keeping her face carefully blank, though she took quick glances about from beneath half-closed eyelids. This sale very much concerned her, since she was the product being discussed, but she had nothing to say in the matter.

She supposed this was a typical sky tower, seeming to float, masked in clouds at times, since its supports were so slender and well concealed, lifting it high above Ty-Kry. However, none of the windows gave on real sky, but each framed a very different landscape, illustrating what must be other planet scenes. Perhaps some were dream remembered or inspired.

There was a living lambil grass carpet around the easirest on which the owner half lay, half sat. But Jabis had not even been offered a pull-down wall seat. And the two other men in attendance on Lord Starrex stood also. They were real men and not androids, which placed the owner in the multi-credit class. One, Tamisan thought was a bodyguard, and the other, younger, thinner, with a dissatisfied mouth, had on clothing nearly equal to that of the man on the easirest but with a shade of difference which meant a lesser place in the household.

Tamisan catalogued what she could see and filed it away for future reference. Most dreamers did not observe much of the world about them. They were too enmeshed in their own creations to care for reality. Most dreamers . . . Tamisan frowned. She *was* a dreamer. Jabis and the Foostmam could prove that. The lounger on the easirest could prove it if he paid Jabis' price. But she was also something more, Tamisan herself was not quite sure what. And that there was a difference in her, she had had mother wit enough to conceal since she had first been aware that the others in the Foostmam's Hive were not able to come cleanly out of their dreams into the here and now. Why, some of them had to be fed, clothed, cared for as if they were not aware they had any bodies!

"Action dreamer." Lord Starrex shifted his shoulders against the padding which immediately accommodated itself to his stirring to give him maximum comfort. "Action dreaming is a little childish—"

Tamisan's control held, but she felt inside her a small flare of anger. Childish was it? She would like to show him just how childish a dream she could spin to enmesh a client. But Jabis was not in the least moved by that derogatory remark from a possible purchaser; it was in his eyes only a logical bargaining move.

"If you wish an E dreamer—" He shrugged. "But your demand to the Hive specified an A."

He was daring to be a little abrupt. Was he so sure of this lord as all that? He must have some inside information which allowed him to be so confident. For Jabis could cringe and belly-down in awe like the lowest beggar if he thought such a gesture needful to gain a credit or two.

"Kas, this is your idea. What is she worth?" Starrex asked indifferently.

The younger of his companions moved forward a step

or two. He was the reason for her being here—Lord Kas, cousin to the owner of all this magnificence; though certainly not, Tamisan had already deduced, with any authority in the household. But the fact that Starrex lay in the easirest was not dictated by indolence, but rather by what was hidden by the fas-silk lap-robe concealing half his body. A man who might not walk straight again could find pleasure in the abilities of an action dreamer.

"She has a ten-point rating," Kas reminded the other.

The black brows which gave a stern set to Starrex's features arose a trifle. "Is that so?"

Jabis was quick to take advantage. "It is so, Lord Starrex. Of all this year's swarm, she rated the highest. It was—is—the reason why we make this offer to your lordship."

"I do not pay for reports only," returned Starrex.

Jabis was not to be ruffled. "A point ten, my lord, does not give demonstrations. As you know, the Hive accrediting can not be forged. It is only because I have urgent business in Brok and must leave for there that I am selling her at all. Though I have had an offer from the Foostmam herself to retain this one for lease-outs—"

Tamisan, had she had anything to wager or someone with whom to wager it, would have set the winning of this bout with her uncle. Uncle? To Tamisan's thinking she had no blood tie with this small insect of a man—with his wrinkled face, his never-still eyes, his thin hands with their half-crooked fingers always reminding one of claws outstretched to grab and grab and grab. Surely her mother must have been very unlike Uncle Jabis, or else how could her father ever have seen aught worth bedding—not for just one night but for half a year—in her?

Not for the first time her thoughts were on the riddle of her parents. Her mother had not been a dreamer—though she had had a sister who had regrettably—for the sake of the family fortune—died in the Hive during adolescent stimulation as an E dreamer. Her father had been from off-world—an alien, though humanoid enough to crossbreed. And he had disappeared again off-world when his desire for star roving had become too strong to master. Had it not been that she had early shown dreamer talent, Uncle Jabis and the rest of the greedy Yeska clan would never have taken any thought of her after her mother had died of the blue plague.

She was crossbred and had intelligence enough to guess early that this had given her the difference between her powers and those of others in the Hive. The ability to dream was an inborn talent. For those of low power, it was an indwelling withdrawal from the world. And those dreamers were largely useless. But the ones who could project dreams to include others—through linkage—brought high prices, according to the strength and stability of their creations. E dreamers who created erotic and lascivious other-worlds once rated more highly than action dreamers. But of late years, the swing had been in the opposite direction, though how long that might hold no one could guess. And those lucky enough to have an A dreamer to sell were pushing their wares speedily lest the market decline.

Tamisan's hidden talent was that she herself was never as completely lost in the dream world as those she conveyed to it. Also—and this she had discovered very recently and hugged that discovery to her—she could in a measure control the linkage so she was never a powerless prisoner forced to dream at another's desire.

She considered now what she knew concerning this Lord Starrex. That Jabis would sell her to the owner of one of the sky towers had been clear from the first. And naturally he would select what he thought would be the best bargain. But, though rumors wafted through the Hive, Tamisan believed that much of their news of the outer world was inaccurate and garbled. Dreamers were roofed and walled from any real meeting with everyday life, their talents feverishly fed and fostered by long sessions with tri-dee projectors and information tapes.

Starrex, unlike most of his class, had been a doer. He had broken the pattern of caste by going off-world on lengthy trips. It was only after some mysterious accident had crippled him that he became a recluse; supposedly hiding a maimed body. And he did not seem like those others who had come to the Hive seeking wares. Of course, it had been the Lord Kas who had summoned them here.

Stretched out on the easirest with that cover of fabulous silk across most of his body, he was hard to judge. But, she thought, standing he would top Jabis, and he seemed to be well muscled, more like his guardsman than his cousin.

He had a face unusual in its planes, broad across the forehead and cheek bones, then slimming to a strong chin which narrowed to give his head a vaguely wedge-shaped line. He was dark-skinned, almost as dark as a space crewman. His hair was black, cut very short so that it was a tight velvety cap, in constrast to the longer strands of his cousin.

His tunic—lutrax of a coppery-rust shade—was of rich material but less ornamented than that of the younger man. Its sleeves were wide and loose, and now and then he ran his hands up his arms, pushing the fabric away from his skin. He wore only a single jewel, a koros stone set in an earring as a drop which dangled forward against his jaw line.

Tamisan did not consider him handsome. But there was something arresting about him. Perhaps it was his air of arrogant assurance, as if in all his life he had never had his wishes crossed. He had not met Jabis before; and perhaps now even Lord Starrex would have something to learn.

Twist and turn, indignant and persuasive, using every trick in a very considerable training for dealing and under-dealing, Jabis bargained. He appealed to gods and demons to witness his disinterested desire to please, his despair at being misunderstood. It was quite a notable act, and Tamisan stored up some of the choicer bits in her mental reservoir for the making of dreams. It was far more stimulating to watch then a tri-dee, and she wondered why this living drama material was not made available to the Hive. Unless, of course, the Foostmam and her assistants feared it, along with any shred of reality which might awaken the dreamers from their conditioned absorption in their own creations.

For an instant or two she wondered if the Lord Starrex was not enjoying it too. There was a kind of weariness in his face which suggested boredom, though that was the norm for anyone wanting a personal dreamer. Then suddenly as if he were tired of it all, he interrupted one of Jabis' more impassioned pleas for celestial understanding of his need for receiving a just price with a single sentence.

"I tire, fellow. Take your price and go." He closed his eyes in dismissal.

2

IT was the guard who drew a credit plaque from his belt, swung a long arm over the back of the easirest for Lord Starrex to plant a thumb on its surface to certify payment, and then tossed it to Jabis. It fell to the floor so the small man had to scrabble for it with his finger claws, and Tamisan saw the look in his darting eyes. Jabis had little liking for Lord Starrex—which did not mean, of course, that he disdained the credit plaque he had to stoop to catch up.

He did not give a glance to Tamisan as he bowed himself out. And she was left standing as if she were an android or a machine. It was the Lord Kas who stepped forward, touched her lightly on the arm as if he thought she needed guidance.

"Come," he said, and his fingers about her wrist drew her after him. The Lord Starrex took no notice of his new possession.

"What is your name?" Lord Kas spoke slowly, emphasizing each word as if he needed to do so to pierce some veil between them. Tamisan guessed that he had had contact with a lower-rated dreamer, one who was always bemused in the real world. Caution suggested that she allow him to believe she was in a similar daze. So she raised her head slowly, and looked at him, trying to give the appearance of one finding it difficult to focus.

"Tamisan," she answered after a lengthy pause. "I be Tamisan."

"Tamisan—that is a pretty name," he said as one would address a dull-minded child. "I am Lord Kas. I am your friend."

But Tamisan, sensitive to shades of voice, thought she had done well in playing bemused. Whatever Kas might be, he was not her friend, at least not unless it served his purpose.

"These rooms are yours." He had escorted her down a hall to a far door where he passed his hand over the surface in a pattern to break some light-lock. Then his grip on her wrist brought her into a high-ceilinged room. There were no windows to break its curve of wall. The place was oval in shape. The center fell in a series of wide, shallow steps to a pool where a small fountain raised a perfumed mist to patter back into a bone-white basin. And on the steps were a number of cushions and soft lie-ons, all of many delicate shades of blue and green. While the oval walls were covered with a shimmer of rippling zidex webbing—pale gray covered with whirls and lines of palest green.

A great deal of care had gone into the making and furnishing of that room. Perhaps she was only the latest in a series of dreamers, for this was truly the rest place—raised to a point of luxury unknown even in the Hive—for a dreamer.

A strip of the web tapestry along the wall was raised, and a personal-care android entered. The head was only an oval ball with faceted eye-plates and hearing sensors to break its surface, its unclothed, humanoid form ivory white.

"This is Porpae," Kas told her. "She will watch over you."

My guard, Tamisan thought. That the care the android would give her would be unceasing and of the best, she did not doubt, any more than that the ivory being would stand between her and any hope of freedom.

"If you have any wish, tell it to Porpae." Kas dropped his hold on her arm, turned to the door. "When the Lord Starrex wishes to dream he will send for you."

"I am at his command," she mumbled the proper response.

She watched Kas leave and then looked to Porpae. Tamisan had good cause to believe that the android was programmed to record her every move. But would anyone here believe that a dreamer had any desire to be free? A dreamer wished only to dream; it was her life, her entire life. And to leave a place which did all to foster such a life—that would be akin to self-killing, something a certified dreamer could not think of.

"I hunger," she told the android. "I would eat."

"Food comes." Porpae went to the wall and swept aside the web once more to display a series of buttons she pressed in a complicated manner.

When the food arrived in a closed tray with the viands each in its own hot or cold compartment, Tamisan ate. She recognized the usual dishes of a dreamer's diet, but better cooked and more tastily served than in the Hive. She ate; she made use of the bathing place Porpae guided her to behind another wall web, and she slept easily and without stirring on the cushions beside the pool where the faint play of the water lulled her gently.

Time had very little meaning in the oval room. She

ate, slept, bathed and looked upon the tri-dees she asked Porpae to supply. Had she been as the others from the Hive, this existence would have been ideal. But instead, when there was no call to display her art, she grew restless. She was prisoner here, and none of the other inhabitants of the sky tower seemed aware of her.

There was one thing she could do, Tamisan decided upon her second waking. A dreamer was allowed—no, required—to study the personality of the master she must serve, if she were a private dreamer and not a leasee of the Hive. She had a right now to ask for tapes concerning Starrex. In fact, it might be considered odd if she did not, and accordingly she called for those. Thus she learned something of her master and his household.

Kas had had his personal fortune wiped out by some catastrophe when he was a child. He had been in a manner adopted by Starrex's father, the head of their clan, and since Starrex's injuries Kas had acted in some fashion as his deputy. The guard was Ulfilas, an off-world mercenary Starrex had brought back from one of his star voyages.

But Starrex, save for a handful of bare facts, remained more or less of an enigma. That he had any human responses to others Tamisan began to doubt. He had gone seeking change off-world, but what he might have found there had not cured his eternal weariness of life. And his personal recordings were meager. She now believed that, to him, any one of his household was only a tool to be used or swept from his path and ignored. He was unmarried and such feminine companionship as he had languidly attached to his household—and that more by the effort of the woman involved than through any direct action on his part—did not last long. In fact, he was so encased in a shell of indifference that Tamisan wondered if there was any longer a real man within that outer covering.

She began to speculate as to why he had allowed Kas to bring her as an addition to his belongings. To make the best use of a dreamer, the owner must be ready to partake, and what she read in these tapes suggested that Starrex's indifference would raise a barrier to any real dreaming.

But the more Tamisan learned in this negative fashion, the more it seemed a challenge. She lay beside the pool in deep thought—though that thought strayed even more than she herself guessed from the rigid mental exercises used by a point ten dreamer. To deliver a dream which would captivate Starrex was indeed a challenge. He wanted action, but her training, acute as it had been, was not enough to entice him. Therefore—*her* action must be able to take a novel turn.

This was an age of oversophistication—when star travel was a fact, when outer action existed in reality. And by these tapes, though they were not detailed as to what Starrex had done off-world, the lord had experienced much—the reality of his time.

So—he must be served the unknown. She had read nothing in the tapes to suggest that Starrex had sadistic or perverted tendencies. And she knew if he were to be reached in such a fashion, she was not the one to do it. Also Kas would have stated such a requirement at the Hive.

There were many rolls of history on which one could draw—but those had also been mined and remined. The future—that again had been overused, frayed. Tamisan's dark brows drew together above her closed eyes. Trite—everything she thought of was trite! Why did she care anyway? She did not even know why it had become so strong a drive to build a dream that, when she was called upon to deliver it, would shake Starrex out of his shell—to prove to him that she was worth her rating. Maybe it was partly because he had made no move to send for her and try to prove her powers, his indifference suggesting that he thought she had nothing to offer.

Tapes—she had the right to call upon the full library of the Hive, and it was the most complete in the star lanes. Why, ships were sent out for no other reason than to bring back new knowledge to feed the imaginations of the dreamers!

History. Her mind kept returning to the past, though it was too threadbare for her purposes. History—what was history? A series of events—actions by individuals, or nations. Actions had results. Tamisan sat up among her cushions. Results of action! Sometimes there were far-reaching results from a single action—the death of a ruler, the outcome of one battle, the landing of a star ship—or its failure to land.

So—

Her flicker of idea became solid. History could have had many roads to travel beside the one already known. Now—could she make use of that?

Why, it had innumerable possibilities! Tamisan's hands clenched the robe lying across her knees. Study—she would have to study! And if Starrex only gave her more time . . . She no longer resented his indifference now. She would need every minute it was prolonged.

"Porpae!"

The android materialized from behind the web.

"I must have certain tapes from the Hive." Tamisan hesitated. In spite of the spur of impatience, she must build smoothly and surely. "A message to the Foostmam: send to Tamisan n' Starrex the rolls of the history of Ty-Kry for the past five hundred years."

The history of a single city and that of the one which based this sky tower! Begin small so she could test and retest her idea. Today a single city, tomorrow a world, and then—who knew—perhaps a solar system! She reined in her excitement. There was much to do. She needed a note recorder—and time. But by the Four Breasts of Vlasta—if she could do it!

It would seem she would have time, though always at the back of Tamisan's mind was the small spark of fear that at any moment the summons to Starrex might come. But the tapes arrived from the Hive and the recorder, so that she swung from one to the other, taking notes from what she learned. Then after the tapes had been returned, she studied those notes feverishly. Now her idea meant more to her than just a device to amuse a difficult master; it absorbed her utterly, as if she were a low-grade dreamer caught in one of her own creations.

When Tamisan realized the danger of this, she broke with her studies and turned back to the household tapes to learn again what she could of Starrex.

But she was again running through her notes when at last the summons came. How long she had been in Starrex's tower she did not know, for days and nights in the oval room were all alike. Only Porpae's watchfulness had kept her to a routine of eating and rest.

It was the Lord Kas who came for her, and she had just time to remember her role of bemused dreamer as he entered.

"You are well and happy?" He used the conventional greeting.

"I enjoy the good life."

"It is the Lord Starrex's wish that he enter a dream." Kas reached for her hand, and she allowed his touch. "The Lord Starrex demands much. Offer him your best, dreamer." He might have been warning her.

"A dreamer dreams," she answered him vaguely. "What is dreamed can be shared."

"True. But the Lord Starrex is hard to please. Do your best for him, dreamer."

She did not answer, and he drew her on, out of the room to a gray shaft and down that to a lower level. The room into which they finally went had the apparatus very familiar to her—a couch for the dreamer, the second for the sharer with the linkage machine between. But here was a third couch. Tamisan looked at it in surprise.

"Two dream, not three?"

Kas shook his head. "It is the Lord Starrex's will that

another shares also. The linkage is of a new model, very powerful. It has been well tested."

Who would be that third? Ulfilas? Was it that Lord Starrex thought he must take his personal guard into a dream with him?

The door swung open again, and Lord Starrex entered. He walked stiffly, one leg swinging wide as if he could not bend the knee nor control the muscles, and he leaned heavily on an android. As the servant lowered him onto the couch, he did not look to Tamisan but nodded curtly to Kas.

"Take you place also," he ordered.

Did Starrex fear the dream state and want his cousin as a check because Kas had plainly dreamed before?

Then Starrex turned to her as he reached for the dream cap, copying the motion by which she settled her own circlet on her head.

"Let us see what you can do." There was a shadow of hosility in his voice, a challenge to produce something which he did not believe she could do.

3

SHE must not allow herself to think of Starrex now, only of her dream. She must create and have no fear that her creation would be less perfect than her hopes. Tamisan closed her eyes, firmed her will and drew into her imagination all the threads of the studies' spinning. She began the weaving of a dream.

For a moment, perhaps two fingers' count of moments, this was like the beginning of any dream and then—

She was not looking on, watching intently, critically, a fabric she spun with dexterity. No, it was rather as if that web suddenly became real and she was caught tightly in it, even as a blue-winged drotail might be enmeshed in a foss-spider's deadly nest curtain!

This was no dreaming such as Tamisan had ever known before, and panic gripped so harshly in her throat and chest that she might have screamed, save that she had no voice left. She fell down and down from a point above, to strike among bushes which took some of her weight, but with an impact which left her bruised and half senseless. She lay unmoving, gasping, her eyes closed, fearing to open them to see that she was indeed caught in a wild nightmare and not properly dreaming.

As she lay there, she came slowly out of her dazed bewilderment; she tried to get control, not only over her fears, but her dreaming powers. Then she opened her eyes cautiously.

An arch of sky was overhead, palidly green, with traces, like long, clutching fingers, of thin gray cloud. As real as any sky might be, did she walk under it in her own time and world. Her own time and world!

The idea she had built upon to astound Starrex came back to her now. Had the fact that she had worked with a new theory, trying to bring a twist to dreaming which might pierce the indifference of a bored man, precipitated this?

Tamisan sat up, wincing at the protest of her bruises, to look about her. Her vantage point was the crest of a small knob of earth. But the land about her was no wilderness. The turf was smooth and cropped, and here and there were outcrops of rock cleverly carved and clothed with flowering vines—some of them; others were starkly bare, brooding. And all faced down slope to a wall.

These forms varied from vaguely acceptable humanoid shapes to grotesque monsters. And Tamisan decided that she liked the aspect of none when she studied them more closely. These were *not* of her imagining.

Beyond the wall began a cluster of buildings. Used to seeing the sky towers and the lesser, if more substantial structures beneath those which were of her own world, these looked unusually squat and heavy. The highest she could see from here was no more than three stories. Men did not build to the stars here, they hugged the earth closely.

But where was *here?* Not her dream—Tamisan closed her eyes and concentrated on the beginnings of her planned dream. That had been about going into another world, born of her imagining, yes—but not this! Her basic idea had been simple enough, if not one which had been used to her knowledge by any dreamer before her. It all hinged on the idea that the past history of her world had been altered many times during its flow—and she had taken three key-points of alteration, studied on what might have resulted had those been given the opposite decision by fate.

Now, keeping her eyes firmly closed against this seeming reality into which she had fallen, Tamisan concentrated with fierce intentness upon her chosen points.

"The Welcome of the Over-Queen Ahta—" she recited the first.

What if the first star ship on its landing had not been accepted as a supernatural event and the small kingdom in which it had touched earth had not accepted its crew as godlings, but rather had greeted them instead with those poisoned darts the spacemen had later seen used? That was her first decision.

"The loss of the Wanderer." That was the second.

A colony ship driven far from its assigned course by computer failure, so that it had had to make a landing here or let its passengers die. If that failure had not occurred and the Wanderer not landed to start an unplanned colony . . .

"The death of Sylt the Sweet-Tongued before he reached the Altar of Ictio."

A prophet who might never have arisen to ruthless power, leading to a blood-crazed insurrection from temple to temple, setting darkness on three-quarters of this world.

She had chosen those points, but she had not even been sure that one might not have canceled out another.

Sylt had led the rebellion against the colonists from

the Wanderer. If the welcome had not occurred . . . Tamisan could not be sure—she had only tried to find a pattern sequence of events and then envision a modern world stemming from those changes.

However—she opened her eyes again—this was not her imagined world! Nor did one in a dream rub bruises, sit on damp sod, feel wind pull at clothes, and allow the first patter of rain to wet hair and robe. She put both hands to her head—what of the dream cap?

Her fingers found a weaving of metal right enough, but there were no cords from it. And for the first time she remembered that she had been linked with Starrex and Kas when this happened.

Tamisan got to her feet to look around her, half expecting to see the other two somewhere near. But she was alone, and the rain was falling heavier. There was a roofed space near the wall, and Tamisan hurried for it.

Three twisted pillars supported a small dome of roof. There were no walls, and she huddled in the very center, trying to escape the wind-borne moisture. She could not keep pushing away the feeling that this was no dream but true reality.

If—if one could dream *true!* Tamisan fought panic and tried to examine the possibilities. *Had* she somehow landed in a Ty-Kry which might have existed had her three checkpoints actually been the decisions she envisioned? If so—could one get back by simply visioning them in reverse?

She shut her eyes and concentrated . . .

There was a sensation of stomach-turning giddiness. She swung out, to be jerked back—swung out, to return once more. Shaking with nausea, Tamisan stopped trying. She shuddered, opening her eyes to the rain. Then again she strove to understand what had happened. That swing had in it some of the sensation of dream breaking. It did! Which meant that she was in a dream. But it was just as apparent that she had been held prisoner here. How? And why? Or—her eyes narrowed a little, though she was looking inward, not at the rain-misted garden before her—by whom?

Suppose—suppose one or both of those who had prepared to share her dream had also come into this place—though not right here—then she must find them. They must return together or the missing one would anchor the others. Find them—and now!

For the first time she looked down at the garment clinging dank and damp to her slender body. It was not the gray slip of a dreamer, for it was long, brushing her ankles. And in color it was a dusky violet, a shade she found strangely pleasing and right.

From its hem to her knees there was a border of intricate embroidery so entwined and ornate that she found it hard to define in any detail, though it seemed oddly enough that the longer she studied it, the more it appeared to be not threads on cloth, but words on a page of manuscript such as she had viewed in the ancient history video tapes. The threads were a metallic green and silver, with only a few minor touches of a lighter shade of violet.

Around her waist was a belt of silver links, clasped by a broad buckle of the same metal set with purple stones. This supported a pouch with a metal top. The dress or robe was laced from the belt to her throat with silver cords run through metal eyelets in the material. And her sleeves were long and full, though from the elbow down they were slit to four parts, those fluttering away from her arms when she raised them to loose the crown.

What she brought away from her head was not the familiar skull cap made to fit over her cropped hair. Rather it was a circlet of silver with inner wires or strips rising to a conical point that added a foot or more to her height. On that point was a beautifully fashioned flying thing, its wings a little lifted as if to take off, the glitter of tiny jewels marking its eyes.

It was so made that, as she turned the crown around, its long neck changed position and the wings moved a fraction. Thus at first she was almost startled enough to drop the circlet, thinking it might just be alive.

But the whole she recognized from one of the history tapes. The bird was the flacar of Olava. Wearing it so meant that she was a Mouth! A Mouth of Olava—half priestess, part sorceress—and oddly enough, entertainer. But fortune had favored her in this; a Mouth of Olava might wander anywhere without question, searching, and seem merely to be about her normal business.

Tamisan ran her hand over her head before she replaced the crown. Her fingers did not find the bristly stubble of a dreamer, but rather soft, mist-dampened strands which curled down long enough to brush her forehead and tuft at the nape of her neck.

She had imagined garments for herself in dreams, of course. But this time she had not provided herself with such, and so the fact that she stood as a Mouth of Olava was not of her willing. But Olava was part of the time of the Over-Queen's rule. Had she somehow swept herself back in time? The sooner she found knowledge of where—and when—she was, the better.

The rain was slackening and Tamisan moved out from under the dome. She bunched up her robe in both hands to climb back up the slope. At its top she turned slowly, trying to find some proof that she had not been tossed alone into this strange world.

Save for the figures of stone and beds of rank-looking growth, there was nothing to be seen. The wall and the dome structure lay below. But when she faced about, there was a second slope leading to a still higher point which was crowned by a roof to be seen only in bits and patches through a screen of oarn trees. The roof had a ridge which terminated at either side in a sharp upcurve, giving the building the odd appearance of an ear on either end. And it was green with a glittering surface, almost brilliantly so in spite of the clouds overhead.

To her right and left Tamisan caught glimpses of the wall curving, and more stone figures with flower or shrub plantings. Gathering up her skirts more firmly, she began to walk up the curve of the higher slope in search of some road or path leading to the roof.

She came across what she sought as she detoured to avoid a thicket of heavy brush in which were impaled huge scarlet flowers. It was a wide roadway paved with small colored pebbles embedded in a solid surface, and it led from an open gateway up the swell of the slope to the front of the rear structure.

In shape the building was vaguely familiar, though Tamisan could not identify it. Unless it resembled something she had seen in the tri-dees. The door was of the same brilliant green as the roof, but the walls were a pale yellow, cut sharply at regular intervals by windows, very narrow, and so tall that they ran from floor to roof level.

Even as she stood there wondering where she had seen such a house before, a woman came out. Like Tamisan she wore a long-skirted robe with laced bodice and slit sleeves. But hers was the same green as that of the door, so that, standing against it, only her head and arms were clearly visible. She gestured with vigor, and Tamisan suddenly realized that it must be she who was being summoned—as if she were expected—

Again she fought down unease. In a dream she was well used to meetings and partings, but always those were of her own devising, did not happen for a purpose which was not of her wish. Her dream people were toys, game pieces, to be moved hither and thither at her will, she being always in command over them.

"Tamisan—they wait—come quickly!" the woman called.

4

TAMISAN was minded in that instant to run in the other direction. But the need to learn what had happened to her made her take what might be the dangerous course of joining the woman.

"Fah—you are wet! This is no hour for walking in the garden. The First Standing asks for a reading from the Mouth. If you would have lavishly from her purse, hurry lest she grows too impatient to wait!"

The door gave upon a narrow entryway, and the woman in green propelled Tamisan toward a second opening directly facing her. She came so into a large room where a circle of couches was centered. By each stood a small table now burdened with dishes which serving maids were bearing away as if a meal had just been concluded. And tall candlesticks, matching Tamisan's own height, stood also between the divans, the candles in each, as thick as her forearm, alight to give forth not only radiance but a sweet odor as they burned.

Midpoint in the divan circle was a tall-backed chair over which arched a canopy. And in that sat a woman, a goblet in her hand. She had a fur cloak pulled about her shoulders hiding almost all of her robe, save that here and there a shimmer of gold caught fire from the candlelight. Only her face was visible in a hood of the same metallic-seeming fabric, and it was that of the very old, seamed with deep wrinkles, sunken of eye.

The divans, Tamisan marked, were occupied by both men and women, the women flanking the chair, the men farthest away from the ancient noblewoman. And directly facing her was a second impressive chair, lacking only the canopy; before it was a table on which stood, at each of its four corners, four small basins, one cream, one pale rose, one faintly blue, and the fourth sea-foam green.

Tamisan's store of knowledge gave her some preparation. This was the setting for the magic of a Mouth, and it was apparent that her service as a foreseer was about to be demanded. What had she done in allowing herself to be drawn here? Could she make pretense her servant well enough to deceive this company?

"I hunger, Mouth of Olava, I hunger—not for that which will feed the body, but for that which satisfies the mind." The old woman leaned forward a little. Her voice might be the thin one of age, but it carried with it the force of authority, of one who has not had her word or desire questioned for a long time.

She must improvise, Tamisan knew. She was a dreamer and she had wrought in dreams many strange things. Let her but remember that now. Her damp skirts clung clammily to her legs and thighs as she came forward, saying nothing to the woman in return, but seating herself in the chair facing her client. She was drawing on faint stirrings of a memory which seemed not truly her own for guidance, though she had not yet realized that fully.

"What would you know, First Standing?" She raised her hands to her forehead in an instinctive gesture, touching forefingers to her temples, right and left.

"What comes to me—and mine." The last two words had come almost as an afterthought.

Tamisan's hands went out without her conscious ordering. She stifled her amazement—this was as if she were repeating an act as well learned as her dreamer's technique had been. With her left hand she gathered up a palm full of the sand from the cream bowl. It was a shade or two darker than the container. She tossed this with a sharp movement of her wrist, and it settled smoothly as a film on the tabletop.

What she was doing was not of her concious mind, as if another had taken charge of her actions. And judging by the way the woman in the chair leaned forward, the hush that had fallen on her companions, this was right and proper.

Without any order from her mind, Tamisan's right hand went now to the blue bowl with its dark blue sand. But this was not tossed. Instead, she held the fine grains in her fist and that upright, passing it slowly over the table top so that a very tiny trickle of grit fed down to make a pattern on the first film.

And it was a pattern, not a random scattering. What she had so drawn was a recognizable sword with a basket-shaped hilt and a slightly curved blade tapering to a narrow point.

Now her hand moved to the pink bowl. The sand she gathered up there was a dark red, more vivid than the other colors, as if she dealt now with flecks of newly shed blood. Once more she used her upheld fist, and the shifting stream, fed from her palm, became a space ship! It was slightly different in outline from those she had seen all her life, but it was unmistakably a ship. And it was drawn on the table top as if it threatened to descend upon the pointed sword. Or was it that the sword threatened it?

She heard a gasp of surprise—or was it fear? But that sound had not come from the woman who had bade her foretell. It must have broken from some other member of the company intent upon Tamisan's painting with the flowing sand.

It was to the fourth bowl now that her right hand moved. But she did not take up a full fistful, rather a generous pinch between thumb and forefinger. She held the sand high above the picture and released it. The green specks floated down—to gather in a sign like a circle with one portion missing.

She stared at that, and it seemed to alter a little under the intentness of her watching. What it had changed to was a symbol she knew well, one which brought a small gasp from her. It was the seal, simplified it was true, but still readable, of the House of Starrex, and it overlaid both the edge of the ship and the tip of the sword.

"Read you this!" The noblewoman demanded sharply.

And from somewhere the words came readily to Tamisan. "The sword is the sword of Ty-Kry raised in defense."

"Assured, assured." The murmur ran along the divans.

"The ship comes as a danger—"

"That thing—a ship? But it is no ship—"

"It is a ship from the stars."

"A woe—woe and woe—" That was no murmur now but a full-throated cry of fright. "As in the days of our fathers when we had to deal with the false ones. Ahta—let the spirit of Ahta be shield to our arms, a sword in our hands!"

The noblewoman made a silencing gesture with one hand. "Enough! Crying to the reverend spirits may bring comfort, but they are not noted for helping those not standing to arms on their own behalf. There have been other sky ships since Ahta's days, and with them we have dealt—to *our* purpose. If another comes, we are forewarned, which is also forearmed. But what lies there in green, O Mouth of Olava, which surprised even you?"

Tamisan had had precious moments in which to think. If it were true as she had deduced, that she was tied to this world by those she had brought with her, then she must find them. And it was clear that they were not of this company. Therefore this last must be made to work for her.

"The green sign is that of a champion, one meant to be mighty in the coming battle. But he shall not be known save when the sign points to him, and it may be that this can only be seen by one with the Eyes."

She looked to the noblewoman, and meeting those old eyes, Tamisan felt a small chill rise in her, one which had not been born from the still damp clothing she wore. For there was that in those two shadowed eyes which questioned coldly and did not accept without proof.

"So should the one with the Eyes you speak of go sniffing all through Ty-Kry and the land beyond the city, even to the boundaries of the world?"

"If need be," Tamisan stood firm.

"A long journey, mayhap, and many step-strides into danger. And if the ship comes before this champion is found? A thin cord I think, O Mouth, on which to hang the future of a city, a kingdom or a people. Look if you will, but I say we have more tested ways of dealing with these interlopers from the skies. But, Mouth, since you have given warning, let it so be remembered."

She put her hands on the arms of her chair and arose, using them to lever her. And so all her company came to their feet, two of the women hurrying to her so that she could lay her hands upon their shoulders to support her out. Without another glance at Tamisan she went, nor did the dreamer rise to see her go. For suddenly she was spent, tired as she had been in the past when a dream broke and left her supine and drained. Only this dream did not break, but kept her sitting before the table and its sand pictures, looking at that green symbol, still caught fast in the web of another world.

The woman in green returned, bearing a goblet in her two hands, offering it to Tamisan.

"The First Standing will go to the High Castle and the Over-Queen. She turned into that road. Drink, Tamisan, and mayhap the Over-Queen herself will ask you for a seeing."

Tamisan? That was her true name. Twice this woman had called her by it. How was it known in a dream? Yet she dared not ask that question or any of the others she needed answers for. Instead she drank from the goblet, finding the liquid hot and spicy, driving the chill from her body.

There was so much she must learn, must know, and she could not discover it save indirectly, lest she reveal what she was and was not.

"I am tired."

"There is a resting place prepared," the woman said. "You have only to come—"

Tamisan had almost to lever herself up as the noblewoman had done. She was giddy, had to catch at the back of the chair. Then she moved after her hostess, hoping desperately to know . . .

5

DID one sleep in a dream, dream upon dream, perhaps? Tamisan wondered about that as she stretched out upon the couch her hostess showed her. Yet when she set aside her crown and laid her head upon the roll which served as a pillow, she was once more alert, her thoughts racing or entangled in such wild confusion that she felt as giddy as she had upon rising from her seer's chair.

The Starrex symbol overlying both that of the sword and the space ship in the sand picture—could it mean that she would only find what she sought when the might of this world met that of the starmen? And had she indeed in some manner fallen into the past where she would relive the first coming of the space voyagers to Ty-Kry? But no, the noblewoman had mentioned past encounters with them which had ended in favor of Ty-Kry.

Tamisan tried to envision a world of her own time, but one in which history had taken a different road. Yet much of that around her was of the past. Did that mean that, without the decisions of her own time, the world of Ty-Kry remained largely unchanged from century to century?

Real, unreal, old, now—she had lost all a dreamer's command of action. Tamisan did not play now with toys which she could move about at will, but rather was caught up in a series of events she could not foresee and over which she had no control. Yet twice the woman had called her by her rightful name—and without willing it she had used the devices of a Mouth of Olava to foretell, as if she had done so many times before.

Could it be? Tamisan closed her teeth upon her lower lip and felt the pain of that, just as she felt the pain of the bruises left by her abrupt entrance into the mysterious here. Could it be that some dreams were so deep, so well woven that they were to the dreamer real? Was this indeed the fate of those "closed" dreamers who were worthless for the Hive? Did they in their trances live a countless number of lives? But she was not a closed dreamer—

Awake! Once more, stretched as she was upon the couch, she used the proper technique to throw herself out of a dream. And once more she experienced that weird nothingness in which she spun sickeningly, as if held helplessly in some void, tied to an anchor which kept her back from the full leap to sane safety. There was only one explanation—that somewhere in this strange Ty-Kry one or both of those who had prepared to share her dream was now to be found and must be sought out before she could return.

So—the sooner that she accomplished, the better! But where should she start seeking? Though a feeling of weakness clung to her limbs, making her move slowly as if she strove to walk against the pull of a strong current, Tamisan arose from the couch. She turned to pick up her Mouth's crown and so looked into the oval of a mirror, startled thus into immobility. For the figure she looked upon as her own reflection was not that she had seen before.

It was not the robe or the crown which had changed her; she was not the same person. For a long time, ever since she could remember, she had had the pallid skin and the close-cropped hair of a dreamer very seldom in the sunlight. But the face of the woman in the mirror was a soft, even brown. The cheekbones were wide, the eyes large, the lips very red. Her brows—she leaned closer to the mirror to see what gave them that odd upward slant and decided that they had been plucked or shaven to produce the effect. Her hair was perhaps three fingers long and not her very fair coloring, but dark and curling. She was not the Tamisan she knew, nor was this stranger the product of her own will.

And it must follow logically that if she did not look like her normal self—then perhaps the two she sought were no longer as she remembered either. Thus her search would be twice the more difficult. Could she ever recognize them?

Frightened now, she sat down on the couch, facing the mirror. No, she dared not even give way to fear. For if she once let it break her control she might be utterly lost. Logic, even in such a world of unlogic, must make her think lucidly.

Just how true was her soothsaying? At least she had not influenced that fall of the sand. Therefore—perhaps the Mouth of Olava did have supernatural powers. She had played with the idea of magic in the past to embroider dreams, but that had been her own creation. Could she use it by will now—since it would seem this unknown self of hers did manage to draw upon some unknown source of power?

Fasten her thoughts upon one of the men, hold him in her mind—could the dream tie pull her to him? Kas or Starrex? All she knew of her master she had learned from tapes, and tapes gave one only superficial knowledge, as if one could study a person going through only half-understood actions behind a veil which concealed more than it displayed. Kas had spoken directly to her, his flesh had touched hers. If she must choose one to draw her, then it had better be Kas.

Kas—in her mind Tamisan built a memory sketch of him as she would build a preliminary picture for a dream. Then suddenly the Kas in her mind flickered and changed. She saw another man. He was taller than the Kas she knew, and he wore a uniform tunic and space boots—his features were hard to distinguish—and that vision lasted only a fraction of time.

The ship! That symbol had lain touching both ship and sword in the sand seeing. And it would be easier to seek a man on the ship than wandering through the streets of a strange city with no better clue than that Starrex—this world's counterpart—might just be here.

So little on which to pin a quest! A ship which might or might not be now approaching Ty-Kry—and which would meet a drastic reception when it landed. Suppose Kas—or his this-world's double—were killed? Would that anchor her here for all time? Resolutely Tamisan pushed such negative speculation to the back of her mind. First things first; the ship had not yet planeted. But when it came she must make sure that she was among those who were preparing for its welcome.

It seemed that having made that decision she was at last able to sleep, for the fatigue which had struck at her in the hall returned a hundredfold, and she fell, back on the couch as one drugged, remembering nothing more until she awakened to find the woman in green standing above her, one hand on her shoulder shaking her gently back to awareness.

"Awake—there is a summons."

A summons to dream, Tamisan thought dazedly, and then the unfamiliar room, the immediate past came completely back to her.

"The First Standing Jassa has summoned." The woman sounded excited. "It is said by her messenger, and he has brought a chair cart for you, that you are to go to the High Castle! Perhaps you will see for the Over-Queen herself! But there is time—I have won it for you—to bathe, to eat, to change your robe. See—I have plundered my own bride chest—" She pointed to a chair over which was spread a robe, not of the deep violet Tamisan now wore, but of a purple-wine. "It is the only one of the proper color—or near it." She ran her hand lovingly over the rich folds.

"But haste!" she added briskly. "As a Mouth you can

claim the need for making ready to appear before high company, but to linger too long will raise the anger of the First Standing."

There was a basin large enough to serve as a bath in the room beyond. And, as well as the robe, the woman brought fresh body linen. So that when Tamisan stood once more before the mirror to clasp her silver belt and assume the Mouth crown, she felt renewed and refreshed and her thanks were warm.

But the woman made a gesture of brushing them aside. "Are we not of the same clan, cousin-kin? Shall one say that Nahra is not open-handed with her own? That you are a Mouth is our clan pride, let us enjoy it through you!"

She brought a covered bowl and a goblet and Tamisan ate a dish of mush-meal into which had been baked dried fruit and bits of what she thought well-chopped meat. It was tasty, and she finished it to the last crumb, just as she emptied the cup of a tart-sweet drink.

"Well away, Tamisan, this is a great day for the clan of Fremont when you go to the High Castle and perhaps stand before the Over-Queen. May it be that the Seeing is not for ill, but for good. Though you are but the Mouth of Olava and not the One dealing fortune to us who live and die."

"For your aid and your good wishing, receive my thanks," Tamisan said. "I, too, hope that fortune comes from misfortune on this day." And that is stark truth, she thought, for I must gather fortune to me with both hands and hold it tight, lest the chancy game I play be lost.

First Standing Jassa's messenger was an officer, his hair clubbed up under a ridged helm to give additional protection to his head in battle, his breastplate enameled blue with the double crown of the Over-Queen, and his sword very much to the fore—as if he already strode the street of a city at war. There was a small grypon between the shafts of the chair cart and two men-at-arms ready, one at the grypon's head, the other holding aside the curtains as their officer handed Tamisan into the chair. He brusquely jerked the curtains shut without asking her pleasure, and she decided that perhaps her visit to the High Castle was to be a secret matter.

But between the curtain edges she caught sight of this Ty-Kry. And, though in parts it was very strange to her, there were enough similarities to provide her with an anchor to the real. The sky towers and other off-world forms of architectures which had been introduced by space travelers were missing. But the streets themselves, the many beds of foliage and flowers, were those she had known all her life.

And the High Castle—she drew a deep breath as they wound out of town and along the river—this—this had been part of her world, too, though then as a ruined and very ancient landmark. Part of it had been slagged in the war of Sylt's rebellion. And it had been considered a place of misfortune, largely shunned, save for off-world tourists seeking the unusual.

But here it was in its pride, larger, more widely spread than in her Ty-Kry, as if the generations who had deserted it in her world had clung to it here, adding ever to its bulk. For it was not a single structure but a city in itself, though it had no merchants nor public buildings, but rather provided homes to shelter the nobles, who must spend part of the year at court, and all their servants, and the many officials of the kingdom.

In its heart was the building which gave it its name, a collection of towers, rising far above the lesser structures at the foot. These were of a gray at their bases which changed subtly as they arose until their tops were a deep, rich blue, while the other buildings in the great pile were wholly gray as to wall, a darker blue as to roof.

The chair creaked forward on its two wheels, the grypon being kept to a steady pace by the man at its head, and passed under the thick arch in the outer wall, then up a street between buildings which, though dwarfed by the towers, were in turn dwarfing to those who walked or rode by them.

There was a second gate, more buildings, a third, and then the open space about the central towers. They had passed people in plenty since entering the first gate. Many were soldiers of the guard, but some of the armed men had worn other colors and insignia, being, Tamisan guessed, the retainers of court lords. And now and then some Lord came proudly, his retinue strung along behind him by threes to make a show which amused Tamisan, as if the number of followers to tread on one's heels enhanced one's importance in the world.

She was handed down with a little more ceremony than she had been ushered into the chair. And the officer offered her his wrist, his men falling in behind as a groom hurried forward to lead off the equipage, thus affording her a tail-of-honor too.

But the towers of the High Castle were so awe-inspiring, so huge a pile, she was glad she had an escort into their heart. The farther they went through halls—so high that it was hard to see their dusky roofs, ill lit by only the big candles in their man-tall holders—the more uneasy she became. As if once within his maze there might be no retreat and she would be lost forever.

6

TWICE they climbed staircases until her legs ached with the effort and the stairs took on the aspect of mountains. Then her party passed into a long hall which was lighted not only by the candle-trees but some thin rays filtering through windows placed so high above their heads that nothing could be seen through them. And Tamisan, in that part of her which seemed familiar with this world, knew this to be the Walk of the Nobles, and the company now gathered here were, nearest, the Third Standing, then the Second and, at the far end of that road of blue carpet onto which her guide led her, First Standing—or rather sitting, there being two arcs of hooded and canopied chairs, with a throne above them on a three-step dais. And the hood over that was upheld by a double crown which glittered with gems, while on the steps were grouped men in the armor of the guard and others wearing bright tunics, their hair loose upon their shoulders.

It was toward that throne that the officer led her and they passed through the ranks of the Third Standing, hearing a low murmur of voices. Tamisan looked neither to right or left. She wished to see the Over-Queen, for it was plain she was being granted full audience. And then—something stirred deep within her as if a small pin pricked. The reason for this she did not know, save that ahead was something of vast importance to her.

Now they were equal with the first of the chairs and she saw that the greater number of those who so sat were women, but not all. And mainly they were of an age to be at least in middle life. So Tamisan came to the foot of the dais, and in that moment she did not go to one knee as did the officer, but rather raised her fingertips to touch the rim of the crown on her head. For with another of those flashes of half recognition, she knew that in this place that which she represented did not bow as did others, but acknowledged only that the Queen was one to whom human allegiance was granted after another and greater loyalty was paid elsewhere.

The Over-Queen looked down with as deeply searching a stare as Tamisan looked up. And what Tamisan saw was a woman to whom she could not set an age; rather she might be either old or young, for the years had not seemed to mark her. The robe on her full figure was not ornate, but a soft pearl color without ornamentation, save that she wore a girdle of silvery chains braided and woven together, and a collarlike necklace of the same metal from which fringed milky gems cut into drops. Her hair was a flame of brightly glowing red in which a diadem of the same creamy stones was almost hidden. As for her face—was she beautiful? Tamisan could not have said. But that she was vitally alive there was no doubt. Even though she sat so quietly now, there was an aura of energy about her suggesting that this was only a pause between the doing of great and necessary deeds. To Tamisan she was the most assertive personality she had ever seen and instantly the guards of a dreamer went into action. To serve such a mistress, Tamisan thought, would sap all the personality from one, so that the servant would become but a mirror to reflect from that surrender onward.

"Welcome, Mouth of Olava who has been uttering strange things." The Over-Queen's voice was mocking, challenging.

"A Mouth says naught, Great One, save what is given it to speak." Tamisan found her answer ready, though she had not consciously formed it in her mind.

"So we are told. Though Gods may grow old and tired. Or is that only the fate of men? But now it is our will that Olava speak again—if that is fortune for this hour. So be it!"

As if that last phrase was an order there was a stir among those standing on the steps of the throne. Two of the guardsmen brought out a table, a third a stool, the fourth a tray on which rested four bowls of sand. These they set up before the throne.

Tamisan took her place on the stool, again put her fingers to her temples. Would this work once more? Or must she try to force a picture in the sand? She felt a small shiver of nerves she fought to control.

"What desires the Great One?" She was glad to hear her voice steady, no hint of her uneasiness in it.

"What chances in—say four passages of the sun?"

Tamisan waited. Would that other personality or power, or whatever it might be, take over? But her hand did not move. Instead that odd, disturbing prick grew the stronger; she was drawn, even as a noose might be laid about her forehead to pull her head around. So she turned to follow the dictates of that pull, to look where something willed her eyes to look. But all she saw was the line of officers on the steps of the throne, and they stared at and through her, none with any sign of recognition by Starrex! She grasped at that hope; but none of them resembled the man she sought.

"Does Olava sleep? Or has His Mouth been forgotten for a space?"

The Over-Queen's voice was sharper, and Tamisan broke that hold on her attention, looked back to the throne and the woman on it.

"It is not meet for the Mouth to speak unless Olava wishes—" Tamisan began, with increasing nervousness until she felt that sensation in her left hand, as if it were not under her control but possessed by another will. She fell silent as it gathered up the brownish sand and tossed it to form a picture's background.

But this time she did not seek next the blue grains; rather her fist dug into the red and moved to paint in the outline of the space ship, above it a single red circle.

Then there was a moment of hesitation, before her fingers strayed to the green, took up a generous pinch and again made Starrex's symbol below the ship.

"A single sun," the Over-Queen read out. "One day until the enemy comes. But what is the remaining word of Olava, Mouth?"

"That there be one among you who is a key to victory. He shall stand against the enemy and under him fortune comes."

"So? And who is this hero?"

Tamisan looked again to the line of officers. Dared she trust to instinct? Something within her urged her on.

"Let each of these protectors of Ty-Kry—" She raised a finger to indicate the officers. "Let each come forward and take up the sand of seeing. Let the Mouth touch that hand and may it then strew the answer—perhaps Olava will so make it clear."

To Tamisan's surprise, the Over-Queen laughed. "As good a way as any perhaps for picking a champion. Though to abide by Olava's choice—that is another matter." And her smile faded as she glanced at the men, as if there was a thought in her mind which disturbed her.

At her nod, they came one by one. Under the shadows of their helmets their faces, being of one race, were very similiar; and Tamisan, studying each, could see no chance of telling which Starrex might be.

Each took up a pinch of green sand, held out his hand palm down and let the grains fall while she set fingertip to the back of that hand. The sand drifted, but in no shape and to no purpose.

It was not until the last man came that there was a difference, for then the sand did not drift, but fell to form again the symbol which was twin to the one already on the table. Tamisan looked up. The officer was staring at the sand rather then meeting her eyes, and there was a line of strain about his mouth, a look about him such as might shadow the face of a man who stood with his back to a wall and a ring of sword points at his throat.

"This is your man," Tamisan said. Starrex? She must be sure—if she could only demand the truth in this instant!

But her preoccupation was swept aside.

"Olava deals falsely!" That cry came from the officer behind her, the one who had brought her here.

"Perhaps we must not think ill of Olava's advice." The Over-Queen's voice had a guttural, feline purr. "It may be his Mouth is not wholly wedded to his service, but speaks for others than Olava at times. Hawarel—so you are to be our champion—"

The officer went to one knee, his hands clasped loosely before him as if he wished all to see he did not reach for any weapon.

"I am no choice, save the Great One's." In spite of the strain visible in his tense body he spoke levelly and without a tremor.

"Great One, *this* traitor—" Two of the officers moved as if to lay hands upon him and drag him away.

"No. Has not Olava spoken?" The mockery was very plain in the Over-Queen's tone now. "But to make sure that Olava's will be carried out, take good care of our champion-to-be. Since Hawarel is to fight our battle with the cursed starmen, he must be saved to do it." Now she looked to Tamisan, who was still startled by the quick turn of events and their hostility to Olava's choice. "Let the Mouth of Olava share with Hawarel this waiting that she may, perhaps instill in Olava's choice the vigor and strength such a battle will demand of our chosen champion." Each time the Over-Queen spoke the last word she made of it a thing of derision and subtle menace.

"The audience is finished." The Over-Queen arose, stepped behind the throne as those about Tamisan fell to their knees; and then she was gone. But the officer who had guided Tamisan was by her side. And Hawarel, once more on his feet, was closely flanked by two of the other guards, one of whom pulled their prisoner's sword from his sheath before he could move. With Hawarel before her, Tamisan was urged from the hall.

At the moment she was pleased enough to go, hoping for a chance to prove the rightness of her guess, that Hawarel and Starrex were the same and she had found the first of her fellow dreamers—was this far onward toward their release.

They traversed more halls until they came to a door which one of Hawarel's guards opened. The prisoner walked through and Tamisan's escort waved her after him.

Then the door slammed shut and at that sound Hawarel whirled around.

Under the beaking fore plate of his helmet his eyes were cold fire and he seemed a man about to leap for his enemy's throat.

"Who—" His voice was only a harsh whisper. "Who set you to my death wishing, witch?"

7

HIS clawed hands were reaching for her throat. Tamisan flung up her arm in an attempt to guard, stumbled back.

"Lord Starrex!" If she had been wrong—if—!

Though his finger tips brushed her shoulders, he did not grasp her. Instead it was his turn to retreat a step or two, his mouth half open in a gasp.

"Witch—witch!" The very force of the words he hurled at her made them like darts dispatched from one of the archaic crossbows of the history tapes.

"Lord Starrex," Tamisan repeated, feeling on more secure ground at seeing his stricken amazement, no longer fearing he would attack her out of hand. His reaction to that name was enough to assure her she was right, though he did not seem prepared to acknowledge it.

"I am Hawarel of the Vanora," he brought out those words as harsh croaking.

Tamisan glanced around. This was a bare-walled room, with no hiding place for a listener. In her own time and place she could have feared many scanning devices. But she thought those unknown to this Ty-Kry. And to win Hawarel-Starrex into cooperation was very necessary.

"You are Lord Starrex," she returned with bold confidence or at least what she hoped was a convincing show of such. "Just as I am Tamisan, the dreamer. And this, wherein we are caught, is the dream you ordered of me."

He raised his hand to his forehead, his fingers encountered his helmet, and he swept it off unheedingly, so that it clanked and skidded across the polished floor. His hair, netted into a kind of protecting cushion, was piled about his head, giving him an odd appearance to Tamisan. It was black and thick, just as his skin was as brown-hued as that of her new body. And without the shadow of the helm she could see his face more clearly, finding in it no resemblance to the aloof master of the sky towers. In a way, it was that of a younger man, one less certain of himself.

"I am Hawarel," he repeated doggedly. "You try to trap me, or perhaps the trap has already closed and you seek now to make me condemn myself with my own mouth. I tell you, I am no traitor—I am Hawarel and my blood oath to the Great One has been faithfully kept."

Tamisan experienced a rise of impatience. She had not thought Lord Starrex to be a stupid man. But it would seem his counterpart here lacked more than just the face of his other self.

"You are Starrex, and this is a dream." If it was not, she did not care to raise that issue now. "Remember the sky tower? You bought me from Jabis for dreaming. Then you summoned me—and Lord Kas—and ordered me to prove my worth."

His brows drew together in a black frown as he stared at her.

"What have they given you or promised, that you do to me?" came his counter-demand. "I am no sworn enemy to you or yours—not that I know."

Tamisan sighed. "Do you deny you know the name Starrex?" she asked.

For a long moment he was silent. Then he turned from her took a stride or two, his toe thumping against his helmet, sending it rolling ahead of him. She waited. He rounded again to face her.

"You are a Mouth of Olava—"

She shook her head, interrupting him. "We have little

time for such fencing, Lord Starrex. You do know that name, and it is in my mind that you also remember the rest, at least in some measure. I am Tamisan the dreamer."

It was his turn to sigh. "So you say."

"So I shall continue to say. And, mayhap as I do, others than you will listen."

"As I thought!" he flashed. "You would have me betray myself."

"If you are truly Hawarel as you state, then what have you to betray?"

"Very well. I am—am two! I am Hawarel and I am someone else who has queer memories and who may well be a night demon come to dispute ownership of this body. There—you have it! Go and tell those who sent you and have me out to the arrow range for a quick ending there. Perhaps that will be better than to continue as a battle field between two different selves."

Perhaps he was not just being obstinate, Tamisan thought. It might be that the dream had a greater hold on him than it did on her. After all she was a trained dreamer, one used to venturing into illusions wrought from imagination.

"If you can remember a little—then listen!" She drew closer to him and began to speak in a lower voice—not that she believed they could be overheard, but it was well to take no chances. Swiftly she gave her account of this whole mad tangle, or what had been her part in it.

When she was done she was surprised to see that a certain hardening had overtaken his features, so that now he looked more resolute, less like one trapped in a maze which had no guide.

"And this is the truth?"

"By what god or power do you wish me to swear to it?" She was exasperated now, frustrated by his lingering doubts.

"None, because it explains what was heretofore unexplainable—what has made my life a hell of doubt these past hours and brought more suspicion upon me. I have been two persons. But if this is all a dream—why is that so?"

"I do not know." Tamisan chose frankness as best befitting her needs now. "This is unlike any dream I have created before."

"In what manner?" he asked crisply.

"It is part of a dreamer's duty to study her master's personality, to suit his desires, even if those be unexpressed and hidden. From what I had learned of you—of Lord Starrex—I thought that too much had been already seen, experienced, known to you. That it must be a new approach I tried, or else you would find that dreaming held no profit.

"Therefore it came to me suddenly that I would not dream of the past, nor of the future, which are the common approaches for an action dreamer, but refine upon the subject. In the past there were times in history when the future rested upon a single decision. And it was in my mind to select certain of these decisions and then envision a world, co-existent with our own, in which those decisions had gone in the opposite direction—trying to see what would be the present-day result of actions in the past."

"And so this is what you tried? And what decisions did you select for your experiment at the rewriting of history?" He was giving her his full attention now.

"I took three. First, the Welcome of the Over-Queen Ahta; second the drift of the Colony ship Wanderer; third, the rebellion of Sylt. Should the Welcome have been a rejection, should the colony ship never reached here, should Sylt have failed—these would produce a world I thought might be interesting to visit—in a dream. So I read what history tapes I could call upon. Thus, when you summoned me to dream I had my ideas ready. But—it did not work as it should have. Instead of spinning the proper dream, creating incidents in good order, I found myself fast caught in a world I did not know, nor build."

As she spoke she watched the change in him. He had lost all the fervent antagonism of his first attack on her. More and more, she could see what she had associated with the personality of Lord Starrex coming through the unfamiliar envelope of the guardsman's body.

"So it did not work properly—"

"No, as I have said, I found myself in the dream, with no control of action, no recognizable creation factors. I do not understand—"

"No? There could be one explanation." The frown line was back between his brows but it was not a scowl aimed at her; rather it was as if he were trying hard to remember something of importance which eluded his efforts. "There is a theory, a very old one—Yes! That of Parallel worlds!"

In her wide use of the tapes she had not come across that and now she demanded the knowledge of him almost fiercely. "What are those?"

"You are not the first—how could you be—to be struck by the notion that sometimes history and the future hang upon a very thin cord which can be twisted this way and that by small chance. There was a theory once advanced that when that chanced it created a second world, one in which the decision was made to the right, when that of the world we know went to the left."

"But—alternated worlds—where—how did they exist?"

"Thus, perhaps." He held out his two hands horizontally one above the other. "In layers. There were even old tales, created for amusement, of men traveling, not back in time, nor forward, but across it from one such world to another."

"But—here we are. I am a Mouth of Olava, nor do I look like myself. Just as to the eye you are not Lord Starrex—"

"Perhaps we are the people we would be if our world had taken the other side of your three decisions. It is a clever device for a dreamer to create, Tamisan."

"Only," she told him now the last truth, "I do not think I have created it. Certainly I can not control it—"

"You have tried to break this dream?"

"Of course! But I am tied here. I think by you and the Lord Kas. Until we three try together, perhaps we can not any of us return."

"And Kas—now you must go searching for him?"

She shook her head. "Kas, I think, is one of the crew on this spacer about to set down. I believe I saw him—though not his face." Now she smiled a little shakily. "It seems that though I am mainly the Tamisan I have always been, yet also do I have some of the powers of a Mouth. Just as you are Hawarel as well as Starrex."

"The longer I listen to you," he announced, "the more I become Starrex. So we must find Kas on the spacer before we wrangle free from this tangle? But that is going to be rather a problem. I am enough of Hawarel to know that the spacer is going to receive the usual welcome dealt off-world ships here—trickery and extinction. Your three points have been as you envisioned them. There was no Welcome, but rather a massacre, no colony ship ever reached here, and Sylt was speared by a contemptuous man-at-arms the first time he lifted his voice to draw a crowd. Hawarel knows this as the truth; as Starrex I am aware there is another truth which did radically change life on this planet. Now, did you seek me out on purpose, your champion tale intended to be our bridge to Kas?"

"No, at least I did not consciously arrange it so. I tell you, I have some of the powers of a Mouth—they take over."

He gave a sharp bark of sound which was not laughter but somewhat akin to it. "By the Fist of Jimsam Taragon, we have it complicated by magic, too! And I suppose you can not tell me just how much a Mouth can do in the way of foreseeing or forearming or freeing us from this trap?"

Tamisan shook her head. "The Mouths were mentioned in the history tapes; they were very important once.

But after Sylt's rebellion they were either killed or disappeared. They were hunted by both sides and most of what we know about them is only legend. I can not tell you what I can do. Sometimes something—perhaps it is the memory and knowledge of this body—takes over and then I do strange things. I neither will nor understand them."

8

HE crossed the room and pulled two stools from a far corner. "We might as well sit at ease and explore what we can of this world's memories. It just might be that united we can learn more than when trying singly. The trouble is—" He reached out a hand and mechanically she touched fingertips to the back of it in an oddly formal ceremony which was not part of her own knowledge. So he guided her to one of the stools and she was glad to sit down.

"The trouble is," he repeated as he dropped on the other stool, stretching out his long legs and tugging at his sword belt with that dangerously empty sheath, "that I was more than a little mixed up when I awoke, if you might call it that—in this body. So that my first reactions must have suggested mental imbalance to those I encountered. Luckily the Hawarel part was in control soon enough to save me. But there is a second drawback to this identity—I am suspect as coming from a province where there has been a rebellion. In fact I am here in Ty-Kry as a distrusted hostage, rather than a member in good standing of the guard. I have not been able to ask questions, and all I have learned is in bits and pieces. The real Hawarel is a quite uncomplicated and simple soldier who is hurt by the suspicion against him and quite fervently loyal to the crown. I wonder how Kas took *his* awakening. If he preserves any remnant of his real self, he ought to be well established by now."

Tamisan, surprised, asked a question to which she

hoped he would give a true and open answer: "You do not like—you have reason to fear Lord Kas?"

"Like? Fear?" She could see that thin shadow of Starrex overlaying Hawarel become more distinct. "Those are emotions. I have had little to do with emotions for some time."

"But you wanted him to share the dream," she persisted.

"True. I may not be emotional about my esteemed cousin, but I am a prudent man. Since it was by his urging, in fact his arrangement, that you were added to my household, I thought it only fair he share in his plan for my entertainment. I know that Kas is very solicitous of his crippled cousin, ready-handed to serve in any way—so generous of time, energy—"

"You suspect him of something?" She thought she had sensed what lay behind his words.

"Suspect? Of what? He has been, as all would assure you freely, and as far as I would allow, my good friend." But there was a closed look about him, warning her off from any further exploration of that.

"His crippled cousin." This time Hawarel repeated those words as if he spoke to himself and not to her. "At least you have done me a small service on the credit side of the scale." Now he did look to Tamisan as he thumped his right leg with a satisfaction which was not of the Starrex she knew. "You have provided me with a body in good working order. Which I may well need, since so far bad has outweighed the good in this world."

"Hawarel—Lord Starrex—" she was beginning when he interrupted her.

"Give me always Hawarel. Remember! There is no need to add to the already heavy load of suspicion surrounding me in these halls."

"Hawarel, then. I did not choose you for the champion; that was done by that power I do not understand, working through me. If they agree—then you have a good chance to find Kas. You may even demand that he be the one you battle."

"Find him how?"

"They may allow me to select the proper one from the off-world force," she suggested. A very thin thread on which to hang any plan of escape, but she could not see a better one.

"And you think that this sand painting will pick him out—as it did me?"

"But it *did* you, did it not?"

"That I can not deny."

"And the first time I foresaw—for one of the First Standing—it made such an impression on her that she had me summoned here to foresee for the Over-Queen."

"Magic!" Again he uttered that half laugh.

"To another worlder, much that the space travelers can do might be termed magic."

"Well enough. I have seen things—yes, I have seen things myself, and not while dreaming either. Very well, I am to volunteer to meet an enemy champion from the ship and then you sand paint out the proper one. If you are successful and do find Kas—then what?"

"It is simple—we wake."

"You take us with you, of course?"

"If we are so linked that we can not leave here without one another—then a single waking will take us all."

"Are you sure you need Kas? After all, I was the one you were planning this dream for."

"We go, leave the Lord Kas here?"

"A cowardly withdrawal you think, my dreamer. But one, I assure you, which would solve many things. However—can you send me through, return for Kas? It is in my mind I would like to know what is happening now for myself—in our own world. Is it not by the dreamer's oath that he for whom the dream is wrought has first call upon the dreamer?"

So he did have some lurking uneasiness tied to Kas!

But in a manner he was right. She reached out before he was aware of what she would do and seized his hand, at the same time using the formula for waking. Once more that mist which was nowhere enveloped her. But it was no use; her first guess had been right—they were still tied. And she blinked her eyes open upon the same room. Hawarel had slumped, was falling from his stool so that she had to go to one knee to support his body with her shoulder or he would have slid full length to the floor. Then his muscles tightened and he jerked erect, his eyes open and blazing into hers with the same cold anger with which he had first greeted her upon entering this room.

"Why—?"

"You asked," she countered.

His lids drooped so she could no longer see that icy anger. "So I did. But I did not quite expect to be so quickly served. Now, you have effectively proven your point—three go or none. And it remains to be seen how soon we can find our missing third."

He asked her no more questions and she was glad, since that whirl into nowhere in the abortive attempt at waking had tired her greatly. She moved the stool a little so her back could rest against the wall and she was farther from him. But in a little while he got to his feet and paced back and forth as if some driving desire for wider action worked in him, to the point where he could not sit still.

Once the door opened, but they were not summoned forth. Instead food and drink were brought to them by one of the guards, the other standing ready with a crossbow at thigh, his eyes ever upon them.

"We are well served." Hawarel opened the lids of bowls and inspected their contents. "It would seem we are of importance. Hail, Rugaard, when do we go forth from this room, of which I am growing very tired?"

"Be at peace, you shall have action enough when the Great One desires it," the officers by the crossbowman answered. "The ship from the stars has been sighted, the mountain beacons have blazed twice. They seem to be aiming for the plain beyond Ty-Kry. It is odd that they are so single-minded and come to the same pen to be taken each time. Perhaps Dalskol was right when he said that they do not think for themselves at all, but carry out the orders of an off-world power which does not allow them independent judgment. Your service time will come. And, Mouth of Olava—" He took a step forward to see Tamisan the better. "The Great One says that it might be well to read the sand on your own behalf. For false seers are given to those they have belittled in such seeing, to be done with as those they have so shamed may decide."

"As is well known," she answered him. "I have not dealt falsely, as shall be seen at the proper time and in the proper place."

When they were gone she was hungry, and so it seemed was Hawarel, for they divided fairly and left nothing in the bowls. When they were done he said, "Since you are a reader of history and know old customs, perhaps you remember one which it is not too pleasant to recall now—that among some races it was the proper thing to dine well a prisoner about to die."

"You choose a heartening thing to think on!"

"No, you choose it, for this is your world, remember that, my dreamer."

Tamisan closed her eyes and leaned her head and shoulders back against the wall. Perhaps she even slept a little, for there was the clang of sudden noise and she gasped out of a doze. The room had grown dark, but at the door was a blaze of light and in that stood the officer, behind a guard of spearmen.

"The time has come," he said.

"The wait has been long." Hawarel stood up, stretching wide his arms as one who has been ready for too long. Then he turned to her and once more offered his wrist. She would have liked to have done without his aid, but she found herself stiff and cramped enough to be glad of it.

They went on a complicated way through halls, down stairs until at last they issued out into the night. And awaiting them was a covered cart much larger than the chair on wheels which had brought her to the castle, this one with two grypons between its shafts.

Into this their guard urged them, drawing the curtains, pegging those down tightly outside, so that even had they wished they could not and looked out. And as the cart creaked out, Tamisan tried to guess by sound where they might be going.

There was little noise to guide her. It was as if they now passed through a town deep in slumber. But in the gloom of the cart she felt rather than saw movement, and then a shoulder brushed hers and a whisper so faint she had to strain to hear it was at her ear.

"Out of the castle—"

"Where?"

"My guess is the field—the forbidden place—"

The memory of the this-world Tamisan supplied explanation. That was where two other spacers had planeted—not to rise again. In fact, the one which had come fifty years ago had never been dismantled but stood, a corroded mass of metal, to be a double warning—to the stars not to invade, to Ty-Kry to be alert against such invasion.

It seemed to Tamisan that their ride would never come to an end. Then there was an abrupt halt which bumped her soundly against the side of the cart, and lights bedazzled her eyes as the end curtains were pulled aside.

"Come, Champion and Champion-maker!"

Hawarel obeyed first and turned to give her assistance once more; but he was elbowed aside as the officer pulled rather than led her into the open. Torches in the hands of spearmen ringed them around. Beyond was a colorful mass of people, with a double rank of guards drawn up as a barrier between those and the dark of the land beyond.

"Up there—" Hawarel was beside her again.

Tamisan raised her eyes, almost blinded by the glare as

a sudden pillar of fire burst across the night sky. A spacer was riding down on tail rockets to make a fin landing.

9

BY the light of those flames, the whole plain was illumined. Beyond stood the hulk of the unfortunate spacer which had last planeted here. And there, drawn up in lines was a large force of spearmen, crossbowmen, officers with the basket-hilted weapons at their sides. However, as they stood they might seem a guard of honor for the Over-Queen, who sat raised above the rest on a very tall chair cart—certainly not an army in battle array.

And those in the ship—they might well look contemptuously on such archaic weapons as useless. How *had* those of Ty-Kry taken the other ship and her crew? By wiles, treachery—as the victims might declare—or by clever tricks, suggested that part of Tamisan who was the Mouth of Olava.

The surface of the ground boiled away under the descent rockets. Then the bright fires vanished, leaving the plain in semi-darkness until their eyes adjusted to the far lesser light of the torches.

There was no expression of awe by the waiting crowd. Though they might be, by their trappings, dress and arms, accounted centuries behind the technical knowledge of the newcomers, they were braced by their history to know that they were not to face gods of unknown powers but mortals with whom they had successfully fought before. What gave them this barrier against the star rovers, Tamisan wondered, and why were they so adverse to any contact with star civilization? Apparently they were content to stagnate at a level of civilization perhaps five hundred years behind her world. Did they not produce any inquiring minds any who desired to do things differently?

The ship was down and gave no outward sign of life,

though Tamisan knew its scanners must be busy feeding back what information they gathered to appear on video-screens. If those had picked up the derelict ship, the newcomers would have so much of a warning. She glanced from the silent bulk of the newly landed spacer to the Over-Queen, just in time to see the ruler raise her hand in a gesture. Four men came forward from the ranks of nobles and guards. Unlike the latter, they wore no body armor nor helms, only short tunics of an unrelieved black. And in the hands of each was a bow—not the crossbow of the troops, but the yet older hand-bow of expert archers.

That part of Tamisan which was of this world knew a catch of breath. For those bows were unlike any other in the land, and those who held them unlike any other archers. No wonder ordinary men and women gave them wide room. For they were a monstrous lot. Over the heads of each was fitted so skillfully fashioned a mask that it seemed no mask at all, rather their natural features, save that the features were not those of human men, but rather copies of the great heads which surmounted, one for each point of the compass, the defensive walls of Ty-Kry. Neither human nor animals, but something of both, and something beyond both.

And the bows they raised were fashioned of treated human bone, strung with cords woven of human hair. The bones and hair of ancient enemies and ancient heroes, so that the intermingled strength of both were ready to serve the living now.

From closed quivers each took a single arrow, and in the torchlight those arrows glittered, seeming to draw and condense radiance until they were shafts of solid light. Fitted to the cords, they had a hypnotic effect, holding one's attention to the exclusion of all else. Tamisan was suddenly aware of that and tried to break the attraction, but at that moment the arrows were fired. And her head turned with all the rest in that company to watch the flight of what seemed to be lines of fire across the dark sky, rising up and up until they were well above the dark ship, then following a curve, to plunge out of sight behind it.

Oddly enough, in their passing they had left great arcs of light behind which did not fade at once, but cast faint gleams on the bubble of the ship. Ingathering—one part of Tamisan's mind supplied—a laying on of ancient power to influence those in the spacer. Though that of her which was a dreamer could not so readily believe in the efficiency of any such ceremony.

There had been sound with the arrows' passing, a shrill high whistling which hurt the ears so that those in that throng put hands to the sides of their heads to shut out the screech. A wind arose out of nowhere and with it a loud crackling. Tamisan looked up to see above the Over-Queen's head a large bird flapping wings of gold and blue, until a closer look said it was no giant bird but rather a banner so fashioned that the wind set it flying to counterfeit the action.

The black-clad archers still stood in a line a little out from the ranks of the guards. And now, though the Over-Queen made no visible sign, those about Hawarel and Tamisan urged them forward until they came to front both those archers and the Over-Queen's tall throne cart.

"Well, champion, is it in your mind to carry out the duties this busy Mouth has assigned you?" There was jeering in the Over-Queen's question, as if she did not honestly believe in Tamisan's prophecy but was willing to allow a dupe to march to destruction in his own way.

Hawarel went to one knee; but as he did so, he swung his empty sword sheath across his knee, making very visible the fact that he lacked a weapon.

"At your desire, Great One, I stand ready. But is it your will that my battle be without even steel between me and the enemy?"

Tamisan saw a smile on the lips of the Over-Queen. And at that moment, she glimpsed a little into this ruler—that it might just please her to will such a fate on Hawarel.

But if the Over-Queen played with that thought for an instant or two, she put it aside. Now she gestured.

"Give him steel, and let him use it. The Mouth has said he is the answer to our defense this time. Is that not so, Mouth?"

And the look she gave to Tamisan had a cruel core.

"He has been chosen in the farseeing. And twice has it read so." Tamisan found the words to answer in a firm voice, as if what she said was an absolutely unchangeable decree.

The Over-Queen laughed. "Be firm, Mouth, put your will behind this choice of yours. In fact, do you go with him, to give him the support of Olava!"

Hawarel had accepted a sword from the officer on his left. Now he arose to his feet, swinging that blade as he saluted with a flourish which suggested that, if he knew he were going to extinction, he intended to march there as one who moved to trumpets and drums.

"The Right be strength to your arm, a shield to your body," intoned the Over-Queen. But there was that in her voice which one might detect to mean that the words she spoke were only ritual, not intended to encourage this champion.

Hawarel turned to face the silent ship. From the burnt and blasted ground about its landing fins arose trails of steam and smoke. Small, red, charring ran in lines away from that ruin. The faint arcs which had remained in the air from the arrow flights were gone now.

As Hawarel moved forward, Tamisan followed a pace or two behind. Though if the ship remained closed to them, with no entrance hatch opened and no ramp run forth, she did not see how they could carry out their plans. And what if that were so, would the Over-Queen expect them to wait hour after hour for some decision from the spacer's commander as to whether or not he would contact them?

Fortunately the spacecrew were more enterprising. Perhaps the sight of that hulk on the edge of the field had given them the need to learn more. The hatch which opened was not the large entrance one, but a smaller door above one of the fins; and from it shot a stunner beam.

Luckily it caught its prey, both Hawarel and Tamisan, before they had reached the edge of the sullenly burning turf, so that their suddenly helpless bodies did not fall into that fire. Nor did they lose consciousness—only the ability to control slack muscles.

Tamisan had crumpled face down, and only the fact that one cheek pressed the earth gave her room to breathe. But her sight was sharply curtailed to the edge of burning grass which crept inexorably on toward her. Seeing that, she forgot all else.

Those moments were the worst she had ever spent. She had conjured up narrow escapes in dreams, but always there had been the knowledge that at the last moment escape *was* possible. Now there was no escape, only her helpless body and the line of advancing fire.

With the suddenness of a blow delivering a shock through her still painful bruises, she was caught, right side and left, by what felt like giant pinchers. As those closed about her body, she was drawn aloft, still face down, the fumes and heat of the burning vegetation choking her. She coughed until the spasm made her sick, spinning in that brutal clutch, being drawn to the spacer, as if the ship had shot forth a robot's arm to pull her in.

She came into a burst of dazzling light. Then hands seized upon her, pulling her down, but holding her upright. The force of the stunner was wearing off; they must have set the beam on lowest power. There was the prickle of feeling returning in her legs and her heavy arms. She was able to lift her head a fraction, to see men in space uniforms about her. They wore helmets as if expecting to issue out on a hostile world, and some of them had the visors closed. Two picked her up easily and carried her along, down a corridor, before dropping her without any gentleness in a small cabin with a suspicious likeness to a cell.

Tamisan lay on the floor, recovering command of her own body and trying to think ahead. Had they taken Hawarel, too? There was no reason to believe they had not. But he had not been put in this cell. She was able to sit up now, her back supported by the wall, and she smiled shakily at her thought that their brave boast of a championship battle had certainly been brought quickly to naught. Not that the Over-Queen's desires might have run far counter to what happened. But she and Starrex had gained this much of their own objective: they were in the ship she believed also held Kas. Only let the three of them make contact and they could leave the dream. And—would their leaving shatter this dream world? How real was it? She was sure of nothing, and there was no reason to worry over side issues. The time had come to concentrate upon one thing only—Kas.

What should she do? Pound on the door of this cell to demand attention—to speak with the commander of this ship? Ask then to see all his crew so she could pick out Kas in his this-world masquerade? She had a suspicion that while Hawarel-Starrex had accepted her story, no one else might.

The important thing was some kind of action to get her free and let her search . . .

The door was actually opening! Tamisan was startled by what seemed a quick answer to her need.

10

THERE was no helmet on the man who stood there, though he wore a tunic bearing the insignia of an upperofficer, slightly different from that Tamisan knew from her own Ty-Kry. He also had a stunner aimed at her, while at his throat was the box of a vocal interpreter.

"I come in peace—"

"With a weapon in hand?" she countered.

He looked surprised; he must have expected a foreign tongue in answer. But she had replied in the Basic which was the second language of all Confederacy planets.

"We have reason to believe that weapons are necessary with your people. I am Glanden Tork of Survey."

"I am Tamisan and a Mouth of Olava." Her hand went to her head and discovered that somehow, in spite of her passage through the air and her lacking-in-ceremony entrance into the ship, her crown was still there. Then she pressed the important question:

"Where is the champion?"

"Your companion?" The stunner was no longer centered on her and his tone had lost some of its belligerency. "He is in safekeeping. But why do you name him champion?"

"Because that is what he is—come to engage *your* selected champion in Right-battle."

"I see. And we select a champion in return, is that it? What is Right-battle?"

She answered his last question first. "If you claim land, you meet the champion of the lordship of that land in Right-battle."

"But we claim no land," he protested.

"You made claim when you set your fiery ship down on the fields of Ty-Kry."

"Your people then consider our landing a form of invasion? But this can be decided by a single combat between champions? And we pick our man—"

Tamisan interrupted him. "Not so. The Mouth of Olava selects—or rather the sand selects—the Seeing selects. That is why I have come, though you did not greet me in honor."

"You select the champion—how?"

"As I have said—by the Seeing."

"*I* do not see, but doubtless it will be made plain in the proper time. And where then is this combat fought?"

"Out there." She waved to what she thought was the

ship walls. "On the land being claimed."

"Logical," he conceded. And then he spoke as if to the air around them. "All that recorded?" Since the air did not answer him, he was apparently satisfied by silence.

"This is your custom, Lady—Mouth of Olava. But since it is not ours, we must discuss it. By your leave we shall do so."

"As you wish." She had this much on her side, he had introduced himself as a member of Survey, which meant that he had been trained in the necessity of understanding alien folkways. And the underlying principle of such training wherever possible was to follow planet customs. If the crew did accept this idea of championship, then they might also be willing to follow it completely. She could demand to see every member of the crew, thus find Kas. And once that was done—break-dream!

But, Tamisan told herself now, do not count on too easy an end to this venture. There was a nagging little doubt lurking in the back of her mind, and it had something to do with those death arrows, with the hulk of the derelict. The people of Ty-Kry, seemingly so weakly defended, had managed through centuries to keep their world free of spacers. When she tried to plumb the Tamisan-of-this-world's memories as to how that was accomplished, she had no answer but what corresponded to magic forces only partly understood. That the shooting of the arrows was the first step in bringing such forces into being she was aware. Beyond that seemed only to lie a belief akin to her Mouth power, and that she did not understand, even when she employed it.

She was accepting all of this, Tamisan realized suddenly, as if this world did exist, that it was not a dream out of her control. Could Starrex's suggestion be the truth, that they had by some means traveled into an alternate world?

Her patience was growing short; she wanted action. Waiting was very difficult. She was sure that scanners of more than one kind were trained on her and she must play the part of a Mouth of Olava, displaying no impatience, only calm confidence in herself and her mission. That she held to as best she could.

Perhaps the time she waited seemed longer than it really was. But Tork returned, to usher her out of the cell and escort her up ladder from level to level. She found the long skirts of her robe difficult to manage. The cabin they came into was large and well furnished, and there were several men seated there. Tamisan looked from one to another searchingly. But she could not tell, she felt none of the uneasiness she had known in the throne room when Hawarel had been present. Of course, that could mean Kas was not one of this group, though a Survey ship did not carry a large crew—mainly specialists of several different callings. There were probably ten, even twenty, more than the six before her.

Tork led her to a chair which had some of the attributes of an easirest, molding it to her comfort as she settled into it.

"This is Captain Lewald, Medico Thrum, Pyscho-Tech Sims, Hist-Techneer El Hamdi." Tork named names and each man acknowledged with a half bow. "I have outlined your proposal to them and they have discussed the matter. By what means will you select a champion from among us?"

She had no sand. For the first time, Tamisan realized that handicap. She would have to depend upon touch alone, but somehow she was sure that would reveal Kas to her.

"Let your men come to me, touching hand to mine," she raised hers to lay it palm up on the table. "When I clasp that of him whom Olava selects, I shall know it."

"It seems simple enough," the Captain returned. "Let us do as the lady suggests." And he leaned forward to rest his own for a minute on hers. There was no response, nor was there any in the others. The Captain called an order on the intercom, and one by one the other members of the crew came to her, touching palm to palm, while Tamisan, with mounting uneasiness, began to believe she had erred. Perhaps only by the sand could she detect Kas. Though she searched the face of each as he took his seat opposite her and laid his hand on hers, she could see no resemblance to Starrex's cousin, nor was there any inner warning her man was here.

"That was the last," the Captain said as the final man arose. "Which is our champion?"

"He is not here." She blurted out the truth, her distress breaking through her caution.

"But you have touched hands with every man on board this ship," the Captain answered her. "Or is this some trick—"

He was interrupted by a sound sharp enough to startle. And the chanted numbers which spilled from the com by his elbow meant nothing to Tamisan but brought the rest in that cabin into instant action. A stunner in Tork's hand caught her before she could rise, and once more she was conscious but unable to move. As the other officers pushed through the door on the run, Tork put out his hand, holding her limp body erect in the chair, while with the other he thumbed some alarm button set into the table.

His summons was speedily answered by two crewmen who carried her along, to thrust her once more into a cabin. This was getting to be far too regular a procedure, Tamisan thought ruefully as they tossed her negligently on a bunk, hardly pausing to see if she landed safely on its surface or not. Whatever that alert had meant, it had certainly once more brought her to the status of prisoner.

Apparently sure of the stunner beam, her guard went out, leaving the door open a crack so that she could hear the pad of running feet, the clangs of what could be secondary alarms.

What possible attack had the forces of the Over-Queen launched against a well-armed and already alert spacer?

Yet it was plain that those men believed themselves in danger and were on the defensive. Starrex—and Kas. Where was Kas? The Captain said she had met all on board. Did that mean that the vision she had earlier seen was false, that the faceless man in the spacer dress was a creature of her too active imagination?

She must not lose confidence. Kas was here—he had to be! She lay now trying vainly to guess by the sounds what was happening. But the first flurry of noise and movement were stilled; there was only silence. Hawarel—where was Hawarel?

The stunner's power was wearing off. She had pulled herself up somewhat groggily when the door of the cabin shot into its wall crack and Tork and the Captain stood there.

"Mouth of Olava, or whatever you truly are," the Captain said with a chill in his voice which reminded Tamisan of Hawarel's earlier rage, "the winning of time may not have been of your devising—this nonsense of Champions and Right-battle—or perhaps it was. Your superiors perhaps deceived you too. At any rate, now it does not matter. They have done their best to make us prisoner and will not reply to our signals for a parley. So we must use you for our messenger. Tell your ruler that we hold her champion and we can readily use him as a key to open gates shut in our faces. We have weapons beyong swords and spears, even beyond those which might not have saved those in that other ship. She can tie us here for a measure of time, but we can solve such bonds. We have not come as invaders, no matter what you believe, nor are we alone. If our signal does not reach our sister ship in orbit above, there will be such an accounting as your race has not seen, nor can conceive of. We shall release you now and you will tell your Queen this. If she does not send those to talk with us before the dawn—then it will be the worse for her. Do you understand?"

"And Hawarel?" Tamisan asked.

"Hawarel?"

"The champion. You will keep him here?"

"As I have said, we have the means to make him a key for your fortress doors. Tell her that, Mouth. From what we have read in your champion's mind you have certain authority here which ought to impress your Queen."

Read from Starrex's mind? What did they mean? Tamisan was suddenly fearful. Some kind of mind probe? But if they did that, then they must know the rest. She was utterly confused now, and found it very hard to center her attention on the matter at hand, that she must relay this defiant message to the Over-Queen. And, since there seemed to be nothing she could do to protest that action, she would do so. Though what reception she might have in Ty-Kry—Tamisan shuddered as Tork pulled her from the bunk and half carried, half led her along.

11

FOR the third time Tamisan sat in prison, but this time she looked not at the smooth walls of a spaceship cabin, but had the ancient stones of the High Castle ringing her in. Captain Lewald's estimation of her influence with the Over-Queen had fallen far wide of the truth, and her plea in favor of a parley with the spacemen had been overruled at once, while the threat concerning their strange weapons and their mysterious use of Hawarel as a "key" was laughed at. The fact that those of Ty-Kry had successfully dealt with this menace in the past made them confident that their same devices would serve as well now. And what those devices were Tamisan had no idea, save that something had happened to the ship before she had been unceremoniously bundled out of it.

Hawarel they had kept on board, Kas had disappeared

—and until she had both to hand she was indeed a captive. Kas—her thoughts kept turning back to the fact he had not been among those who had faced her. Yet Lewald had assured her that she had seen all his crew—

Wait! She set herself to recall his every word—what had he said? "You have touched hand with every man aboard this ship." But he had not said all the crew. Had there been one outside the ship? All she knew of space travel she had learned from tapes. But those had been very detailed as they needed to be to supply the dreamers with factual background and inspiration from which to build fantasy worlds. This spacer claimed to be a Survey vessel and not operating alone. Therefore—it might really have a companion in orbit, and there Kas could be. But, if that were so, she had no chance of reaching him.

Now if this were only a true dream—Tamisan sighed, leaned her head back against the dank stone of the wall and then jerked away from that support as its chill struck into her shoulders. Dreams—

Suppose—she sat upright, alert and a little excited—suppose she could dream within a dream—and find Kas that way? Was it possible? You could not tell until you proved it in one manner or another. She had no stabilizer, no booster. But those were only needed when a dream was shared. She might venture as well on her own. But if she dreamed within a dream, could she do aught to set matters right? Why ask questions she could not answer until it was put to the proof?

She stretched out on the stones of the cell floor, resolutely blocking off those portions of her mind which were aware of the present discomfort of her body. Instead, she began the deep, even breathing of a dreamer, fastening her thoughts on the pattern of self-hypnosis which was the door to her dream. But all she had as a goal was Kas and he as he was in his real person. So poor a guide!

She was going under—she could still dream!

Walls built up around her. Only these were of a translucent material through which flowed soft and pleasing colors. It could not be a space ship. Then the scene wavered, and swiftly Tamisan thrust aside that doubt which might puncture the dream fabric. The walls sharpened, fixed into a solid state: this was a corridor, facing her a door.

She willed to see beyond and was straightway, after the manner of a proper dream, in that chamber. Here the walls were hung with the same sparkling web stuff which had lined her chamber in the sky tower. Seeking Kas, she had returned to her own world. But she held the dream, curious as to why her aim had brought her here. Had she been wrong, and had Kas never come with her? But if that were so, why had she and Starrex been marooned in the other dream?

There was no one in the chamber, but she felt that faint pull drawing her on. She sought Kas and there was that which promised he was here. A second room. Entering, she was startled. For this she knew and well—it was the room of a dreamer. And Kas stood by an empty couch, while the other was occupied.

The dreamer wore a sharing crown, but what rested on the other couch was not any second sleeper but a squat box of metal, to which her dream cords were attached. And Tamisan was not the dreamer! She had expected to see herself. Instead the entranced was one of the locked minds, the blankness of her countenance was unmistakeable. Dream force was being created here by an indreamer, and seemingly it was harnessed to that box.

Given such clues, Tamisan projected the rest. This was not the same dreaming chamber where she had fallen asleep; rather it was a smaller room. And Kas was very much awake, intent upon some dials on the box top. The indreamer and the box, locked so together, could be holding them in the other world. But what of that faint vision of Kas in Ship's uniform? To mislead her? Or was *this* a misleading dream, dictated by the suspicions she had detected in Starrex concerning his cousin? For this was the logical reasoning from such suspicions, that she had been sent with Starrex into a dream world and therein locked by this indreamer and machine—real or dream?

Was she now visible to Kas? If this were a dream, she should be. If she had come back to reality— Her head reeled under the listing of things which might be true, untrue, half true. To prove at least one small fraction, she moved forward and laid her hand on that of Kas as he leaned over to make some small adjustment to the box.

He gave a startled exclamation, jerked his hand from under hers and glanced around. But, though he stared straight at her, it was plain he saw nothing; she could be as disembodied as a spirit in one of the old tales. Yet if he had not seen her, he had felt something.

Again he leaned over the box, eyeing it intently as if he thought he must have felt some shock or emanation from it. The dreamer never moved. Save for the slow rise and fall of her breathing, which told Tamisan she was indeed deep in her self-induced and created world, she might have been dead. Her face was very wan and colorless. Seeing that, Tamisan was uneasy. This tool of Kas's had been far too long in an uninterrupted dream. She would have to be awakened if she made no move to break it for herself. One of the dangers of indreaming was this possible loss of the power to break a dream. That occurring, the guardian must break it. Most of the dreamers' caps provided the necessary stimulus to do so. Only the cap of this dreamer's head had certain modifications Tamisan had never seen before, and these might prevent breaking—

What would happen if Tamisan could evoke waking? Would that also release her—and Starrex—wherever he might be now—from *their* dream, return them to the proper world? She was well drilled in the technique of deep dream break. But those she had used when she stood in reality beside a victim who had overstayed the proper dream time.

She reached out a hand, touched the pulse on the sleeper's throat and applied slight massage. But though her hands seemed corporal and solid to her, there was no response in the other. To prove a point, Tamisan aimed a finger, thrusting it deeply as she could into the pillow on which the dreamer's head rested. Her finger did not dent that soft roundness, but rather went into it, as if her flesh and bone had no substance.

There was yet another way. It was harsh and used only in cases of extremity. But to Tamisan this could be no else. She put those unsubstantial fingers on the temples of the sleeper, just below the rim of the dream cap, and concentrated on a single command. Awake!

The sleeper stirred, her features convulsed and a low moan came from her. Kas uttered an exclamation, hung over his box, his fingers busy pushing buttons with a care which suggested he was about a very delicate task.

"Awake!" Tamisan commanded with such force as she could summon.

The sleeper's hands arose very slowly, unsteadily from her sides and wavered up toward the cap, though her eyelids did not raise. Her expression was now one of pain. And Kas, breathing hard and fast, kept to his adjustments on the box.

So they fought their silent battle for possession of the dreamer. And slowly Tamisan was forced to concede that whatever force lay in that box, it overrode all the technique she knew. But, the longer Kas kept this poor wretch under, the weaker she would grow. Death would be the answer, though perhaps that did not trouble him.

If she could not wake the dreamer, break the bonds

which she was certain now were what tied her and Starrex to that other world, then she must somehow get at Kas himself. He had responded to her touch before—therefore he might just—

Tamisan slipped away from the head of the couch and came to stand beside Kas. He straightened up, a faith relief mirrored on his face as he studied the dreamer, and apparently his box reported that there was no longer any disturbance.

Now Tamisan raised her hands to either side of his head, spreading wide her fingers so they might in some way ape the expanse of a dreamer's cap, and then brought them swiftly down to cover his head, putting firm touch on his temples though she could not exert real pressure there.

He gave a muffled cry and tossed his head from side to side as if to free himself from a cloud. But Tamisan, with all the determination of which she was capable, held fast.

She had already seen this done once in the Hive. However then it had been used on a docile and willing subject and both the controlled and the dreamer had been on the same plane of existence. Now she could only hope that she could disrupt Kas' train of thought long enough to make him release the dreamer himself. So she brought to bear all her will to that purpose. He was not only shaking his head from side to side now, making it very hard to keep her fingers in the proper position, but he was swaying back and forth, his hands up, clawing as if to tear her hold away, though it appeared he could not touch her any more than she could lay firm grip on him.

That fund of energy which had enabled her to create strange worlds and hold them for a fellow dreamer was bent to the task of influencing Kas. But to her dismay, though he ceased his frenzied movements and his clawing for the hands he could not clutch grew feebler, and though his eyes closed and his face screwed into such an expression of horror and rejection that it was that of a frightened child, he did not move to the box.

Instead, he slumped forward so suddenly that Tamisan was taken wholly unaware, falling half across the divan. And in that fall he flailed out with an arm to send the box smashing to the floor, its weight dragging the cap in turn from the dreamer.

She drew several deep breaths, her haggard face now displaying a small trace of returning color. Tamisan, still startled at the results of her efforts to influence Kas, began to wonder if she might have made matters worse. She did not know how much the box had to do with their transportation to the alternate world and whether, if it was broken, they would ever be able to return or not.

There was one precaution, if she could take it. If she returned to that prison cell in the High Castle—as she must do or leave Starrex-Hawarel lost forever—then to leave Kas here, perhaps able again to use his machine—no! But how—since *she* could not—

11

TAMISAN looked to the stirring dreamer. The girl was struggling from the depths of so deep a stratum of unconsciousness that she was not aware of what lay about her. In this state she might be pliable. Tamisan could only try.

Leaving Kas, she went back to the dreamer. Once more, touching the girl's forehead, she sought to influence.

The dreamer sat up with such slow movements of body and limbs as one might use if almost unbearable weights were fastened to every muscle. In a painfully slow gesture, she raised her hands to her head, groping for the cap no longer there. Then she sat, her eyes still shut, while Tamisan drew heavily on her own strength to deliver a final set of orders.

Blindly, for she never opened her eyes, the dreamer felt along the edge of the couch on which she had lain, until her hand swept against the cords which fastened the cap to the box. Her lax fingers fumbled and then tightened as she gave a feeble jerk, then another, until both cords pulled free. Holding those still in one hand, she slipped from the couch in a forward movement which brought her to her knees, the upper part of her body on the other couch, one cheek touching that of the unconscious Kas.

The strain on Tamisan was very great. She was wavering in her control now; several times those weak hands fell limply as her hold on the dreamer ebbed. But each time she found some small surge of energy which brought them back into action again. So that at last the cap was on Kas, the cords which had connected it to the box in a half coil on which the dreamer's head rested.

So big a chance and with such poor equipment! Tamisan could not be sure of any results, she could only hope. Tamisan had released her command of the dreamer, who now lay against the couch on one side as Kas half lay on the other. She summoned all that she had, all that she sensed she had always possessed, that small difference in dream power she had secretly cherished. Once more she touched the forehead of the sleeping girl and broke her own dream within a dream!

This was like climbing a steep hill with an intolerably heavy burden lashed to one's aching back—like being forced to pull the dead weight of another body through a swamp which sucked one ever down. It was such an effort as she could not endure—

Then that weight was gone, and the relief of its vanishing was such that Tamisan did not for a space more than just savor the fact that it did not drag at her. She opened her eyes at last and even that small movement required an effort which left her spent.

She was not in the sky tower. These walls were stone.

And the light was dusky, coming wanly from a slit high in the opposite wall. The High Castle from which she had dreamed her way back to her own Ty-Kry, the dream within a dream. But how well had she wrought there?

For the present, she was too tired to even think connectedly. Bits and pieces of all she had seen and done since she had awakened first in this Ty-Kry floated through her mind, not making any concrete pattern.

It was the mind picture of Hawarel's face as she had seen it last while they marched toward the spacer which roused her from that uncaring drift—Hawarel and the threat the Captain had made and which the Over-Queen had pushed aside. If Tamisan had truly broken the lock Kas had set up to keep them here, then it would be escape—but now there was in her no strength. She tried to remember the formula for breaking, and knew a stroke of chilling fear when her memory proved faulty. She could not do it now—she must have more time to rest both mind and body. Now she was hungry, thirsty, with such a need for both food and drink that it was a torment. Did they mean to leave her here without any sustenance?

Tamisan lay still, listening. And then she inched her head around slowly to view the deeper dusk of her surroundings at floor level. She was not alone!

Kas!

Had she been successful and pulled Kas with her? And if so—was it that he had no counterpart in this world as she and Starrex had found, so that he was still his old self?

However, she did not have time to explore that possibility, for there was a loud grating, followed by a line of light marking an opening door. In the beam of a torch stood that same officer who had earlier been her escort. Using her hands to brace up her body, Tamisan raised herself. But at the same time there was a cry from the far corner.

Someone moved there, raising a head and showing features she had last seen in the sky tower. Kas—and in his rightful body! He was scrambling to his feet. The officer and the guardsman behind him in the doorway, stared at the other-worlder as if they could not believe their eyes. Kas shook his head to clear away some mist and then—

His lips pulled back from his teeth in a terrible rictus which was no smile. There was a small laser in his hand. She could not move; he was going to burn her! In that moment she was so sure of it that she did not even know fear, only waited for the crisping of her flesh.

But the aim of that weapon raised beyond her and fastened on the doorway. Under it, both officer and guard went down. With one hand on the wall to steady himself, Kas pulled along until he came to her. He stood away from the stone then, transferred his laser to the other hand and reached down to hook fingers in the robe where it covered her shoulder.

"On—your—feet." He mouthed the words with difficulty, as if his exhaustion nearly equalled hers. "I do not know how—or why—or who—"

The torch dropped from the charred hand which had carried it to give them much curtailed light. But Kas swung her around, thrusting his face very close to hers. He stared at her intently, as if by the very force of his glare he could strip aside the mask this other world body made for her, force the old Tamisan into sight.

"You are Tamisan—it can not be otherwise! I do not know how you did this, demon-born." He shook her with a viciousness which struck her painfully against the wall. "Where—is—he?"

All that came from her parched throat were harsh sounds without meaning.

"Never mind." Kas stood straighter now and there was more vigor in his voice. "Where he is—there shall I find him. Nor shall I lose you, demon-born, since you are my way back. And for Lord Starrex here there will be no guards, no safe shields. Perhaps this is the better way after all!" He slapped her face, his palm bruising her flesh, once more thumping her head back against the wall so that the rim of the Mouth crown bit into her scalp and she cried out in pain.

"Speak! Where is this place. Answer me."

"The High Castle of Ty-Kry," she croaked out.

"And what do you in this hole?"

"I am prisoner to the Over-Queen."

"Prisoner? What do you mean? You are a dreamer, this is your dream. Why are you a prisoner?"

Tamisan was so shaken she could not marshal words easily as she had done to explain to Starrex. And she thought, a little dazedly, that Kas might not accept her explanation anyway.

"Not—wholly—a dream," she got out.

He did not seem surprised. "So the control has that property, has it—to impose a sense of reality. Then—" His eyes blazed into hers. "You can not control this dream, is that it? Again fortune favors me, it seems. Where is Starrex now?"

She could give him a truthful answer and she was glad of that. As it seemed to her now, she could not speak falsely with any hope of belief. It was as if he could see straight into her mind with those demanding eyes of his. "I do not know."

"But he is in this dream—somewhere?"

"Yes."

"Then you shall find him for me, Tamisan. And speedily. Do we have to search this High Castle?"

"He was, when I saw him last, outside."

She kept her eyes turned from the door, from what lay there. But now he hauled her toward that and she was afraid she was going to be sick. Where they might be in the interior of the small city which was the High Castle, she did not know. Except that those who had brought her here had not taken her on to the core towers, but had turned aside along the first of the gateways and gone down a long flight of stairs. She doubted if they would be able to walk out again as easily as Kas thought to do.

"Come." He pulled at her, dragging her on, kicking aside what lay in the door. She closed her eyes tightly as he brought her past. But the stench of death was so strong that she staggered, retching, with his hand ever dragging at her, keeping her on her feet and reeling ahead.

Twice she watched glassily as he burned down opposition. And his luck at keeping surprise on his side held. They came to the foot of the stairs and climbed. Tamisan held to one hope—now that she was on her feet and moving she found a measure of strength returning, so that she no longer feared falling, if Kas released his hold upon her. When they were out at last in the night, with the damp smell of the underways wafted away by a rising wind, she felt clean and renewed and was able to think.

Kas might have been able to get her this far because of her weakness. So to his eyes she must continue to counterfeit that, until she had a chance to act. It could be that his weapon, so alien to this world and thus so effective, might well cut their way to Starrex. But that did not mean that once they had reached him she need obey Kas. And somehow she also felt that face to face Kas would be less confident of success.

It was not a guard that halted them now but a massive gate, such a barrier as was meant to hold. Kas examined the bar and laughed, before he raised the laser and sent a needle-thin beam to cut as he needed. There was a shout from above and Kas, almost lanquidly, swung the beam to a narrow stair leading from the ramparts, laughing again as there came a choked scream and the sound of a falling body.

"Now!" Kas put his shoulder to the gate and it swung,

more easily than Tamisan would have thought possible for its weight. "Where is Starrex? And if you lie—" His smile was a very evil one.

"There." Tamisan was sure of her direction and she pointed to where there was a distant blaze of torches about the shadow bulk of the grounded spacer.

13

"A spacer!" Kas paused.

"Besieged by these people," Tamisan informed him. "And Starrex is a hostage on board, if he still lives. They have threatened to use him in some manner as a weapon and the Over-Queen, as far as I know, does not care."

Kas turned on her. His evil merriment had vanished, his smile was rather now a snarl, and he shook her back and forth. "It is your dream—control it!"

For a moment, Tamisan hesitated. Should she try to tell him what she believed the truth? Kas and his other world weapon might be her only hope of reaching Starrex now. Could he be persuaded to a frontal attack if he thought that was their only chance of reaching their goal? On the other hand, if she admitted she could not break this dream, he might well burn her down out of hand and take his chances.

"Your meddling has warped the pattern, Lord Kas. I can not control some elements. Nor can I break the dream until I have Lord Starrex with me—since we are pattern-linked in this sequence."

Her steady reply seemed to have some effect on him. Though he gave her one more punishing shake and uttered an obscenity, he looked on to the torches and the half-seen bulk of the ship, a certain calculation in his eyes.

They made a lengthly detour, away from most of the torches, coming up across the open land to the south of the ship. There was a graying in the sky and a hint that dawn might perhaps be not too far away. Now that they could see better, it was apparent that the ship was sealed. No hatch opened on its surface, no ramp ran out. And surely the laser in Kas's hand was not going to burn their way in, in the manner he had opened the gate of the High Castle.

Apparently the same difficulty presented itself to Kas, for he halted her with a jerk while they were still in the shadows well away from the line of torches forming a square around the ship. They sheltered in a small dip in the ground surveying the scene.

The torches were no longer held by men, but had been planted in the ground at regular intervals, and they were as large as outsize candles. The colorful mass which had marked the Over-Queen and her courtiers on Tamisan's first visit to the landing field was gone, leaving only a perimeter line of guardsmen in wide encirclement of the sealed ship.

Why did the spacemen just not lift and planet elsewhere? Unless that confusion in the last moments when she had been on board the spacer meant that they could not do so. They had spoken then of a sister ship in orbit above. It would seem that it had made no move to aid them, though she had no idea how much time had elapsed since last she had been here.

Now Kas turned on her again. "Can you get to Starrex—reach him a message?" he demanded.

"I can try. For what reason?"

"Have him ask for us to come to him." Kas had been silent for a moment before replying. Was he so stupid as to believe that she would not give a warning with whatever message she could so deliver? Or had he precautions against that?

But *could* she reach Starrex? She had gone into the secondary dream to make contact with Kas. There was no time nor preparation for such a move now. She could only use the mental technique for inducing a dream and see what happened thereby. She said as much to Kas, promising no success.

"Be about what you can do—now!" he told her roughly.

Tamisan closed her eyes to think of Hawarel as she had seen him last, standing beside her on this very field. And she heard a gasp from Kas. Opening her eyes she saw Hawarel, even as he had been then—or rather a pallid copy of him, wavering and indistinct, already beginning to fade, so she spoke in a swift gabble:

"Say we come from the Queen with a message, that we must see the Captain—"

The shimmering outline of Hawarel faded into the night. She heard Kas mutter angrily. "What good will that ghost do?"

"I can not tell. If he returns to that of which he is a part, he can carry the message. For the rest—" Tamisan shrugged. "I have told you this is no dream I can control. Do you think if it were, we two would stand here in this fashion?"

His thin lip parted in one of his mirthless grins.

"You would not, I know, dreamer!"

His head went from left to right as he slowly surveyed the line of planted torches and the men standing on guard between them. "Do we move closer to this ship, expect them to open to us?"

"They used a stunner to take us before," Tamisan saw fit to warn him. "They might do so again."

"Stunner," he gestured with the laser. Tamisan hoped his answer would not be a headlong attack on the ship with that.

But instead, he used it as a pointer to motion her on toward the torch line. "If they do open up," he commented, "I shall be warned."

Tamisan gathered up the long skirt of her robe. It was torn by rough handling, frayed in strips at the hem where she could be tripped if she caught those rags between her feet. And the rough brush growing knee-high about them caught at it so that she stumbled now and again, urged on continually by Kas' pulling when he dug his fingers painfully into her already bruised shoulder.

So they reached the torch line. The guards there faced inward to the ship and in this increase of light Tamisan could see that they were all bowmen, armed with crossbows, not with those of bone which the black-tunicked men had earlier used. Bolts against the might of the ship! The answer seemed laughable, a jest to delight the simple. Yet, the ship lay there and Tamisan could well remember the consternation of those men who had been questioning her within it.

Now—

There was a dark spot on the hull of the ship and a hatch suddenly swung open! A battle hatch—though she had only seen those via tape study.

"Kas—they are going to fire!" With a laser beam from such, they could crisp everything on this field, perhaps clear back to the walls of the High Castle!

She tried to turn in his grasp, to race back and away, knowing already that such a race was lost before she took the first lunging stride. But he held her fast.

"No muzzle," he said.

Tamisan strained to see through the poor, flickering light. Perhaps it was a lightening of the sky which did make clear that there was no muzzle projecting to spew a fiery death across them all. But that was surely a gun port.

As quickly as it had appeared, that opening was closed. The ship was again sealed tightly.

"What—?"

"Either they can not use it," Kas answered her half question, "or they have thought better of doing so. Which means, by either count, we have a chance. Now—stay you here! Or else I shall come looking for you in a manner you shall not relish, and never believe that I can not find you!" Nor did something in Tamisan dispute that.

She stood. After all, apart from Kas' threats, where did she have to go? If she were sighted by any of the guards, she might either be returned to prison or dealt with summarily in another fashion. And she had to reach Starrex if she were to escape.

But she watched Kas make good use of the interest which riveted the eyes of the guards on the ship. He crept, with more ease than she thought possible for one used to the luxury living of the sky towers, behind the nearest man.

What weapon he used she could not see; it was not the laser. Instead he straightened to his full height behind the unsuspecting guard, reached out an arm and seemed only to touch the stranger on the neck. Immediately the fellow collapsed without a sound, though Kas caught him before he had fallen to the ground and dragged him backward to the slight depression in the field where Tamisan waited.

"Quick!" Kas ordered. "Give me his cloak and helm!"

He ripped off his own tunic with its extravagantly padded shoulders, while Tamisan knelt to fumble with a great brooch, freeing the enveloping cloak of the guard. Kas snatched it out of her hands, dragged the rest of it loose from under the limp body and pulled it around him, taking up the helm and settling it on his head with a tap. Then he took up the crossbow.

"Walk before me," he told Tamisan. "If they have a field scanner on in the ship, I want them to see a prisoner under guard. That may bring them to a parley. It is a thin chance, but our best—"

He could not guess that it might be a better chance than he hoped, Tamisan knew, since he did not know that she had been once within the ship and the crew might be expecting some such return with a message from the Over-Queen. But to walk out boldly, past the line of torches—surely Kas' luck would not hold so well; they would be seen by the other guards before they were a quarter of the way to the ship. But she had not any other proposal to offer in exchange.

This was no adventure such as she had lived through in dreams. She believed that if she died now, she died indeed and would not wake unharmed in her own world. And her flesh crawled with a fear which made her mouth go dry and her hands quiver as they held wet and tight upon the folds of her robe. Any second now—she would feel the impact of a bolt—hear a shout of discovery—be—

But still Tamisan tottered forward and heard, with danger-alerted ears, the faint crunch of boots which was Kas behind. His contempt for a danger which was only too real for her made her wonder, fleetingly, if he did indeed still believe this a dream she could control, and need not then watch for any one but her. But she could not summon words to impress on him his woeful mistake.

So intent was she upon some attack from behind that she was not really conscious of the ship towards which they went. Until, suddenly she saw another of those ports open and steeled herself to feel the numbing charge of a stunner.

However, again an attack she feared did not come. The sky was growing lighter even if there was no sign of sunrise. Instead the first drops of a storm began to fall. And under that onslaught of moisture from lowering clouds, the torches hissed and sputtered, finally flickering out, so that the gloom was hardly better than twilight.

14

THEY came close enough to the ship to board, were one of the ramps lowered to them. There they stood waiting, while Tamisan felt the rise of almost hysterical laughter inside her. What an anticlimax if the ship refused to acknowledge them! They could not stand here forever and there was no chance they could battle a way inside. Kas' faith in her communication with that ghost of Hawarel had been too high.

But even as she was sure that they made an absurd

failure, there was a sigh of sound from well above them. The port hatch wheeled back into the envelope of the ship's wall, and a small ramp, hardly more than a steep ladder, swung creaking out and dropped to hit the charred ground not far from them.

"Go!" Kas prodded her forward.

With a shrug, Tamisan went. She found it hard to climb with the heavy, frayed skirts dragging her back. But by using her hands to pull along the single rail of the ramp, she made progress. Why had not the rest of the guards along that watching line of torches moved? Had it been that Kas' half disguise had indeed deceived them, and they thought that Tamisan had been sent under orders to parley a second time with the ship's people?

She was nearly at the hatch now and could see the suited men in the shadows above waiting. They had tanglers ready to fire, prepared to spin the webs to enmesh them both as easily handled prisoners. But before those slimy strands spun forth to touch—patterned as they were to seek flesh to anchor—both the waiting spacemen jerked right and left, clutched with already dead hands at the breasts of charred tunics from which arose small, deadly spirals of smoke.

They had expected a guard armed with a bow; they had met Kas' laser, to the same undoing as the guardsmen at the castle. Kas' shoulder in the middle of her back sent her sprawling, to land half over the bodies of the two who had awaited them.

She heard a scuffle and was kicked and rolled aside, fighting the folds of her own long skirt, trying to get out of the confines of the hatch pocket. Somehow, on her hands and knees, she made it forward, since she could not retreat. Now she fetched up against the wall of a corridor and managed to pull around to face the end of the fight.

The two guards lay dead. But Kas held the laser on a third man. Now, without glancing around, he gave an order which she mechanically obeyed.

"The tangler—here!"

Still on her hands and knees, Tamisan crawled far enough back into the hatch compartment to grip one of those weapons. The second—she eyed it with awakening need for some protection herself, but Kas did not give her time to reach it.

"Give it to me—now!"

Still holding the laser pointed steadily at the middle of the third spaceman, he groped back with his other hands. She had no choice—no choice—but she did!

If Kas thought he had her thoroughly cowed— Swinging the tangler around without taking time to aim, Tamisan pressed the firing button.

The lash of the sticky weaving spun through the air, striking the wall from which it dropped away, then one arm of the motionless captive, who was still under Kas' threat; there it clung, across his middle. And then it spun through the air until it clasped Kas' gun hand, his middle, his other arm, adhering instantly, tightening with its usual efficiency and tying captor to captive.

Kas struggled against those ever-tightening bands to bring the laser around to beam on Tamisan, though whether he would have used it even in his white hot rage, she did not know. It was enough that the tangler made it so she could keep from his line of fire. Having ensnared them enough to render them both harmless for a time, Tamisan drew a deep breath and relaxed somewhat.

She had to be sure of Kas. She had loosed the firing button of the tangler as soon as she saw that he could not use his arms. Now she raised the weapon, and with more of a plan, tied his legs firmly together. He kept on his feet, but he was as helpless as if they had managed to turn a stunner beam on him.

Warily, she approached him. And guessing her intent, he went into wild wrigglings, trying to bring the adhesive tangler strands in contact with her flesh also. But she stooped and tore at the already fringed and frayed hem of her robe, ripping up a strip as high as her waist, winding this about her arm and wrist to make sure she could not be so entrapped.

In spite of his struggles, she managed to get the laser out of his hold, and for the second time knew a surge of great relief. He made no sound, but his eyes were wild and his lips so tightly drawn against his teeth, his mouth slightly open, that a small trickle of spittle oozed from one corner to wet his chin. Looking at him dispassionately, Tamisan thought him near insane at that moment.

The spacecrewman was moving. He hitched along as she swung around with the laser as a warning, his shoulders against the wall keeping him firmly on his feet, his unbound legs giving him more mobility, though the cord of the tangler anchored him to Kas. Tamisan glanced around, searching for what he appeared so desperate to reach. There was a com box.

"Stand where you are! For now—" she ordered.

The threat of the laser kept him frozen. With that still trained on him, she darted short glances over her shoulder to the hatch opening. Sliding along the wall in turn, the tangler thrust loosely into the front of her belt, she managed with one arm to slam the hatch door and give a turn to its locking wheel.

Now— Using the laser as a pointer she motioned the crewman to the com, but the immobile Kas was too much of an anchor. Dared she free the crewman by even so much? There was no other way. She motioned with one hand.

"Stand well away."

He had said nothing during their encounter, but he obeyed with an agility which suggested he liked the sight of that weapon in her hand even less than he had liked it when Kas had held it. He stretched to the limit the cord would allow so she was able to burn it through.

Kas spit out a series of obscenities which were only a meaningless noise as far as Tamisan was concerned. Until he was released, he was no more now than a well-anchored bundle—helpless. But the crewman had importance.

She gestured him on to the com, reaching it before him. Now she played the best piece she had in this desperate game.

"Where is Hawarel? The native who was brought on board?"

He could lie, of course, and she would not know it. But it seemed he was willing to answer, probably because he thought that the truth would strike her worse than any lie.

"They have him in the lab—conditioning him." And he grinned at her with some of the evil malignancy she had seen in Kas.

She remembered the Captain's earlier threat to make of Hawarel a tool to use against the Over-Queen and her forces. Was she too late? But there was only one road to take and that was the one she had chosen in those few moments when she had taken up the tangler and used it for herself.

"You will call." She spoke as she might to one finding it difficult to understand her. "And you will say that Hawarel will be released, brought here—now!"

"Why?" the crewman returned with visible insolence. "What will you do? Kill me? Perhaps, but that will not defeat the Captain's plans. He will be willing to see half the crew burned—"

"That may be true." She nodded. Not knowing the Captain, she could not tell whether or not that was a bluff. "But will his sacrifice then save his ship?"

"What can you do?" began the crewman and then he paused. His grin was gone; now he looked at her speculatively. In her present guise she perhaps did not look formidable enough to threaten the ship, but he could not be sure. And one thing she knew from her own time and place—a spaceman learned early to take nothing for granted on a new planet. It might well be that she did have command over some unknown force.

"What can I do? There is much." She took quick advantage of that hesitation. "Have you been able to raise the ship?" She plunged on, hoping very desperately that she had made the right guess. "Have you been able to communicate with your other ship, or ships, in orbit?"

His expression was her answer, one which fanned her hope into a bright blaze of excitement. The ship *was* grounded, had some sort of a hold on it which they had not been able to break!

"The Captain won't listen." He was sullen now.

"I think he will. Tell him that we get Hawarel—here—and himself—or else we shall truly show you what happened to that derelict across the field."

Kas had fallen silent. He was watching her, not with quite the same wariness of the crewman, but with an emotion she was not able to read. Surprise? Or did it mask some sly thought of taking over her bluff, captive though he was?

"Talk!" The need for hurry rode Tamisan now. By this time those above would wonder why their captives had not been brought before them. Also, outside, the Over-Queen's men would certainly have reported that Tamisan and a seeming guard had entered the ship. From both sides enemies might be closing in.

"I can not set the com," her prisoner answered.

"Tell me then!"

"The red button—"

But she thought she had seen a slight shift in his eyes. Tamisan raised her hand, to press the green button instead. Without accusing him of the treachery she was sure he had tried, she said again, more fiercely:

"Talk!"

"Sannard here." He put his lip close to the com. "They—they have me. Rooso and Cambre are dead. They want the native."

"In good condition," hissed Tamisan, "and now!"

"They want him now, in good condition," Sannard repeated. "They threaten the ship."

There came no acknowledgment from the com in return. Had she indeed pressed the wrong button because she was overly suspicious? What was going to happen? Time—she could not wait on time!

"Sannard—" the voice from the com was metallic, without human inflection or tone.

But Tamisan gave the crewman a push which sent him sliding back along the wall until he bumped into Kas and the binds of both men immediately united to make them one struggling package. Tamisan spoke into the com.

"Captain, I do not play any game. Send me your prisoner or look upon that derelict you see and say to yourself that will be your ship. For this is so, as true as I stand here now, with your man as my captive. Also—send Hawarel alone, and pray to whatever immortal powers you believe sit in judgment over your actions that he can so come! Time grows very short and there is that which will act if you do not, and to a purpose you shall not relish!"

The crewman, whose legs were still free, was trying to kick away from Kas. But his struggles instead sent them both to the floor in a heaving tangle. Tamisan's hand dropped to her side as she leaned against the wall, breathing heavily. With all her will she wanted to control action as she did in a dream, but only fate did that now.

15

THOUGH she sagged against the wall, Tamisan felt rigid, as if she were in a great encasement of su-steel. And, as time moved at so slow a pace as not to be measured normally, that prisoning hold on her body and spirit grew. The crewman and Kas had ceased their struggles. She could not see the crewman's face, but that which Kas turned to her had a queer, distorted look. As if before her eyes, though not through any skill of hers, he was indeed changing, taking on the aspect of another man. Since her return to the sky tower in the second dream she had known he was to be feared. Now, in spite of the fact that his body was securely imprisoned, she found herself edging away, as if by the very intentness of that hostile stare he could aim a weapon to bring her down. But he said nothing, lay as broodingly quiet and impassive as though he had foreknowledge of utter failure for her.

She knew so little, Tamisan thought, she who had always taken pride in her learning, in the wealth of lore she had drawn into furnishing her memory for action dreaming. The spacecrew might have some way of flooding this short corridor with a noxious gas, or using a hidden ray linked with a scanner to finish them. Tamisan found herself running her hands along the walls, studying the unbroken surface a little wildly, striving to find where death might enter quietly and unseen.

There was another bulkhead door at the end of this short corridor; at a few paces away from the outer hatch a ladder ascended to a closed trap. Her head turned constantly, until she regained a firmer control of herself, from one of those entrances to the other. They had only to wait to call her bluff—only to wait.

Yes! They had waited and they were—

The air about her was changing, there was a growing scent in it. Not unpleasant—but even a fine perfume would have seemed a stench from the dungheap when it reached her nostrils under these present conditions! Also the light which radiated from the jointure of the corridor roof and ceiling was altering. It had been that of a moderately sunlit day, now it was bluish. So under it her own brown skin took on an eerie look. She had lost her throw! Maybe, if she could open the hatch again, let in the outer air—

Tamisan tottered to the hatch, gripped the locking

wheel and brought her strength to bear. Kas was writhing again, trying to break loose from his unwilling partner. But oddly enough the crewman lay limp, his head rolling when Kas' heaving disturbed the lay of his body, but his eyes were closed. And, at the same time Tamisan braced against the wall, her full strength turned on the need for opening the door, she knew a flash of surprise. Was it her overvivid imagination alone which made her believe that she was in danger? When she rested to draw a deep breath—

Why—in her startlement she could have cried out aloud. She did utter a small sound. She was gaining strength, not losing it. Every lungful of that scented air she breathed in—and she was breathing deeper, more slowly as if her body desired such nourishment—was a restorative.

Kas, too? She turned to glance at him again. Where she breathed deeply, with lessening apprehension, he was gasping, his face ghastly in the change of light. And then, even as she watched, his struggles ended, his head fell back so that he lay as inert as the crewman he sprawled across.

So whatever change was in progress here, it affected Kas and the crewman—that latter faster than the former —but not her. And now her trained imagination took another leap. Perhaps she had not been so far wrong in threatening those on this ship with danger. Though she had no guess as to how it was done, this could be another strange weapon in the armament of the Over-Queen.

Hawarel? The spacemen had probably never intended to send him. Dared she go to seek him? Tamisan wavered, one hand on the hatch wheel, looking to the ladder and the other door. If all within this ship save she had reacted to the strange air, there would be none to stop her. But if she fled the ship, she would face the loss of the keys to her own world—Starrex and Kas. In addition, she might be met by some evil fate at the hands of the Over-Queen. She had broken prison, and—if they did not know of Kas—had left dead men behind her. As the Mouth of Olava, she shuddered from the judgment which would be rendered one deemed to have practiced wrongful supernatural acts.

Resolutely, Tamisan went to the door at the end of the corridor. It was really true that she had no choice at all. She must find Starrex, somehow bring him here, so that they three could be together and win a small space of time in which to arrange a dream breaking—or she was totally defeated.

She loosened her belt a little so she could draw up her robe through it, shortening the hampering length, leaving her legs freer. There was the tangler and Kas' laser. In addition was this mounting feeling of strength and well being, though an inner warning suggested she not trust to overconfidence.

The door gave under her push and she looked out upon a scene which first startled and then reassured her. There were crewmen in the corridor. But they lay prone as if they had been caught while on their way to the hatch. Lasers—of a slightly different pattern than that Kas had brought—had fallen from their hands, and three of the four wore tanglers.

Tamisan picked her way carefully around them, gathering up all those weapons in a fold of her robe, as if she were some maiden in a field gathering an armload of spring flowers. The men were alive, she saw as she stooped closer, but they breathed evenly as if peacefully asleep.

She took one of the tanglers, discarding the one she had used, fearing its charge might be near exhaustion. As for the rest of the collection, she dropped them at the far end of the passageway and turned the beam of Kas' weapon on them; she left behind a metal mass of no use to anyone.

Her idea of the geography of the ship was scanty. She would simply have to explore and keep exploring until she found Starrex. But she would start at the top and work down. So she found a level ladder, three times coming upon a sleeping crewman. Each time she made sure he was disarmed before she left him.

The blue shade of the light was growing deeper, giving a very weird cast to the faces of the sleepers. Making sure her robe was tightly kilted up, Tamisan began to climb. She had reached the third level when she heard the sound, the first she had noted in this too-silent ship since she had left the hatchway.

She stopped to listen, deciding it came from somewhere in the level into which she had just climbed. With laser in hand, she tried to use it as a guide, though it was misleading—and might have come from any one of the cabins. Each door she passed Tamisan pushed open. There were more sleepers—some stretched in bunks, others on the floors or seated at tables with their heads lying on those surfaces. But she did not halt now to collect weapons. The need to be about her task, free of this ship, built in her as sharp as might a slaver's lash laid across her shrinking shoulders.

Suddenly the sound grew louder as she came to a last door and pushed it. Now she looked into a cabin not meant for living but perhaps for a kind of death. Two men in plain tunics were crumpled by the threshold. As if they had had some limited warning of danger to come and had tried to flee, but fallen before they could reach the corridor. Behind them was a table and on that a body, very much alive, struggling with dogged determination against confining straps.

Though his long hair had been clipped and the stubble of it shaven to expose the full nakedness of his entire scalp, there was no mistaking Hawarel. He not only fought against the clamps and straps which held him to the table, but in addition he jerked his head with sharp, short pulls, to dislodge disks fastened to his forehead, and from there, by wire, to a vast box of a machine which filled one-quarter of the cabin.

Tamisan stepped over the inert men, reached the side of the table and jerked the disks away from the prisoner's head; perhaps his determined struggles had already loosened them somewhat. His mouth had opened and shut as she came to him as if he were forming words she could not hear, or he could not voice. But as the apparatus came away in her hands, he gave a cry of triumph.

"Get me loose!" he commanded. She was already examining the under part of the table for the locking mechanism of those straps and clamps. It was only seconds before she was able to obey his order.

He sat upright, bare to the waist, and she saw beneath, where his shoulders and the upper part of his spine had rested on the table, a complicated series of disks.

"Ah!" Before she could move he scooped up the laser she had laid on the edge of the table when she had freed him. And the gesture he made with it might not have been only to indicate the door and the need for hurry, but perhaps also was a warning that with a weapon in his hands he now thought he was in command of the situation.

"They sleep—everywhere," she told him. "And Kas—he is a prisoner."

"I thought you could not find him—he was not one of the crew."

"He was not. But I have him now, and with him we can return."

"How long will it take?" Starrex was down on one knee, searching the two men on the floor.

"I can not tell." She gave him the truth. "But—how long will these sleep? Their unconsciousness is, I think, some trick of the Over-Queen's."

"It came unexpectedly for them," Starrex agreed. "And you may be right that this is only preliminary to taking over the ship. I have learned this much, that their instruments and much of their equipment has been affected so they can not trust them. Otherwise—" His Hawarel face was grim under its bluish, deadman's coloring. "Otherwise I would not have survived this long as myself."

"Let us go!" Now that she had miraculously—or so it seemed to her—succeeded, Tamisan was even more uneasy, wanting nothing to spoil their escape.

16

THEY found their way back to the corridor before the hatch while the ship still slept. Starrex knelt by Kas and then looked with astonishment at Tamisan. "But this is the real Kas!"

"It is Kas, real enough," she agreed. "And there is a reason for that. But need we discuss it now? If the Over-Queen's men come to take this ship—I tell you her greeting to us may be worse than any you have met here. I remember enough of the Tamisan who is the Mouth of Olava to know that."

He nodded. "Can you break dream now?"

She looked around her a little wildly. Concentration—no, somehow she could not think so clearly. It was as if the exultation of fumes of that scented air had awakened in her was draining. And with that sapping went what she needed most.

"I—I fear not."

"It is simple then." He stopped again to examine the tangle cords. "We shall have to go to where you can." She saw him set the laser on its lowest beam to burn through the cords which united Kas to the crewman, though he did not free his cousin from the rest of his bonds.

But what if they marched out of the hatch into a waiting party of the Over-Queen's guards? They had the tangler, the laser, and perhaps—just perhaps—the half smile of fortune on their side. They would have to risk it.

Tamisan opened the inner door of the pressure chamber. The dead men lay there as they had fallen. Fighting nausea, she dragged one aside to make room for Starrex, who carried Kas over his shoulder, moving slowly under that burden, a fold of cloak well wrapped about the prisoner to prevent any contact between the cords and Starrex's own flesh. The outer hatch was open and beyond—

A blast of icy rain, with the added bite of the wind which drove it, struck viciously at them. It had been dawn when Tamisan had entered the ship, but outside now the day was no lighter. The torches had been extinguished. Tamisan could see no lights. Shielding her eyes against the wind and the rain, she tried to make out the line of guards.

Perhaps the severe weather had driven them all away. She was sure no one was waiting at the foot of the ramp, unless they were under the fins of the ship, sheltering there. And that chance would have to be taken. She said as much and Starrex nodded.

"Where do we go?"

"Anywhere away from the city. Give me but a little shelter and time."

"Vermer's Hand over us and we can do it," he returned. "Here—take this!"

He kicked an object across the metal plates of the deck and she saw it was one of the lasers used by the crewmen. She picked it up in one hand, the tangler in her other. Burdened as he was by Kas, Starrex could not lead the way. She must now play in real life such an action role as she had many times dreamed. But this held no amusement, only a wish to scuttle quickly into any form of safety wind and rain would allow her.

The ramp being at such a steep angle, she feared slipping on it and had to belt the tangler, hold on grimly with one hand and go much more slowly than her fast-beating heart demanded, anxious lest Starrex in turn might lose footing and slam into her, carrying them both on to disaster.

The strength of the storm was such that it was a battle

to gain step after step, even though she reached the ground without mishap. Tamisan was not sure in which direction she must head now to avoid the Castle and the city. Her memory seemed befuddled by the storm and she could only guess. Also she was afraid of losing contact with Starrex; as slowly as she went, he dragged even more behind.

Then she stumbled against an upright stake. She put out her hand and fumbled along it enough to know that this was one of the rain-quenched torches. It heartened her a little to learn that they had reached the barrier and that no guards stood here. Perhaps the storm was a life saver for the three of them.

Tamisan lingered, waiting for Starrex to catch up. Now he caught at the torch, steadying himself as if he needed that support.

His voice came in wind-deadened gusts, labored. "I may have in this Hawarel a good body, but I am not a heavy duty android. We must find your shelter."

There was a dark shadow to her left; it could be a coppice. Even trees or tall brush could give them some measure of relief.

"Over there." She pointed, but did not know if, in this gloom, he could see it.

"Yes." He straightened a little under the burden of Kas, staggering in the direction of the shadow.

They had to beat their way into the vegetation. Tamisan, having two arms free, broke the path for Starrex. She might have used the laser to cut, but the ever-present fear that they might need the charges for future protection kept her from a waste of their slender resources for defense.

At last, at the cost of branch-whipped and thorn-ripped weals in their flesh, they came into a space which was a little more open. Starrex allowed his burden to fall to the ground.

"Can you break dream now?" He squatted down beside Kas, as she dropped to sit panting near him.

"I can—"

But she got no farther. There was a sound which cut through even the tumult of the storm, and that part of them which was allied to this world knew it for what it was, the warning of a hunt. And—since they *were* able to hear it—they must be the hunted!

"The Itter Hounds!" He put their peril into words.

"And they run for us!" Mouth of Olava or not, when the Itter Hounds coursed on one's track there was no defense, for they could not be controlled once they were loosed to chase.

"We can not fight them."

"Do not be too sure of that," he answered. "We have the lasers, weapons not of this world. The weapon which put the ship's crew to sleep did not vanquish us; so might an off-world weapon react the other way here—"

"But Kas—" She thought she had found a weak point in his reasoning, much as she wanted to believe he had guessed rightly.

"Kas is in his own form, which is perhaps more akin to the crewmen now than to us. And, by the way, how is it that he is?"

She kept her tale terse, but told him of her dream within a dream and how she had found Kas. She heard him laugh.

"I was right then in thinking my dear cousin might well be at the center of this web! However, now he is as completely enmeshed as the rest of us. As a fellow victim he may be more cooperative."

"Entirely so, my noble lord!" The voice out of the dark between them was composed.

"You are awake then, cousin. Well, we would be even more awake. There is a struggle here in progress between two sets of enemies who are both willing to make us a third. We had better travel swiftly elsewhere if we would save our skins. What of it, Tamisan?"

"I must have time."

"What I can do to buy it for you, I will!" That carried the force of a sworn oath. "If the lasers act outside the laws of this world, it may be that they can even stop the Itter Hounds. But to get to it!"

She had no proper conductor, nothing but her will and the need. Putting out her hands she touched the bare, wet flesh of Starrex's shoulder, was more cautious in seeking a hold on Kas, lest she encounter one of the tangle cords. Then she exerted her full will and looked far in, not out.

It was no use, her craft failed her. There was that momentary sensation of suspension between two worlds. Then she was back in the dark brush where the growing walls did not hold off the rain.

"I can not break the dream. There is no energy machine to step up the power." But she did not add that perhaps she might have done it for herself alone.

Kas laughed then. "It would seem my sealer still works in spite of all your meddling, Tamisan. I fear, my noble lord, you will have to prove the effectiveness of your weapons after all. Though you might set me free and give me arms, necessity making allies of us after all."

"Tamisan!" Starrex's voice was one to bring her out of the dull anguish of her failure. "This dream—remember, it may not be a usual dream after all. Could another world door be opened?"

"Which world?" At that moment her memories of reading and viewing tapes were a whirl in her head. And the voiceless call of the Itter Hounds to which *this* Tamisan was attuned made her whole body cringe and shiver, addled her thinking even more.

"Which world? Any one—think, girl, think! Take a single change if you must, but think!"

"I can not. The Hounds—aheee—they come—they come! We are meat for the fangs of those who course the Dark Runnels under moonless skies! We are lost!" The Tamisan who dreamed slipped into the Mouth of Olava, and the Mouth of Olava vanished in turn, and she was only a naked, defenseless thing crouching under the shadow of a death against which she could raise no shield. She was—

Her head rocked, the flesh of her cheeks stung as she swayed from the slaps dealt her by Starrex.

"You are a dreamer!" His voice was imperative. "Dream now then as you have never dreamed before! For there is that in you which can do this, if you will it."

It was like the action of that strange scented air in the ship; her will was reborn, her mind steadied. Tamisan the dreamer pushed out that other weak Tamisan. But—what world? A point—give her but a decision point in history!

"Yaaaah—" the cry from Starrex's throat was not now meant to arouse her. Perhaps it was the battle challenge of Hawarel.

There was a pallid snout, about which hung a dreadful sickening phosphorescence, thrust through the screen of brush. She sensed rather than saw Starrex fire the laser at it.

A decision—water beating in on her. Wind rising as if to claw them out of the poor refuge to be easy meat for the hunters. Drowning—sea—sea—the Sea Kings of Nath!

Feverishly she seized upon that. But she knew so little of the Sea Kings who had once held the lace of islands east of Ty-Kry. They had threatened Ty-Kry itself—so long ago that that war was legend, not true history. And they had been tricked, their king and his war chiefs taken by treachery.

The Ill Cup of Nath. Tamisan forced herself to remember, to hold on that. And, with her choice made, again her mind steadied. She threw out her hands, once more touching Starrex and Kas, though she did not choose the latter; her hand went without her conscious bidding as if he must be included or all would fail.

The Ill Cup of Nath—this time it would not be drunk!

Tamisan opened her eyes. Tamisan—no—she was Tam-sin! She sat up and looked about her. Soft covering of pale green fell away from her bare body. And, inspecting that same body, she saw that her skin was no longer warmly brown but was instead a pearl white. What she sat within was a bed place fashioned in the form of a great shell, the other half of it arching over head to form a canopy.

Also—she was not alone. Cautiously, she turned a little to survey her sleeping companion. His head was somewhat hidden from her so that she could see only a curve of shoulder as pale as her own, hair curled in a tight fitting cap, the red-brown shade of storm-tossed seaweed.

Warily, very warily, she put out a fingertip, touched it to his hunched shoulder—and knew! He sighed, began to roll over toward her. Tamisan smiled and clasped her arms under her small, high breasts.

She was Tam-sin, and this was Kilwar, who had been Starrex and Hawarel—but was now Lord of LockNer of the Nearer Sea. But, there had been a third! Her smile faded as memory sharpened. Kas! Anxiously she looked about the room, its nacre-coated walls, its pale green hangings, all familiar to Tam-sin.

No Kas. Which did not mean that he might not be lurking somewhere about, a disruptive factor if his nature held true.

A warm arm swung up about her waist. Startled she looked down into green eyes, sea-green eyes, eyes which knew her—and which also knew that other Tamisan. Below those very knowledgeable eyes lips smiled.

"I think," his voice was familiar and yet strange, "that this is going to be a very interesting dream, my Tam-sin."

She allowed herself to be drawn down beside him. Perhaps—no, surely—he was right.

Wizards' Worlds

1

CRAIKE'S swollen feet were agony, every breath he drew fought a hot band imprisoning his laboring lungs. He clung weakly to a rough spur of rock in the canyon wall, swayed against it, raking his flesh raw on the stone. That weathered red and yellow rock was no more unyielding than the murderous wills behind him. And the stab of pain in his calves no less than the pain of their purpose in his dazed mind.

He had been on the run so long, ever since he had left the E-Camp. But until last night—no, two nights ago—when he had given himself away at the gas station, he had not known what it was to be actually hunted. The will-to-kill which fanned from those on his trail was so intense it shocked his Esper senses, panicking him completely.

Now he was trapped in wild country, and he was city born. Water—Craike flinched at the thought of water. Espers should control their bodies, that was what he had been taught. But there come times when cravings of the flesh triumph over will.

He winced, and the spur grated against his half-naked breast. They had a "hound" on him right enough. And that brain-twisted Esper slave who fawned and served the mob masters would have no difficulty in trailing him straight to any pocket into which he might crawl. A last remnant of rebellion sent Craike reeling on over the gravel of the long-dried stream bed.

Espers had once been respected for their "wild talents," then tolerated warily. Now they were used under guard for slave labor. And the day was coming soon when the fears of the normals would demand their extermination. They had been trying to prepare against that.

First they had worked openly, petitioning to be included in spaceship crews, to be chosen for colonists on the moon and Mars; then secretly when they realized the norms had no intention of allowing that. Their last hope was flight to the waste spots of the world, those refuse places resulting from the same atomic wars which had brought about the birth of their kind.

Craike had been smuggled out of an eastern E-Camp provided with a cover, sent to explore the ravaged area about the one-time city of Reno. Only he had broken his cover for the protection of a girl, only to learn, too late, she was bait for an Esper trap. He had driven a stolen speeder until the last drop of fuel was gone, and after that he had kept blindly on, running, until now.

The contact with the Esper "hound" was clear; they must almost be in sight behind. Craike paused. They were not going to take him alive, wring from him knowledge of his people, recondition him into another "hound." There was only one way, he should have known that from the first.

His decision had shaken the "hound." Craike bared teeth in a death's-head grin. Now the mob would speed up. But their quarry had already chosen a part of the canyon wall where he might pull his tired and aching body up from one hold to another. He moved deliberately now, knowing that when he had lost hope, he could throw aside the need for haste. He would be able to accomplish his purpose before they brought a gas rifle to bear on him.

At last he stood on a ledge, the sand and gravel some fifty feet below. For a long moment he rested, steadying himself with both hands braced on the stone. The weird beauty of the desert country was a pattern of violent color under the afternoon sun. Craike breathed slowly; he had regained a measure of control. There came shouts as they sighted him.

He leaned forward and, as if he were diving into the river which had once run there, he hurled himself outward to the clean death he sought.

Water, water in his mouth! Dazed, he flailed water until his head broke surface. Instinct took over, and he swam, fought for air. The current of the stream pulled him against a boulder collared with froth, and he arched an arm over it, lifting himself, to stare about in stupified bewilderment.

He was close to one bank of a river. Where the colorful cliff of the canyon had been there now rolled downs thickly covered with green growth. The baking heat of the desert had vanished; there was even a slight chill in the air.

Dumbly Craike left his rock anchorage and paddled ashore, to lie shivering on sand while the sun warmed his battered body. What HAD happened? When he tried to make sense of it, the effort hurt his mind almost as much as had the "hound's" probe.

The Esper Hound! Craike jerked up, old panic stirring. First delicately and then urgently, he cast a thought-seek about him. There was life in plenty. He touched, classified and disregarded the flickers of awareness which mingled in confusion—animals, birds, river dwellers. But nowhere did he meet intelligence approaching his own. A wilderness world without man as far as Esper ability could reach.

Craike relaxed. Something had happened. He was too tired, too drained to speculate as to what. It was enough that he was saved from the death he had sought, that he was HERE instead of THERE.

He got stiffly to his feet. Time was the same, he thought—late afternoon. Shelter, food—he set off along the stream. He found and ate berries spilling from bushes where birds raided before him. Then squatting above a side eddy of the stream, he scooped out a fish, eating the flesh raw.

The land along the river was rising, he could see the beginning of a gorge ahead. Later, when he had climbed those heights, he caught sight through the twilight of the fires. Four of them burning some miles to the southwest, set out in the form of a square!

Craike sent out a thought probe. Yes—men! But an alien touch. This was no hunting mob. And he was drawn to the security of the fires, the camp of men in the dangers of the night. Only, as Esper, he was not one with them but an outlaw. And he dare not risk joining them.

He retraced his path to the river and holed up in a hollow not large enough to be termed a cave. Automatically he probed again for danger. Found nothing, but animal life. He slept at last, drugged by exhaustion of mind and body.

The sky was gray when he roused, swung cramped arms, stretched. Craike had awakened with the need to know more of that camp. He climbed once again to the vantage point, shut his eyes to the early morning and sent out a seeking.

A camp of men far from home. But they were not hunters. Merchants—traders! Craike located one mind among the rest, read in it the details of a bargain to come. Merchants from another country, a caravan. But a sense of separation grew stronger as the fugitive Esper sorted out thought streams, absorbed scraps of knowledge thirstily. A herd of burden-bearing animals, nowhere any indication of machines. He sucked in a deep breath—he was—he was in another world!

Merchants traversing a wilderness—a wilderness? Though he had been driven into desert the day before, the land through which he had earlier fled could not be termed a wilderness. It was overpopulated because there were too many war-poisoned areas where mankind could not live.

But from these strangers he gained a concept of vast, barren territory broken only by small, sparse, strips of cultivation. Craike hurried. They were breaking camp. And the impression of an unpeopled land they had given him made him want to trail the caravan.

There was trouble! An attack—the caravan animals stampeded. Craike received a startlingly vivid mind picture of a hissing, lizard thing he could not identify. But it was danger on four scaled feet. He winced at the fear in those minds ahead. There was a vigor of mental broadcast in these men which amazed him. Now, the lizard thing had been killed. But the pack animals were scattered. It would take hours to find them. The exasperation of the master trader was as strong to Craike as if he stood before the man and heard his outburst of complaint.

The Esper smiled slowly. Here—handed to him by Fate—was his chance to gain the good will of the travelers. Breaking contact with the men, Craike cast around probe webs, as a fisher might cast a net. One panic-crazed animal and then another—he touched minds, soothed, brought to bear his training. Within moments he heard the dull thud of hooves on the mossy ground, no longer pounding in a wild gallop. A shaggy mount, neither pony nor horse of his knowledge, but like in ways of each, its dull hide marked with a black stripe running from the root of shaggy mane to the base of its tail, came toward him, nickered questionly. And then fell behind Craike, to be joined by another and another, as the Esper walked on—until he led the full train of runaways.

He met the first of the caravan men within a quarter of a mile and savored the fellow's astonishment at the sight. Yet, after the first surprise the man did not appear too amazed. He was short, dark of skin, a black beard of wiry, tightly curled hair clipped to a point thrusting out from his chin. Leggings covered his limbs, and he wore a sleeveless jerkin laced with thongs. This was belted by a broad strap gaudy with painted designs, from which hung a cross-hilted sword and a knife almost as long. A peaked cap of silky white fur was drawn far down so that a front flap shaded his eyes, and another, longer strip brushed his shoulders.

"Many thanks, Man of Power—" The words he spoke were in a clicking tongue, but Craike read their meaning mind to mind.

Then, as if puzzled on his closer examination of the Esper, the stranger frowned, his indecision slowly turning hostile.

"Outlaw! Begone, horned one!" The trader made a queer gesture with two fingers. "We pass free from your spells—"

"Be not so quick to pass judgment, Alfric—"

The newcomer was the Master Trader. As his man, he wore leather, but there was a gemmed clasp on his belt. His sword and knife hilt were of precious metal, as was a badge fastened to the fore of his yellow and black fur head gear.

"This one is no local outlaw." The Master stood, feet apart, studying the fugitive Esper as if he were a burden pony offered as a bargain. "Would such use his power for our aid? If he is a horned one—he is unlike any I have seen."

"I am not what you think—" Craike said slowly, fitting his tongue to the others' alien speech.

The Master Trader nodded. "That is true. And you intend us no harm; does not the sun-stone so testify?" His hand went to the badge on his cap. "In this one is no evil, Alfric, rather does he come to us in aid. Have I not spoken the truth to you, stranger from the wastes?"

Craike broadcast good will as strongly as he could. And they must have been somewhat influenced by that.

"I feel—he DOES have the power!" Alfric burst forth.

"He has power," the Master corrected him. "But has he striven to possess our minds as he could do? We are still our own men. No—this is no renegade Black Hood. Come!"

He beckoned to Craike, and the Esper, the animals still behind him, followed on into the camp where the rest of the men seized upon the ponies to adjust their packs.

The Master filled a bowl from the contents of a three-legged pot set in the coals of a dying fire. Craike gulped an excellent and filling stew. When he had done, the Master indicated himself.

"I am Kaluf of the Children of Noe, a far trader and trail master. Is it your will, Man of Power, to travel this road with us?"

Craike nodded. This might all be a wild dream. But he was willing to see it to its end. A day with the caravan, the chance to gather more information from the men here, should give him some inkling as to what had happened to him and where he now was.

2

CRAIKE'S day with the traders became two and then three. Esper talents were accepted by this company matter-of-factly, even asked in aid. And from the travelers he gained a picture of this world which he could not reconcile with his own.

His first impression of a large continent broken by widely separated holdings of a frontier type remained. In addition there was knowledge of a feudal government, petty lordlings holding title to lands over men of lesser birth.

Kaluf and his men had a mild contempt for their customers. Their own homeland lay to the southeast, where, in some coastal cities, they had built up an overseas trade, retaining its cream for their own consumption, peddling the rest in the barbarous hinterland. Craike, his facility in their click speech growing, asked questions which the Master answered freely enough.

"These inland men know no difference between Saludian silk and the weaving of the looms in our own Kormonian quarter." He shrugged in scorn at such ignorance. "Why should we offer Salud when we can get Salud prices for Kormon lengths and the buyer is satisfied? Maybe—if these lords ever finish their private quarrels and live at peace so that there is more travel and they themselves come to visit in Larud or the other cities of the Children of Noe, then shall we not make a profit on lesser goods."

"Do these Lords never try to raid your caravans?"

Kaluf laughed. "They tried that once or twice. Certainly they saw there was the profit in seizing a train and paying nothing. But we purchased trail rights from the Black Hoods, and there was no more trouble. How is it with you, Ka-rak? Have you lords in your land who dare to stand against the power of the Hooded Ones?"

Craike, taking a chance, nodded. And knew he had been right when some reserve in Kaluf vanished.

"That explains much, perhaps even why such a man of power as you should be adrift in the wilderness. But you need not fear in this country, your brothers hold complete rule—"

A colony of Espers! Craike tensed. Had he, through some weird chance, found here the long-hoped-for refuge of his kind. But where *was* here? His old bewilderment was lost in a shout from the fore of the train.

"The outpost has sighted us and raised the trade banner." Kaluf quickened pace. "Within the hour we'll be at the walls of Sampur. Illif!"

Craike made for the head of the line. Sampur, by the reckoning of the train, was a city of respectable size, the domain of a Lord Ludicar with whom Kaluf had had mutually satisfactory dealings for some time. And the

Master anticipated a profitable stay. But the man who had ridden out to greet them was full of news.

Racially he was unlike the traders, taller, longer of arm. His bare chest was a thatch of blond-red hair as thick as a bear's pelt, long braids swung across his shoulders. A leather cap, reinforced with sewn rings of metal, was crammed down over his wealth of hair, and he carried a shield slung from his saddle pad. In addition to sword and knife, he nursed a spear in the crook of his arm, from the point of which trailed a banner strip of blue stuff.

"You come in good time, Master. The Hooded Ones have proclaimed a horning, and all the outbounders have gathered as witnesses. This is a good day for your trading, the Cloudy Ones have indeed favored you. But hurry, the Lord Ludicar is now riding in and soon there will be no good place from which to watch—"

Craike fell back. Punishment? An execution? No, not quite that. He wished he dared ask questions. Certainly the picture which had leaped into Kaluf's mind at the mention of "horning" could not be true!

Caution kept the Esper aloof. Sooner or later his alien origin must be noted, though Kaluf had supplied him with a fur cap, leather jerkin, and boots from the caravan surplus.

The ceremony was to take place just outside the main gate of the stockade, which formed the outer rampart of the town. A group of braided, ring-helmed warriors hemmed in a more imposing figure with a feather plume and a blue cloak, doubtless Lord Ludicar. Thronging at a respectful distance were the townfolk. But they were merely audience; the actors stood apart.

Craike's hands went to his head. The emotion which beat at him from that party brought the metallic taste of fear to his mouth, aroused his own memories. Then he steadied, probed. There was terror there, broadcast from two figures under guard. Just as an impact of Esper power came from the three black-hooded men who walked behind the captives.

He used his own talent carefully, dreading to attract the attention of the men in black. The townsfolk opened an aisle in their ranks, giving free passage to the open moorland and the green stretch of forest not too far away.

Fear—in one of those bound, stumbling prisoners it was abject, the same panic which had hounded Craike into the desert. But, though the other captive had no hope, there was a thick core of defiance, a desperate desire to strike back. And something in Craike arose to answer that.

Other men, wearing black jerkins and no hoods, crowded about the prisoners. When they stepped back Craike saw that the drab clothing of the two had been torn away. Shame, blotting out fear, came from the smaller captive. And there was no mistaking the sex of the curves that white body displayed. A girl, and very young. A violent shake of her head loosened her hair to flow, black and long, clothing her nakedness. Craike drew a deep breath as he had before that plunge into the canyon. Moving quickly he crouched behind a bush.

The Black Hoods went about their business with dispatch, each drawing in turn certain designs and lines in the dust of the road until they had created an intricate pattern about the feet of the prisoners.

A chant began in which the townspeople joined. The fear of the male captive was an almost visible cloud. But the outrage and anger of his feminine companion grew in relation to the chant, and Craike could sense her will battling against that of the assembly.

The watching Esper gasped. He could not be seeing what his eyes reported to his brain! The man was down on all fours, his legs and arms stretched, a mist clung to them, changed to red-brown hide. His head lengthened oddly, horns sprouted. No man, but an antlered stag stood there.

And the girl—?

Her transformation came more slowly. It began and then faded. The power of the Black Hoods held her, fastening on her the form they visualized. She fought. But in the end a white doe sprang down the path to the forest, the stag leaping before her. They whipped past the bush where Craike had gone to earth, and he was able to see through the illusion. Not a red stag and a white doe, but a man and woman running for their lives, yet already knowing in their hearts there was no hope in their flight.

Craike, hardly knowing why he did it or who he could aid, followed, sure that mind touch would provide him with a guide.

He had reached the murky shadow of the trees when a sound rang from the town. At its summoning he missed a step before he realized it was directed against those he trailed and not himself. A hunting horn! So this world also had its hunted and its hunters. More than ever he determined to aid those who fled.

But it was not enough to just run blindly on the track of stag and doe. He lacked weapons. And his wits had not sufficed to save him in his own world. But there he had been conditioned against turning on his hunters, hampered, cruelly designed from birth to accept the quarry role. That was not true here.

Esper power—Craike licked dry lips. Illusions so well done they had almost enthralled him. Could illusion undo what illusion had done? Again the call of the horn, ominous in its clear tone, rang in his ears, set his pulses to pounding. The fear of those who fled was a cord, drawing him on.

But as he trotted among the trees Craike concentrated on his own illusion. It was not a white doe he pursued but the slim, young figure he had seen when they stripped away the clumsy stuff which had cloaked her, before she had shaken loose her hair veil. No doe, but a woman. She was not racing on four hooved feet, but running free on two, her hair blowing behind her. No doe, but a maid!

And in that moment, as he constructed that picture clearly, he contacted her in thought. It was like being dashed by sea-spray, cool, remote, very clean. And, as spray, the contact vanished in an instant, only to return.

"Who are you?"

"One who follows," he answered, holding to his picture of the running girl.

"Follow no more, you have done what was needful!" There was a burst of joy, so overwhelming a release from terror that it halted him. Then the cord between them broke.

Frantically Craike cast about seeking contact. There was only a dead wall. Lost, he put out a hand to the rough bark of the nearest tree. Wood things lurked here, them only did his mind touch. What did he do now?

His decision was made for him. He picked up a wave of panic again—spreading terror. But this was the fear of feathered and furred things. It came to him as ripples might run on a pool.

Fire! He caught the thought distorted by bird and beast mind. Fire which leaped from tree crown to tree crown, cutting a gash across the forest. Craike started on, taking the way west, away from the menace.

Once he called out as a deer flashed by him, only to know in the same moment that this was no illusion but an animal. Small creatures tunnelled through the grass. A dog fox trotted, spared him a measuring gaze from slit eyes. Birds whirred, and behind them was the scent of smoke.

A mountain of flesh, muscle and fur snarled, reared to face him. But Craike had nothing to fear from any animal. He confronted the great red bear until it whined, shuffled its feet and plodded on. More and more creatures crossed his path or ran beside him for a space.

It was their instinct which brought them, and Craike, to a river. Wolves, red deer, bears, great cats, foxes and all the rest came down to the saving water. A cat spat at the flood, but leaped in to swim. Craike lingered on the bank.

The smoke was thicker, more animals broke from the wood to take to the water. But the doe—where was she?

He probed, only to meet that blank. Then a spurt of flame ran up a dead sapling, advance scout of the furnace. He yelped as a floating cinder stung his skin and took to the water. But he did not cross, rather did he swim upstream, hoping to pass the flank of the fire and pick up the missing trail again.

3

SMOKE cleared as Craike trod water. He was beyond the path of the fire, but not out of danger. For the current against which he had fought his way beat here through an archway of masonry. Flanking that arch were two squat towers. As an erection it was far more ambitious than anything he had seen during his brief glimpse of Sampur. Yet, as he eyed it more closely, he could see it was a ruin. There were gaps in the narrow span across the river, a green bush sprouted from the summit of the far tower.

Craike came ashore, winning his way up the steep bank by handholds of vine and bush no alert castellan would have allowed to grow. As he reached a terrace of cobbles stippled with bunches of coarse grass, a sweetish scent of decay drew him around the base of the tower to look down at a broad ledge extending into the river. Piled on it were small baskets and bowls, some so rotted that only outlines were visible. Others new and all filled with mouldering food stuffs. But those who left such offerings must have known that the tower was deserted.

Puzzled Craike went back to the building. The stone was undressed, yet the huge blocks which formed its base were fitted together with such precision that he suspected he could not force the thin blade of a pocket knife into any crack. There had been no effort at ornamentation, at any lighting of the impression of sullen, brute force.

Wood, split and insect bored, formed a door. As he put his hand to it Craike discovered the guardian the long-ago owners of the fortress had left in possession. His hands went to his head, the blow he felt might have been physical. Out of the stronghold before him came such a wave of utter terror and dark promise as to force him back. But no farther than the edge of the paved square about the building's foundation.

Grimly he faced that challenge, knowing it for stored emotion and not the weapon of an active will. He had his own defense against such a formless enemy. Breaking a dead branch from a bush, he twisted about it whisps of the sun-bleached grass until he had a torch of sorts. A piece of smoldering tinder blown from the fire gave him a light.

Craike put his shoulder to the powdery remnants of the door, bursting it wide. Light against dark. What lurked there was nourished by dark, fed upon the night fears of his species.

A round room, bare except for some crumbling sticks of wood, a series of steps jutting out from the wall to curl about and vanish above. Craike made no move toward further exploration, holding up the torch, seeking to see the real, not the threat of this place.

Those who had built it possessed Esper talents. And they had used that power for twisted purposes. He read terror and despair trapped here by the castellans' art, horror, an abiding fog of what his race considered evil.

Tentatively Craike began to fight. With the torch he brought light and heat into the dark and cold. Now he struggled to offer peace. Just as he had pictured a girl in flight in place of the doe, so did he now force upon those invisible clouds of stored suffering calm and hope. The gray window slits in the stone were uncurtained to the streaming sunlight.

Those who had set that guardian had not intended it to hold against an Esper. Once he began the task, Craike found the opposition melting. The terror seeped as if it sank into the floor wave by wave. He stood in a room which smelt of damp and, more faintly, of the rotting food piled below its window slits; but now it was only an empty shell.

Craike was tired, drained by his effort. And he was puzzled. Why had he fought for this? Of what importance to him was the cleansing of a ruined tower?

Though to stay here had certain advantages. It had been erected to control river traffic. Though that did not matter for the present, just now he needed food more—

He went back to the rock of offerings, treading a wary path through the disintegrating stuff. Close to the edge he came upon a clay bowl containing coarsely ground grain and, beside it, a basket of wilted leaves filled with overripe berries. He ate in gulps.

Grass made him a matted bed in the tower, and he kindled a fire. As he squatted before its flames, he sent out a questing thought. A big cat drank from the river. Craike shuddered away from that contract with blood lust. A night-hunting bird provided a trace of awareness. There were small rovers and hunters. But nothing human.

Tired as he was Craike could not sleep. There was the restless sensation of some demand about to be made, some task waiting. From time to time he fed the fire. Towards morning he dozed, to snap awake. A night creature drinking, a screech overhead. He heard the flutter of wings echo hollowly through the tower.

Beyond—darkness—blank, that curious blank which had fallen between him and the girl. Craike got to his feet eagerly. That blank could be traced.

Outside it was raining, and fog hung in murky bands among the river hollows. The blank spot veered. Craike started after it. The tower pavement became a trace of old road he followed, weaving through the fog.

There was the sour smell of old smoke. Charred wood, black muck clung to his feet. But his guide point was now stationary as the ground rose, studded with outcrops of rock. So Craike came to a mesa jutting up into a steel-gray sky.

He hitched his way up by way of a long-ago slide. The rain had stopped, but there was no hint of sun. And he was unprepared for the greeting he met as he topped the lip of a small plateau.

A violent blow on the shoulder whirled him halfway around, and only by a finger's width did he escape a fall. A cry echoed his, and the blank broke. She was there.

Moving slowly, using the same technique he knew to soothe frightened animals, Craike raised himself again. The pain in his shoulder was sharp when he tried to put much weight upon his left arm. But now he saw her clearly.

She sat cross-legged, a boulder at her back, her hair a rippling cloud of black through which her hands and arms shown starkly white. She had the thin, three-cornered face of a child who has known much harshness; there was no beauty there—the flesh had been too much worn by spirit. Only her eyes, watchful-wary as those of a feline, considered him bleakly. In spite of his beam of good will, she gave him no welcome. And she tossed another stone from hand to hand with the ease of one who had already scored with such a weapon.

"Who are you?" she spoke aloud.

"He who followed you," Craike fingered the bruise wound on his shoulder, not taking his eyes from hers.

"You are no Black Hood." It was a statement not a question. "But you, also, have been horned." Another statement.

Craike nodded. In his own time and place he had indeed been "horned."

Just as her thrown stone had struck without warning, so came her second attack. There was a hiss. Within striking distance a snake flickered a forked tongue.

Craike did not give ground. The snake head expanded,

fur ran over it; there were legs, a plume of tail fluffed. A dog fox yapped once at the girl and vanished. Craike read her recoil, the first faint uncertainty.

"You have the power!"

"I have power," he corrected her.

But her attention was no longer his. She was listening to something he could hear with neither ear nor mind. Then she ran to the edge of the mesa. He followed.

On this side the country was more rolling, and across it now came mounted men moving in and out of mist pools. They rode in silence, and over them was the same blanketing of thought as the girl had used.

Craike glanced about. There were loose stones, and the girl had already proven her marksmanship with such. But they would be no answer to the weapons the others had. Only flight was no solution either.

The girl sobbed once, a broken cry so unlike the iron will she had shown that Craike started. She leaned perilously over the drop, staring down at the horsemen.

Then her hands moved with desperate speed. She tore hairs from her head, twisted and snarled them between her fingers, breathed on them, looped them with a stone for weight, casting the tangled mass out to land before the riders.

The mist curled, took on substance. Where there had been only rock there was now a thicket of thorn, so knotted that no fleshed creature could push through it. The hunters paused, then they rode on again, but now they drove a reeling, naked man, a man kept going by a lashing whip whenever he faltered.

Again the girl sobbed, burying her face in her hands. The wretched captive reached the thorn barrier. Under his touch it melted. He stood there, weaving drunkenly.

A whip sang. He went to his knees under its cut, a trapped animal's wail on the wind. Slowly, with a blind seeking, his hands went out to small stones about him. He gathered them, spread them anew in patterns. The girl had raised her head, watched dry-eyed, but seething with hate and the need to strike back. But she did not move.

Craike dared lay a hand on her narrow shoulder, feeling through her hair the chill of her skin, while the hair itself clung to his fingers as if it had the will to smother and imprison. He tried to pull her away, but he could not move her.

The naked man crouched in the midst of his pattern, and now he chanted, a compelling call the girl could not withstand. She wrenched free of Craike's hold. But as she went she spared a thought for the man who had tried to save her. She struck out, her fist landing on the stone bruise. Pain sent him reeling back as she went over the rim of the mesa, her face a mask which no friend nor enemy might read. But there was no resignation in her eyes as she was forced to the meeting below.

4

BY the time Craike reached a vantage point the girl stood in the center of the stone ring. Outside crouched the man, his head on his knees. She looked down at him, no emotion showing on her wan face. Then she dropped her hand on his thatch of wild hair. He jerked under that touch as he had under the whip which had printed the scarlet weals across his back and loins. But he raised his head, and from his throat came a beast's mournful howl. At her gesture he was quiet, edging closer to her as if seeking some easement of his suffering.

The Black Hood drew in. Craike's probe could make nothing of them. But they could not hide their emotions as well as they concealed their thoughts. And the Esper recoiled from the avid blood lust which lapped at the two by the cliff.

A semicircle of the black-jerkined retainers moved too. And the man who had led them lay on the earth now, moaning softly. But the girl faced them, head unbowed. Craike wanted to aid her. Had he time to climb down the cliff? Clenching his teeth against the pain movement brought to his shoulder, the Esper went back, holding a mind shield as a frail protection.

Directly before him now was one of the guards. His mount caught Craike's scent, stirred uneasily, until the quieting thought of the Esper held it steady. Craike had never been forced into such action as he had these past few days; he had no real plan now, it must depend upon chance and fortune.

As if the force of her enemies' wills had slammed her back against the rock, the girl was braced by the cliff wall, a black and white figure.

Mist swirled, took on half substance of a monstrous form, was swept away in an instant. A clump of dried grass broke into flame, sending the ponies stamping and snorting. It was gone, leaving a black smudge on the earth. Illusions, realities—Craike watched. This was so far beyond his own experience that he could hardly comprehend the lightning moves of mind against mind. But he sensed these others could beat down the girl's resistance at any moment they desired, that her last futile struggles were being relished by those who decreed this as part of her punishment.

And Craike, who had believed that he could never hate more than he had when he had been touched by the fawning "hound" of the mob, was filled with a rage tempered into a chill of steel determination.

The girl went to her knees, still clutching her hair about her, facing her tormenters with her still-held defiance. Now the man who had wrought the magic which had drawn her there crawled, all humanity gone out of him, wriggling on his belly back to his captors.

Two of the guards jerked him up. He hung limp in their hands, his mouth open in an idiot's grin. Callously, as he might tread upon a worm, the nearest Black Hood waved a hand. A metal axe flashed, and there came the dull sound of cracking bone. The guards pitched the body from them so that the bloodied head almost touched the girl.

She writhed, a last frenzied attempt to break the force which pinned her. Without haste the guards advanced. One caught at her hair, pulling it tautly from her head.

Craike shivered. The thrill of her agony reached him. This was what she feared most, fought so long to prevent. If ever he must move now. And that part of his brain which had been feverishly seeking a plan went into action.

Ponies pawed, reared, went wild with panic. One of the Black Hoods swung around to face the terrorized animals. But his own mount struck out with teeth and hooves. Guardsmen shouted, and above their cries arose the shrill squeals of the animals.

Craike stood his ground, keeping the ponies in terror-stricken revolt. The guard who held the handful of hair slashed at the tress with his knife, severing it at a palm's distance away from her head. But in that same moment she moved. The knife leaped free from the man's grasp, while the severed hair twined itself about his hands, binding them until the blade buried itself in his throat; and he went down.

One of the Black Hoods was also finished, tramped into a feebly squirming thing by the ponies. Then from the ground burst a sheet of flame which split into balls, drifting through the air or rolling along the earth.

The Esper wet his lips—that was not his doing! He did not have to feed the panic of the animals now; they were truly mad. The girl was on her feet. Before his thought could reach her she was gone, swallowed up in a mist which arose to blanket the fire balls. Once more she cut their contact; there was a blank void where she had been.

Now the fog thickened. Through it came one of the ponies, foam dripping from its blunt muzzle. It bore down on Craike, eyes gleaming red through a tangled forelock. With a scream it reared.

Craike's hand grabbed a handful of mane as he leaped, avoiding teeth and hooves. Then, somehow, he gained the pad saddle, locking his fingers in the coarse hair, striving to hold his seat against the bucking enraged beast. It broke into a run, and the Esper plastered himself to the heaving body. For the moment he made no attempt at mind control.

Behind, the Black Hoods came out of their stunned bewilderment. They were questing feverishly, and he had to concentrate on holding his shield against them. A pony fleeing in terror would not excite them; a pony under control would provide them with a target.

Later he could circle about and try to pick up the trail of the witch girl. Flushed with success, Craike was sure he could provide her with a rear guard no Black Hood could pass.

The fog was thick, and the pace of the pony began to slacken. Once or twice it bucked half-heartedly, giving up when it could not dislodge its rider. Craike drew his fingers in slow, soothing sweeps down the sweating curve of its neck.

There were no more trees about, and the unshod hooves pounded on sand. They were in a dried water course, and Craike did not try to turn from that path. Then his luck ran out.

What he had ignorantly supposed to be a rock ahead, heaved up seven feet or more. A red mouth opened in a great roar. He had believed the bear he had seen fleeing the fire to be a giant, but this one was a nightmare monster.

The pony screamed with an almost human note of despair and whirled. Craike gripped the mane again and tried to mind control the bear. But his surprise had lasted seconds too long. A vast clawed paw struck, ripping across pony hide and human thigh. Then Craike could only cling to the running mount.

How long he was able to keep his seat he never knew.

Then he slipped; there was a throb of pain as he struck the ground, to be followed by blackness.

It was dusk when he opened his eyes, fighting agony in his head, his leg. But later there was moonlight. And that silver-white spotlighted a waiting shape. Green slits of eyes regarded him remotely. Dizzily he made contact.

A wolf—hungry—yet with a wariness which recognized in the prone man an enemy. Craike fought for control. The wolf whined, then it arose, its prick ears sharp cut in the moonlight, its nose questing for the scent of other, less disturbing prey, and it was gone.

Craike edged up against a boulder and sorted out sounds. The rush of water. He moved a paper-dry tongue over cracked lips. Water to drink—to wash his wounds—water!

With a groan Craike worked his way to his feet, holding fast to the top of the rock when his torn leg threatened to buckle under him. The same inner drive which had kept him going through the desert brought him down to the river.

By sunrise he was seeking a shelter, wanting to lie up, as might the wolf, in some secret cave until his wounds healed. All chance of finding the witch girl was lost. But as he crawled along the shingle, leaning on a staff he had found in drift wood, he kept alert for any trace of the Black Hoods.

It was midmorning on the second day that his snail's progress brought him to the river towers. And it took another hour for him to reach the terrace. Gaunt and worn, his empty stomach complaining, he wanted nothing more than to sink down in the nest of grass he had gathered and cease to struggle.

Perhaps he might have done so had not a click-clack of sound from the river put him on the defensive, his staff now a club. But these were not Black Hoods. Farmers, local men bound for the market of Sampur with products of their fields. They had paused, were making a choice among the least appetizing of their wares for a tribute to be offered to the tower demon.

Craike hitched stiffly to a point where he could witness that sacrifice. But when he assessed the contents of their dugout, the heaping basket piled between the paddlers, his hunger took command.

Fob off a demon with a handful of meal and a too-ripe melon, would they? With three haunches of cured meat and all that other stuff on board!

Craike voiced a roar which could have done credit to the red bear, a roar which altered into a demand for meat. The paddlers nearly lost control of their crude craft. But one reached for a haunch and threw it blindly on the refuse-covered rock, while his companion added a basket of small cakes into the bargain.

"Enough, little men—" Craike's voice boomed hollowly. "You may pass free."

They needed no urging, they did not look at those threatening towers as their paddles bit into the water, adding impetus to the pull of the current.

Craike watched them well out of sight before he made a slow descent to the rock. The effort he was forced to expend warned him that a second such trip might be impossible, and he inched back to the terrace dragging both meat and cakes.

The cured haunch he worried into strips, using his pocket knife. It was tough, not too pleasant to the taste and unsalted. But he found it more appetizing than the cakes of baked meal. With this supply he could afford to lie up and favor his leg.

About the claw rents the flesh was red and puffed. Craike had no dressing but river water and the leaves he had tied over the tears. Sampur was beyond his power to reach, and to contact men traveling on the river would only bring the Black Hoods.

He lay in his grass nest and tried to sort out the events

of the past few days. This was a land in which Esper powers were allowed free range. He had no idea of how he had come here, but it seemed to his feverish mind that he had been granted another chance—one in which the scales of justice were more balanced in his favor. If he could only find the girl, learn from her—

Tentatively, without real hope, he sent out a questing thought. Nothing. He moved impatiently, wrenching his leg, so that his head swam with pain. Throat and mouth were dry. The lap of water sounded in his ears. Water—he was thirsty again. But he could not crawl down slope and up once more. Craike closed his eyes wearily.

5

CRAIKE'S memory of the hours which followed thereafter was dim. HAD he seen a demon in the doorway? A slavering wolf? A red bear?

Then the girl sat there, cross-legged as he had seen her on the mesa, her cloak of hair about her. A hand emerged from the cloak to lay wood on the fire. Illusions?

But would an illusion turn to him, put firm, cool fingers upon his wound, somehow driving out by touch the pain and fire which burned there? Would an illusion raise his head, cradling it against her so that the soft silk of her hair lay against his cheek and throat, urging on him liquid out of a crude bowl? Would an illusion sing softly to herself while she drew a fish-bone comb back and forth through her hair, until the song and the sweep of the comb lulled him into a sleep so deep that no dream walked there?

He awoke, clear headed. Yet that last illusion lingered. For she came from the sun-drenched world without, a bowl of fruit in her hand. For a long moment she stood gazing at him searchingly. But when he tried mind contact, he met that wall. Not unheeding—but a refusal to answer.

Her hair was now braided. But about her face the lock

which the guardsman had shorn made an untidy fringe. While around her thin body was a strip of hide, purposefully arranged to mask all femininity.

"So," Craike spoke rustily, "you are real—"

She did not smile. "I am real. You no longer dream with fever."

"Who are you?" He asked the first of his long-hoarded questions.

"I am Takya." She added nothing to that.

"You are Takya, and you are a witch—"

"I am Takya, and I have the power." It was an assertion of fact rather than agreement.

She settled in her favorite cross-legged position, selected a fruit from her bowl and examined it with the interest of a housewife who has shopped for supplies on a limited budget. Then she placed it in his hand before she chose another for herself. He bit into the plumlike globe. If she would only drop her barrier, let him communicate in the way which was fuller and deeper than speech.

"You also have the power—"

Craike decided to be no more communicative than she. He replied to that with a curt nod.

"Yet you have not been horned—"

"Not as you have been. But in my own world, yes."

"Your world?" Her eyes held some of the feral glow of a hunting cat's. "What world, and why were you horned there, man of sand and ash, power?"

Without knowing why Craike related the events of the days past. Takya listened, he was certain, with more than ears alone. She picked up a stick from the pile of firewood and drew patterns in the sand and ash, patterns which had something to do with her listening.

"Your power was great enough to break a world wall." She snapped the stick between two fingers, threw it into the flames.

"A world wall?"

"We of the power have long known that different

worlds lie together in such a fashion." She held up her hand with the fingers tight lying one to another. "Sometimes there comes a moment when two touch so closely that the power can carry one through. If at that moment there is a desperate need for escape. But those places of meeting can not be readily found, and the moment of their touch can lay only for an instant. Have you in your world no reports of men and women who have vanished almost in sight of their fellows?"

Remembering old tales he nodded.

"I have seen a summoning from another world," she continued with a shiver, running both hands down the length of her braids as if so she evoked a shield for both mind and body. "To summon so is a great evil, for no man can hold in check the power of something alien. You broke the will of the Black Hoods when I was a beast running from their hunt. When I made the serpent to warn you off, you changed it into a fox. And when the Black Hoods would have shorn my power—" she looped the braids about her wrists, caressing, treasuring them against her small breasts, "again you broke their hold and set me free for a second time. But this you could not have done had you been born into this world, for our power must follow set laws. Yours lies outside out patterns and can cut across those laws—even as the knife cut this—" She touched the rough patch of hair at her temple.

"Follow patterns? Then it was those patterns in stone which drew you down from the mesa?"

"Yes. Takyi, my womb-brother, whom they slew there, was blood of my blood, bone of my bone. When they crushed him, then they could use him to draw me, and I could not resist. But in the slaying of his husk they freed me—to their great torment, as Tousuth shall discover in time."

"Tell me of this country. Who are the Black Hoods and why did they horn you? Are you not of their breed since you have the power?"

But Takya did not answer at once in words. Nor did she, as he had hoped, lower her mind barrier.

Her fingers now held one long hair she had pulled from her head, and this she began to weave in and out, swiftly intricately, in a complicated series of loops and crossed strands. After a moment Craike did not see the white fingers, nor the black hair they passed in loops from one to another. Rather did he see the pictures she wrought in her weaving.

A wide land, largely wilderness. The impressions he had gathered from Kaluf and the traders crystalized into vivid life. Small holdings here and there, ruled by petty lords, new settlements carved out by a scattered people moving up from the south in great wheeled wains, bringing flocks and herds, their carefully treasured seed. Stopping here and there for a season to sow and reap, until they decided upon a site for their final rooting. Tiny city-states, protected by the Black Hoods—the Esper born who purposefully interbred their own gifted stock, keeping their children apart.

Takya and her brother coming, as was sometimes—if rarely—true, from the common people. Carefully watched by the Black Hoods. Then discovered to be a new mutation, condemned as such to be used for experimentation. But for a while protected by the local lord who wanted Takya.

But he might not take her unwilling. For the power that was hers as a virgin was wholly rift from her should she be forced. And he had wanted that power, obedient to him, as a check upon the monopoly of the Black Hoods. So with some patience he had set himself to a peaceful wooing. But the Black Hoods had moved first.

Had they accomplished her taking, the end they had intended for her was not as easy as death. And she wove a picture of it, with all its degradation and shame stark and open, for Craike's seeing.

"Then the Hooded ones are evil?"

"Not wholly." She untwisted the hair and put it with care into the fire. "They do much good, and without them people would suffer. But I, Takya, am different. And after me, when I mate, there will be others also different. How different we are not yet sure. The Hooded Ones want no change, by their thinking that means disaster. So they would use me to their own purposes. Only I, Takya, shall not be so used!"

"No, you shall not." The vehemence of his own outburst startled him. Craike wanted nothing so much at that moment than to come to grips with the Black Hoods, who had planned this systematic hunt.

"What will you do now?" He asked more calmly, wishing she would share her thoughts with him.

"This is a strong place. Did you cleanse it?"

He nodded impatiently.

"So I thought. That was also a task one born to this world might not have performed. But those who pass are not yet aware of the Cleansing. They will not trouble us, but pay tribute."

Craike found her complacency irritating. To lie up here and live on the offerings of river travelers did not appeal to him.

"This stone piling is older work than Sampur and much better," she continued. "It must have been a fortress for some of those forgotten ones who held lands and then vanished long before we came from the south. If it is repaired no lord of this district would have so good a roof."

"Two of us to rebuild it?" he laughed.

"Two of us—working thus."

A block of stone, the size of a brick, which had fallen from the sill of one of the needle-narrow windows, arose slowly in the air, settled into the space from which it had tumbled. Illusion or reality? Craike got to his feet and lurched to the window. His hand fell upon the stone which moved easily in his grasp. He took it out, weighed it, and then gently returned it to its place. Not illusion.

"But illusion too—if need be." There was, for the first time, a warm note of amusement in her tone. "Look on your tower, river lord!"

He limped to the door. Outside it was warm, sunny, but it was a site of ruins. Then the picture changed. Brown drifts of grass vanished from the terrace, the fallen stone was all in place. A hard-faced sentry stood wary-eyed on a repaired river arch. Another guardsman led out ponies saddle-padded and ready, other men were about garrison tasks.

Craike grinned. The sentry on the arch lost his helm, his jerkin. He now wore the tight tunic of the Security Police, his spear was a gas rifle. The ponies misted, and in their place a speedster sat on the stone. He heard her laugh.

"*Your* guard, *your* traveling machine. But how grim, ugly. This is better!"

Guards, machine, all were swept away. Craike caught his breath at the sight of delicate winged creatures dancing in the air, displaying a joy of life he had never known. Fawns, little people of the wild, came to mingle with such shapes of beauty and desire that at last he turned his head away.

"Illusion," her voice was hard, mocking.

But Craike could not believe that what he had seen had been born from hardness and mockery.

"All illusions. We shall be better now with warriors. As for plans, can you suggest any better than to remain here and take what fortune sends—for a space?"

"Those winged dancers—where?"

"Illusions!" She returned harshly. "But such games tire one. I do not think we shall conjure up any garrison before they are needed. Come, do not tear open those wounds of yours anew, for healing is no illusion and drains one even more of the power."

The clawed furrows were healing cleanly, though he would bear their scars for life. He hobbled back to the grass bed and dropped upon it, but regretted the erasure of the sprites she had shown him.

Once he was safely in place, Takya left with the curt explanation she had things to do. But Craike was restless, too much so to remain long inside the tower. He waited until she had gone and then, with the aid of his staff, climbed to the end of the span above the river. From here the twin tower on the other bank looked the same as the one from which he had come. Whether it was also haunted Craike did not know. But, as he looked about, he could see the sense of Takya's suggestion. A few illusion sentries would discourage any ordinary intrusion.

Takya's housekeeping had changed the rock of offerings. All the rotting debris was gone and none of the odor of decay now offended the nostrils at a change of wind. But at best it was a most uncertain source of supply. There could not be too many farms upriver, nor too many travelers taking the water way.

As if to refute that, his Esper sense brought him sudden warning of strangers beyond the upper bend. But, Craike tensed, there were no peasants bound for the market at Sampur. Fear, pain, anger, such emotions heralded their coming. There were three, and one was hurt. But they were not Esper, nor did they serve the Black Hoods. Though they were, or had been, fighting men.

A brutal journey over the mountains where they had lost comrades, the finding of this river, the theft of the dugout they now used so expertly—it was all there for him to read. And beneath that something else, which, when he found it, gave Craike a quick decision in their favor—a deep hatred of the Black Hoods! Outlaws, very close to despair, keeping on a hopeless trail because it was not in them to surrender.

Craike contacted them subtly. They must not think

they were heading into an Esper trap! Plant a little hope, a faint suggestion that there was a safe camping place ahead, that was all he could do at present. But so he drew them on.

"No!" A ruthless order cut across his line of contact, striking at the delicate thread with which he was playing the strangers in. But Craike stood firm. "Yes, yes, and yes!"

He was on guard instantly. Takya, mistress of illusion as she had proved herself to be, might act. But surprisingly she did not. The dugout came into view, carried more by the current than the efforts of its crew. One lay full length in the bottom, while the bow paddler had slumped forward. But the man in the stern was bringing them in. And Craike strengthened his invisible, unheard invitation to urge him on.

6

BUT Takya had not yet begun to fight. As the dugout swung in toward the offering ledge one of the Black Hoods' guardsmen appeared there, his drawn sword taking fire from the sun. The fugitive steersman faltered until the current drew his craft on. Craike caught the full force of the stranger's despair, all the keener for the hope of moments before. The Esper irritation against Takya flared into anger.

He made the illusion reel back, hands clutching at his breast from which protruded the shaft of an arrow. Craike had seen no bows here, but it was a weapon to suit this world. And this should prove to Takya he meant what he had said.

The steersman was hidden as the dugout passed under the arch. There was a scrap of beach, the same to which Craike had swum on his first coming. He urged the man to that, beaming good will.

But the paddler was almost done, and neither of his companions could aid him. He drove the crude craft to the bank, and its bow grated on the rough gravel. Then he crawled over the bodies of the other two and fell rather than jumped ashore, turning to pull up the canoe as best he could.

Craike started down. But he might have known that Takya was not so easily defeated. Though they maintained an alliance of sorts she accepted no order from him.

A brand was teleported from the tower fire, striking spear-wise in the dry brush along the slope. Craike's mouth set. He tried no more arguments. They had already tested power against power, and he was willing to so battle again. But this was not the time. However the fire was no illusion, and he could not fight it, crippled as he was. Or could he?

It was not spreading too fast—though Takya might spur it by the forces at her command. Now—there was just the spot! Craike steadied himself against a mound of fallen masonry and swept out his staff, dislodging a boulder and a shower of gravel. He had guessed right. The stone rolled to crush out the brand, and the gravel he continued to push after it smothered the creeping flames.

Red tongues dashed spitefully high in a sheet of flame, and Craike laughed. THAT was illusion. She was angry. He produced a giant pail in the air, tilted it forward, splashed its contents into the heart of that conflagration. He felt the lash of her rage, standing under it unmoved. So might she bring her own breed to heel, but she would learn he was not of that ilk.

"Holla!" That call was no illusion, it begged help.

Craike picked a careful path downslope until he saw the dugout and the man who had landed it. The Esper waved an invitation and at his summons the fugitive covered the distance between them.

He was a big man of the same brawny race as those of Sampur, his braids of reddish hair hanging well below his wide shoulders. There was the raw line of a half-healed wound down the angle of his jaw, and his sunken eyes were very tired. For a moment he stood downslope from Craike, his hands on his hips, his head back, measuring the Esper with the shrewdness of a canny officer who had long known how to judge and handle raw levies.

"I am Jorik of the Eagles' Tower." The statement was made with the same confidence as the announcement of rank might have come from one of the petty lords. "Though," he shrugged, "the Eagles' Tower stands no more with one stone upon the other. You have a stout lair here—" he hesitated before he concluded, "friend."

"I am Craike," the Esper answered as simply, "and I am also one who has run from enemies. This lair is an old one, though still useful."

"Might the enemies from whom you run wear black hoods?" countered Jorik. "It seems to me that things I have just seen here have the stink of that about them."

"You are right. I am no friend to the Black Hoods."

"But you have the power—"

"I have power," Craike tried to make the distinction clear. "You are welcome, Jorik. So all are welcome here who are no friends to Black Hoods."

The big warrior shrugged. "We can no longer run. If the time has come to make a last stand, this is as good a place as any. My men are done." He glanced back at the two in the dugout. "They are good men, but we were pressed when they caught us in the upper pass. Once there were twenty hands of us," he held up his fist and spread the fingers wide for counting. "They drew us out of the tower with their sorcerers' tricks, and then put us to the hunt."

"Why did they wish to make an end to you?"

Jorik laughed shortly. "They dislike those who will not fit into their neat patterns. We are free mountain men, and no Black Hood helped us win the Eagles' Tower; none aided us to hunt. When we took our furs down to the valley they wanted to levy tribute. But what spell of theirs trapped the beasts in our dead-falls, or brought them to our spears? We pay not for what we have not bought. Neither would we have made war on them. Only, when we spoke out and said it so, there were others who were encouraged to do likewise, and the Black Hoods must put an end to us before their rule was broken. So they did."

"But they did not get all of you," Craike pointed out. "Can you bring your men up to the tower? I have been hurt and can not walk without support or I would lend you a hand."

"We will come." Jorik returned to the dugout. Water was splashed vigorously into the face of the man in the bow, arousing him to crawl ashore. Then the leader of the fugitives swung the third man out of the craft and over his shoulder in a practiced carry.

When Craike had seen the unconscious man established on his own grass bed, he stirred up the fire and set out food. While Jorik returned to the dugout to bring in their gear.

Neither of the other men were of the same size as their leader. The one who lay limp, his breath fluttering between his slack lips, was young hardly out of boyhood, his thin frame showing bones rather than muscled flesh under the rags of clothing. The other was short, dark-skinned, akin by race to Kaluf's men, his jaw sprouting a curly beard. He measured Craike with suspicious glances from beneath lowered red lids, turning that study to the walls about him and the unknown reaches at the head of the stair.

Craike did not try mind touch. These men were rightly suspicious of Esper arts. But he did attempt to reach Takya, only to meet that nothingness with which she cloaked her actions. Craike was disturbed. Surely now that she was convinced he was determined to give the harborage to the fugitives, she would oppose him. They had nothing to fear from Jorik and his men, but rather would gain by joining forces.

Until his wounds were entirely healed he could not go far. And without weapons they would have to rely solely upon Esper powers for defense. Having witnessed the efficiency of the Hooded Ones' attack, Craike doubted a victory in any engagement to which those masters came fully prepared. He had managed to upset their spells merely because they had not known of his existence. But the next time he would have no such advantage.

On the other hand the tower could be defended by force of arms. With bows— Craike savored the idea of archers giving a Hooded force a devastating surprise. The traders had had no such arm, as sophisticated as they were. And he had seen none among the warriors of Sampur. He'd have to ask Jorik if such were known.

In the meantime he sat among his guests, watching Jorik feed the semi-conscious boy with soft fruit pulp and the other man wolf down dried meat. When the latter had done, he hitched himself closer to the fire and jerked a thumb at his chest.

"Zackuth," he identified himself.

"From Larud?" Craike named the only city of Kaluf's people he could remember.

The dark man's momentary surprise had no element of suspicion. "What do you know of the Children of Noe, stranger?"

"I journeyed the plains with one called Kaluf, a Master Trader of Larud."

"A fat man who laughs much and wears a falcon plume in his cap?"

"Not so," Craike allowed a measure of chill to ice his reply. "The Kaluf who led this caravan was a lean man who knew the edge of a good blade from its hilt. As for cap ornaments—he had a red stone to the fore of his. Also he swore by the Eyes of the Lady Lor."

Zackuth gave a great bray of laughter. "You are no stream fish to be easily hooked, are you, tower dweller? I am not of Larud, but I know Kaluf, and those who travel in his company do not wear one badge one day and another the next. But, by the looks of you, you have fared little better than we lately. Has Kaluf also fallen upon evil luck?"

"I traveled safely with his caravan to the gates of

Sampur. How it fared with him thereafter I can not tell you."

Jorik grinned and settled his patient back on the bed. "I believe you must have parted company in haste, Lord Ka-rak?"

Craike answered that with the truth. "There were two who were horned. I followed them to give what aid I could."

Jorik scowled, and Zackuth spat into the fire.

"We were not horned; we have no power," the latter remarked. "But they have other tricks to play. So you came here?"

"I was clawed by a bear," Craike supplied a meager portion of his adventures, "and came here to lie up until I can heal me of that hurt."

"This is a snug hole," Jorik was appreciative. "But how got you such eating?" He popped half a fruit into his mouth and licked his juicy fingers. "This is no wilderness feeding."

"The tower is thought to be demon-haunted. Those taking passage down stream leave tribute."

Zackuth slapped his knee. "The Gods of the Waves are good to you, Lord Ka-rak, that you should stumble into such fortune. There is more than one kind of demon for the haunting towers. How say you, Lord Jorik?"

"That we have also come into luck at last, since Lord Ka-rak has made us free of this hold. But perhaps you have some other thought in your head?" He spoke to the Esper.

Craike shrugged. "What the clouds decree shall fall as rain or snow," he quoted a saying of the caravan men.

It was close to sunset, and he was worried about Takya. He could not believe that she had gone permanently. And yet, if she returned, what would happen? He had been careful not to use Esper powers. Takya would have no such compunctions.

He could not analyze his feelings about her. She disturbed him, awoke emotions he refused to face. There was a certain way she had of looking sidewise— But her calm assumption of superiority pricked beneath his surface armor. And the antagonism fretted against the feeling which had drawn him after her from the gates of Sampur. Once again he sent out a quest-thought and, to his surprise, was answered.

"They must go!"

"They are outlaws, even as we. One is ill, the others worn with long running. But they stood against the Black Hoods. As such they have a claim on roof, fire and food from us."

"They are not as we!" Again arrogance. "Send them or I shall drive them. I have the power—"

"Perhaps you have the power, but so do I!" He put all the assurance he could muster into that. "I tell you, no better thing could happen then for us to give these men aid. They are proven fighters—"

"Swords can not stand against the power!"

Craike smiled. His plans were beginning to move even as he carried on this voiceless argument. "Not swords, no, Takya. But all fighting is not done with swords or spears. Nor with the power either. Can a Black Hood think death to his enemy when he himself is dead, killed from a distance, and not by mind power his fellows could trace and be armored against.

He had caught her attention. She was acute enough to know that he was not playing with words, that he knew of what he spoke. Quickly he built upon that spark of interest. "Remember how your illusion guard died upon the offering rock when you would warn off these men?"

"By a small spear." She was contemptuous again.

"Not so." He shaped a picture of an arrow and then of an archer releasing it from the bow cord, of its speeding true across the river to strike deep into the throat of an unsuspecting Black Hood.

"You have the secret of this weapon?"

"I do. And five such arms are better than two, is that not the truth?"

She yielded a fraction. "I will return. But they will not like that."

"If you return, they will welcome you. These are no hunters of witch maidens—" he began, only to be disconcerted by her obvious amusement. Somehow he had lost his short advantage over her. Yet she did not break contact.

"Ka-rak, you are very foolish. No, these will not try to mate with me, not even if I willed it so. As you will see. Does the eagle mate with the hunting cat? But they will be slow to trust me, I think. However, your plan has possibilities, and we shall see."

7

TAKYA had been right about her reception by the fugitives. They knew her for what she was, and only Craike's acceptance of her kept them in the tower. That and the fact, which Jorik did not try to disguise, that they could not hope to go much farther on their own. But their fears were partly allayed when she took over the nursing of the sick youngster, using on him the same healing power she had produced for Craike's wound. By the new day she was feeding him broth and demanding service from the others as if they had been her liegemen from birth.

The sun was well up when Jorik came in whistling from a dip in the river.

"This is a stout stronghold, Lord Ka-rak. And with the power aiding us to hold it, we are not likely to be shaken out in a hurry. Doubly is that true if the Lady aids us."

Takya laughed. She sat in the shaft of light from one of the narrow windows, combing her hair. Now she looked over her shoulder at them with something approaching a pert archness. In that moment she was more akin to the women Craike had known in his own world.

"Let us first see how the Lord Ka-rak proposes to defend us." There was mockery in that, enough to sting, as well as a demand that he make good his promise of the night before.

But Craike was prepared. He discarded his staff for a hold on Jorik's shoulder, while Zackuth slogged behind. They climbed into the forest. Craike had never fashioned a bow, and he did not doubt that his first attempts might be failures. But, as the three made their slow progress, he explained what they must look for and the kind of weapon he wanted to produce. They returned within the hour with an assortment of wood lengths with which to experiment.

After noon Zackuth grew restless and went off, to come back with a deer, visibly proud of his hunting skill. Craike saw bowstrings where the others saw meat and hide for the refashioning of foot wear. For the rest of the day they worked with a will. It was Takya, who had the skill necessary for the feathering of the arrows after Zackuth netted two black river birds.

Four days later the tower community had taken on the aspect of a real stronghold. Many of the fallen stones were back in the walls. The two upper rooms of the tower had been explored, and a vast collection of ancient nests had been swept out. Takya chose the topmost one for her own abode and, aided by her convalescing charge, the boy Nickus, had carried armloads of sweet-scented grass up for both carpeting and bedding. She did not appear to be inconvenienced by the bats that still entered at dawn to chitter out again at dusk. And she crooned a welcome to the snowy owl that refused to be dislodged from a favorite roost in the very darkest corner of the roof.

River travel had ceased. There were no new offerings on the rock. But Jorik and Zackuth hunted. And Craike tended the smoking fires which cured the extra meat against coming need, while he worked on the bows. Shortly they had three finished and practiced along the terrace, using blunt arrows.

Jorik had a true marksman's eye and took to the new weapon quickly, as did Nickus. But Zackuth was more clumsy, and Craike's stiff leg bothered him. Takya was easily the best shot when she would consent to try. But while agreeing it was an excellent weapon, she preferred her own type of warfare and would sit on the wall, braiding and rebraiding her hair with flying fingers, to watch their shooting at marks and applaud or jeer lightly at the results.

However, their respite was short. Craike had the first warning of trouble. He awoke from a dream in which he had been back in the desert panting ahead of the mob. Awoke, only to discover that some malign influence filled the tower. There was a compulsion on him to get out, to flee into the forest.

He tested the silences about him tentatively. The oppression which had been in the ancient fort at his first coming had not returned, that was not it. But what?

Someone moved restlessly in the dark.

"Lord Ka-rak?" Nickus' voice was low and hoarse, as if he struggled to keep it under control.

"What is it?"

"There is trouble—"

A bulk which could only belong to Jorik heaved up black against the faint light of the doorway.

"The hunt is up," he observed. "They move to shake us out of here like rats out of a nest."

"They did this before with you?" asked the Esper.

Jorik snorted. "Yes. It is their favorite move to battle. They would give us such a horror of our tower that we will burst forth and scatter. Then they can cut us down as they wish."

But Craike could not isolate any thought beam carrying that night terror. It seeped from the walls about them. He sent probes unsuccessfully. There was the pad of feet on the stairs, and then he heard Takya call:

"Build up the fire, foolish ones. They may discover that they do not deal with those who know nothing of them."

Flame blossomed from the coals to light a circle of sober faces. Zackuth caressed the spear lying across his knees, but Nickus and Jorik had eyes only for the witch maid as she knelt by the fire, laying out some bundles of dried leaf and fern. Her thoughts reached Craike.

"We must move or these undefended ones will be drawn out from here as nut meats are picked free from the shell. Give me of your power—in this matter I must be the leader."

Though he resented anew her calm assumption of authority, Craike also recognized in it truth. But he shrank from the task she demanded of him. To have no control over his own Esper arts, to allow her to use them to feed hers—it was a violation of a kind, the very thing he had so feared in his own world that he had been willing to kill himself to escape it. Yet now she asked it of him as one who had the right!

"Forced surrender is truly evil—but given freely in our defense this is different." Her thoughts swiftly answered his wave of repulsion.

The command to flee the tower was growing stronger. Nickus got to his feet as if dragged up. Suddenly Zackuth made for the door, only to have Jorik reach forth a long arm to trip him.

"You see," Takya urged, "they are already half under the spell. Soon we shall not be able to hold them, either by mind or body. And then they shall be wholly lost—for ranked against us now is the high power of the Black Hoods."

Craike watched the scuffle on the floor and then, still reluctant and inwardly shrinking, he limped around the fire to her side, lying down at her gesture. She threw on the fire two of her bundles of fern, and a thick, sweet smoke curled out to engulf them. Nickus coughed, put his hands uncertainly to his head and slumped, curling up as a tired child in deep slumber. And the struggle between Jorik and his man subsided as the fumes reached them.

Takya's hand was cool as it slipped beneath Craike's jerkin, resting over his heart. She was crooning some queer chant, and, though he fought to hold mind contact, there was a veil between them as tangible to his inner senses as the fern smoke was to his outer ones. For one wild second or two he seemed to see the tower room through her eyes instead of his own, and then the room was gone. He sped bodiless across the night world, casting forth as a hound on the trail.

All that had been solid in his normal sight was now without meaning. But he was able to see the dark cloud of pressure closing in on the tower and trace that back to its source, racing along the slender thread of its spinners.

There was another fire, and about it four of the Black Hoods. Here, too, was scented smoke to free minds from bodies. The essence which was Craike prowled about that fire, counting guardsmen who lay in slumber.

With an effort of will which drew heavily upon his strength, he concentrated on the staff which lay before the leader of the company. Setting upon it his own commands.

It flipped up into the air, even as its master roused and clutched at it, falling into the fire. There was a flash of blue light, a sound which Craike felt rather than heard. The Hooded Ones were on their feet as their master stared straight across the flames to Craike's disembodied self. His was not an evil face, rather did it hold elements of nobility. But the eyes were pitiless, and Craike knew that now it was not only war to the death between them, but war beyond death itself. The Esper sensed that this was the first time that other had known of his existence, had been able to consider him as a factor in the tangled game.

There was a flash of lightning knowledge of each other,

and then Craike was again in the dark. He heard once more Takya's crooning, was conscious of her touch resting above the slow, pulsating beat of his heart.

"That was well done," her thought welcomed him. "Now they must meet us face to face in battle."

"They will come." He accepted the dire promise that Black Hood had made.

"They will come, but now we are more equal. And there is not the Rod of Power to fear."

Craike tried to sit up and discovered that the weakness born of his wounds was nothing to that which now held him.

Takya laughed with some of her old mockery. "Do you think you can make the Long Journey and then romp about as a fawn, Ka-rak? Not three days on the field of battle can equal this. Sleep now and gather again the inner power. The end of this venture is still far from us."

He could no longer see her face, the glimmer of her hair veiled it, and then that shimmer reached his mind and shook him away from consciousness; and he slept.

It might have been early morning when he had made that strange visit to the camp of the Black Hoods. By the measure of the sun across the floor it was late afternoon when he lifted heavy eyelids again. Takya gazed down upon him. Her summons had brought him back, just as her urging had sent him to sleep. He sat up with a smile, but she did not return it.

"All is right?"

"We have time to make ready before we are put to the test. Your mountain captain is not new to this game. Matters of open warfare he understands well, and he and his men have prepared a rude welcome for those who come. And," her faint smile deepened. "I, too, have done my poor best. Come and see."

He limped out on the terrace and for a moment was startled. Illusion, yes, but some of it was real.

Jorik laughed at the expression on Craike's face, inviting the Esper with a wave of the hand to inspect the force he captained. For there were bowmen in plenty, standing sentinel on the upper walls, arch, and tower, walking beats on the twin buildings across the river. And it took Craike a few seconds to sort out the ones he knew from those who served Takya's purposes. But the real had been as well posted as their illusionary companions. Nickus, for his superior accuracy with the new weapon, held a vantage point on the wall, and Zackuth was on the river arch where his arrows needed only a short range to be effective.

"Look below," Jorik urged, "and see what shall trip them up until we can pin them."

Again Craike blinked. The illusion was one he had seen before, but that had been a hurried erection on the part of a desperate girl; this was better contrived. For all the ways leading to the river towers were cloaked with a tangled mass of thorn trees, the spiked branches interlocking into a wall no sword, no spear could hope to pierce. It might be an illusion, but it would require a weighty counterspell on the part of the Hooded Ones to clear it.

"She takes some twigs Nickus finds, and a hair, and winds them together, then buried all under a stone. After she sings over it—and we have this!" Jorik babbled. "She is worth twenty hands—no, twice twenty hands, or fighting men, is the Lady Takya! Lord Ka-rak, I say that there is a new day coming for this land when such as you two stand up against the Hooded Ones."

"Aaaay—" The warning was soft but clear, half whistle, half call, issuing from Nickus' lofty post. "They come!"

"So do they!" That was a sharp echo from Zackuth. "And down river as well."

"For which we have an answer." Jorik was undisturbed.

Those in the tower held their fire. To the confident

attackers it was as such warfare had always been for them. If half their company was temporarily halted by the spiny maze, the river party had only to land on the offering rock and fight their way in, their efforts reinforced by the arts of their Masters.

But, as their dugout nosed in, bow cords sang. There was a voiceless scream which tore through Craike's head as the hooded man in its bow clutched at the shaft protruding from his throat and fell forward into the river. Two more of the crew followed him, and the rest stopped paddling, dismayed. The current pulled them on under the arch, and Zackuth dropped a rock to good purpose. It carried one of the guardsmen down with it as it hit the craft squarely. The dugout turned over, spilling all the rest into the water.

Zackuth laughed; Jorik roared.

"Now they learn what manner of blood letting lies before them!" he cried so that his words must have reached the ears of the besiegers. "Let us see how eagerly they come to such feasting."

8

IT was plain that the Black Hoods held their rulership by more practical virtues than just courage. Having witnessed the smashing disaster of the river attack, they made no further move. Night was coming, and Craike watched them withdraw downstream with no elation. Nor did Jorik retain his cheerfulness.

"Now they will try something else. And since we did not fall easily into their jaws, it will be harder to face. I do not like it that we must so face it during the hours of dark."

"There will be no dark," Takya countered. One slim finger pointed at a corner of the terrace, and up into the gathering dusk leaped a pencil of clear light. Slowly she turned and brought to life other torches on the roof of the tower over the river, on the arch spanning the water, on the parapet— And in that radiance nothing could move unseen.

"So!" Her fingers snapped, and the beacons vanished. "When they are needed, we shall have them."

Jorik blinked. "Well enough, Lady. But honest fire is also good, and it provides warmth for a man's heart as well as light for his eyes."

She smiled as a mother might smile at a child. "Build your fire, Captain of Swords. But we shall have ample warning when the enemy comes." She called. A silent winged thing floated down and alighted on the arm she held out to invite it. The white owl, its eyes seeming to observe them all with intelligence, snapped its wicked beak as Takya stared back at it. Then with a flap of wings, it went.

"From us they may hide their thoughts and movements. But they can not close the sky to those things whose natural home it is. Be sure we shall know, and speedily, when they move against us."

They did not leave their posts however. And Zackuth readied for action by laying up pieces of rubble which might serve as well as his first lucky shot.

It was a long night, wearing on the tempers of all but Takya. Time and time again Craike tried to probe the dark. But a blank wall was all he met. Whatever moves the Black Hoods considered, they were protected by an able barrier.

Jorik took to pacing back and forth on the terrace, five strides one way, six the other, and he brought down his bow with a little click on the time-worn stones each time he turned.

"They are as busy hatching trouble as a forest owl is in hatching an egg! But what kind of trouble?"

Craike had schooled himself into an outward patience. "For the learning of what we shall have to wait. But why do they delay—?"

Why did they? The more on edge he and his handful of defenders became, the easier meat they were. And he had not doubt that the Black Hoods were fertile in surprise. Though, judging by what Takya and Jorik reported, they were not accustomed to such determined and resourceful opposition to their wills. Such opposition would only firm their desire to wipe out the rebels.

"They move," Takya's witch fires leaped from every point she had earlier indicated. In that light she sped across the terrace to stand close to Jorik and Craike, close to the parapet wall. "This is the lowest hour of the night when the blood runs slow and resistance is at its depth. So they choose to move—"

Jorik snapped his bow cord, and the thin twang was a harp's note in the silence. But Takya shook her head.

"Only the Hooded Ones come, and they are well armored. See!" She jumped to the parapet and clapped her hands.

The witch light shown down on four standing within the thorn barrier, staring up from under the shadow of their hoods. An arrow sang, but it never reached its mark. Still feet away from the leader's breast it fell to the earth.

But Jorik refused to accept defeat. With all the force of his arm he sent a second shaft after the first. And it, too, landed at the feet of the silent four. Craike grasped at Takya, but she eluded him, moving to call down to the Hooded Ones:

"What would you, men of power—a truce?"

"Daughter of evil, you are not alone. Let us speak with your lord."

She laughed, shaking out her unbound hair, rippling it through her fingers, gloatingly. "Does this show that I have taken a lord, men of power? Takya is herself, without division, still. Let that hope die from your hearts. I ask you again, what is it you wish—a truce?"

"Set forth your lord, with him we will bargain."

She smoothed back her hair impatiently. "I have no lord, I and my power are intact. Try me and see, Tousuth.

Yes, I know you Tousuth, the Master, and Salsbal, Bulan, Yily—" she told them off with a pointed finger, a child counting out in some game.

Jorik stirred and drew in a sharp breath, and the men below shifted position. Craike caught thoughts—to use a man's name in the presence of hostile powers, that was magic indeed.

"Takya!" It was a reptile's hiss.

Again she laughed. "Ah, but the first naming was mine, Tousuth. Did you believe me so poor and power lost that I would obey you tamely? I did not at the horning, why should I now when I stand free of you? Before you had to use Takyi to capture me. But Takyi is gone into the far darkness, and over me now you can lay no such net! Also I have summoned one beside me—" Her hand closed on Craike's arm, drawing him forward.

He faced the impact of those eyes meeting them squarely. Raising his hand he told them off as the girl had done:

"Tousuth, Master of women baiters, Salsbal, Bulan, Yily, the wolves who slink behind him. I am here, what would you have of me?"

But they were silent, and he could feel them searching him out, making thrusts against his mind shield, learning in their turn that he was of their kind; he was Esper born.

"What would you have?" he repeated more loudly. "If you do not wish to treat—then leave the night undisturbed for honest men's sleep."

"Changeling!" It was Tousuth who spat that. It was his turn to point a finger and chant a sentence or two, his men watching him with confidence.

But Craike, remembering that other scene before Sampur, was trying a wild experiment of his own. He concentrated upon the man Takya had named Yily. Black cloak, black hood making a vulture's shadow against the rock. Vulture—vulture!

He did not know that he had pointed to his chosen victim, nor that he was repeating that word aloud in the same intonation as Tousuth's chant. "Vulture!"

Cool hand closed about his other wrist, and from that contact power flowed to join his. It was pointed, launched—

"Vulture!"

A black bird flapped and screamed, arose on beating wings to fly at him, raw red head outstretched, beak agape. There was the twang of a bow cord. A scream of agony and despair and a black-cloaked man writhed out his life on the slope by the thorn thicket.

"Good!" Takya cried. "That was well done, Ka-rak, very well done! But you can not use that weapon a second time."

Craike was filled with a wild elation, and he did not listen to her. his finger already indicated Bulan and he was chanting: "Dog—"

But to no purpose. The Black Hood did not drop to all fours, he remained human; and Craike's voice faded. Takya spoke in swift whisper:

"They are warned, you can never march against them twice by the same path. Only because they were unprepared did you succeed. Ho, Tousuth," she called, "do you now believe that we are well armed? Speak with a true tongue and say what you want of us."

"Yes," Jorik boomed, "you can not take us, Master of power. Go your way, and we shall go ours—"

"There can not be two powers in any land, as you should know, Jorik of the Eagles' towers, who tried once before to prove that and suffered thereby. There must be a victor here—and to the vanquished—naught!"

Craike could see the logic in that. But the Master was continuing: "As to what we want here—it is a decision. Match your power against ours, changeling. And since you have not taken the witch, use her also if you wish. In the end it will come to the same thing, for both of you must be rendered helpless."

"Here and now?" asked Craike.

"Dawn comes, it will soon be another day. By sun or shadow, we care not in such a battle."

The elation of his quick success in that first try was gone. Craike fingered the bow he had not yet used. He shrank inwardly from the contest the other proposed, he was too uncertain of his powers. One victory had come from too little knowledge. Takya's hand curled about his stiff fingers once again. The impish mockery was back in her voice, ruffling his temper, irritating him into defiance.

"Show them what you can do, Lord Ka-rak, you who can master illusions."

He glanced down at her, and the sight of that cropped lock of hair at her temple gave him an odd confidence. Neither was Takya as all-powerful as she would have him believe.

"I accept your challenge," he called. "Let it be here and now."

"WE accept your challenge!" Takya's flash of annoyance, her quick correction, pleased him. Before the echo of her words died away she hurled her first attack.

Witch fire leaped down slope to ring in the three men, playing briefly along the body of the dead Yily. It flickered up and down about their feet and legs so they stood washed in pallid flame. While about their heads darted winged shapes which might have been owls or other night hunters.

There was a malignant hissing, and the slope sprouted reptiles, moving in a wave. Illusions? All—or some. But designed, Craike understood, to divert the enemy's minds. He added a few of his own—a wolfish shape crouching in the shadow—leaping—to vanish as its paws cut the witch fire.

Swift as had been Takya's attack, so did those below parry. An oppressive weight, so tangible that Craike looked up to see if some mountain threatened them from overhead, began to close down upon the parapet. He heard a cry of alarm. There was a black cloud to be seen now, a giant press closing upon them.

Balls of witch fire flashed out of the light pillars, darted at those on the parapet. One flew straight at Craike's face, its burning breath singeing his skin.

"Fool!" Takya's thought was a whip lash, "Illusions are only real for the believer."

He steadied, and the witch ball vanished. But he was badly shaken. This was outside any Esper training he had had, it was the very thing he had been conditioned against. He felt slow, clumsy, and he was ashamed that upon Takya must the burden of their defense now rest.

Upon her—Craike's eyes narrowed. He loosened her hold on him, did not try to contact her. There was too much chance of self-betrayal in that. His plan was utterly wild, but it had been well demonstrated that the Black Hoods could only be caught by the unexpected.

Another witch ball hurtled at him, and he leaped to the terrace, landing with a force which sent a lance of pain up his healing leg. But on the parapet a Craike still stood, shoulder to shoulder with Takya. To maintain that illusion was a task which made him sweat as he crept silently away from the tower.

He had made a security guard to astonish Takya, the wolf, all the other illusions. But they had been only wisps, things alive for the moment with no need for elaboration. To hold this semblance of himself was in some ways easier, some ways harder. It was easier to make, for the image was produced of self-knowledge, and it was harder, for it was meant to deceive masters of illusion.

Craike reached the steps to the rock of the offerings. The glow of the witch lights here was pale, and the ledge below dark. He crept down, one arrow held firmly in his hand.

Here the sense of oppression was a hundredfold worse,

and he moved as one wading through a flood which entrapped limbs and brain. Blind, he went to all fours, feeling his way to the river.

He set the arrow between his teeth in a bite which indented its shaft. A knife would have been far better, but he had no time to beg Jorik's. He slipped over, shivering as the chill water took him. Then he swam under the arch.

It was comparatively easy to reach the shingle where the dugout of the Black Hoods had turned over. As he made his way to the shore he brushed against water-soaked cloth and realized he shared this scrap of gravel with the dead. Then, arrow still between his teeth, Craike climbed up behind the Black Hoods' position.

9

THE thorn hedge cloaked the rise above him. But he concentrated on the breaking of that illusion, wading on through a mass of thorns, intact to his eyes, thin air at his passing. Then he was behind the Black Hoods. Takya stood, a black and white figure on the wall above, beside the illusion Craike.

Now!

The illusion Craike swelled a little more than life size, while his creator gathered his feet under him, preparatory to attack. The Craike on the wall altered—anything to hold the attention of Tousuth for a crucial second or two. Monster grew from man, wings, horns, curved tusks, all embellishments Craike's imagination could add. He heard shouts from the tower.

But with the arrow as a dagger in his hand, he sprang, allowing himself in that moment to see only, to think only of a point on Tousuth's back.

The head drove in and in, and Tousuth went down on his knees, clutching at his chest, coughing. While Craike, with a savagery he had not known he possessed, leaned ont he shaft to drive it deeper.

Fingers hooked about Craike's throat, cutting off air, dragging him back. He was pulled from Tousuth, loosing his hold on the arrow shaft to tear at the hands denying him breath. There was a red fog which even the witch lights could not pierce and the roaring in his head was far louder than the shouts from the tower.

Then he was flat on the ground, still moving feebly. But the hands were gone from his throat, and he gasped in air. Around him circled balls of fire, dripping, twirling, he closed his eyes against their glare.

"Lord—Lord!"

The hail reached him only faintly. Hands pulled at him, and he tried to resist. But when he opened his eyes it was to see Jorik's brown face. Jorik was at the tower—how had Craike returned there? Surely he HAD attacked Tousuth? Or was it all illusion?

"He is not dead."

Whether or not that was said to him, Craike did not know. But his fingers were at his throat and he winced from his own touch. Then an arm came under his shoulders, lifting him, and he had a dizzy moment until earth and gray sky settled into their proper places.

Takya was there, with Nickus and Zackuth hovering in the background of black jerkined guardsmen who stared back at her sullenly over the bodies of the dead. For they were all dead—the Hooded Ones. There was Tousuth, his head in the sand. And his fellows crumpled beside him.

The witch girl chanted, and in her hands was a cat's cradle of black strands. The men who followed Tousuth cringed, and their fear was a cloud Craike could see. He grabbed at Jorik, won to his feet, and tried to hail Takya. But not even a croak came from his tortured throat. So he flung himself at her, one hand out like a sword blade to slash. It fell across that wicked net of hair, breaking it, and went to close upon Takya's wrist in a crushing grip.

"Enough!" He could get out that command mind to mind.

She drew in upon herself as a cat crouches for a spring, and spat, her eyes green with feral lusting fire. But he had an answer to that, read it in her own spark of fear at his touch. His hands twined in her hair.

"They are men," he pulled those black strands to emphasize his words, "they only obeyed orders. We have a quarrel with their masters, but not with them!"

"They hunted, and now they shall be hunted!"

"I have been hunted, as have you, witch woman. And while I live there shall be no more such hunts—whether I am hound or quarry."

"While you live—" her menace was ready.

Suddenly Craike forced out a hoarse croak meant for laughter. "You, yourself, Takya, have put the arrow to this bow cord!"

He kept one hand tangled in her hair. But with the other he snatched from her belt the knife she had borrowed from Nickus and not returned. She screamed, beat against him with her fists, tried to bite. He mastered her roughly, not loosing his grip on that black silk. And then in sweeps of that well-whetted blade he did what the Black Hoods had failed in doing, he sawed through those lengths.

"I am leaving you no weapons, Takya. You shall not rule here as you have thought to do—" The exultation he had known when he had won his first victory against the Black Hoods was returning a hundredfold. "For a while I shall pull those pretty claws of yours!" He wondered briefly how long it would take her hair to regrow. At least they would have a breathing spell before her powers returned.

Then, his arm still prisoning her shoulders, the mass of her hair streaming free from his left hand, he turned to face the guardsmen.

"Tell them to go," he thought, "taking their dead with them."

"You will go, taking these with you," she repeated aloud, stony calm.

One of the men dropped to his knees by Tousuth's body, then abased himself before Craike.

"We are your hounds, Master."

Craike found his voice at last. "You are no man's hounds—for you are a man. Get you gone to Sampur and tell them that the power is no longer to make hind nor hound. If there are those who wish to share the fate of Tousuth, perhaps when they look upon him as dead they will think more of it."

"Lord, do you come also to Sampur to rule?" the other asked timidly.

Craike laughed. "Not until I have established my lordship elsewhere. Get you back to Sampur and trouble us no more."

He turned his back on the guardsmen and, drawing the silent Takya, still within the circle of his arm, with him, started back to the tower. The bowmen remained behind, and Craike and the girl were alone as they reached the upper level. He paused then and looked down into her set, expressionless face.

"What shall I do with you?"

"You have shamed me and taken my power from me. What does a warrior do with a female slave?" She formed a stark mind picture, hurling it at him as she had hurled the stone on the mesa.

With his left hand he whipped her hair across her face, smarting under that taunt.

"I have taken no slave, nor any woman in that fashion, nor shall I. Go your way, Takya, and fight me again if you wish when your hair has grown."

She studied him, and her astonishment was plain. Then she laughed and clutched at the hair, tearing it free from his grasp, bundling it into the front of her single garment.

"So be it, Ka-rak. It is war between us. But I am not

departing hence yet a while." She broke away, and he could hear the scuff of her feet on the steps as she climbed to her own chamber in the tower.

"They are on their way, Lord, and they will keep to it." Jorik came up. He stretched. "It was a battle not altogether to my liking. For the honest giving of blows from one's hand is better than all this magic, potent as it is."

Craike sat down beside the fire. He could not have agreed more heartily with any suggestion. Now that it was over he felt drained of energy.

"I do not believe they will return," he wheezed hoarsely, very conscious of his bruised throat.

Nickus chuckled, and Zackuth barked his own laughter.

"Seeing how you handled the Lady, Lord, they want nothing more than to be out of your grasp and that as speedily as possible. Nor, when those of Sampur see what they bring with them, do I think we shall be sought out by others bearing drawn swords. Now," Jorik slapped his fat middle, "I could do with meat in my belly. And you, Lord, have taken such handling as needs good food to counter."

There was no mention of Takya, nor did any go to summon her when the meat was roasted. And Craike was content to have it so. He was too tired for any more heroics.

Nickus hummed a soft tune as he rubbed down his unstrung bow before wrapping it away from the river damp. And Craike was aware that the younger man glanced at him slyly when he thought the Esper's attention elsewhere. Jorik, too, appeared highly amused at some private thoughts, and he had fallen to beating time with one finger to Nickus' tune. Craike shifted uncomfortably. He was an actor who had forgotten his lines, a novice required to make a ritual move he did not understand. What they wanted of him he could not guess, for he was too tired to mind touch. He only wanted sleep, and that he sought as soon as he painfully swallowed his last bite. But he heard through semistupor a surprised exclamation from Nickus.

"He goes not to seek her—to take her!"

Jorik's answer held something of approval in it. "To master such as the Lady Takya he will need full strength of power and limb. His is the wisest way, not to gulp the fruits of battle before the dust of the last charge is laid. She is his by shearing, but she is no meek ewe to come readily under any man's hand."

Takya did not appear the next day, nor the next. And Craike made no move to climb to her. His companions elaborately did not notice her absence as they worked together, setting in place fallen stones, bringing the tower into a better state of repair, or killing deer to smoke the meat. For as Jorki pointed out:

"Soon comes the season of cold. We must build us a snug place and have food under our hands before then." He broke off and gazed thoughtfully down stream. "This is also the fair time when countrymen bring their wares to market. There are traders in Sampur. We could offer our hides, even though they be newly fleshed, for salt and grain. And a bow—this Kaluf of whom you have spoken, would he not give a good price for a bow?"

Craike raised an eyebrow. "Sampur? But they have little cause to welcome us in Sampur."

"You and the Lady Takya, Lord, they might take arms against in fear. But if Zackuth and I went in the guise of wandering hunters—and Zackuth is of the Children of Noe, he could trade privately with his kin. We must have supplies, Lord, before the coming of the cold, and this is too fine a fortress to abandon."

So it was decided that Jorik and Zackuth were to try their luck with the traders. Nickus went to hunt, wreaking havoc among the flocks of migrating fowl, and Craike held the tower alone.

As he turned from seeing them away, he sighted the owl wheel out from the window slit of the upper chamber, its mournful cry sounding loud. On sudden impulse he went inside to climb the stair. There had been enough of her sulking. He sent that thought before him as an order. She did not reply. Craike's heart beat faster. Was—had she gone? The rough outer wall, was it possible to climb down that?

He flung himself up the last few steps and burst into the room. She was standing there, her shorn head high as if she and not he had been the victor. When he saw her Craike stopped. Then he moved again, faster than he had climbed those stairs. For in that moment the customs of this world were clear, he knew what he must do, what he wanted to do. If this revelation was some spell of Takya's he did not care.

Later he was aroused by the caress of silk on his body, felt her cool fingers as he had felt them drawing the poison from his wounds. It was a black belt, and she was making fast about him, murmuring words softly as she interwove strand with strand about his waist until there was no beginning nor end to be detected.

"My chain on you, man of power." Her eyes slanted down at him.

He buried both his hands in the ragged crop of hair from which those threads had been severed and so held her quiet for his kiss.

"My seal upon you, witch."

"What Tousuth would have done, you have accomplished for him," she observed pensively when he had given her a measure of freedom once again. "Only through you may I now use my power."

"Which is perhaps well for this land and those who dwell in it," he laughed. "We are now tied to a common destiny, my lady of river towers."

She sat up running her hands through her hair with some of her old caress.

"It will grow again," he consoled.

"To no purpose, except to pleasure my vanity. Yes, we are tied together. But you do not regret it, Ka-rak—"

"Neither do you, witch." There was no longer any

barrier between their minds, as there was none between their bodies. "What destiny will you now spin for the two of us?"

"A great one. Tousuth knew my power-to-come. I would now realize it." Her chin went up. "And you with me, Ka-rak. By this," her hand rested lightly on the belt.

"Doubtless you will set us up as rulers over Sampur?" he said lazily.

"Sampur!" she sniffed. "This world is wide—" Her arms went out as if to encircle all which lay beyond the tower walls.

Craike drew her back to him jealously. "For that there is more than time enough. This is an hour for something else, even in a warlock's world."

Mousetrap

REMEMBER that old adage about the man who built a better mousetrap and then could hardly cope with the business which beat a state highway to his door? I saw that happen once—on Mars.

Sam Levatts was politely introduced—for local color—by the tourist guides as a "desert spider." "Drunken bum" would have been the more exact term. He prospected over and through the dry lands out of Terraport and brought in Star Stones, Gormel ore, and like knickknacks to keep him sodden and mostly content. In his highly scented stupors he dreamed dreams and saw visions. At least his muttered description of the "lovely lady" was taken to be a vision, since there are no ladies in the Terraport dives he frequented and the females met there are far from lovely.

But Sam continued a peaceful dreamer until he met Len Collins and Operation Mousetrap began.

Every dumb tourist who steps into a scenic sandmobile at Terraport has heard of the "sand monsters." Those which still remain intact are now all the property of the tourist bureaus. And, brother, they're guarded as if they were a part of that cache of Martian royal jewels Black

Spragg stumbled on twenty years ago. Because the monsters, which can withstand the dust storms, the extremes of desert cold and heat, crumble away if so much as a human fingertip is poked into their ribs.

Nowadays you are allowed to get within about twenty feet of the "Spider Man" or the "Armed Frog" and that's all. Try to edge a little closer and you'll get a shock that'll lay you flat on your back with your toes pointing Earthwards.

And, ever since the first monster went drifting off as a puff of dust under someone's hands, the museums back home have been adding to the cash award waiting for the fellow who can cement them for transportation. By the time Len Collins met Sam that award could be quoted in stellar figures.

Of course, all the bright boys in the glue, spray and plastic business had been taking a crack at the problem for years. The frustrating answer being that when they stepped out of the rocket over here, all steamed up about the stickability of their new product, they had nothing to prove it on. Not one of the known monsters was available for testing purposes. Every one is insured, guarded, and under the personal protection of the Space Marines.

But Len Collins had no intention of trying to reach one of these treasures. Instead he drifted into Sam's favorite lapping ground and set them up for Levatts—three times in succession. At the end of half an hour Sam thought he had discovered the buddy of his heart. And on the fifth round he spilled his wild tale about the lovely lady who lived in the shelter of two red rocks—far away—a vague wave of the hand suggesting the general direction.

Len straightway became a lover of beauty panting to behold this supreme treat. And he stuck to Sam that night closer than a Moonman to his oxy-supply. The next morning they both disappeared from Terraport in a private sandmobile hired by Len.

Two weeks later Collins slunk into town again and booked passage back to New York. He clung to the port hotel, never sticking his head out of the door until it was time to scuttle to the rocket.

Sam showed up in the Flame Bird four nights later. He had a nasty sand burn down his jaw and he could hardly keep his feet for lack of sleep. He was also—for the first time in Martian history—cold and deadly sober. And he sat there all evening drinking nothing stronger than Sparkling Canal Water. Thereby shocking some kindred souls half out of their wits.

What TV guy doesn't smell a story in a quick change like that? I'd been running the dives every night for a week—trying to pick up some local color for our 6 o'clock casting. And the most exciting and promising thing I had come across so far was Sam's sudden change of beverage. Strictly off the record—we cater to the family and tourist public mostly—I started to do a little picking and prying. Sam answered most of my feelers with grunts.

Then I hit pay dirt with the casual mention that the Three Planets Travel crowd had picked up another shocked cement dealer near their pet monster, "The Ant King." Sam rolled a mouthful of the Sparkling Water around his tongue, swallowed with a face to frighten all monsters, and asked a question of his own.

"Where do these here science guys think all the monsters come from?"

I shrugged. "No explanation that holds water. They can't examine them closely without destroying them. That's one reason for the big award awaiting any guy who can glue them together so they'll stand handling."

Sam pulled something from under the pocket flap of his spacealls. It was a picture, snapped in none too good a light, but clear enough.

Two large rocks curved toward each other to form an almost perfect archway and in their protection stood a woman. At least her slender body had the distinctly graceful curves we have come to associate with the stronger half of the race. But she also had wings, outspread in a grand sweep as if she stood on tiptoe almost ready to take off. There were only the hints of features—that gave away the secret of what she really was—because none of the sand monsters ever showed clear features.

"Where—?" I began.

Sam spat. "Nowhere now." He was grim, and his features had tightened up. He looked about ten years younger and a darn sight tougher.

"I found her two years ago. And I kept going back just to look at her. She wasn't a monster like the rest of 'em. She was perfect. Then that—" Sam lapsed into some of the finest space-searing language I have ever been privileged to hear—"that Collins got me drunk enough to show him where she was. He knocked me out, sprayed her with his goo, and tried to load her into the back of the 'mobile. It didn't work. She held together for about five minutes and then—" He snapped his fingers. "Dust just like 'em all!"

I found myself studying the picture for a second time. And I was beginning to wish I had Collins alone for about three minutes or so. Most of the sand images I had seen I could cheerfully do without—they were all nightmare material. But, as Sam had pointed out, this was no monster. And it was the only one of its type I had ever seen or heard about. Maybe there might just be another somewhere—the desert dry lands haven't been one quarter explored.

Sam nodded as if he had caught that thought of mine right out of the smoky air.

"Won't do any harm to look. I've noticed one thing about all of the monsters—they are found only near the rocks. Red rocks like these," he tapped the snapshot, "that have a sort of blue-green moss growin' on 'em." His eyes focused on the wall but I had an idea that he was seeing beyond it, beyond all the sand barrier walls in Terraport, out into the dry lands. And I guessed that he wasn't telling all he knew—or suspected.

I couldn't forget that picture. The next night I was back at the Flame Bird. But Sam didn't show. Instead rumor had it that he had loaded up with about two months' supplies and had gone back to the desert. And that was the last I heard of him for weeks. Only, his winged woman had crept into my dreams and I hated Collins. The picture was something—but I would have given a month's credits—interstellar at that—to have seen the original.

During the next year Sam made three long trips out, keeping quiet about his discoveries, if any. He stopped drinking and he was doing better financially. Actually brought in two green Star Stones, the sale of which covered most of his expenses for the year. And he continued to take an interest in the monsters and the eternal quest for the fixative. Two of the rocket pilots told me that he was sending to Earth regularly for everything published on the subject.

Gossip had already labeled him "sand happy." I almost believed that after I met him going out of town one dawn. He was in his prospector's crawler and strapped up in plain sight on top of his water tanks was one of the damnedest contraptions I'd ever seen—a great big wire cage!

I did a double take at the thing when he slowed down to say good-by. He saw my bug-eyes and answered their protrusion with a grin, a wicked one.

"Gonna bring me back a sand mouse, fella. A smart man can learn a lot from just watchin' a sand mouse, he sure can!"

Martian sand mice may live in the sand—popularly they're supposed to eat and drink the stuff, too—but they are nowhere near like their Terran namesakes. And nobody with any brains meddles with a sand mouse. I almost dismissed Sam as hopeless then and there and wondered what form the final crack-up would take. But when he came back into town a couple of weeks later—minus the cage—he was still grinning. If Sam had held any grudge against me, I wouldn't have cared for that grin—not one bit!

Then Len Collins came back. And he started in right away at his old tricks—hanging around the dives listening to prospectors' talk. Sam had stayed in town and I caught up with them both at the Flame Bird, as thick as thieves over one table, Sam lapping up imported rye as if it were Canal Water and Len giving him cat at the mouse hole attention.

To my surprise Sam hailed me and pulled out a third stool at the table, insisting that I join them—much to Collins' annoyance. But I'm thick-skinned when I think I'm on the track of a story and I stuck. Stuck to hear Sam spill his big secret. He had discovered a new monster, one which so far surpassed the winged woman that they couldn't be compared. And Collins sat there licking his chops and almost drooling. I tried to shut Sam up—but I might as well have tried to can a dust storm. And in the end he insisted that I come along on their expedition to view this fabulous wonder. Well, I did.

We took a wind plane instead of a sandmobile. Collins was evidently in the chips and wanted speed. Sam piloted us. I noticed then, if Collins didn't, that Sam was a lot less drunk than he had been when he spilled his guts in the Flame Bird. And, noting that, I relaxed some—feeling a bit happier about the whole affair.

The red rocks we were hunting stood out like fangs—a whole row of them—rather nasty looking. From the air there was no sign of any image, but then those were mostly found in the shadow of such rocks and might not be visible from above. Sam landed the plane and we slipped and slid through the shin-deep sand.

Sam was skidding around more than was necessary and he was muttering. Once he sang—in a rather true baritone—just playing the souse again. However, we followed along without question.

Collins dragged with him a small tank which had a hose attachment. And he was so eager that he fairly crowded on Sam's heels all the way. When at last Sam stopped short he slid right into him. But Sam apparently didn't even notice the bump. He was pointing ahead and grinning fatuously.

I looked along the line indicated by his finger, eager to see another winged woman or something as good. But there was nothing even faintly resembling a monster—unless you could count a lump of greenish stuff puffed up out of the sand a foot or so.

"Well, where is it?" Collins had fallen to one knee and had to put down his spray gun while he got up.

"Right there." Sam was still pointing to that greenish lump.

Collins' face had been wind-burned to a tomato red but now it darkened to a dusky purple as he stared at that repulsive hump.

"You fool!" Only he didn't say "fool." He lurched forward and kicked that lump, kicked it good and hard.

At the same time Sam threw himself flat on the ground and, having planted one of his oversize paws between my shoulders, took me with him. I bit into a mouthful of grit and sand and struggled wildly. But Sam's hand held me pinned tightly to the earth—as if I were a laboratory bug on a slide.

There was a sort of muffled exclamation, followed by an odd choking sound, from over by the rocks. But, in spite of my squirming, Sam continued to keep me more or less blindfolded. When he at last released me I was burning mad and came up with my fists ready. Only Sam wasn't there to land on. He was standing over by the rocks, his hands on his hips, surveying something with an open and proud satisfaction.

Because now there *was* a monster in evidence, a featureless anthropoidic figure of reddish stuff. Not as horrible as some I'd seen, but strange enough.

"Now—let's see if his goo does work this time!"

Sam took up the can briskly, pointed the hose tip at the monster, and let fly with a thin stream of pale bluish vapor, washing it all over that half-crouched thing.

"But—" I was still spitting sand between my teeth and only beginning to realize what must have happened. "Is that—that thing—"

"Collins? Yeah. He shouldn't have shown his temper that way. He kicked just once too often. That's what he did to her when she started to crumple, so I counted on him doing it again. Only, disturb one of those puff balls and get the stuff that's inside them on you and—presto—a monster! I got on to it when I was being chased by a sand mouse a couple of months back. The bugger got too close to one of those things—thinking more about dinner than danger, I guess—and whamoo! Hunted me up another mouse and another puff ball—just to be on the safe side. Same thing again. So—here we are! Say, Jim, I think this *is* going to work!" He had drawn one finger along the monster's outstretched arm and nothing happened. It still stood solid.

"Then all those monsters must once have been alive!" I shivered a little, remembering a few of them.

Sam nodded. "Maybe they weren't all natives of Mars—too many different kinds have been found. Terra was probably not the first to land a rocket here. Certainly the antmen and that big frog never lived together. Some day I'm going to get me a stellar ship and go out to look for the world my lady came from. This thin air could never have supported her wings.

"Now, Jim, if you'll just give me a hand, we'll get this work of art back to Terraport. How many million credits are the science guys offering if one is brought back in one piece?"

He was so businesslike about it that I simply did as he asked. And he collected from the scientists all right—

collected enough to buy his stellar ship. He's out there now, prospecting along the Milky Way, hunting his winged lady. And the unique monster is in the Interplanetary Museum to be gaped at by all the tourists. Me—I avoid red rocks, green puff balls, and never, never kick at objects of my displeasure—it's healthier that way.

Were-Wrath

KROBIE meat! Krobie meat!

She who had once been the Lady Thra and was now a brown bone of a woman as worn as one of the carrion birds she snarled at in a harsh whisper, dug her fist into the muck at the foot of the first forest tree. A sharp stone cut into her palm. She welcomed that pain as she made herself watch the scene in the valley below where a man kicked his way into death's peace.

Rinard, shy, slow spoken, hard of muscle if slightly dull of wit, one of that fighting tail who had broken out of Lanfort at its taking, riding and fighting at her back. Now he, the last of them all, was gone at the hands of these haughty, cruel northerners who would have no more refugees to threaten their own private raids and wars. She was all alone.

A black running hound on a blood-red banner—she would remember that. Oh, aye, she would hold that in mind and some day—her hand closed into a tight lock upon the stone, taking the hurt of it to seal the vow she made—though she might have little chance to keep it.

The forest was her only chance. They had cut her off from the open lands. It was both dark and thick and there were storm clouds gathering. She arose, settling her sword belt more easily, shrugged the weight of her pack straight.

There were rumors that some made a living in this place of grim dark trees. But it was evil-mouthed by most. Though she had seen greater evils caused by men with blood reek and fire, and the dusk beyond seemed to promise shelter.

Men were alien to this forest, that she had also heard. Well enough. In her heart she felt alien to her own kind, no beast could present a greater threat.

Her face was sharp featured beneath the shadow of a cap over-sewn with metal rings, and she had long forgot the luxury of clean linen, her present world was a harsh one. But there was a path opening before her, a narrow slot marked here and there by paw or hoof but with no trace of boot track.

The silence here brought odd thoughts to mind. This was a place in which to hide, aye, but one with a secret life of its own so that now and then Thra glanced over a shoulder seeking something she felt lurked and watched. Her uneasiness grew the stronger with every step she took as she listened keenly for sounds of pursuit.

Now the trail widened, and, in spite of the clouds and the gloom beneath the trees, more light showed ahead. She came out into a glade where two of the giant trees had crashed and now lay together, the tangled mass of branches of the one twined past any freeing with the upturned roots of the other.

Backed to this root-branch maze was a hut rough and yet sturdy, part of it being walled with stone, and its roof looking strong enough for a storm shelter.

To her right a basin had been formed of the same stone and into that poured a gurgle of water, welcome sight for her dry throat and dusty body.

Thra, screened by bushes, studied the scene before her. There was a crude chimney on the cabin but neither scent nor sign of smoke. Two dark slits, hardly wider than her own hand, flanked the bark-covered door—she sensed no life here.

A large butterfly spiraled down, its brilliant golden wings banded with sable. Out of a tangle of small plants sprang a gray beast, but its leap was not quick enough. Not until it landed, baffled of its prey, was Thra able to identify it as a cat.

The beast settled on the fallen trunk of the nearest tree, elevated a hind leg to wash with the meticulous care of one uninterested in butterflies. Thra took an impulsive step into the open. The cat looked well fed, its presence here argued habitation. Pausing in its washing the cat eyed her speculatively. Into Thra's mind—

"Two-legs—a new two-legs—" There was critical appraisal in that.

Nor was she completely startled by such an invasion. Since she had entered the forest anything seemed possible. This place had its own life. But—she wet her lips with the tip of her tongue—the thought of addressing this furred creature as she might one of her own kind was difficult to accept.

The cat looked from her to the cabin and back again before she ventured hoarsely:

"Someone lives here?" To her own ears her voice was too loud.

"The den is empty—now."

Thra drew a deep breath. To be answered so! She advanced to the side of the basin, went down on one knee, her right hand still near her sword hilt, as she cupped water into the other, half lapped at its freshness.

The cat continued to watch as she pulled forth her water bag, dumped what remained of its murky contents and filled it. Having made sure of that future supply, Thra settled herself cross-legged to face the cat. There was a slumberous content in this clearing which subtly eased both her mind and her body. She was aware of herb scents borne by the rising wind and yawned—to catch herself sharply.

Sorcery wooing her? She had fled too long from danger to trust anything or anyone. Pulling to her feet, she went towards the cabin still keeping eye on the cat.

Its gray body made no hostile move, the ears were not laid back against the skull, no warning hiss sounded. Thra set hand to the door on which no latch string dangled out in welcome. However, at the pressure of her fingers, it swung inward, moving easily.

In spite of the storm clouds the clearing light reached now within, spreading before her like a carpet. A single room. To her right was the rough fireplace. Board formed a bunk place. Over that was a shelf. There was also a box or coffer, a section of log hollowed out. More shelves supported an array of mugs and bowls, some of wood, others lopsidedly fashioned of fire-burned clay.

Yet there was another piece of furniture in the room and it was enough to center full attention. All the rest was ill made, without true craft. This armorie might have come from a high lord's castle. Fashioned of reddish wood it was carved with the skill of a master artist, following no general pattern, rather with a story deep chiseled. The carving hid the opening of the door for she could discern neither crack nor hinge.

Twists of leaf garlands formed frames for squares, each of which embodied an intricate scene. Some of the tiny people so depicted were no taller than her fingernail. Here rode a company of men with hounds in the full cry of a hunt. While that which fled before them—

Thra stooped closer. Even in the cabin's gloom the carven pictures were visible. That which fled hunched its shoulder, and the head did not seem altogether human in outline.

She shivered. There were old tales aplenty in Greer. Men and women—in ancient days they were said to have shared lordship with—others. That which fled here, which was partly like unto herself—was also something else. Thra turned quickly to the next picture.

The squares *were* allied. Here that which ran had dropped to all fours, upper limbs had become shaggy, the hands were paws.

What of the upper panels? Thra straightened to look. Here was one of a forest glade containing a pool beside which lounged a youth bare of body. He dabbled one hand, leaning over to gaze into the water's mirror. So skillful had been the craftsman who had wrought this that Thra never doubted he had taken a living likeness for his model. The scene was one of peace and content.

However in the next square the head of the lounger was up as if startled, he might be listening. In the next—the beginning of the hunt. One saw so well pictured the baying of hounds one could almost hear their cries—

"Found! Found! And away—!"

So the boy from the pool changed. Still, oddly, as Thra followed the pictured story from one square to the next, she found nothing threatening or wrong in the alteration. Rather her sympathy was all for the pursued. He was the hunted—even as she herself had been. She found herself scratching with a fingernail at the foremost hound as if to claw it away.

Now she squatted on her heels to see the finish the better, unaware that her heart was beating faster, her breath came raggedly as if she too ran that course.

A sharp hiss jerked her attention from the last scene. The cat stood just within the open door, staring in turn at the armorie. Thra looked back to the cupboard. In the last square the runner had thrown up a desperate forepaw to hook claws about a loop of low-hanging vine.

"Two legs," Thra spoke aloud, using the cat's designation, "or four legs?"

"Both—neither—"

The answer was instant but one she could not understand. The cat still watched the armorie.

"Both, yet neither?" Thra shifted to view the right-hand side of the armorie. Only there was no continuation of the hunt such as she had expected to find.

Rather she looked at a small, deeply incised scene of a room, as if she were a giantess spying through a window. Here was no hunt, not even a peaceful lounger.

Instead, stretched on a bed was a woman, attendants gathered about her. A maid fed wood to a fire on the hearth over which hung a kettle. Such was the detail of the scene. Thra could near hear the bubbling of the water. What she saw was a bold representation of a birthing.

Quickly she sought the next square. Here the babe had safely arrived, held up for the mother to view. Only there were expressions of aversion, horror, on the faces of all those gathered there, even upon that of the mother.

A child so greeted—why? Thra hurriedly went to the next square. A man was now present, one of high degree by his ornamental robe. His face was stern set, and, plainly by his orders, one of the nurses was placing the blanket-wrapped baby in a rush basket.

The fourth scene—another man, a huntsman by his clothing and gear, was mounted on one of those ponies used for transport of game. This rider stooped to take the basket from the nurse, while the stern-faced man watched.

Now a forest—which suggested by the skill of the carver just such a one as held Thra now—dark and secret. Here was the hunter leaning sidewise once more in his saddle to drop the basket into a stand of rank growth.

So far the story was plain enough. She had heard, even in the south where life had once been easier, old and grim tales. Men did not slay those of their own blood, but a newborn babe conveniently left in a wild place—gone before being presented to the Kin— Yes, that might well have been done. She returned to that earlier scene—horror

—truly that had been also in the mother's face. This babe must have been recognized at once as something monstrous.

Left abandoned, then what? Thra traced with her finger the vine wreathing the hunter at his cruel task. Some fault in the wood had here produced a streak of darker hue and the artist had taken advantage of it to add to the somberness of the picture.

Then—next—from a bush showed a face, or was it a beast's eager muzzle?

Man or animal, or both together? Next that lurker had come into the open and the mixture was plain. A furred, animal-like head with pricked and large pointed ears, supported on human shoulders giving way to a woman's full breasts.

She who advanced out of hiding appeared more human in the next scene where she had gathered to her the babe so that a small eager mouth had found one of her nipples. There was peace, joy, on the animal woman's near human face.

In other scenes the baby grew with its foster mother, played, lived seemingly happy and content. Until in the last scene of all a boy, at that age between youth and manhood, stood staring at a huddled body on the ground, a body from which stood a cruel arrow.

Thus he had been deprived of a mother and then—on the fore of the armorie—hunted himself. Thra was not aware that her jaw had set grimly and her hand had gone to sword hilt again. What of the panels on the other side—she hurried to look.

Here were the wreathing vines again dividing the familiar squares but all of those were blank! Except for the very first one where there were only scratches, perhaps marking out a general sketch of a scene yet to be completed. She squinted closely at those, feeling cheated of the rest of the tale. So much so that she thudded her fist home on the meaningless marks.

As flesh met wood there sounded a sharp sound and the well-concealed door of the armorie began to swing open, folding back.

Light! At first, bemused, Thra thought there must be a torch inside. Then she saw that radiance issued from the wooden walls which had been highly polished. To her nostrils came a clean scent such as she had once known to be used in the laying up of fine clothing.

The color of the inner wood was a clear ivory. There was no hint of mustiness nor dust. Nor could she, on investigation, see any hinge or latch.

However, it was what hung within which caught her full attention. Two pegs set at her own shoulder height were there, one on either side. From one depended a sword. The hilt was plain of any gem setting, seemingly made of the same ivory which lined the cabinet. Its pommel was wrought into the head of a beast—such as was neither man nor animal. A plain scabbard shielded the blade—and the belt was of white leather studded with small yellow gems.

Against the opposite wall was looped a second belt. This was of sleek black fur—thick and plushy, so shiny it might still be a part of the coat of some well-kept, cleanly beast. It was near four fingers wide, and, though it supported no weapon, there was a large clasp for its fastening made to match the head of the sword pommel. Save that this human-animal countenance was snarling, its open mouth revealing curved tusks ready to rend and tear.

Though the metal of the buckle was dark other colors played across its surface, red, orange, like flames, icy blue, the gold of the sky at sunset.

Thra put out her hand, then snatched it back, for, as her fingers passed within the armorie, they tingled and smarted. There was some protection here she could not understand.

Power—the power of a blade which could become awesome when the hilt fitted a hand trained to wield such a weapon. The other—more power she did not understand, from which she shrank. How long had these hung here waiting—and for whom?

The bare side of the armorie was frustrating. She shivered, it would have been better for her had she never stumbled upon such a mystery. Even though the cabin was shelter. Still she was not uneasy enough, as yet, to leave that. There was—

Thra sought the right word—waiting! Aye, that was it! Here hung these waiting—but not for her. Someone else—who?

On impulse she looked to the cat. It no longer lounged at ease. The light from the open door of the cabin had grown less. Was this an early coming of evening or the storm at hand? The animal gazed into the open, the tip of its tail swung slowly back and forth.

"Four-legs—" she began. Instantly the cat looked to her. "Whom do you wait?"

"Wait?" The cat's head lifted a fraction. "Two-legs–four-legs—both pass in their own time."

"But you remain?"

"I remain," the shared thought concurred.

There had been no cat picture in all that carving. Still Thra was sure that the animal before her had some part in the mystery. The cabin looked long deserted—

"Who?" This time her voice sounded unnaturally loud but not loud enough to drown out a roll of thunder. At least she would remain here until the storm was over. She shucked off her pack.

If she expected any answer to her half question, she was to be disappointed. The cat withdrew to face out again into the rain. Thra, used to making the most of any meager comfort, moved swiftly past the crouching animal to pull grass, break off small thornless branches, to be dumped into the bed place. She would sleep this night in better ease than she had for some time.

There was even a stack of dusty wood lengths by the

hearth and these she used for a fire. Honest flames leaping there banished some of the strangeness of the cabin. The roll of thunder grew louder, there came a crack of lightning so near the jaggered light seemed about to probe inward for her.

Thra pushed shut the door as rain slanted across the floor. The fire provided only a palm-sized light, yet in the dusk the interior of the open armorie gave off a continuous glow.

The cat had not moved, its head still pointed towards the door. While that feeling that she awaited some portentous happening fed her uneasiness. To steady her thoughts, her shaking hands, Thra dug the last of her trail rations from her pack. Two journey cakes, now near stone hard, were there. She hammered a piece from the larger with the pommel of her belt knife. Her other provision was a short stick of hard dried meat, that she cut into thin slivers.

One of the clay pots from the shelf gave her a chance to crumble the cake and meat into some water, forming a mess she hoped to find more palatable than it looked. Thra spun out these preparations as long as she could, the cat paying no attention to her actions.

The storm continued to loose its fury. Thra heard a distant sound which must have marked the fall of another of the giant trees. She crowded closer to the fire, holding her sun-browned hands to the flames, though she shivered more from what she guessed might happen than from any cold.

At last she drew both sword and knife and laid them close to hand, for the cat's doorwise stare added to her disquiet. Also she edged farther around that she, too, might watch that portal. Once she arose and strove to move the armorie itself for a barrier, but its weight was beyond her shifting.

She ate the unappetizing mush with her fingers, found it no worse than much of the food she had eaten in the immediate past. Putting the bowl to one side she sat waiting, her hands loosely clasped about her knees. Unable to stand her own imaginings any longer she asked aloud:

"Who comes?"

For the first time the cat turned its eyes toward hers. "Long waited, perhaps come at last. Take you that sword, two-legs?" Distinctly it nodded towards the weapon hanging in the armorie.

"I hold by my own steel." She dropped hand to her blade. "What or who comes? Tell me, four-legs!"

The cat had turned its full attention to the armorie.

"There hangs power—"

"Still I hold by what I know!" Thra repeated. To be sitting thus, exchanging thoughts with a cat—had some fell fever fallen on her when she entered this misbegotten woodland, or was she indeed ensorceled? Patience she had learned in a hard school during the past years and patience only might serve her now, until she discovered more.

That feeling of otherness which had been with her since she had come beneath these trees was growing sharper even though the storm seemed to be retreating. The cat showed no fear—perhaps that curiosity which men said was a strong trait in these beasts kept it here to watch her blunder into some web unknown to her.

Thra might not be forest wise but she had stood sentry too many nights, every sense alert, to be mistaken now. Something was outside. There came a snuffling, faint but unmistakeable, as if the nose of some creature swept close along the bottom crack of the door.

She arose, sword in hand, her dark brows ascowl as she edged over to set her back to the armorie, ready to front whatever might force a way in. The lips in her gaunt face flattened against her teeth as if she could snarl like her furred companion. However the cat, itself, faced the door with no sign of anger or fear.

That snuffling ceased, but, as surely as if she could see

through the door, Thra believed the other still crouched there. As the cat, it waited.

"You speak of power," she said, "Is it of claw and fang now out there?"

"Perhaps." To her astonishment the cat leaped straight for the armorie, brushing past her. Its teeth fastened upon the belt of fur, but all its energy could not pull that free from the peg on which it hung.

Hardly knowing whether she was reckless and foolhardy, or doing what was only right Thra braved the warning prickle in her hand and reached inside to slip free the strip. It seemed to her that the fur arched upwards to meet her touch as might an animal seeking a caress.

The belt fell, still tight-held by the cat, and that animal backed away from the cupboard dragging it towards the door. Did it seek to deliver that prize to the lurker? With a stride Thra gained the door, her sword pointed at the cat.

"I do not know what game you would play," she said. "But here I am master—"

"You are but one sent." Words near as sharp as her own blade cut into her mind. "There is but one master!"

She could have easily spitted the animal, or kicked it aside. There was no good reason to let it outside to what waited. Save within her brute force still did not entirely rule. So she slipped along the wall to be shelted from the door as it opened and then pushed to let in a burst of rain-sweet wind.

From without sounded a strange cry, one which sent a chill along her half-crouched back. Thra wanted badly to see what stood there in the storm dark but she did not move, only gripped her sword the more fiercely.

As if that sound was a summons, trailing still the belt from its jaws, the cat sprang into the dark. Thra waited tensely. The light from the fire was small help and the edge of the door a screen.

Someone stepped within. She could strike now and

make sure. Even as that thought came to her the cat flashed once more into the full warmth of the fire, shaking itself vigorously.

Wet leather, her nose wrinkled at that acrid scent, also a strange musky odor as if he who wore such garments had lived unclean for a long time. For this was a man, not topping her in height more than an inch or so. He might be facing the cat and the fire, but Thra was sure he was well aware of just where she stood.

Aware but not alarmed. That realization awoke in her a spark of anger. Woman she might be, and wanderer without a following, but she was still a force to be reckoned with—as he would discover!

His arms hung loosely by his sides, there was no sword, not even the gleam of a knife hilt at his belt. As her own, his clothing was leather but worse worn. On the shoulders tatters had peeled away, as they had also about his legs and thighs. His feet were bare, splotched with mud which he tracked on the floor.

Around his slender waist was the belt—its length of silky fur in contrast to the rest of him. For his hair was a tangle of greasy strings knotted with dried leaves and small twigs—he might have rooted in a thicket for weeks on end.

Thra fought to bring up her sword, aiming its point between those rack-thin shoulders. She had seen before men sunk to this extremity of neglect—many in the south. They could not be trusted, nor could one call them beasts, for beasts were far more cleanly and merciful than such.

Still, though Thra was sure he knew she menaced him, he did not turn his head, rather dropped to his bony knees before the fire, raising both palms to the heat. She had a confused memory of how men had once knelt so in places of worship. Did this refuse then worship fire—or only what it signified—shelter, food, warmth—plunder?

That he continued to ignore her meant one of two things—that he was not alone, but the forerunner of a party of like outcasts—or he possessed some means of defense which did not depend upon weapons.

Those outstretched hands, was there something odd about the nails—were they not unusually long and sharp? Thra wanted him to turn his head so that she might clearly see his features—human—or strange?

The cat settled on the hearth, its back to the fire, tail curled over forepaws. Thra could wait no longer, her voice was unnaturally loud in the room.

"Who are you?" She was not sure of her question until she had voiced that demand.

He glanced back over his shoulder at last, showing her three-quarters of his face. She had expected to see a tangle of beard as wild as the crop on his head but his cheeks were smooth as a boy's, though weather-browned to a dark shade. There was an oddity about his features. Perhaps it lay in the slantwise set of his brows, the narrow, forward thrust of his chin. His frowsy hair grew downward in a peak between his eyes to nearly meet the brows.

Those eyes—green or yellow—or a mixture of both? Thra had never seen their like in the face of any man of Greer. While his mouth looked too wide, his lips very dark red and glistening. Small points of teeth showed against those, almost as if he had fangs sprouting from his jaws.

Yet for all its alienness it was not a face to disgust one, nor did it bear the signs of degradation or idiotic mindlessness which she had expected to see. When he spoke his voice was not only low-pitched but calm, even gentle:

"You have my thanks, Lady of Lanlat—"

Her sword quivered in her hold. Who in this northern land could still call her by that name? Was he some other refugee? Had she once met him long ago at some feastings? No, once met this man could never be forgot.

"There is no more Lanlat—" she returned harshly. "But I have asked—who are you?"

His hands moved in a vague gesture she could not understand. "I do not know—"

Some drifter from a lost battle? She had heard of men head wounded so they could not remember, but were afterwards like new-born children, having to learn again how to live.

"How came you here?"

At least he should be able to answer that, unless his wits were so disordered that even recent events were lost to him.

"I have always been—" His voice trailed away as he continued to regard her with a kind of eager curiosity. In his clear eyes she could detect nothing of a sleeping mind but rather eager intelligence.

Her sword point touched the pounded earth of the floor. In spite of his foul clothing, wild appearance, he had such a quiet air of certainty that he could be one wearing a disguise.

His hands had gone now to his belt where he ran fingers back and forth across the sleek fur as one might caress a beloved animal—or reassure himself that a treasure long denied, long lost, had been safely returned.

"Always been?" Doggedly she kept to her point.

He nodded. An errant lock of hair fell across his face and he brushed it aside. Not soon enough. Thra held her breath for an instant. Just so—her eyes flickered to the door of the armorie and away again. No—this was no refugee from her own land. He was—she moved her shoulders along the wall, setting more of a distance between them.

"*What* are you?" Her voice was a whisper. Still, among the wild thoughts now churning in her mind, there was no fear—rather wonder. This surely—grown somewhat older—was the youth of the carving—the one who had fled the hunters.

"Why do you ask that?" It was his voice which rang loud and sharp. "When you already know—if you allow yourself to face the truth." His head inclined the slightest toward the open armorie door.

Thra moistened lips with tongue tip. "I have seen that," she, too, indicated the door. "You are like the hunted one. But—"

He raised hands from his belt, flexed his fingers full in the subdued glow of the fire. Those were claws with wet earth clinging to them, not overlong human nails.

"You have heard of my kind?"

Thra could not answer at once. What were old legends compared with this? Though the forest had such an ill name her mind refused to connect such tales with this slender young man. Legend suggested that such as he were a dark menace of sorcery, yet in her there was no shrinking. She had met many of her own kind who carried with them a far greater stench of pure evil.

His lips drew back so those fang-sharp teeth showed clearly as he stood there straight and tall, as one facing an enemy about to make an assault on a poorly defended last redoubt.

"I am *were.*" He might have been shouting a battle slogan against all the world which she represented.

Silence, one so deep that she heard a leaf flutter across the floor inward from the open door. Once more his tongue swept across his lips. He looked almost sly—dangerous. Still in her she felt no menace and she held his gaze locked to hers.

"Do you not understand, Lady Thra? Or are our kind not known in the south for the dreaded thrice-damned stock we are? Do you lack cursed forests there?"

Her sword point scratched a half-remembered protective pattern on the well-packed earth. But what had such to do with turning aside the possible wrath of one who claimed his blood?

"You put your trust in steel?" Those slanting brows near vanished beneath the fringe of rough hair. "Ah, but steel, no matter how cunningly forged, cannot harm *us.* Though hounds may chase to pull us down, yet no true arrow nor spear can kill. We can feel pain but not death—

save by silver. Silver or," his hands quivered, "fire."

"Yet you warm yourself by that," Thra returned. "Is this not your home? Yet you bring your enemy fire into it."

His wide mouth stretched in a wry smile.

"You see me in a guise wherein fire is servant not master. Ah, Grimclaw," he addressed the cat, "who have you summoned here? A lady who shows no fear, does not tremble nor look upon me as if I differed from those of her own kind, one who walks—"

"Two-legged?" Thra interrupted. "How is it that you greet me by my name, stranger? I am new come into these lands, only this day into your forest." She still held the thought that he might be one who had lost his wits from some battle injury.

"This is my talent—" Even as the cat had before him, he projected his unspoken answer into her mind.

That her thoughts could be so invaded was, to her, a kind of ravishment, such a blow as she had never taken before. She stiffened against showing outwardly her repugnance but rage rose icily within her.

He no longer even looked in her direction, instead he moved a little closer to the armorie, gazing intently at the sword still hanging there. But, if that weapon was his as the belt seemed to be, he made no attempt to arm himself with it. Perhaps he had run four-legged so long that he clung to fangs and claws as his proper weapons.

"I have to thank you." Though he spoke aloud this time she thought that was a concession on his part. "I have been long afield and there are those to whom I am welcome prey. That you have brought me this much freedom," his fingers once more sought the circlet of fur about him, "is almost more than I had dared hope for. Perhaps there is some meaning in this. We are only the playthings of strange forces. And you chose a poor refuge here, why, my lady?"

Need he ask when he could read her mind and she

could not shut him out? Thra longed to turn her sword on him—to banish so this—this *thing* who could know her in a way so unnatural. Was her every thought and feeling open to him now?

"I cannot enter where you hate—" His voice was low. "It was when I skulked outside and must know who or what waited here that I did that. We have our own oaths which we do not break!" There was high pride in him, such pride as matched her own, and she felt herself responding when she did not want to yield. "Do you wish such an oath from me, lady?"

What did he awaken in her—feelings and beliefs she thought long slain? She shook her head, instead accepting this self-confessed forest monster as she would one of her own rank in the old days.

"So—what brought you here?" He returned to his first question.

"A beast pack which marches under the banner of a running hound—" she spat forth the words and thumped the point of her sword into the earth. "My freedom was hard bought—the last of my liegemen hangs from a tree in the valley. Your lords hunt to ill deaths."

His eyes glowed flame bright for an instant.

"A running hound—aye!" Once more his lips shaped a snarl which was feral. "Roth is abroad then or—" he scowled, "since time moves different here within the wood and years sometimes speed without noting—one of his get. They live with fear as their armor and their weapons, but lately they have not tried the forest ways. Perhaps now the hounds will course again—on your trail, lady!"

He showed no sign of uneasiness, rather spoke eagerly as if he looked forward to some contest.

"It might be so." She did not enlarge upon that, wondering if she would also be considered prey by some of the forest dwellers.

"This is a place of fear," he continued. "My brothern

lair here, and yet even we do not know all the dark dangers which pad the trails." He weighed her with a bold and fierce gaze but she was not to be eyed down so. Instead she returned her sword to its sheath, showing him hands as bare as his own.

"Devils and dangers I have seen amany and the worst of them are two-legged and name themselves men." She laughed harshly. "You have made free with my name, how then are you called?"

"I am Farne—and there is another name, only that your throat cannot voice. Grimclaw here is my marshal, the holder of my castle. I have not recently been resident in this part of my domain. Lady Thra, I offer you guest right."

He stooped to catch the lower end of one of the smaller branches half-consumed by the fire, holding it aloft so that flame sprouted from its tip as it might from a wax taper.

"I light you to your chamber," he began formally and then laughed. "I fear you shall have to take us as we are, which is in ill condition. But at least—" Still holding his improvised taper he passed her to the door, to return a moment later swinging by their feet a brace of wood fowl.

"Even Roth might relish these—"

"Roth?" That was the second time he had mentioned that name. "His badge is the running hound? Roth of—" She waited.

"Farne," he had settled on his heels before the fire drawing from a break between stones a knife with which he set about cleaning the fowl. "What is a name? It can be given to a thing, a place, a woman, a man. Those with the old knowledge claim that a name has power—that it can be used for or against that which bears it. But who truly knows?"

There was so much more she wanted to learn. What of the tale carved on the armorie of the babe abandoned in the wilds, the youth later hunted. Was it *his* story which was thus portrayed?

"The sword—" She pointed to that which hung in the cupboard. "Is that also of Farne?"

His head turned so suddenly she blinked and dropped hand to knife hilt. Then he voiced a throaty sound like a growl, while the cat hissed.

"What have you heard of Farne?"

"Nothing save your own words," she replied. "I saw the raiders at their work and lost a good friend to them. But yonder does hang a sword and its pommel is a head which is strange. While on two sides of that armorie is carven a tale clearly enough. Therefore I ask—does that blade fit your hand?"

"My heritage? Perhaps, lady, when the time is right. For now I wear that which is closer to me." He touched the furred belt. "That," he nodded to the sword, "has a purpose which will come." He arose from where he had set quarters of the fowls on improvised spits and went to the armorie.

"A purpose into which Farne enters?" Thra prodded him.

His shoulders tensed. She had a momentary feeling that this was all a dream. Then he caught at the door and with a sharp push sent it shut.

"Let it hang! I will not have it yet—perhaps never. There are traps and traps, and those who are hunted learn to sniff them out—or die."

Their meal was sizzling and he divided it fairly, laying it in the bowls from the shelf. Thra licked fingers scorched by hot grease before she began to chew the meat avidly from the bones.

Night had come fully but Farne made no move to close the door. Also he paused now and then as if to listen. Perhaps his ears were better attuned to the normal forest sounds so he could detect the unusual. Thra heard the squalling cry of some furred hunter that had missed its prey, the hooting of an owl. And always there was the drip of moisture and the rustle of branch.

When he had finished Farne went to that crude tree-trunk box against the far wall, pawing through its contents to select an armload of fresh clothing. Saying nothing he went out into the night.

Thra licked her fingers well and fed wood to the fire. She was tired and this was shelter. She looked to that bunk she had filled with bedding. The cat was washing its face, though now and then its ears twitched as it picked up some sound.

There would soon be need for more wood if the fire was to burn through the night, but there was no use seeking that in the soaked outer world. Farne—a part of Thra wondered at her own calm acceptance of him. There were the old tales—she had heard more of them as she and Rinard had prowled closer to the forest.

They had been seeking more knowledge of this very wood as well as supplies when they had been trapped in the raided village. Thra had believed Rinard close on her heels, but the poor fool had stood his ground, apparently believing that he served her so, as she had discovered too late. Rinard—forcibly she put him out of her mind now. Had the raiders sighted her, tracked her later?

"Hunters—" Thra was not even aware she said that aloud until the cat answered her.

"Not yet. But a hunt comes, yes. Those others seek always for *him!*"

"Often?" she pressed.

"Often enough. Until he chooses—" But there were no more mind words added to that. Thra felt that in another place a door had closed—firmly. She would learn no more—at least for now.

Those stories of the werefolk were awesome. And Farne might be only one of many. She shifted uneasily as the were appeared to materialize out of the dark. He was dressed in fresh leather as sleek as the belt he still wore. Twigs and mud had been brushed out of his hair, the grime washed from his hands and face. He walked with assurance, and with that same air of authority he began to question Thra about the raid upon the village.

"It would seem that Roth, or he who holds the Hound rule, grows overbold," Farne mused when she had done. "To this shelter—" he gestured with one hand, "you are welcome, rough though it is. But I would advise you not to remain here in the forest." He added that decisively and Thra knew resentment. There he stood fingering that belt of his and looking at her as if she were a green girl who had never heard an alarm bell.

"The forest—" He hesitated. "Oh, yes, there are those who *have* sought refuge here but mainly they are the unwary, the ignorant. Tomorrow I shall show you a trail leading westward out of Roth's way, and so see you free of this land. But tonight I have that which I must do." He turned on his heel and, with no other farewell, was gone again into the dark, the cat bounding after him.

Thra crouched in a dusk which was hardly thinned by the light of the dying fire. Her body ached with fatigue, her eyelids were heavy, yet in this place dared she yield to sleep? Tonight there was no Rinard to share the watch turn about.

She fed the last of the wood to the fire and laid down close to the hearth, drawing both sword and knife, to place them where her hand could fall easily. Thra closed her eyes knowing that, trust or no trust, she could not continue without rest.

However she dreamed and in that dream she fled, a hunted thing without any defense against the force on her trail. Yet within her rage flared so hot she felt as if her whole body was aflame. There arose before her a dark wall of vines much interwoven and the terror of the chase flung her full at that. The vines writhed and wreathed, reached, clutched her in an unbreakable grip. She fought and tore at that growth, her hands rent in turn by thorns. Now she was held fast as the din of the hunt drew nearer and she heard a triumphant blast of horn.

Blast of horn! Thra opened eyes—not upon a mass of imprisoning greenery, though the dream seemed still real for a second or two and her hands were up and out flailing the air. This was a dim and shadowed room—the only light, wan and limited, came through two narrow slits of windows.

As she pulled herself up, her body slick with sweat beneath her worn garments, she heard it clearly—a horn!

Hunters! On her own trail or merely loose in the forest? She dared not remain where she was lest she be trapped, yet to seek a path through the wood without a guide was also a lost cause.

She stumbled as she stooped for her weapons, and her hand, flung out to balance her, slapped the side of the armorie. For the second time the door swung open.

No furred belt—where was that now—and its wearer? But the sword— Her own blade would be the better for a smith's sharpening and it was well worn. Since Farne had chosen not to take this then why could she not arm herself the better?

Thra listened. The horn sounded once again and she could not deceive herself—its blatant blast was closer. She must be out and away. Slamming her own weapon into its sheath and kicking her pack towards the door, she reached for the armorie sword.

Her flesh tingled almost as if flames licked at her. But she had set weapon swinging back and forth. Only when she tried to grab for it her hand had no strength, fingers numb, with that numbness spreading up her wrist into her arm. She who had scoffed at tales of sorcery was helpless. Fear pushed her away from the slow swing of that sheathed blade.

A third call of the horn and now it was answered by a clear bay and then a second. Thra shivered. Men she could and had faced when necessity drover her to it, but hounds —with them she would have little chance. She swung around to survey the cabin. One entrance, those narrow slits of windows—it offered defense of a kind save there was no bar for the door and she had nothing to build a barricade. Only to venture out—with hounds ready to trail—

Knife, sword, she had no other weapons, she pushed aside the pack and shut the door. No bolt—it could be easily forced.

Thra fingered her knife. There was a way of escape if it came to a last desperate moment—by her own hand. To wait to be ravished by hound or huntsman—was that a coward's choice? How could she—?

A loud baying with a note in that deep belling which startled her. Eagerness, such cry as a hound might give when its prey was in sight. Yet that had not come from just without the cabin as she had expected, rather it was farther away—to the west. It was answered by a chorus of other cries trailing away from her. She hardly dared to believe that the hunt had turned. Now her shoulder grazed the armorie.

She stood before the deep carving of the door. The were who had fled—the hunters who followed. Farne's trail, had it this morning crossed hers, setting a counter-scent to draw the hounds? She frowned, breathing a little faster as if, though she had not stirred from the cabin, she had indeed run a quarry's hard pace.

Farne—she did not doubt he had been hunted before. This was his country, he would know every rock, tree, shrub of it—be fully aware of any hole giving refuge. Yes, the sound was lessening—the hunt drew westward—she need only wait until she could hear no more and then head east.

Why had he done this? Had it been by chance? Somehow Thra doubted that as she reached for her pack again. By rights he owed her no favors. True, she had, by chance, opened the armorie and the cat had taken the belt—but was that so great a service—?

So far had her thoughts gone when she was startled by

what was no hound's triumphant bay—rather a deep-throated howl. Not one of pain—rather anger and—fear!

It was drowned out almost instantly by the frenzied yapping of dogs and the shouts of men. Something—Farne?—was at bay. The shouting grew louder but she could not distinguish words. With bared sword in one hand she pulled open the cabin door.

Across the clearing leaped a flash of gray. The cat was within the hut before she truly saw it. Rearing up on its hind legs it pawed forcibly at the closed door of the armorie. Its ears were flat to its skull and it was snarling steadily. Now it turned its head a fraction and its eyes sought her.

"Trap!" The word sprang into her mind with the force of a blow.

That howl sounded again from the distance. Thra listened. This quarrel was none of hers. Farne, a were, was an enemy to her kind. That he had not harmed her—had offered the gesture of guesting rights—what difference did that make now? One sword against a hound pack and the men who followed it—what could that avail?

"Nothing—" she said aloud, to answer the pressure rising in her mind, what the cat would force upon her. "This is no ploy for me—"

There was no answer in words, instead for a moment which might have been lifted out of real time she saw—not this hut, the furious cat—but rather another scene.

A net which writhed with the wild struggles of what it contained, a beast with a foam-flecked mouth which strove to snap at the cords which so bound it and who flinched from that weaving. Now she could see that it was no true net, rather hide strips interwoven with linked chains which had a silver glint.

Silver!

Memory stirred as that picture broke. What had Farne said—the silver was the bane of his kind.

"That is so!" She saw no prisoner now, rather the cat

still reared against the cupboard, its claws busy striving to rip the wood apart.

Guessing the secret of the armorie from her two former experiences Thra slapped the uncarven side and the door opened. The cat leaped, attempting to pull down the sword. But it could only set that swinging. Thra thrust the point of her own weapon within and caught the loop of the belt, pulling it towards her.

The sheathed blade slid down and the cat crouched before her snarling. Once free of the armorie the weapon appeared to draw light, and the eyes of the head which formed the pommel glinted as might the eyes of a living beast.

Thra let the weapon slip to the floor. She expected the cat to catch it up as it had the belt, but instead the animal stood guard, gazing straight at her.

"What would you have of me?" she demanded.

No reply flashed into her mind, no picture rose in answer. Once more the din of the hunt swelled—almost as if that was her reply.

"Take it if that is what is needed!" she urged.

The cat did not move. Though no words formed in Thra's mind there was a growing compulsion.

"No! Your Farne is no cup brother of mine, nor liegeman. What have I to do with him? One sword cannot stand against a hound pack and huntsmen. I shall not—"

Yet, even as she made that denial, there was rising in her something which she could not understand. Ensorcelment? She fought in vain but she stooped, utterly against her true will, to take up the sword belt.

The cat arose from its crouch and uttered what was undoubtedly a yowl of promised battle. It held her gaze for a long moment before it headed towards the door.

She turned as if another will possessed her, using her body awkwardly and against every instinct. Thra, her own sword drawn, the belt of the sheathed one in her other hand, followed the cat, at first stumblingly and then with the even tread of one who goes to face some act of sworn duty.

Grimclaw sped ahead, not taking the faint path which had led her here but rounding one of the fallen trees and heading straight through the brush which filled the small clearing.

The clamor of the hunt had not dwindled. Apparently the hounds and their masters were not on the move. As she went in that direction Thra continued to fight the will—the thing which forced her to serve its purpose. Sweat gathered at the rim of her ring-sewn cap, made tracks down her face.

She was one. Before her—how many? If she exhausted her strength in fighting this compulsion what might that cost her later? She abandoned that inner struggle, allowed that which possessed her full rein.

The din of the hounds slacked off but the voices of the men grew clearer. Someone was roaring orders to lower that, fasten this—get on with it.

Grimclaw stopped short to look back at her. Thra dropped to her knees and crawled forward through brush toward another clearing. With all the stealth she had learned during her wandering she covered that ground and used her sword tip to lift a branch of leafy shrub that she might see.

Five men, two of them now occupied with cuffing back the hounds, setting leashes to their collars. He who was doing the roaring stood to one side overlooking the labors of two of his fellows who were awkwardly striving to wind closer a net encompassing a still upright and struggling captive.

Thra recognized with an icy chill of full anger the badges these hunters wore—the running hound. But five of them and four hounds—against her—! She had no cross-bow even, nothing except her sword—she could not attack these!

"Leave be!" ordered the roarer at last. He approached the captive to inspect the bonds tying the net to a tree.

"The beast is well caught and my lord will want to see the rest of it. Jacon, get you to camp, you and Ruff, taking those hounds. M'lord will not favor any who care not for *them.* And we do not know how many of such beasts slink hereabouts—"

"'Twould be better to haul the were with us—" began one of those who had been busy by the tree.

Bull throat laughed. "It is well caught. M'lord truly had the proper secret for that after all these years. Silver they cannot break. See how it twists itself even now so that bare bits touch it not."

The prisoner so enfolded was writhing constantly, and, between the voices of the hounds being cuffed into order and those of the men, Thra caught desperate panting sounds which could only have come from the captive.

"Silver and—fire." There was brutal satisfaction in that strong voice. Aye, it was by *his* order that Rinard had been hung—with men shouting wagers on how long he would kick before death was merciful. Thra would have given all she possessed at that moment for a crossbow—he was so good a target standing there with his thumbs hooked in his belt, a grin stretching lips near hidden by a greasy beard. "There will be a handsome fire perhaps of m'lord's own lighting—and good ale drunk this night!"

The two men he watched stepped back from their captive. In spite of the seeming helplessness of the netted creature, they appeared to have little liking for being near it. Thra started at a cold touch on her hand and was fearful that she might have so betrayed herself. It was Grimclaw.

"Behind—" the word blazed in her mind.

Behind what? It was hard to believe that those restless hounds had not already scented her or the cat. Away—get away before they, too, were trapped. Part of her mind seemed to scream that, but to no avail.

"Behind!" The cat's order was emphatic. It crouched upon its belly, one paw advanced gingerly to draw it forward and then the other. So it angled away from her and the hounds. Also it was plain that she was expected to follow.

Thra hesitated. As she did so the man who had given the orders slouched across to stand by the netted creature. He leaned down to pick up an end of the rope which clearly showed the silver knotted in it. With evil deliberation he thrust this toward the captive, inserting the end through the mesh of the net.

She both heard and felt—the cry rang in her mind worse than a wound, and a searing pain stroked her left cheek, leaving stinging agony behind. What was aimed at the captive had also touched her.

On hands and knees, using all the skulker's skills she had learned, Thra followed the slinking cat. They moved away from the clearing even as the men led away the leashed hounds, but only so for a short distance before the cat made a deliberate turn to the left. "Behind" was plain now, they were heading to the rear of those trees where the net had been anchored. She had to bite down upon her lower lip, call upon full strength not to betray herself as the transfered torture of the captive continued to scorch her own flesh.

Grimclaw halted. There were no more spurts of pain, maybe the hound master had tired of his game. She could hear a heavy breathing—perhaps from the prisoner.

Longing to be elsewhere Thra was still bound to obey that other will. Not too far away a twist of brown and silver was looped about an upstanding tree root—surely one of the anchors of the net.

With the blade of her own sword between her teeth, Thra reached for her belt knife. The rope was thick and she feared that, even if she could sever that, the metal within would not break. But, as the strands parted, the silver did not seem so hard as she had feared—it must be unusually pure and so more workable. She pried and pulled loose an end, twisting that back and forth until it broke.

As the rope end swung free Grimclaw reached up and

caught it between ready jaws stretching it taut while Thra, with all the caution she could summon, started on the next.

"Two more—but two more!" No invasion of her thoughts by Grimclaw, that had come from the captive. Thra did not resent his message, rather threw open her mind as well as she could for a picture of what must be done.

She followed the rope to her left—there was a second loop to be loosened, then hurriedly knotted about a branch to give the appearance of being untouched. She was sawing at the third when there came a shout in the clearing setting both Thra's hands to tear frenziedly at the bonds.

"Netted, by the Fangs of Rane! Netted as any beast!"

Gloating in that voice—and it was not the bull roar of the hunters' leader. Perhaps this was his lord.

"Were—" The tone of voice made the word an obscenity.

"Kinsman—" That answer was Farne's, she could never have mistaken his voice even though she had already been sure he was the captive.

"Beast—devil begotten—"

"Begotten by your blood, kinsman—do *you* claim devil's blood?"

Thra laid hand to the last knot of rope and gave a jerk into which she put all the force she could summon. The silver mesh sawed at her fingers cruelly but she twisted, not caring. As she fought another voice broke in:

"'Ware, m'lord. Perhaps there may be more of his breed nearby. On guard, you dolts, on guard!"

The cord parted leaving bleeding gouges in her fingers. She curled hand around sword hilt in spite of the pain. The sword she had dragged with her from the hut lay at her feet. Grimclaw burst from the bushes wild-eyed to stand before her.

"Give me the spell spear!" That was the lord's voice. "And you—stand near the brush toward any devils this one may summon. Give me room for a cast now—"

Thra staggered back as a body swung at her. He who had been hanging in the net was free. And this was not the man who had left her in the hut but a furred, four-footed thing which had no right to run in a sane world.

Without thought Thra aimed a blow at the creature. Its yellow eyes blazed as it skidded to a halt and from the hairy throat came a deep warning growl.

Could it possess her by its will? Thra set her back to the broad trunk of a tree. Between them lay the sword from the armorie. The yellow eyes shifted from her to that. The beast advanced a paw towards the belt and then drew back as if it, as well as silver, carried some malignant spell.

Then the lord of the hunters thrust through the brush, though he came warily, a spear held at ready. Farne, if indeed it was Farne, showed fangs. But the man's eyes had flickered on to Thra. She had but a moment to duck sidewise before that spear thudded between her arm and her side. Instantly she scrambled on, seeking to set the tree between them.

"There be another! This one yet unwitched!"

The bushes in the direction Thra had headed tossed and crackled as some one forced a path through to bring them face to face. Farne moved—was before her again.

She steadied herself against the tree. Better take a spear through her here and now than fall helpless into their hands. She was already damned in their eyes and wanted to die cleanly.

The man now facing her was much younger than the leader of the hunters. Slim and agile, there was that about him which proclaimed some kinship with Farne when the latter walked two-legged. Only the eyes were different. Beneath the edging of a helm his were as blue and cold as winter ice.

He was also armed with a spear but now he pounded the butt of that against the forest muck and whipped out a sword of light-colored metal. Was that also forged of silver?

He thought to take her alive then, perhaps for a fate

like that promised Farne. Would his liegemen help to net her while she fought their lord?

"So this one does not run on all fours. What does such a devil know of skill with steel?"

"M'lord, watch yourself. These creatures deal in foul witchery—" That was the leader of the hunters. "They can make a man see what is not—"

Thra kept silent. If they believed her were they would indeed be wary of ensorcelment and in their wariness might lay some small chance for her. Not, she knew grimly, that she would be fortunate to live through this encounter, but it was far better to die on steel.

"Watch *you* well!" ordered the lord. "Since this one would use a blade so shall I. Mayhap I can thus prove that such are not to be so dreaded as foolish tales would have us believe." He lunged at her with the confidence of one who has yet to meet his match.

Blade rang against blade. Thra saw a shift in those cold eyes. Had he truly thought to bring her down with that simple thrust? Was it ignorant self-confidence past belief, or knowledge that he had won many times before?

Her worn blade shivered with that contact and she feared meeting a second such blow would shatter that too-often honed length. That other sword from the armorie, how far away now did it lie? She thought of Grimclaw—could the cat drag it to her? The cat had claimed the weapon from the cupboard yet her own hand had burned when she reached for it. Could one depend upon anything dark with witchery?

Thra fought defensively and kept the tree ever at her back. The point of that other weapon seemed to flicker in her very eyes and there was a sharp pain along her cheek. Where was Farne? She was sure he had been there at the beginning of this duel yet it would seem that the men had not sighted him— No time for that now—this battle was her own.

She fixed the picture of the sword in her mind. If

Grimclaw read her thoughts now would he answer her? Then there was a flash of thought which did not seem aimed at her but did come like a third dancing blade to join the battle. Sword—to take the sword—to choose—

It was not her desire, something more powerful even than fear had awakened in her. There was denial, and anger, and yes, a touch of terror. The ancient enemy—the sword— No, rend, tear, take payment for the wrong thus. Fang right, claw right—those were best—always best!

There was no animal cry but out of the bushes sprang a form which fastened upon one of the watching men. For only a second Thra spared a glance towards that struggle, heard sounds from others in the brush. Payment for that glance came with a blow upon her shoulder, which drove the mail painfully inward, bruising, though it did not cut the rings.

"Thus and thus—" He who fought sent the point again flickering into her face. She countered his stroke and her sword snapped, leaving but a jagged fragment in her hand. He laughed then and moved in for the kill.

"Thus!" he cried for the third time and that was a sentence of death, or so she hoped. Instead his blade cut painfully across her fingers so she dropped her hold on her broken weapon.

"What I promise I do. Do you take this one—" He turned his head a fraction to give that order.

Thra's knife came up toward her own throat. She was ready to press the point home when pain shot through her head and she would have fallen had not the tree supported her.

No pain of body—no—a deeper, stronger pain, such as her kind had never been meant to bear. She heard a voice cry aloud in torment and despair against a fate which could not be denied—but the voice was not hers.

Nor did Thra appear to suffer alone. The lord who had bested her staggered, his sword fell from his hand as he put both to his head. His mouth twisted in a wordless scream.

From where the brush had been beaten down by Farne's charge someone rose. He flung up his head, sending his hair back from his face, a face which wavered and changed even as they stared at him. Man not beast now, he leaped forward and in his hand was the other sword clear of its sheath, its blade giving off a reddish glow as if it were a shaft of Hell fire.

There were cries. Men ran but Thra did not try to move and her knife was still ready in her hand.

The lord half twisted to face the swordsman. He visibly drew a deep breath and stooped to seize again his own weapon as if he had already regained full control of body and mind. Of his followers only one flaccid body remained on the ground.

"Well met, ill met, kinsman!" Farne smiled slowly. He stood waiting attack even as she had earlier done.

There was a wild rage in the other's eyes. Thra thought that for this lord of the hounds the whole world had suddenly narrowed to confrontation with this single man-beast.

The glow in Farne's blade spread. His fingers, locked about the hilt, reddened, the flush wreathed about his wrist, reached up his arm. In Thra a fire seemed to burn. She caught her breath and choked down a cry of agony. If this was the cost of using the weapon to her who only stood aside, what must it be to Farne himself? For she was certain that what she felt was a reflection of that he had to bear now.

Instead he cried aloud on the edge of human rage yet still with an animal note. If the young lord thought that he faced easy meat he was made speedily aware of his mistake, for the fire blade kept play in a way which Thra, with all her knowledge of weapons, marveled to see.

Only for seconds she watched and then she remembered the others. What of the men who had gone with the hounds, the rest? No matter how skillful Farne might be he could not hope to stand against four or more of them.

Dropping her sheared sword she leaped for the body in the brush.

Red ruin above a torn throat, she looked no higher. But she had her hands on a spear haft. Above the clash of weapons behind her she heard a stifled moan.

There was a second man in the bushes. He half-lay, face stark, a mangled arm across his breast, looking at her wild-eyed as she came to him, his good hand awkwardly fumbling with a short hunting sword. She took that from him easily, wrenching it free, for her own arming.

While he spat meaningless words at her she staggered back, still afire, straight into the path of another running to the fight.

"Die, devil!"

She was still not at ready and he was about to cut her down when he shrieked aloud and threw up his hands, the wounded man echoing his cry. This pain in her head—she could hardly see. However on hands and knees Thra scrambled away as a heavy body crashed down. To make certain of his helplessness she brought the heavy pommel of the sword on the nape of his neck as his helm loosened and rolled away.

For a moment she simply crouched, sobbing for breath, hardly daring to believe she yet lived. The pain was now no longer a torment; rather a steady fire which strengthened her in a way she could not understand.

Out of a tangle of tall grass came Grimclaw. As he passed the legs of the man before her a paw aimed a quick blow claws out. Thra used the spear to aid her to her feet where those other two still fought with skill and desperation. Thrusting the hunting sword close to hand in the ground she stood with the spear at ready, to hold the lists. Grimclaw stationed himself beside her.

Mastery of steel—Thra knew that she watched two evenly matched fighting men of top skill. And they could almost have been brothers from one birthing. That strange cast of Farne's features had faded away. He was smiling slightly, yellow eyes alight—only the color of those differing from his enemy.

The blaze from his blade now formed a nebulous glow about his whole body through which the sword moved like a darting tongue. Were they so evenly matched that they might fight forever without giving way? Thra could detect no sign of fatigue, no lighting of the clang of weapons.

She had no more that thought then when the flame-wreathed blade appeared to turn of itself in Farne's hand. The weapon might command the man not the man the weapon. There was a hard clang of sound and the lord's sword spun out of his grip to strike against the trunk of the tree where Thra had sheltered. He stood bare handed, with no change of expression, as if he now waited stocially that thrust at throat or breast which would put an end to him.

As the fire blade turned point down Farne caught and held those other chill eyes.

"Blood calls to blood," he said slowly.

The other's mouth contorted. He spat and the spittle flecked the trampled leaves by Farne's boots.

"Beast calls not to true man!" He flung up his head in harsh pride. "Kill if you will but think not that aught between us can ever be altered—runner in the night!"

Farne swung the sword, not towards the other but as if he weighed something in his hand and that weight dragged heavy upon him. He shook his head.

"Run no more," he said slowly. "The choice has been forced upon me at last. I may well have lost more than I gain—"

"I do not understand you," broke in the other impatiently. "Kill me—you win nothing, beast—"

Farne, to Thra's surprise, nodded. "Nothing," he agreed. "Did you think I challenged your rulership with this?" Again he waved the sword.

That light which had blazed along it was gone. But the

strangeness did not return to his face. Now he stepped back and away from the other.

"This much is true. You live, kinsman, by my leave."

The other scowled and took a step forward as if he wished to drag Farne down by strength alone.

"Also," once more the forest man shifted his grip on the sword, "I have at last come into my inheritance. No, kinsman, do not fear that you shall be dispossessed of your lands, your ill-ruled people—not yet. But the 'beast' you have been pleased to hunt is gone. Try your tricks again at your will, they shall net you naught. Take up your liegemen and get you gone. This forest has an ill name among your kind that was not lightly earned, nor shall it be forgot."

Deliberately he sheathed the sword and held its belt in one hand. The other he put to the wide buckle of the furred belt.

As Farne's fingers touched that buckle it burst open. The metal over which the strange colors had played flaked away. Fur loosened from scaling hide and shifted through the air, the hide itself slipped and fell from about his body, to lie in bits upon the ground. Then he fastened the sword belt in its place.

The lord watched through narrowed eyes.

"You have given me quarter—I asked it not, I shall not accept it!" His voice was harsh challenge.

"Accept or not as you wish," Farne shrugged. "You stand on land which I know and which knows me. I have made my choices—yours shall be yours only, and you shall answer for them."

He turned his head to look to Thra. What he had just said, she thought, was meant in its latter part as much for her as for the lord.

She swallowed. Life was always choices and somehow she knew she faced a mighty one now. As she settled the sword she had taken into the empty scabbard at her belt she saw on the ground a wisp of dirty fur.

Two belts and a man, there was a meaning she could guess at. But in this forest one need not be surprised at anything. She made her choice.

As Farne moved forward she fell in at his right hand, Grimclaw padding into the shadow of the great trees at his left.

By a Hair

YOU say, friend, that witchcraft at its strongest is but a crude knowledge of psychology, a use of a man's own fear of the unknown to destroy him? Perhaps it may be so in modern lands. But me, I have seen what I have seen. More than fear destroyed Dagmar Kark and Colonel Andrei Veroff.

There were four of them, strong and passionate: Ivor and Dagmar Kark, Andrei Varoff and the Countess Ana. What they desired they gained by the aid of something not to be seen nor felt nor sensed tangibly, something not in the experience of modern man.

Ivor was an idealist who held to a cause and the woman he thought Dagmar to be. Dagmar, she wanted power—power over the kind of man who could give her all her heart desired. And so she wanted Colonel Andrei Varoff.

And Varoff, his wish was a common one, though odd for one of his creed. When a man has been nourished on the belief that the state is all, the individual nothing, it is queer to want a son to the point of obsession. And, though Varoff had taken many women, none had produced a child he could be sure was his.

The Countess Ana, she wanted justice—and love.

The four people had faith in themselves, strong faith. Besides, they had it in other things—Ivor in his cause and his wife, Varoff in a creed. And Dagmar and Ana in something very old and enduring.

It could not have happened in this new land of yours, to that I agree; but in my birth country it is different. All this came to be in a narrow knife slash of a valley running from mountains to the gray salt sweep of the Baltic. It is true that the shadow of the true cross has lain over that valley since the Teutonic knights planted it on the castle they built in the crags almost a thousand years ago. But before the white Christ came, other, grimmer gods were worshipped in that land. In the fir forest where the valley walls are steep, there is still a stone altar set in a grove. That was tended, openly at first, and later in secret, for long after the priests of Rome chanted masses in the church.

In that country the valley is reckoned rich. Life there was good until the Nazis came. Then the Count was shot in his own courtyard, since he was not the type of man to suffer the arrogance of others calmly, and with him Hudun, the head gamekeeper, and the heads of three valley households. Afterwards they took away the young Countess Ana.

But Ivor Kark fled to the hills and our young men joined him. During two years, perhaps a little more, they carried on guerrilla warfare with the invader, just as it happened in those days in all the countries stamped by the iron heel.

But to my country there came no liberation. Where the Nazi had strutted in his pride, the Bear of the north shambled, and stamped into red dust those who defied him. Some fled and some stayed to fight, believing in their innocence that the nations among the free would rise in their behalf.

Ivor Kark and his men, not yet realizing fully the doom come upon us, ventured out of the mountains. For a time it appeared that the valley, being so small a community, might indeed be overlooked. In those few days of freedom Ivor found Dagmar Llov.

Who can describe such a woman as Dagmar with words? She was not beautiful; no, seldom is it that great beauty brings men to their knees. Look at the portraits of your historical charmers, or read what has been written of Cleopatra, of Theodora and the rest. They have something other than beauty, these fateful ones: a flame within them which kindles an answer in all men who look upon them. But their own hearts remain cold.

Dagmar walked with a grace which tore at you, and when she looked at one sidewise. . . . But who can describe such a woman? I can say she had silver, fair hair which reached to her knees, a face with a frost white skin, but I cannot so make you see the Dagmar Llov that was.

Because of his leadership in the underground, Ivor was a hero to us. In addition, he was good to look upon: a tall whip of a man, brown, thin, narrow of waist and loins, and broad of shoulder. He had been a huntsman of the Count's, and walked with a forester's smooth glide. Above his widely set eyes his hair grew in a sharp peak, giving his face a disturbingly wolfish cast. But in his eyes and mouth there was the dedication of a priest.

Being what she was, Dagmar looked upon those eyes and that mouth, and desired to trouble the mold, to see there a difference she had wrought. In some ways Ivor was an innocent, but Dagmar was one who had known much from her cradle.

Also, Ivor was now the great man among us. With the Count gone, the men of the valley looked to him for leadership. Dagmar went to him willingly and we sang her bride song. It was a good time, such as we had not known for years.

Others came back to the valley during those days. Out of the black horror of a Nazi extermination camp crawled a pale, twisted creature, warped in body, perhaps also in mind. She who had once been the Countess Ana came quietly, almost secretly, among us again. One day she had not been there, and the next she was settled in the half-ruinous gate house of the castle with old Mald, who had been with her family long before her own birth.

The Countess Ana had been a woman of education before they had taken her away, and she had not forgotten all she had learned. There was no doctor in the valley; twenty families could not have supported one. But the Countess was versed in the growing of herbs and their healing uses, and Mald was a midwife. So together they became the wise women of our people. After a while we forgot the Countess Ana's deformed body and ravaged face, and accepted her as we accepted the crooked firs growing close to the timberline. Not one of us remembered that she was yet in years a young woman, with a young woman's dreams and desires, encased in a hag's body.

It was late October when our fate came upon us, up river in a power boat. The new masters would set in our hills a station from which their machines could spy upon the outer world they feared and hated; and to make safe the building of that station they sent ahead a conqueror's party. They surprised us and something had drained out of the valley. So many of our youth were long since bleached bones that, save for a handful, perhaps only the number of the fingers on my two hands, there was no defiance; there was only a dumb beast's endurance. Within three days Colonel Andrei Varoff ruled from the castle as if he had been Count, lord of a tired, cowed people.

Three men they hauled from their homes and shot on the first night, but Ivor was not one. He had been warned and, with the core of his men, had taken again to the mountains. But he left Dagmar behind, by her own will.

Mald and the Countess were warned, too. When Varoff marched his pocket army into the castle, the gate house was deserted; and those who thereafter sought the wise women's aid took another path, up into the black-green of the fir forest and close to a long stone partly buried in the ground within a circle of very old oaks, which had not grown so by chance. There in a game-station hut, those in need could find what they wanted, perhaps more.

Father Hansel had been one of the three Varoff shot out of hand, and there was no longer an open church in the valley. What went on in the oak glade was another matter. First our women drifted there, half ashamed, half defiant, and later they were followed by their men. I do not think the Countess Ana was their priestess. But she knew and condoned. For she had learned many things.

The wise women began to offer more than just comfort of body. It was a queer wild time when men in their despair turned from old belief to older ones, from a god of love and peace, to a god of wrath and vengeance. Old knowledge passed by word of mouth from mother to daughter was recalled by such as Mald, and keenly evaluated by the sharper and better-trained brain of the Countess Ana. I will not say that they called upon Odin and Freya (or those behind those Nordic spirits) or lighted the Beltane Fire. But there was a stirring, as if something long sleeping turned and stretched in its supposed grave.

Dagmar, for all her shrewd egotism (and egotism such as hers is dangerous, for it leads a man or woman to believe that what they wish is right), was a daughter of the valley. She was moved by the old beliefs; and because she had her price, she was convinced that all others had theirs. So at night she went alone to the hut. There she watched until the Countess Ana left. It was she who carried news and a few desperately gained supplies to those in hiding, especially Ivor.

Seeing the hunched figure creep off, Dagmar laughed spitefully, making a secret promise to herself that even a man she might choose to throw away would go to no other woman. But since at present she needed aid and not ill-will, she put that aside.

When the Countess was out of sight, Dagmar went in to Mald and stood in the half-light of the fire, proud and tall, exulting over the other woman in all the sensual strength and grace of her body, as she had over the Countess Ana in her mind.

"I would have what I desire most, Andrei Varoff," she said boldly, speaking with the arrogance of a woman who rules men by their lusts.

"Let him but look on you. You need no help here," returned Mald.

"I cannot come to him easily; he is not one to be met by chance. Give me that which will bring him to me by his own choice."

"You are a wedded wife."

Dagmar laughed shrilly. "What good does a man who must hide ever in a mountain cave do me, Old One? I have slept too long in a cold bed. Let me draw Varoff, and you and the valley will have kin within the enemy's gate."

Mald studied her for a long moment, and Dagmar grew uneasy, for those eyes in age-carved pits seemed to read far too deeply. But, without making any answer in words, Mald began certain preparations. There was a strange chanting, low and soft but long, that night. The words were almost as old as the hills around them, and the air of the hut was thick with the scent of burning herbs.

When it was done Dagmar stood again by the fire, and in her hands she turned and twisted a shining, silken belt. She looped it about her arm beneath her cloak and tugged at the heavy coronet of her braids. The long locks Mald had shorn were not missed. Her teeth showed in white points against her lip as she brought out of her pocket some of those creased slips of paper our conquerors used for money.

Mald shook her head. "Not for coin did I do this," she said harshly. "But if you come to rule here as you desire, remember you *are* kin."

Dagmar laughed again, more than ever sure of herself. "Be sure that I will, Old One."

Within two days the silken belt was in Varoff's hands,

and within five Dagmar was installed in the castle. But in the Colonel she had met her match, for Varoff found her no great novelty. She could not bend him to her will as she had Ivor, who was more sensitive and less guarded. But, being shrewd, Dagmar accepted the situation with surface grace and made no demands.

As for the valley women, they spat after her, and there was hate in their hearts. Who told Ivor I do not know, though it was not the Countess Ana. (She could not wound where she would die to defend.) But somehow he managed to get a message to Dagmar, entreating her to come to him, for he believed she had gone to Varoff to protect him.

What that message aroused in Dagmar was contempt and fear: contempt for the man who would call her to share his harsh exile and fear that he might break the slender bond she had with Varoff. She was determined that Ivor must go. It was very simple, that betrayal, for Ivor believed in her. He went to his death as easily as a bullock led to the butcher, in spite of warnings from the Countess Ana and his men.

He slipped down by night to where Dagmar promised to wait and walked into the hands of the Colonel's guard. They say he was a long time dying, for Andrei Varoff had a taste for such treatment for prisoners when he could safely indulge it. Dagmar watched him die; that, too, was part of the Colonel's pleasure. Afterward there was a strange shadow in her eyes, although she walked with pride.

It was two months later that she made her second visit to Mald. But this time there were two to receive her. Yet in neither look, word, nor deed, did either show emotion at that meeting; it was as if they waited. They remained silent, forcing her to declare her purpose.

"I would bear a son." She began as one giving an order. Only—confronted by those unchanging faces she faltered and lost some of her assurance. She might even have turned and gone had the Countess Ana not spoken in a cool and even voice.

"It is well known that Varoff desires a son."

Dagmar responded to that faint encouragement. "True! Let me be the one to bear the child and my influence over him will be complete. Then I can repay—it is true, you frozen faces!" She was aroused by the masks they wore. "You believe that I betrayed Ivor, not knowing the whole of the story. I have very little power over Varoff now. But let me give him a son; then there will be no limit on what I can demand of him—none at all!"

"You shall bear a son; certainly you shall bear a son," replied the Countess Ana. In the security of that promise Dagmar rejoiced, not attending to the finer shades of meaning in the voice which uttered it.

"But what you ask of us takes preparation. You must wait and return when the moon once more waxes. Then we shall do what is to be done!"

Reassured, Dagmar left. As the door of the hut swung shut behind her, the Countess Ana came to stand before the fire, her crooked shape making a blot upon the wall with its shadow.

"She shall have a son, Mald, even as I promised, only whether thereafter she will discover it profitable—"

From within the folds of her coarse peasant blouse, she brought out a packet wrapped in a scrap of fine but brown-stained linen. Unfolding the cloth, she revealed what it guarded: a lock of black hair, stiff and matted with something more than mud. Mald, seeing that and guessing the purpose for which it would be used, laughed. The Countess did not so much as smile.

"There shall be a son, Mald," she repeated, but her promise was no threat. There was a more subtle note, and in the firelight her eyes gleamed with an eagerness to belie the ruin of her face.

Within two days came the night she had appointed and Dagmar with it. Again there was chanting and things done in secret. When Dagmar left at dawn she smiled a thin smile. Let her but bear a child and they would see, all would see, how she would deal with those who now dared to look crosswise after her and spit upon her footprints! Let such fools take heed!

Shortly thereafter it became known that Dagmar was with child. Varoff could not conceal his joy. During the months which followed he made plans to send her out of the valley, that his son might be born with the best medical care; and he loaded her with gifts. But the inner caution of an often-disappointed man made him keep her prisoner.

Dagmar did not leave the valley. She could not make the rough trip by river and sea. The road over the mountain was but a narrow track, and just before Varoff prepared to leave with her there was such a storm as is seldom seen at that time of year. A landslide blotted out the road. The Colonel cursed and drove his own soldiers and the valley men to dig a way through, but even he realized it could not be cleared in time.

So he was forced to summon Mald. His threats to her were cold and deadly, for he had no illusions concerning the depth of the valley's hatred. But the old woman bore his raving meekly, and he came to believe her broken enough in spirit to be harmless. Thus, though he still suspected her, he brought her to Dagmar and bade her use her skill.

For a night and a day Dagmar lay in labor, and what she suffered must have been very great. But greater still was her determination to be the one to place a living son in the arms of Andrei Varoff.

In the evening the child was born, its thin cry echoing from the walls of the ancient room like the wail of a tormented soul. Dagmar clawed herself up.

"Is it a boy?" she demanded hoarsely.

Mald nodded her white head. "A boy."

"Give him to me and call—"

But there was no need to complete that order for Andrei Varoff was already within the chamber and Dagmar greeted him proudly, the baby in the curve of her arm. As he strode to the bedside she thrust away the swaddling blanket and displayed the tiny body fully. But her eyes were for Varoff rather than for the child she had schemed to make a weapon in her hand.

"Your son—" she began. Then something in Varoff's eyes as he stared down upon the child chilled her as if naked steel, ice cold, had been plunged into her sweating body.

For the first time she looked upon the baby. This was her key, a son for Varoff.

Her scream, thin and high, tore through the storm wind moaning outside the narrow window. Andrei loomed over her as she cowered away from what she read in his eyes, in the twist of his thick lips.

It was Mald who snatched the baby and sped from that room, at a greater speed than her years might warrant, to be joined by another within a secret way of the castle. The twisted, limping figure took the child eagerly into long empty arms, to hold it tenderly as a long-desired gift.

But neither of the two Mald left were aware of her flight. What was done there cannot be told, but before the coming of dawn Varoff shot himself.

Where is the magic in all this, besides the muttering of old woman? Just this: when Dagmar demanded a son from the Countess Ana, she indeed obtained her desire. But the child she bore had fine black hair growing in a sharp peak above a wolf cub's face—a face which Andrei Varoff and Dagmar Kark had excellent reason to know well. Who fathered Dagmar's child, a man nigh twelve months dead? And who was its true mother? Think carefully, my friend.

Not a pretty story, eh? But, you see, old gods do not tend to be mild when called on to render justice.

All Cats Are Gray

STEENA of the Spaceways—that sounds just like a corny title for one of the Stellar-Vedo spreads. I ought to know; I've tried my hand at writing enough of them. Only this Steena was no glamorous babe. She was as colorless as a lunar planet—even the hair netted down to her skull had a sort of grayish cast, and I never saw her but once draped in anything but a shapeless and baggy gray spaceall.

Steena was strictly background stuff, and that is where she mostly spent her free hours—in the smelly, smoky, background corners of any stellar-port dive frequented by free spacers. If you really looked for her you could spot her—just sitting there listening to the talk—listening and remembering. She didn't open her own mouth often. But when she did, spacers had learned to listen. And the lucky few who heard her rare spoken words—these will never forget Steena.

She drifted from port to port. Being an expert operator on the big calculators, she found jobs wherever she cared to stay for a time. And she came to be something like the masterminded machines she tended—smooth, gray, without much personality of their own.

But it was Steena who told Bub Nelson about the Jovan moon rites—and her warning saved Bub's life six months later. It was Steena who identified the piece of stone Keene Clark was passing around a table one night, rightly calling it unworked Slitite. That started a rush which made ten fortunes overnight for men who were down to their last jets. And, last of all, she cracked the case of the *Empress of Mars.*

All the boys who had profited by her queer store of knowledge and her photographic memory tried at one time or another to balance the scales. But she wouldn't take so much as a cup of canal water at their expense, let alone the credits they tried to push on her. Bub Nelson was the only one who got around her refusal. It was he who brought her Bat.

About a year after the Jovan affair, he walked into the Free Fall one night and dumped Bat down on her table. Bat looked at Steena and growled. She looked calmly back at him and nodded once. From then on they traveled together —the thin gray woman and the big gray tomcat. Bat learned to know the inside of more stellar bars than even most spacers visit in their lifetimes. He developed a liking for Vernal juice, drank it neat and quick, right out of the glass. And he was always at home on any table where Steena elected to drop him.

This is really the story of Steena, Bat, Cliff Moran, and the *Empress of Mars,* a story which is already a legend of the spaceways. And it's a damn good story, too. I ought to know, having framed the first version of it myself.

For I was there, right in the Rigel Royal, when it all began on the night that Cliff Moran blew in, looking lower than an antman's belly and twice as nasty. He'd had a spell of luck foul enough to twist a man into a slug snake, and we all knew that there was an attachment out for his ship. Cliff had fought his way up from the back courts of Venaport. Lose his ship and he'd slip back there—to rot. He was at the snarling stage that night when he picked out a table for himself and set out to drink away his troubles.

However, just as the first bottle arrived, so did a visitor. Steena came out of her corner, Bat curled around her shoulders stolewise, his favorite mode of travel. She crossed over and dropped down, without invitation, at Cliff's side. That shook him out of his sulks. Because Steena never chose company when she could be alone. If one of the man-stones on Ganymede had come stumping in, it wouldn't have made more of us look out of the corners of our eyes.

She stretched out one long-fingered hand, set aside the bottle he had ordered, and said only one thing. "It's about time for the *Empress of Mars* to appear."

Cliff scowled and bit his lip. He was tough, tough as jet lining—you have to be granite inside and out to struggle up from Venaport to a ship command. But we could guess what was running through his mind at that moment. The *Empress of Mars* was just about the biggest prize a spacer could aim for. But in the fifty years she had been following her queer derelict orbit through space, many men had tried to bring her in—and none had succeeded.

A pleasure ship carrying untold wealth, she had been mysteriously abandoned in space by passengers and crew, none of whom had ever been seen or heard of again. At intervals thereafter she had been sighted, even boarded. Those who ventured into her either vanished or returned swiftly without any believable explanation of what they had seen—wanting only to get away from her as quickly as possible. But the man who could bring her in—or even strip her clean in space—that man would win the jackpot.

"All right!" Cliff slammed his fist on the table. "I'll try even that!"

Steena looked at him, much as she must have looked at Bat that day Bub Nelson brought him to her, and nodded. That was all I saw. The rest of the story came to me in pieces, months later and in another port half the system away.

Cliff took off that night. He was afraid to risk waiting —with a writ out that could pull the ship from under him. And it wasn't until he was in space that he discovered his passengers—Steena and Bat. We'll never know what happened then. I'm betting Steena made no explanation at all. She wouldn't.

It was the first time she had decided to cash in on her own tip and she was there—that was all. Maybe that point weighed with Cliff, maybe he just didn't care. Anyway, the three were together when they sighted the *Empress* riding, her deadlights gleaming, a ghost ship in night space.

She must have been an eerie sight because her other lights were on too, in addition to the red warnings at her nose. She seemed alive, a Flying Dutchman of space. Cliff worked his ship skillfully alongside and had no trouble in snapping magnetic lines to her lock. Some minutes later the three of them passed into her. There was still air in her cabins and corridors, air that bore a faint corrupt taint which set Bat to sniffing greedily and could be picked up even by the less sensitive human nostrils.

Cliff headed straight for the control cabin, but Steena and Bat went prowling. Closed doors were a challenge to both of them and Steena opened each as she passed, taking a quick look at what lay within. The fifth door opened on a room which no woman could leave without further investigation.

I don't know what had been housed there when the *Empress* left port on her last lengthy cruise. Anyone really curious can check back on the old photo-reg cards. But there was a lavish display of silk trailing out of two travel kits on the floor, a dressing table crowded with crystal and jeweled containers, along with other lures for the female which drew Steena in. She was standing in front of the dressing table when she glanced into the mirror—glanced into it and froze.

Over her right shoulder she could see the spider-silk cover on the bed. Right in the middle of that sheer, gossamer expanse was a sparkling heap of gems, the dumped contents of some jewel case. Bat had jumped to the foot of the bed and flattened out as cats will, watching those gems, watching them and—something else!

Steena put out her hand blindly and caught up the nearest bottle. As she unstoppered it, she watched the mirrored bed. A gemmed bracelet rose from the pile, rose in the air and tinkled its siren song. It was as if an idle hand played. . . . Bat spat almost noiselessly. But he did not retreat. Bat had not yet decided his course.

She put down the bottle. Then she did something which perhaps few of the men she had listened to through the years could have done. She moved without hurry or sign of disturbance on a tour about the room. And, although she approached the bed, she did not touch the jewels. She could not force herself to do that. It took her five minutes to play out her innocence and unconcern. Then it was Bat who decided the issue.

He leaped from the bed and escorted something to the door, remaining a careful distance behind. Then he mewed loudly twice. Steena followed him and opened the door wider.

Bat went straight on down the corridor, as intent as a hound on the warmest of scents. Steena strolled behind him, holding her pace to the unhurried gait of an explorer. What sped before them was invisible to her, but Bat was never baffled by it.

They must have gone into the control cabin almost on the heels of the unseen—if the unseen had heels, which there was good reason to doubt—for Bat crouched just within the doorway and refused to move on. Steena looked down the length of the instrument panels and officers' station seats to where Cliff Moran worked. Her boots made no sound on the heavy carpet, and he did not glance up but sat humming through set teeth, as he tested the tardy and reluctant responses to buttons which had not been pushed in years.

To human eyes they were alone in the cabin. But Bat still followed a moving something, which he had at last made up his mind to distrust and dislike. For now he took a step or two forward and spat—his loathing made plain by every raised hair along his spine. And in that same moment Steena saw a flicker—a flicker of vague outline against Cliff's hunched shoulders, as if the invisible one had crossed the space between them.

But why had it been revealed against Cliff and not against the back of one of the seats or against the panels, the walls of the corridor or the cover of the bed where it had reclined and played with its loot? What could Bat see?

The storehouse memory that had served Steena so well through the years clicked open a half-forgotten door. With one swift motion, she tore loose her spaceall and flung the baggy garment across the back of the nearest seat.

Bat was snarling now, emitting the throaty rising cry that was his hunting song. But he was edging back, back towards Steena's feet, shrinking from something he could not fight but which he faced defiantly. If he could draw it after him, past that dangling spaceall . . . He had to—it was their only chance!

"What the . . ." Cliff had come out of his seat and was staring at them.

What he saw must have been weird enough: Steena, bare-armed and bare-shouldered, her usually stiffly-netted hair falling wildly down her back; Steena watching empty space with narrowed eyes and set mouth, calculating a single wild chance. Bat, crouched on his belly, was retreating from thin air step by step and wailing like a demon.

"Toss me your blaster." Steena gave the order calmly—as if they were still at their table in the Rigel Royal.

And as quietly, Cliff obeyed. She caught the small weapon out of the air with a steady hand—caught and leveled it.

"Stay where you are!" she warned. "Back, Bat, bring it back."

With a last throat-splitting screech of rage and hate, Bat twisted to safety between her boots. She pressed with thumb and forefinger, firing at the spaceall. The material turned to powdery flakes of ash—except for certain bits which still flapped from the scorched seat—as if something had protected them from the force of the blast. Bat sprang straight up in the air with a screech that tore their ears.

"What . . .?" began Cliff again.

Steena made a warning motion with her left hand. *"Wait!"*

She was still tense, still watching Bat. The cat dashed madly around the cabin twice, running crazily with white-ringed eyes and flecks of foam on his muzzle. Then he stopped abruptly in the doorway, stopped and looked back over his shoulder for a long, silent moment. He sniffed delicately.

Steena and Cliff could smell it too now, a thick oily stench which was not the usual odor left by an exploding blaster shell.

Bat came back, treading daintily across the carpet, almost on the tips of his paws. He raised his head as he passed Steena, and then he went confidently beyond to sniff, to sniff and spit twice at the unburned strips of the spaceall. Having thus paid his respects to the late enemy, he sat down calmly and set to washing his fur with deliberation. Steena sighed once and dropped into the navigator's seat.

"Maybe now you'll tell me what in the hell's happened?" Cliff exploded as he took the blaster out of her hand.

"Gray," she said dazedly, "it must have been gray—or I couldn't have seen it like that. I'm color-blind, you see. I can see only shades of gray—my whole world is gray. Like Bat's—his world is gray, too—all gray. But he's been compensated, for he can see above and below our range of color vibrations, and apparently so can I!"

Her voice quavered, and she raised her chin with a new air Cliff had never seen before—a sort of proud acceptance. She pushed back her wandering hair, but she made no move to imprison it under the heavy net again.

"That is why I saw the thing when it crossed between us. Against your spaceall it was another shade of gray—an outline. So I put out mine and waited for it to show against that—it was our only chance, Cliff.

"It was curious at first, I think, and it knew we couldn't see it—which is why it waited to attack. But when Bat's actions gave it away, it moved. So I waited to see that flicker against the spaceall, and then I let him have it. It's really very simple. . . ."

Cliff laughed a bit shakily. "But what *was* this gray thing. I don't get it."

"I think it was what made the *Empress* a derelict. Something out of space, maybe, or from another world somewhere." She waved her hands. "It's invisible because it's a color beyond our range of sight. It must have stayed in here all these years. And it kills—it must—when its curiosity is satisfied." Swiftly she described the scene, the scene in the cabin, and the strange behavior of the gem pile which had betrayed the creature to her.

Cliff did not return his blaster to its holder. "Any more of them aboard, d'you think?" He didn't look pleased at the prospect.

Steena turned to Bat. He was paying particular attention to the space between two front toes in the process of a complete bath. "I don't think so. But Bat will tell us if there are. He can see them clearly, I believe."

But there weren't any more and two weeks later, Cliff, Steena and Bat brought the *Empress* into the lunar quarantine station. And that is the end of Steena's story because, as we have been told, happy marriages need no chronicles. Steena had found someone who knew of her gray world and did not find it too hard to share with her—someone besides Bat. It turned out to be a real love match.

The last time I saw her, she was wrapped in a flame-red cloak from the looms of Rigel and wore a fortune in Jovan rubies blazing on her wrists. Cliff was flipping a three-figured credit bill to a waiter. And Bat had a row of Vernal juice glasses set up before him. Just a little family party out on the town.

Swamp Dweller

I am Quintka blood, no matter my mother. Shame-shorn of skull, snow-pale of skin, her body criss-crossed by lash scarring, her leg torn by hound's teeth, lying in a ditch, she bore me, to hide me in leaves before death came. The Calling was mine from the first breath I drew, as it is with all the Kin, and Lari, free ranging that day, heard, pawing me free, giving me the breast with her own current nurseling, before loping back to Garner himself to show her new cubling.

Quintka I plainly was by my wide yellow eyes and silver hair. Though my mother was of no race known to Garner, and he was a far-traveled man.

The Kin paid her full death honors, for it was plain she had fought for my life. Children are esteemed among the Kin, who breed thinly, for all our toughness of body and quickness of mind, gifts from Anthea, All Mother.

Thus did I foster with Kin and Second-Kin, close to Ort, Lari's cubling, though he was quicker to find his feet and forge for himself. However, I mind-spoke all the beast ones, and tongue-spoke the Kin; thus all accepted me fully.

Before I passed my sixth winter I had my own team of trained ones, Ort as my seconding. I was able to meet the high demands of Garner, for he accepted only the best performers.

Because I was able so young, the clan prospered. Those not of the blood seemed bemused that beasts such as orzens and fal, and quare, clever after their own fashion, head-topping me by bulk of bodies, would obey me. Many a lord paid good silver to have us entertain.

Nor had we any fears while traveling, such as troubled merchant caravans that must hire bravos to their protection. For all men knew that the beasts who shared our covered wagons, or tramped the roads beside us were, in themselves, more formidable weapons than any men could hope to forge.

Once a year we came to Ithkar Fair—knowing that we would leave with well-filled pouches. For Garner's shows were in high demand. Lords, even the high ones of the temple, competed in hiring us.

However, it was not alone for that profit we came. There were dealers who brought rare and sometimes unknown beasts—strange and fearsome, or beautiful and appealing—from the steppes of the far north or by ships plying strange seas. These we sought, adding to our clan so.

Some we could not touch with the Calling, for they had been so mishandled in their capture or transport as to retreat far behind fear and hate, where the silent speech could not reach. Those were a sorrow and despair to us all. Though we ofttimes bought them out of pity, we could not make them friends and comrades. Rather did we carry them away from all that meant hurt and horror and sung them into peace and rest forever. This also being one of the duties Anthea, All Mother, required of us.

I was in my seventeenth year, perhaps too young and too aware of my own powers, when we came that memorable time to Ithkar. There was no mandate laid upon me to mate—even though the Kin was needful of new blood—but there were two who watched me.

Feeta's son by Garner—Wowern. Also there was Sim,

who could bend any horse to his will, and whose riding was a marvel, as if youth and mount were of one flesh. Only to me my team was still the closer bond, and I felt no need to have it otherwise.

The fair-wards at the entrance hailed us as they might some lord, though we scattered no gold. From his high seat the wizard-of-the-gate, ready to make certain no dark magic entered, broke his grave mask with a smile, waved to Feeta, who also makes magic, but of a healing kind. Our weapons were few and Garner had them already sheathed and bundled, as well as the purse for our fee ready, so there was no waiting at the barrier.

We would pay a courtesy visit to the temple later, but, since we were not merchants dealing in goods, we made only a silver offering. Now we pushed on into that section where there were beasts and hides, and all that had to do with living things. Our yearly place was ready for us—a fair-ward waiting, having kept that free for our coming. Him we knew, too, being Edgar, a man devoted to Feeta, who had cured his hound two seasons back. He tossed his staff in the air to pay us homage and called eager questions.

We all had our assigned tasks, so we moved with the speed of long practice, setting up the large tent for the showing, settling in our Second-Kin. They accepted that here they must keep to cages and picket lines, even though this was, in a manner, an insult to them. But they understood that outside the Kin they were not as clan brothers and sisters, but sometimes feared. I know that some, such as Ily, the mountain cat, and Somsa, the horned small dragon, were amused to play dangerous—giving shudders to those who came to view them.

I had finished my part of the communal tasks when Ort padded to me, squatting back on his powerful hindquarters, his taloned forepaws lightly clasped across his lighter belly fur. His domed head, with its upstanding crest of stiff, dark blue fur, was higher than mine when he reared thus.

"Sister-Kin . . ."—the thoughts of beasts do not form words, but in the mind one easily translates—"there is wrong here. . . ."

I looked up quickly. His broad nostrils expanded, as if drawing in a scent that irked him. Our senses are less in many ways than those of the Second-Kin, and we learn early to depend upon what they can read by nose, eye, or ear.

"What wrong, Brother-Kin?"

Ort could not shrug as might one of my own species, but the impression of such a gesture reached me. There was as yet only simple uneasiness in his mind; he could not pin it to any source. Still I was alerted, knowing that if Ort had made such a judgment, others would also be searching. Their reports would come to those among the Kin with whom they felt the deepest bond.

The Calling we did not use except among ourselves and the Second-Kin—and that I dared not attempt now. But as I dressed for fairing, I tried to open myself to any fleeting impression. A vigorous combing fluffed out hair usually banded down, and I placed on midforehead the blue gem I had bought at this same fair last year, which adhered to one's flesh, giving forth a subtle perfume.

Ort still companied me. Mai, Erlia, and Nadi, the other girls, were in and out of our side tent. But there was no light chatter among us. The tree cat, that rode as often as was possible on Nadi's shoulder, switched its ringed tail back and forth, a sure sign of uneasiness, and Mai looked abstracted, as if she were listening to something afar. She was like Sim with horses, though also she had two Fos deer from the mountain valleys in her team.

It was Erlia who turned from the mirror to face the rest of us squarely.

"There is . . ." She hesitated for a moment with her head suddenly to one side, almost as if she had been hailed. Still facing so, she added, "There is darkness here—something new."

"A distress Calling?" suggested Mai, her face shadowed by concern. She faced that portion of the fairgrounds where dealers in beasts had their stands and where we had found those in pain and terror before. Erlia shook her head.

"No Calling—this rather would hide itself—" She brushed her hand across her face as if pushing aside an unseen curtain that she might sense the better.

She was right. Now it reached me. There are evil odors to sicken one, and evil thoughts like dirty fingers to claw into the mind. This was neither, yet it *was* there, a whiff of filth, an insidious threat—something I had never met before. Nor had these, my kinswomen, for they all faced outward with a look of questing.

We pushed into the open, uneasy, needing some council from any who might know more. Ort snarled. The red glare of awakening anger came into his large-pupiled eyes, while the tree cat gave a yowl and flattened its ears.

Wowern, his trail clothing also changed, stood there, his hand resting on the head of his favorite companion, the vasa hound that he had bought at this same fair last year—then a slavering, fighting-mad thing who had needed long and patient handling to become as it now was. That, too, was head up, sniffing, as Wowern frowned, his hand seeking the short knife that was all fair custom allowed him as a weapon. As we joined him he glanced around.

"There is danger." The vasa lifted lip in such a snarl as I had not seen since Wowern had won its trust at long last.

"Where and what?" I asked. For I could not center fully on that tinge of evil. Sorcery? But such was forbidden, and there was every guard against it. Not only was there a witch or wizard by every gate to test against the import of such, but those priests who patrolled with the fair-wards of frequent intervals had their own ways of sniffing out dire trouble.

Wowern shook his head. "Only . . . it is here." He made answer, then added sharply, "Let us keep together.

The Second-Kin"—once more his hand caressed the hound's head—"must remain here. Garner has already ordered it so, for Feeta urges caution. We may go to the dealers, but take all heed in our going."

I was not so pleased. All of us usually spread out and explored the fair on our own. Within the breast pocket of my overtunic I had my purse, and I had thoughts on what I wanted to see. Though first, of course, we would visit the dealers in beasts.

Heeding orders, we moved off as a group, Sim joining us. Nadi set the tree cat in its own cage, and Ort returned reluctantly to the tents. I felt the growth of uneasiness in him, his rising protest that I go without him.

There were other beast shows along the lane where our own camp had been set up. One was manned by the people from the steppes who specialize in the training of their small horses. Then there was a show of bright-winged birds, taught to sing in harmony, and at the far end, the place of Trasfor's clan—no bloodkin to us, yet of our own race. There we were hailed by one hurrying into our path.

Color glowed on Erlia's cheeks when he held out hands in a kinsman's welcome.

"Thasus!" she gave him greeting. I believed that this was something she wished and was sure would happen. By the light in his golden eyes, she was right.

"All is well?" He broke the gaze between the two of them, speaking to all of us as if we had parted only yesterday. "The All Mother has spread her cloak above you?"

Wowern laughed, giving Erlia a tiny push toward Thasus. "Over this one at least. You need have no fear for her, brother."

Erlia did not respond to his gentle attempt at teasing. Her head turned away and on her face lay again a shadow of distress. I had caught it, also, stronger, more determined—that echo of darkness and all evil.

This time it was as if I had actually picked up a foul

scent—the kind that clung to swamps, places of death and decay ruled by tainted water. Then it was gone, and I wondered if I had only made a guess without foundation. There are those who sell reptiles and crawling things, yes. But they are set apart from our beasts and have their own corner. One which I, for one, did not spend time in exploring. Yet I was sure this was no stench of animal or of any living thing—

It was gone as quickly as it had come, leaving only that ever-present uneasiness. Still, I dropped a little behind and tried in a very cautious way—not really Calling—to pin upon that hint of evil.

"What is with you, Kara?" Wowern matched his stride to mine.

"I do not know." That was true, yet deep within me something stirred. I was certain that never before had this unknown touched me. Still . . .

Once again I caught that rank stench. It was stronger, so that I wavered—and, without being aware of what I did, steadied myself by a touch on Wowern's arm. He, in turn, started as might a horse suddenly reined in.

"What—" he began again as I swung halfway about to face an opening between two smaller stalls.

"This way!" As certain as if a Calling drew me, I pushed into that narrow opening, heedless whether the rest of the Kin followed or not.

Ahead was a second line of booths fronting another lane. From these came the chatter of smaller animals, squawks and screams of birds. This was the beginning of the area where merchants and not showmen ruled. Yet it was toward none of these that that trace of need—for need did lie beneath the overlayer of evil—drew me.

I entered the section I had always hitherto shunned—that portion of the mart where dealers in reptiles and scaled life gathered. Dragons I knew, yes, but they are warm-blooded in spite of the scaled bodies and in their way sometimes far more intelligent than my own species. But the crawlers, the fang-jawed, armor-plated creatures, were to me wholly alien.

"What—" Again Wowern broke my preoccupation. I threw out a hand, demanding silence.

The afternoon was nearly spent. Flares outside booths and stalls blazed up—adding their acrid odor—not enough to cover the ill smells of the wares. A deep, coughing bellow drowned out whatever protest my companion might have uttered. Whether the others of our company still followed I did not know nor care.

I stood before a tent perhaps a third the size of ours. But where the leather and stiff woven walls we favored were brilliantly colored, gay to the eye, these walls were uniformly a sickly gray, overcast with a yellow that made me think of decay and pustulant nastiness.

Over the tent-flap the light of a torch brought to life a device such as might be the mark of a noble house. However, even when one stared directly at this (it was as dull as tarnished and unkempt metal) it was difficult for the eye to follow its convolutions. This might be a secret seal only a mage could interpret.

Shivering, I looked away. There was an impression of dark shadow angling forth, as might the tentacle of an obscene creature questing for prey. Still, I must pass under, for what I sought lay within.

No merchant stood to solicit buyers. Nor was there any glow of lamp. What did issue as I walked slowly, more than half against my will, toward that dark opening was the effulgence of a swampland wherein lay evil and death.

There *was* light after all—a greenish gleam flaring as I passed the flap. I could see, fronting me, a short table of the folding sort, some lumpish stools, like frozen clots of mud. Around the walls of the tent were cages, and from them came a stealthy, restless rustling. Those within were alert . . . and dangerous.

I had no desire to walk along those cages, peer at their occupants. I had no wish to be here at all. Still, my body—or an inner part of me—would not allow me back into the open air. Out of the gloom, which pooled oddly in corners as if made up of tangible hangings, emerged a figure so muffled by a thickly folded robe, so encowled about the head, that I could not have said whether I fronted man or woman.

The green glow that filled the tent, except in those shadowed corners, appeared to draw in about the newcomer, forming an outline, yet not illuminating to any great extent. There was an answering glow of dullish light from the breast of the robe. A pendant rested there—gold, I thought, but dull. I could make out (as if it were purposefully expanding and drawing color just to catch my eyes) the shape of a head—beautiful but still evil. The eyes were half-covered with heavy lids, only I had the fancy that beneath was true sight, so I was being regarded by something reaching through the metal—regarded and measured.

"Lady." The voice from beneath the hood, shaped by lips I still could not see, was clear. "You would buy." It was not a true question, rather a statement, as if any bargain we might make was already concluded.

Buy? What? I wanted nothing from any of those cages whose contents I still could not see. Buy? . . .

My gaze was pulled—away from the robe-hidden seller—until I looked over his or her left shoulder. There was one cage apart from the rest, a large one. And within it—

As one walks in one of those troubled dreams wherein one is compelled to a task one dreads, I moved forward, though I still had enough control over my shivering body to make a wide circle, not approaching either that table or the one who stood by it.

The cage was before me and here the shadows were thick curtains—the light did not reach. Nor could I discern any movement. Yet there was life there—that I knew.

I heard a sound from the merchant, out of my sight

unless I turned my head. Did he speak or call? Certainly what he uttered was in no tongue I knew.

In the air above the cage appeared a ball of sickly yellow which cast light—no flame of any honest torch.

A creature crouched low upon the floor of the cage, so bent in upon itself that at first it was difficult to see any exact shape. Its skin was a dirty gray, like the tent walls, not scaled, but warty and wrinkled, hanging in folds. There were four limbs—for now it uncoiled to rise. When it reached its full height, it stood erect on hind limbs, its feet webbed and flat. It was taller than I, matching Wowern's inches.

There was a thick growth of ugly yellow wattles about the throat and a ragged comb-crest of the same upon its rounded head. The forelimbs reached forward as massively clawed digits closed about the bars of the cage, scratching along the metal. There was no chin, rather a wide mouth like that of a frog, above that a single slit, which must serve it as a nostril. Only—the eyes . . .

In that hideous nightmare of a face they were so startling that they brought a gasp from me, for they were a clear green—like wondrous gems in an ugly and degrading setting. Nor were the pupils slitted as one would expect in a reptile or amphibian—but round, somehow as human as my own. Also . . . in them lay intelligence—intelligence and such pain as was a knife thrust into me when our gaze locked.

What the creature was I could not tell. Certainly I had never seen its like before. A flutter of movement to my left and the robed merchant moved closer. From one of those long sleeves issued a hand as pale as that of any fine lady very slender and long of finger. This waved in a surprisingly graceful gesture toward the still silent captive.

"A rare bargain, lady. You shall not see the like of this perhaps again in your lifetime."

"What is it—and from where?" Wowern's voice was loud and harsh. He moved in upon my right and I could sense his growing uneasiness, his desire that we both be away from this hidden-faced one and his or her strange wares.

"What is it?" the other repeated. "Ah. It is so rare we have not yet put name to it. From where? The east."

Then I felt cold. All who roved knew what lay to the east—that swampland so accursed that no one ventures into it—about which all kinds of evil legends and tales have been told for generations.

"A bargain," the merchant repeated when neither of us made comment. "All know of the Quintka—that you delight in your trained beasts—that you seek ever new ones to add to your company. Here is one which will bring many flocking to see it. It is not stupid, I think you can train it well."

Those green eyes—how they demanded that I look upon them! That feeling of pain, of sorrow so deep that there were no words to express it—flowed from them to me.

"It is a monster!" Wowern caught my arm in a grip so tight that his nails near scored my flesh. I could sense fear rising in him—not for himself but for me. He strove to pull me back a step or two, meaning, I understood, to take me out of this place.

"Five silver bits, lady."

The caged creature made no sound; I felt rather than saw its compelling gaze shift a fraction. It looked now to the robed one, and within those green eyes was a flare of deep and abiding hatred. Within *me* arose an answer.

Those eyes, did they trouble me with some fleeting memory? How could they? This was an unknown monster. Yet at that moment this feeling of emotion was as much a true Calling as if mind-words passed. Our meeting was meant to be.

I brought out my purse. Wowern's hold on me tightened. He protested fiercely but I did not listen. Rather I jerked free, and, without the usual bargaining, I counted forth those bits. Not into that long-fingered graceful hand; rather, I turned and tossed them on the tabletop. I wanted no close contact with the merchant. Nor did I want to linger here, for it seemed those heavy shadows reached farther and farther, drawing out of the tainted air any hint of freshness, leaving me breathless.

"Loose—" I got out that part order, past a thickening of my throat, not sure that even a Quintka could control such a creature. Still, when I met again those eyes so wrongly set in that hideous face, I was not afraid.

The robed one uttered a queer sound, almost as if he or she had choked down jeering laughter. There was no move to draw any bolt or bar locking that cage. Instead, the slender hand went to the pendant lying heavy on the robe, fingers closed tightly about that, hiding the beautiful, vile face from view.

There sped a puff of darkness from that hand—thrusting outward to the bars of the cage. The creature had retreated, standing with shoulders a little hunched. I smelled a sickly sweetness which made my head swim—though I stood well away from that black tongue.

It wreathed about the bars and they were gone. For a long moment the creature remained where it was. From all the other cages about uprose not only a frenzied rustling, as if the other captives aroused to demand their own freedom but also gutteral grunts and croakings, hissings—

That thing I had so madly purchased shambled forward. I was aware, without turning my head, that the robed one moved even more quickly, retreating into a deeper core of shadow. That retreat pleased me, made me less aware of my own recklessness. Did this merchant fear the late captive? If so, no such fear was mine. For the first time I spoke to the monster, using the same firm tone I would with any new addition to my team.

"Come!"

Come it did—treading deliberately on hind legs as if that came naturally, its taloned paw-hands swinging at its sides. I turned, sure within myself that where I went it would follow.

However, once outside that tent I paused, for whatever compulsion had gripped me faded. Also, I realized that I could not return to our own place openly. Even though the twilight gathered in, this creature padding at my heels, as if he were a well-trained tree cat, was far too obvious and startling. Though it was often the custom for one of the Quintka to parade a member of his or her personal team through the fair lanes as an inducement for a show, none of us had ever so displayed a creature like unto this.

Wowern wore his trainer's cloak hooked at the throat, thrown back over his shoulders. I had not brought mine. The feeling that we must attract as little attention as possible made me turn to him. There was no mistaking the frown on his face, the stubborn set of his chin.

"Wowern . . ." It irritated me to ask any favor; still, I was pressured into an appeal. "Your cloak?"

His scowl was black, his hand at the buckle of that garment, as if to defend himself against my snatching it from him. Behind him the monster stood quietly, his eyes no longer on me, for his bewattled head was raised as he stared at the device above the tent-flap door.

At that moment I swayed. What reached me was akin to a sharp blow in the face, a blast of raw hatred so deep—so intense—as to be as sharp as a danger Calling! Wowern must also have been struck by it. Hand to knife hilt, slightly crouching, he swung half-about, ready to defend himself. Only there was no attack, just the creature, its arms still dangling loosely at its sides, staring upward.

His eyes narrowed, his scowl fading into something else, an intentness of feature as if he strained to listen, Wowern surveyed that other. Then, with his left hand, for he still kept grip upon the knife, he snapped open cloak buckle and swiftly spun the folds of cloth about the creature in such a skillful fashion that its head was covered as well as its body to the thick and warty-skinned thighs.

"Come!" He gave the order now. Again he seized upon my arm with a grasp I could not withstand, propelling me forward to the opening of the same narrow side lane that had brought us here, taking no note of the muffled creature, as if he were entirely certain it would follow. Thus we came back to the place of the Kin, Wowern choosing our path, which lay amid such pockets of shadow as he could find. I allowed him this leadership, for I was in a turmoil within myself.

I realized that we two had been alone. The others of our company must have gone on when I had been seized by the need to hunt out the dismal, shadowed tent. Which was good—for the moment, I could have made no real explanation of why I had done what I did.

Ort met me at the edge of our stand, his head forward, voicing that anxious, half-growling sound he always used when I left him. Sighting what accompanied us, he snarled, lifting lip to show gleaming teeth, his claws well extended as he brought up both paws in the familiar stance of challenge. Before I could send a mind-message, his growl, which had risen to a battle cry, was cut off short. I saw his nostrils expand, though since we had left that foul tent I had not been aware of any odor from the creature.

Now Ort fell back, not as one afraid, rather as one puzzled, confronted by a mystery. I picked up the bewilderment which dampened his anger, confused him to a point I had never witnessed before.

"Brother-Kin," I mind-reached him. Though the muffled monster betrayed no sign of anger, I wanted no trouble. Ort had never been jealous of any of my team. He knew well that he was my seconding, that between the two of us there was a close bond which no other could hope to break. "Brother-Kin, this is one who . . ." I hesitated and then plunged on, because I was as sure as if it had been told me that I spoke the truth. "Has been ill-used—"

Ort shuffled his huge hind paws; his eyes were still on the creature as now Wowern caught his cloak by the edge and whipped it away from that ugly body, plainly revealed in the torchlight.

The monster made no sound, but its bright eyes were fast on Ort. I saw my Brother-Kin blink.

"Sister . . ." There was an oddness in Ort's sending. "This one—" His thought closed down so that I caught nothing more for a long moment. Then he came into my mind more clearly. "This one is welcome."

The stranger might be welcome to Ort, but with Garner and the rest of the clan it was a different matter. I was told that I had far overstepped the bonds of permissiveness, taking upon myself rights none had dared before. I think that Garner would have speedily dispatched my monster to his former master and cage, save that Feeta, who had been silently staring at my purchase, broke into his tirade. The rest of the clan had also been facing me accusingly, as if, for the first time in my life, they judged me no Kin at all.

"Look to Ort," Feeta's voice arose, "to Ily, Somsa—" She pointed to each of the Second-Kin as she spoke.

We stood in that lesser tent where our smaller teammates were caged, or leashed, according to fair custom. What she made us aware of was the silence of all those four-footed ones, the fact that they regarded the newcomer round-eyed—and that they had broken mind-link with us.

Garner paused in mid-word, to stare from one to another of those seconding our teams. I felt his thought, striving to establish linkage. The flush of anger faded from his face. In its place came a shadow of concern, which deepened as he beat against stubbornly held barriers.

Feeta took a short pace forward, raising her right hand so that her forefinger touched the forehead of the monster at a point between its brilliant eyes. Then she spoke to me alone, as if all there were only the three of us—healer, monster, and I.

"Kara . . ."

I knew what she summoned me to do. In spite of the deep respect and obedience she could always claim from me, I wanted to refuse. Such a choice was denied me. Was it the power of those green eyes that drew me, or the weight of Feeta's will down-beating mine? I could not have said as I went to her, taking her place as she moved aside. My hand came up that my finger, in turn, filled the place where hers had touched.

There was a sick whirling, almost as if the world about me was rent by forces beyond my reckoning. Also, I sensed once more that overshadow of faint memory out of nowhere. This was like being caught in a vast, sticky web—utterly foul, utterly evil, threatening every clean and decent thought and impulse. Entrapped I was, and there could be no loosing of that bond. No! There was also resistance, near beaten under, still not destroyed.

The net was not mine. That much I learned in a breath or two of time. Just as that stubborn, near despairing resistance was not born from any strength within *me!*

Danger—a murky vision of thick darkness, within which crawled unseen perils all so obscenely alien to my kind as to make the very imagining of them fearsome. Danger—a tool, a weapon launched, set to strike—but a tool that could turn in the user's hand, a weapon whose edge might well cut the wielder.

"What threatens us?" I demanded aloud, even as I also hurled that thoughtwise, threading it into that wattled head through my touch.

I felt Feeta catch my free hand, hold it in a tight grip between both of hers. From the creature came a pulsating flow—sometimes sharp and clear, sometimes fading, as if the one who sent it must fight for every fraction of warning.

Evil, dark, strong, rising like a wave— There lurked

within that darkness the beautiful face of the pendant. It leered, slavered, anticipated—was arrogantly sure of victory. I heard a gasp from Feeta—a single word of recognition.

"Thotharn!"

Her naming made my vision steady, become clearer. Names are potent things, and to call them aloud, our wise people tell us, can act as a focus point for power.

Thotharn I might not know, though of him I had heard, uneasy whispering for the most part, passed from one traveler to another as veiled warnings. There were the Three Lordly Ones upon whose threshold Ithkar stood, there were other presences within our world which my kind recognized and paid homage to—did not *we* look to the All Mother? But Thotharn was the dark, all that man feared the most, shifting westward from swamplands into which no man, save he be outlawed and damned, dared stray.

It is an old, old land—the swamp country. We who tread the roads collect tales upon tales. It is said there was once a mighty nation in the east—greater than any existing today, when small lordlings hold their own patches of land jealously and fight short, bitter wars over the ownership of a field or some inflated pride. The north was ravaged when I was a small child, by the rise of a conqueror who sought to bring diverse holdings under one rule. But he was slain, and his patchwork of a kingdom died with him, by blood and iron.

Only in the east was no tale of a lordling with ambition. No—there was far more, a rulership that impressed itself on all the land and under which men lived in a measure of peace, no lord daring then to raise sword against his neighbor. There came an end, and tradition said this end was born of evil, nourished in evil, dying evilly, even before the Three Lordly Ones came to us. With the breaking of this power the land fell into the depths of night for a space. All manner of foulness raved and ravaged unchecked. Was Thotharn a part of that? Who knows now?

But in these past few years rumor spread again his name—first in whispers, and then openly.

Thotharn's priests walked our roads. They did not preach aloud, as did the friars or the wise ones who serve All Mother, striving thus to better the lives of listeners. Nor did they shut themselves into a single temple pile and impress their weight of service demands as did those who outwardly acclaim the Three Lordly Ones. They simply walked, and were . . . while from them spread an unease and then a drawing—

From the creature I touched flared red rage, strong enough to burn my mind. Thotharn—yes! That name awakened this emotion. But it was *against* the dread lord of shadows that that blaze was aroused. Whatever this creature might be, he was no hand of the east.

No hand. It caught at my turn of thought, seized upon it, hurled it back to me, changed after a fashion. Obey the will of Thotharn—no, not that, ever! When I acknowledged that fraction of half appeal, that need to make clear what lay inside the other's brain and heart, there was a swell of triumph through the sending—a quick flare like a shout of "Yes, yes!"

I spoke aloud again. Perhaps some part of me wanted to do so, that I make very sure of what I learned.

"They believe you serve them? . . ."

Again a burst of agreement. There is this about mind-send: a man may cloak his values and his desires when he uses words, but there can be no hiding of the truth while sending. Any barrier becomes in itself a warning and injects suspicion. That this hideous thing out of the swampland could hide from me in thought was not to be believed. But, knowing this, why then would any follower of Thotharn—such as the robed merchant must surely be—thrust upon a Quintka possessing sending powers a creature so easily read?

That thought, also, was picked up. The churning within the other became chaotic in eagerness to answer.

Thoughts were so intermingled, came so swiftly, that I could not sort one from the other. I heard far off, as if she were now removed from me, though still our hands were locked, a gasped moan from Feeta. I guessed that it was only our linkage, her power and mine together, that made this exchange possible at all.

There were scraps of information—that the robed one of Thotharn knew of the Quintka, had marked them because of their far traveling, the fact that they were readily welcome in lords' keeps, even the temples—that the people who gathered for our showings were many in all parts of the land. Where a wandering priest or priestess of suspect learning could not freely go, one linked with us might penetrate. However, the swamplanders did not truly know the Quintka. They accepted us as trainers of beasts, not realizing that, to us in our own circles, there was no Kin and beast—two things forever separated—rather there was Kin and Second-Kin linked by bonds they did not dream existed.

This one had been prepared (the plan had been a long time in the making—and it was their first such) to be sent out as a link between their great ones, who did not leave the swamp, and the world they coveted so strongly. The first—there would be others. The robed one I had dealt with—I learned in that half-broken communication with my purchase—had believed *I* was under the influence of Thotharn's subtle scents and pressures when I bought it—that when I left, already I was a part, too!

"Why do you betray so easily your masters?" I strove to find some flaw in this flood of explanation. "You were made for what you do, yet now you freely tell us that you are a thing designed to be all treachery and betrayal—"

"Made!" Again a flare of intense anger—so painfully projected into my mind that I flinched and near dropped my finger contact. "Made!"

In that bitter repetition I understood. This thing, in spite of all its grotesque ugliness, was near mad from the usage it had received. It had lain under Thotharn's yoke without hope—now it took the first opportunity to strike back, even though any blow it might deliver could not be a direct one. Perhaps it also had not realized the Quintka had their own defenses.

It was even as I caught this that there dropped a sudden curtain of silence. But not before, it seemed to me, a whiff of foul air blew between me and this purchase of mine. The green eyes half closed, then opened fully. In them I read appeal—an agony of appeal.

Feeta loosed her grip, caught at my wrist, jerking me back from that touch which had brought us such knowledge.

"What is it?" I rounded upon her.

"They are questing—they might learn," she half spat at me. Never had I seen her so aroused. "Is that not so? Blink your eyes if I speak the truth!" She spoke directly to the creature.

Lids fell over those green eyes, rested so for a breath as if to make very sure that we would understand, then arose again.

I heard a swift, deep-drawn breath from Garner where he stood, feet a little apart, as one about to face an enemy charge. Feeta spoke without turning her eyes from the swamp thing.

"You mind-heard?"

Garner bared his teeth as Ort might do. "I heard. So these crawlers in the muck would think to so use *us!"*

"To plan is not to do." I did not know from whence those words came to me but I spoke them, before I addressed the swamp dweller.

"These you serve, do they have a way of setting a watch upon you? Blink in answer!"

Again, deliberately those eyes closed and reopened.

"Do they know of our linkage? Blink twice if this is not so." I waited, cold gathering within me, fearing one answer, but hoping for another. That came—two measured blinks.

"So . . ." Garner expelled breath in a mighty puff. He dropped a hand on Feeta's shoulder and drew her to him. The tie between them was so old and deep that I did not wonder he had been able to link with her during that exchange. "Now what do we do?"

I had one answer, though whether he would accept it or not I could not tell. "To return this would arouse their suspicions, lead them to other plans."

He snorted. "Think you that I do not understand that?" He regarded the creature measuringly. Then he made his decision.

"This one is yours, Kara. Upon you rests the burden."

Which, of course, was only fair.

Garner and the others left me with the self-confessed spy of evil. Only Second-Kin—Ort, the rest of the beasts—remained. They continued to watch the stranger with unrelenting stares.

We had no cage large enough to accommodate the being, and somehow it did not seem fitting to set a rope loop about its neck, tether it with the four-footed ones. Where was I to keep it? Soon would come time for the night shows, and it should be under cover before our patrons came to look at the animals as was the regular custom.

Ort answered the problem with action that surprised me greatly. He padded to the baskets of act trappings set along one side of the tent, came back to me, a wadding of cloth in his forepaws. I shook out a cape with a hood, old and worn, which had been used to top and protect the stored "costumes" our teams wore. It was a human garment and the folds appeared adequate to cover the creature.

Wowern had already taken back his cloak; now I flung this musty-smelling length about the thing's shoulders, fastened the rusty throat buckle. To my astonishment the creature, as if it were indeed a man and not grotesque beast, used its forepaws to pull the hood up over its misshapen head, well forward so that its ugliness was completely hidden. I could almost believe that I fronted a man—not a monster.

Ort chirped, one of those sounds my human throat could not equal. Our disguised one swung about, stumping after my seconding, out of the tent and into the shadows beyond. With an exclamation I hurried after.

Ort apparently had no such thing as escape in mind, nor did the other, who was certainly powerful enough to leave if it wished, deviate from the path shown it. Rather, it squatted down at the end of the row where our mounts were tied, concealed behind the bales of hay now stacked as a back wall. In those shadows the dull gray of the cloak was hidden, one would not have known that anything sheltered there.

The horses and ponies had stirred uneasily at first, but Ort paced down their line, giving voice to that soothing throat hum which he had used many times over to reassure nervous beasts. They accepted this newcomer because of his championship.

I hurried to change clothing, catching up some cold food to eat between the doffing of one robe, the donning of another, the fastening of buckles, the setting of sham jewels about my throat, wrists, and in hair strings. Nadi and Erlia were already prepared and on their way to lead forth their teams, but Mai stood before our mirror applying a thicker red to her lips.

"What do you plan to do?" she asked bluntly. "To carry with us a spy—even though it seems to have no liking for its true master—that is to endanger all of us. Why do you bring this upon us, Kara?" There was no softness in her voice, rather hostility in the eyes that met mine within the mirror.

"I—I had no choice." To me that was truth. I had clearly been drawn to the merchant's booth; once there I had been enspelled. . . . Enspelled? I shivered, the cold was well within me now and I could not rid myself of it.

"No choice?" She was both scornful and angry. "This is foolishness. Would you say you are englamored by this bestial ugliness out of the dark? Ha, Kara, you cannot expect the rest of us to risk its presence."

She swept away and I knew that she gave a truthful warning. Those of the clan would not long accept—even at Garner's and Feeta's bidding, if I could depend upon that—this addition to our party. I did not want it, either. I—

Yet I had paid that silver without a question. Unless . . . Again I shivered and stood very still, my hands clasped tightly on the handle of my team leader's wand. Unless there was something in *me* which that robed one had been able to touch, to tame to his or her will, even as I lead my team! If that were so, then what flaw lay inside me that evil could reach out so easily and twist to its own usage? At that moment I knew fear so sharp it made me waver where I stood, throw out a hand to the edge of the mirror table and hold fast, for it seemed that the very earth moved under my feet.

I heard the thump of drums in the show tent. Habit set me into motion without thought. Nadi was dancing with her long-legged birds now—next I must be ready with my marchers. I staggered a little, still under the touch of that fear. Ort awaited me, his hand drum slung about his thick neck. Behind him, in an ordered row, were Oger, Ossan, Obo, Orn—just as they had been for months and years. Tall all of them, their talons displayed in order to astound the audiences, their bush combs aloft, and their long necks twining back and forth to the beat of the drums.

Nadi's music faded. She would be issuing from the other side of our stage. I breathed deeply twice, steadying my nerves—putting out of my mind with determination all except that which was immediately before me—the need to give my part of the show.

We had finished the first appearance of the evening and Garner was talking to several who wore the shoulder ribbons and house marks of lords, making arrangements for private performances. Those would be steady for us all during the two ten-days we were in Ithkar. However, another stood in the lesser light just at the edge of the torch beams as if waiting his or her turn at bargaining. Enveloped in a cloak, it might well be a woman—and of that I was sure when a hand bearing a ring-bracelet came out of hiding to draw closer the cloak. She made no effort to push forward until Garner had finished and the others were gone. I saw her speak and Garner raise his head, stare across the crowded yard between our tents where fairgoers came to see closer our teammates. He looked at me, nodded, and I could not escape that silent order.

So I went to join him and the other. Her gem-backed hand touched her hood, pushing it back a little. I saw a face, deeper brown in color—some southern-born lady, I thought. Her features were thin and sharp, with an impatient line between her straight brows. No beauty—but one who was obeyed when it pleased her to give orders.

"Speak with this one." Garner was also impatient. "What we know is her doing." He left abruptly. The lady regarded me as I would a beast unknown—curious, perhaps. However, there was a sting in that survey. I lifted my chin and eyed her as boldly back.

"You made a purchase." She spoke abruptly. There was a slurring in her speech new to me. "It was one not meant for you."

"I was asked a price and I paid. The merchant seemed satisfied," I returned. This might be the answer to our problem. If she wanted the swamp dweller, then let her have him. But I would not strike any bargain until I knew more. At this moment it seemed to me that I saw between the two of us those wide green eyes.

"Paugh!" Her lips moved then as if she would spit, as

might any common fair drab, highborn though she seemed. "That merchant exceeded his instructions. I have come" —a second hand appeared from beneath her robe, in it a purse weighing heavy by the look—"to buy what is rightfully mine. Where is he?"

"Safe enough." I made no move to take that purse. The hand holding it had come fully under the light and on the forefinger I saw the ring—the same smiling face of the merchant's pendant formed its bezel.

"Summon him." She moved a little, almost as if she wanted to be well away from us. "Summon him at once!"

Had they then learned, these followers of Thotharn, that the swamp creature had betrayed their purpose, and so were eager to reclaim him? What would be his fate at their hands? I knew that Garner would report to the temple all we had learned. These could reclaim the creature, slay it, and deny all. What proof would we have then that they had tried to move so against the peace of Ithkar?

"I—" Fear I had known, even disgust, when I had made that purchase; still, I would betray no living thing. For the Quintka might not deny refuge to the Second-Kin. Second-Kin—a swamp creature out of the dark land? Yet Ort and the others had made it welcome after their own fashion, and their instincts I trusted.

"Summon him!" Her order was sharp; she waved the bag back and forth so it gave out a clink of metal. It must be well filled with coin. "I give you four—five times what you paid. He is mine—bring him hither!"

I heard the guttural throat sound from Ort and looked over my shoulder. My Brother-Kin led a cloaked shape into the open, the swamp creature. Still, Ort lifted his lips a little, showing fangs, and I knew that what he did was not in obedience to such as she who stood with me, nor even to me. He moved for himself—and perhaps another.

Those who had come to see the animals had passed along—I heard the boom of a gong signaling the second part of our performance and the thud of hooves as the horses moved out into the circular space beyond. We were alone now—the four of us.

"Ran . . ." Her voice was far different from that with which she had addressed me. "Ran, I came as I had promised—freedom!" She swung up the purse to give forth again that clinking.

I saw a warty paw in the open, tugging at the hood so it fell free upon his broad shoulders. His nightmare face was clear. She bit her lip and could not suppress the shadow of distaste, near of loathing. She is not, the thought flashed into my head, as good an actress as she believes.

"Take it!" Again she shoved the bag in my direction.

I put my hands behind my back as the green eyes turned toward me. I could not pick up any clear mind-speech, and I dared not touch him to establish linkage. But somehow I felt again that blaze of red rage—not for me, but for this woman.

"I will not," I said firmly. Though I could not find any true reason why—except those eyes.

"You shall!" She thrust her head forward and her hood fell away, her eyes bored into me. Then I saw her gaze change a fraction; she caught her breath. "No . . ." Her voice was a half whisper. "Not that—the blood—"

I am no voice of the All Mother, I wear no robe of the Three Lordly Ones—I am no shaman of any tribe. Still, there awoke in me then something that I had sensed twice before this day—an ancient knowledge. Nor was that of the Quintka. Partly of their blood I might be—yet who knew what other strain my dead mother had granted me?

What I did came in that moment as natural as breathing—I brought forth both hands as I took two quick steps toward my monster. He pawed at the buckle of his cloak and that fell away from him, leaving his nightmare body bare. My hands fell to his shoulders, the roughness of his skin was harsh under mine. He had to bend a little from his height. All that filled the world now were his green eyes—and in them was a flashing light of eagerness, of hope reborn, of pain now fading—

> *"By the thorn and by the tree,*
> *By the moon and by the sea,*
> *By the truth and by the right,*
> *By the touch and by the sight,*
> *Let that which is twisted,*
> *Straightened be.*
> *That the imprisoned go free!"*

I pressed my lips to the slimy cold of his toad mouth. Fighting revulsion—pushing it utterly from me.

When I drew back I cried aloud—words that had no meaning, yet were of power—and I felt that power fill me until I could hold no more. My fingers crooked, bit into his odious flesh. I tore with my nails— The skin parted, as might rotted cloth. As cloak so old that nothing was left but tatters, that skin gave to my frantic hands, rent, and fell away.

No monster, but a man—a true man—as I shredded from him that foul overcovering. I heard a shriek behind me—a keening that arose and arose. Then the man I had freed flung out one arm, to set me behind him, confronting the woman. She had her beringed hand up, held close to her lips, ugly and open, as she mouthed words across the surface of that head-set ring. Frantically she spilled forth spells. His hand shot out, caught hers. He twisted her finger, pulled free the ring, flung it to the ground.

There was a barking cry from Ort. One of his ponderous hind feet swept between the two at ground level, stamped that circlet into the beaten earth.

The woman wailed, then spat in truth, before she fled. Where the ring had been pounded there arose a small thread of smoke. Ort leaned forward and spat in turn, full upon the thread, setting it into nothingness.

"So be it!" A deep voice.

A well-muscled arm swooped, fingers caught up the cloak, once more twisting it about a bare body, but this time a human body. "So be it."

"You are a man—" The power that had filled me vanished as quickly as it had come. I was left with only amazement and a need to understand.

He nodded. Gone from him was all but the eyes—those were rightly his, marking him even through the foulness of the spell. "I am Ran Den Fur—a fool who went where no man ventured, and by my folly I learned. Now . . ." He gazed about him. I saw the cloak move as he drew a deep breath, as if inhaling new life to rid him of the old. "I shall live again—and perhaps I have put folly behind me."

He looked at me with the same intentness as when he had tried to link earlier.

"I have much to thank you for, lady. We shall have time—now—even in the shadow of Thotharn, we still have time."